UNSCROLLED

54 WRITERS AND ARTISTS WRESTLE WITH THE TORAH

UNSCROLLED

54 WRITERS AND ARTISTS WRESTLE WITH THE TORAH

a REBOOT book

WORKMAN PUBLISHING
NEW YORK

EDITED BY ROGER BENNETT

TO RACHEL LEVIN AND AMICHAI LAU-LAVIE,
WHO BUILT REBOOT WITH THE LOVE AND CARE BEZALEL
DEVOTED TO CONSTRUCTING THE TABERNACLE,
ALTHOUGH WITH FEWER DOLPHIN SKINS

Library of Congress Cataloging-in-Publication Data:
Unscrolled : 54 writers and artists wrestle with the Torah : a reboot book /edited by Roger Bennett.
    p. cm.
  ISBN 978-0-7611-6919-2 (alk. paper)
1. Bible. Pentateuch—Criticism, interpretation, etc. I. Bennett, Roger, editor.
  BS1225.52.U47 2013
  222'.106—dc23   2013026700

Cover design by Raquel Jaramillo and Jean-Marc Troadec
Interior design by Jean-Marc Troadec
Typographic illustrations by Vaughn Andrews and James Williamson

Translation of Hebrew courtesy of the *JPS Hebrew–English TANAKH* (1999)

Photo credits: p. 124 (from left to right), iStockphoto: Antagain, Digoarpi, lauriek; pp. 209
and 210, photos courtesy of Jamie Glassman; p. 217, photo courtesy of Amichai Lau-Lavie;
p. 281, photos courtesy of Larry Smith; pp. 350 and 351, photos courtesy of Bonni Benrubi Gallery;
and p. 358, *Missed Connections* (2011) © Sophie Blackall. Commissioned by MTA Arts for Transit
and Urban Design.

Workman books are available at special discounts when purchased in bulk for premiums and sales
promotions as well as for fund-raising or educational use. Special editions or book excerpts can
also be created to specification. For details, contact the Special Sales Director at the address below,
or send an email to specialmarkets @ workman.com.

Workman Publishing Company, Inc.
225 Varick Street
New York, NY 10014-4381
workman.com

WORKMAN is a registered trademark of Workman Publishing Co., Inc.
Printed in the United States of America
First printing September 2013
10 9 8 7 6 5 4 3 2 1

CONTENTS

INTRODUCTION

EVERY BOOK HAS A FOUNDING STORY. LIKE the Bible itself, this volume originated on a mountaintop, though without the pomp, fire, and cloud of Mount Sinai. In slightly less theatrical surrounds, it was born amid the snow-tipped Wasatch Mountain range outside Park City, Utah.

The Reboot network (see page 372) has met there every year since 2002, bringing together an eclectic mix of characters to discuss how generational changes in technology, community, and meaning have transformed American Jewish identity. Over the years, the conversation has catalyzed the creation of more than a hundred varied projects and programs. This book is one such product—the outcome of a discussion that began in 2011, when Damon Lindelof invited the group to consider the Genesis tale of Abraham's binding of Isaac.

In a room full of talkative writers, technologists, and social activists, the perplexing story of a father willing to sacrifice his son to prove the depth of his belief was like conversational catnip.

An animated discussion encompassing godly commands, false prophecy, dodgy parenting, blind faith, and human justice ensued.

The conversation forced the group to confront a number of questions, most glaringly, how long it had been since they had last read a biblical text. The majority had stumbled through the *Tibetan Book of the Dead*, *The Prophet*, or *Siddhartha* in their college years, but if they retained any sense of the Bible, it was typically a vague memory, forged in youth, of crudely constructed, sanitized tales badly told—a stark contrast to the nuanced narrative they now grappled with together. A second session was scheduled to explore the story of the Tower of Babel. One on Moses and the burning bush quickly followed.

And so the idea for *Unscrolled* was born: an experiment to see what questions and ideas would emerge if fifty-four game individuals each wrestled with a single section of the Torah—the first five books of the Bible—from the rollicking, human stories of Genesis, to the nation building of Exodus; the blood, organs, and ritual sacrifices of Leviticus; the confusion of Numbers; and the dramatic climax of Deuteronomy.

The idea is far from original. The Torah is typically read in fifty-four sections in synagogues around the world over the course of a lunisolar year. Each public reading, chanted aloud, is traditionally accompanied by a *Dvar Torah* (literally a "word of Torah") in which a member of the congregation steps up to deliver a personal interpretation of the story. This riff can focus on anything, from a single word or detail, to an overarching examination of character or the entire story line.

Consider this, then, as a book of unorthodox *Divrei Torah*, offered up in the spirit of the rabbinical assertion that there are infinite interpretations of the Torah and that everyone who stood at Mount Sinai saw a "different face" of the text.

A word on the book's format: Each chapter contains a synopsis of the biblical section, including the particular verse that inspired the contributor's interpretation that follows. The synopsis is faithful to the biblical text. If you find your blood boiling because the number of Israelite men leaving Egypt is recorded along with a reference to the children and cattle who accompanied them, yet women are not mentioned, that is the original text talking.

Know also that although we are eternally indebted to each contributor and the spirit of creative adventure he or she brought to the project, the reaction triggered by the text and interpretation—be it enjoyment, frustration, amusement, or anger—is the point. Our highest hope is that this volume will cause you to follow this biblical text along with us throughout the year and wrestle with the narrative to come to your own conclusions—a ritual that has been faithfully followed for more than three thousand years.

Roger Bennett
New York City
@unscrolled
unscrolled.org

PART ONE

GEN

ESIS

A DIZZYING RACE FROM THE STORY of creation through the tales of the Patriarchs— Abraham! Isaac! Jacob!—Genesis is a crushed cluster of classic biblical stories served up at nose-bleed pace.

The narrative charges through the primeval story, Adam and Eve, and Noah and the flood before lingering on the covenant-entwined life of Abraham, Isaac, and Jacob (with all-too-fleeting mention of matriarchs Sarah, Rebekah, Leah, and Rachel).

In arguably the Torah's most complete book, the characters are humanly portrayed and the stories well crafted. Ranging in emotion from the horror of Isaac's binding, to the suffering of Lot, the romance of Rebekah, and the soap-operatic tale of Jacob's rise to power, the tales never lose their narrative thread, leaving a reader eager to move from cliff-hanger to cliff-hanger.

כי ידע אלהים כי ביום אכלכם ממנו
ונפקחו עיניכם והייתם כאלהים ידעי טוב ורע:

"God knows as soon as you eat of it your eyes will be opened and
you will be like divine beings who know good and bad." —Genesis 3:5

B'REISHIT (*"In the beginning"*)
GENESIS 1:1–6:8

IN THE BEGINNING: **GOD CREATES HEAVEN AND** earth, light and darkness, day and night, and then proceeds to embellish the project on a daily basis. The land is separated from water to establish earth and sea. Then trees, fruit, and other plants are crafted. The stars are next to be added, along with the sun and moon.

The waters are packed with sea creatures, the land with wildlife, and the sky with birds, all of which will reproduce.

Then comes the big one. God creates humanity—both male and female are a reflection of the creator's image—blessing them with the mandate to become fertile masters of the world, in control of every other living creature.

To cap this week of stunning productivity, God blesses the seventh day, declares it holy, downs the tools, and stops work.

THE RISE AND FALL OF MANKIND

A more detailed retelling of the creation of the human race is now provided. The male prototype is crafted from the dust on the ground. God breathes life into his soul by blowing into his nostrils, causing man to snap to attention.

God selects the garden of Eden as man's habitat—a paradise containing all the food anyone could eat. A tree of life sprouts in the center, alongside the tree of good and bad knowledge. God inserts man into this setting with simple instructions: "Help yourself to anything, but whatever you do, don't eat from the tree of knowledge—it will kill you."

While man goes about the time-consuming task of naming every animal, God realizes it is not a good idea for him to be alone. After putting man to sleep, God extracts a rib and fashions it into woman, a name man creates. Both are stark naked, but their nudity does not bother them in the slightest.

A canny serpent soon manages to persuade woman to consider eating from the tree of knowledge. The snake's key point is that knowing *everything* will elevate humans to God's level. With her interest piqued, woman proceeds to eat from the tree, feeding her husband, too. As soon as they have eaten, they look down, realize they are naked, and experience a sudden burst of shame. Fig leaves are quickly fashioned into loincloths, and they are nude no more.

When they hear God approaching, both man and woman attempt to hide. God calls out to man, who admits he is hiding because he is embarrassed by his naked state. God shrewdly inquires if this sudden self-consciousness is a sign that man and woman have eaten from the forbidden tree of knowledge. Man confesses that he ate, but only because woman urged him to do so. Woman passes the buck on to the serpent, claiming it seduced her.

God's punishment is immediate. The serpent can now move only by crawling on its belly. Woman is condemned to suffer the intense pain of childbirth, and man will now have to work the land to grow whatever they require to eat. Humans will also be mortal from now on. To make sure of this, God kicks the pair out of Eden so they will not be tempted to eat from the tree of life and names them: Adam and Eve.

OFFSPRING AND MURDER ARE INVENTED ALMOST SIMULTANEOUSLY

Adam and Eve proceed to have two sons: Abel, a shepherd, and Cain, a farmer. The two make offerings to God. Cain uses his fruit. Abel gives up his

best sheep. God favors the lamb offering, which upsets Cain so much that
God is compelled to chide him. "Don't
be angry. You can do better," God
explains. "Good and bad are yours to
choose, but sin is intoxicating, and it
is up to you to resist it."

The warning does Cain no good.
The next thing we know, he has killed
his brother in the field. When God
inquires about Abel's whereabouts
and Cain plays dumb, replying, "I don't
know; am I my brother's keeper?" God
busts him. Once more punishment is
dispensed instantaneously. From that
day on, Cain will struggle to farm and
will be forced to wander the world rest-
lessly. A panicked Cain is concerned
that other men will enforce vigi-
lante justice to avenge his crime. God
thoughtfully places "the mark of Cain"
on his head to warn others that they
should not touch him.

THINGS AREN'T WHAT THEY USED TO BE

Cain takes a wife and proceeds to have
a child, Enoch. He also builds a city and
names it after his son. His descendants
are listed, creating an impression of a
world that is filling up with people over
time. Adam and Eve also have another
son, Seth. Several generations of his
descendants are listed, along with their
life spans, which are as long as 969 years.
They culminate in Noah, who has three
sons: Shem, Ham, and Japheth, all born
when he is at the ripe old age of 500.

The story ends on a dark note.
Monitoring all that has been created,
God is appalled by the wickedness
that fills the human mind. Filled with
regret, the Lord considers destroying
the entire creation, right down to the
very last bird. But humanity has one
last hope: a character named Noah,
who still finds favor with the Lord.

JOSH RADNOR

I believe in God. I try to feel the room before I blurt that out in conversation, but . . . it's a feature of my personality and a fact of my life. I've long wanted to do away with ideology and the punishing male trickster deity of my youth and get to the heart of the heart of the matter. Who is God? Who are we? What are we doing here? And how can we do it with a little more grace and guidance? Healing my broken perceptions of the divine, hitting the "install update" button and awakening to a new vision of God—that's what this prayer is for me.

REVISION

1 Lord, hear my prayer—

1 My mind is filled with falsehoods about You.
2 Today let me rewrite.
3 Give me the courage to delete the rotten first second third and hundredth drafts
4 That deny You,
5 That blame You,
6 That slander You.
7 It is time.

1 Guide me to write a different, better story.
2 Teach me the true meaning of the garden, the snake, the apple, and the fall.
3 Scrub from my mind the lazy oft-told tales of punishment, trickery, and abandonment.
4 Let me retire the ego's clichés and distortions, O Lord, and bid farewell to the misconceived central character:
5 the psychopathic, jealous trickster,
6 the crude caricature of paternal retribution,
7 the off-planet deity watching over us impassively, folded-armed, while we rot and writhe, our cries falling on deaf God ears.

7

1 I declare this vision of God to be false, and I ask that any remnants of this lie be erased from the crevices of my consciousness.

1 Let me learn anew. Let not the guilting of grandparents lead me to fear and reject the guidance of the other:
2 The Sikh,
3 The Sufi,
4 The Shaman,
5 The Hindu,
6 The Buddhist,
7 The Christian,
8 The Gnostic,
9 The Kabbalist.
10 If it is wise and true
11 —If it bears Your cosmic fingerprints and the quiet perfection of Your voice—
12 I will listen.

1 Let me live with the compassion of Buddha and Quan Yin and Mother Mary,
2 Let me write with the sacred clarity of Rumi and Hafiz, Wordsworth and Blake.

3 Teach me to surrender like Mohammed and pray like David,
4 To be fiery like Rama and fierce like Jesus.

1 May I not fall into the deification of any man—for You alone are God—but may I let the example of their light guide my path.

1 When I am weeping like Arjuna on the inner battlefield, may beautiful blue Krishna—the divine charioteer—lift me up and remind me of the Truth:

1 *I am That.*
2 *Thou are That. All this is That.*
3 *That alone Is and there is nothing else but That.*

1 Let me remember the divine dance of the Mother-Father, always, lest I fall into the dog-eat-dog foolishness upon which so much cruelty and injustice is based.

1 (When the Father said, "Let there be light," the Mother answered, "And there was light.")

1 Erase the imprint of atheism from my mind, Lord.
2 And while You're at it, please remove: guilt, shame, anxiety, depression, comparison, competition, vanity, arrogance, and sloth.

---

1 Let the false prophets and holy bullies turn inward.
2 May they recognize the battle is never outside themselves.
3 For You do not exist in the world of opposites.

---

1 The madness of this world is our own.
2 We created it, we perpetuated it.
3 You do not endorse it.
4 You are innocent.
5 We have created You in our image.
6 Forgive us.

---

1 How am I to know I am being heard?
2 Because I am speaking to myself.

---

1 You and I are not separate.

---

1 Heal the wound in my psyche that stubbornly claims otherwise,
2 For this is the ego's

well-constructed and persistent lie:
3 You are alone you are alone you are alone.

---

1 Like a train schedule blaring on a loudspeaker, it is repeated. Over and over.
2 Daring us to relent and believe that which is false.

---

1 The bite of that apple was terrible indeed.
2 It convinced us we were not You.

---

1 Let me bear the weight of the responsibility for these errors of thought, speech, action, and perception as I learn to walk the razor's edge of virtue.

---

1 May I always hear the steady vigilance and unending love of Your voice guiding me home.

---

1 All else falls away.
2 Only that which is unchanging is True.

---

1 Thank You, Mother-Father God,
2 for this new beginning.

עַל כֵּן קָרָא שְׁמָהּ בָּבֶל כִּי שָׁם בָּלַל יְהוָה שְׂפַת
כָּל הָאָרֶץ וּמִשָּׁם הֱפִיצָם יְהוָה עַל פְּנֵי כָל הָאָרֶץ:

"That is why it was called Babel, because there the Lord confounded
the speech of the whole earth; and from there the Lord scattered them
over the face of the whole earth."—Genesis 11:9

NOAH ("*Noah*")
GENESIS 6:9–11:32

I T'S ONE OF THE GREAT DIY PROJECTS OF ALL time. Noah is reintroduced as a righteous man who "walks with God." He lives at a time in which the earth is in such an anarchical state, God reveals an intention to destroy humanity. Noah is instructed to prepare for a flood by constructing an immense ark and then filling it with his family—wife, sons, and their partners—as well as animals of every kind, both male and female. Noah may be 600 years old, but he does what he is told and prepares for a forthcoming deluge, which God claims will last for forty days and forty nights.

The rains begin and last as long as predicted. Water swallows up even the highest mountains, covering the land for almost six months. Every human being and all of the earth's creatures are wiped out. The only remaining forms of life exist within the belly of the ark.

In the seventh month, the waters finally begin to recede, and the vessel comes to rest on Mount Ararat. Noah employs a dove to test the flood level. The first time it goes out, it circles back, unable to find a resting place.

Seven days later, it brings an olive branch back in its mouth, which Noah considers a good sign. A week later, the bird does not return.

After little more than a year, Noah disembarks and sets the animals free. God instructs him to be fertile, and Noah responds by offering a sacrifice in God's honor. The Lord sets out a series of laws that Noah must follow and promises never again to destroy humanity, unleashing a mighty rainbow as a mark of that intent.

DON'T DRINK AND FARM

Noah becomes a farmer, but drinks far too much wine while planting his vineyard. Ham, Noah's youngest son, discovers his father passed out and naked in his tent and tells his other brothers. Those two treat their father with a lot more respect than Ham, covering his nudity while taking great pains to ensure they don't glimpse him in this vulnerable state.

When Noah recovers and realizes how his youngest son has behaved, he curses him, dictating that Ham's descendants will be Canaan, a slave nation to his brothers' offspring.

Despite this unfortunate incident, Noah lives an additional 350 years, finally passing away at the ripe old age of 950. His sons' progeny become nations that populate the entire earth.

THE CITY AND TOWER OF BABEL

Every human speaks the same language until the population in one of the regions decides to build a city that will gain renown by hosting a tower that soars up into the heavens. God is angered by the vanity of this concept. Disappointed that the residents have abused the power of communication, God scatters the citizens across the earth, forcing them to speak different languages so they can no longer automatically understand one another. The building project ceases, and God calls the place Babel, which would become a pun, as it was the town that compelled the world's languages to be mixed.

Shem's descendants are listed through the generations until we learn of a man named Abram, heading out for Canaan with his wife, Sarai, who is, regrettably, childless.

AIMEE BENDER

THIRTY-SEVEN STATEMENTS ON BABEL

I My first word was *What?*

II I ask my writing class to list words they love. Then to list words they hate. The hate list is fun. Every year, someone says moist and everyone cringes. They can hardly stand it! Usually someone puts shit on their love list, and another student across the room puts shit on the hate list.

III Amichai, an Israeli scholar, tells me that the word for ark, teva, can also mean "word." Teva means "sacred container," something holding the seed for life, and Noah's ark was definitely that, but it could also be translated as "word," a box containing a sacred meaning. So according to that interpretation, Noah got those animals two by two, the elephants, the cheetahs, the marmots, the radiant eels, and he put them all on a word.

IV A few lines later, it's the Tower of Babel. The people were building a tower, and everyone spoke the same language.

V God came in and was angry at the power of the united human front and made the one language into many languages. "There the Lord confounded the speech of the whole earth."

VI It must've been different then. Just because you speak the same language doesn't mean you can understand the person.

VII We had that bad spat in the deli. You thought I meant that I wanted to go with you to the cop movie. But I didn't say that! I knew it was a moment for you to have special time with your friend! I said I wanted to go with you to the next cop movie. You didn't hear me. Maybe I forgot to say "next." It took us an HOUR to get through it. You looked so upset. I was crying.

VIII   We both speak English.

IX   My friend has a daughter. When her daughter was born, she was blonde with light eyes. My friend has dark hair and dark eyes. She was so surprised. She had expected a child who would look a little like Anne Frank, as my friend looks a little like Anne Frank, as many Jewish women do. But her daughter looked more like Aunt Katie from Nevada.

X   "Do you know what I mean?" "You know?" "Does that make sense?"

XI   "I'm so surprised!" said my friend on the phone. "Who is this person?"

XII   Ants operate as a string of neurons. The ant brain is spread out amongst the group of ants. Before the Tower of Babel was broken, all the people must've been of one mind, kind of like a group of tower-building ants. We were not so separate if we all truly spoke the same language, if we all could really communicate that clearly, if all our words were the same. We were groupthink. We were oneness.

XIII   Then my friend reconsidered. I could hear the gurgling baby sounds on the other side of the phone line. "I don't know her yet," she admitted. "If she had looked like Anne Frank, I would've assumed that I knew her, that she was just like me."

XIV   If you see an ant separate from its line of ants, it will wander around. If it does not find the group again, it will die.

XV   André Breton, father of surrealism, wrote in 1924 in his brilliant *Surrealist Manifesto*, "Keep reminding yourself that literature is the saddest road that leads to everything."

XVI   What the hell is he talking about?

XVII I have it on the wall in my office. I read it and reread it. Why the saddest road?

XVIII Here it is in its original French: *Dites-vous bien que la littérature est un des plus tristes chemins qui mènent à tout.*

XIX Flaubert says, "[N]one of us can ever express the exact measure of our needs, or our ideas, or our sorrows, and human speech is like a cracked kettle on which we beat out tunes for bears to dance to, when we long to move the stars to pity."

XX Tripping and falling and flubbing and rephrasing.

XXI Flaubert's talking gorgeously about the inadequacy of our tools, but I enjoy thinking of bears in a forest, dancing.

XXII Metaphor is beautiful. It is also failure. Simile: *It is like, the sun is like, your body is like, my heart is like.* This is one of our very best ways to describe experience, which is at its core a way to admit we cannot directly ever describe experience.

XXIII In the story, God gave us our separateness.

XXIV My friend's daughter is not my friend. Even if she had looked like Anne Frank, she would not have been my friend. It was actually helpful that they looked so different, so there would be no confusion over who was who.

XXV We came in on a word. We were all the same mind, speaking the same words. Then God made us different.

XXVI It is sad.

XXVII It is also true.

XXVIII It is also kind of relieving. We were never ants to begin with.

XXIX We try and try. Try to communicate. Try again. Misunderstand again.

xxx   That other fight we had on the way to the national park? Awful! I cannot believe you said that! When I say, "Turn right," I mean "turn right"!

xxxi   There is the bear waltz. And the bear Charleston.

xxxii   The tower crashed. After the dust cleared, the people looked around, bewildered, coughing. They all began talking at once. It was loud and confusing. Some sounds were guttural. Some fluid. Someone was singing a song no one had ever heard before, to a melody that had no match.

xxxiii   I was weeping on the ground and a man walked by. "We're through," I said. "It's over!" Babies were crying in the distance. Someone threw a handful of pebbles at the sky. The man sat on a rock next to me. He was wearing a beret and smoking a cigarette. "Do you speak English?" I asked, even though that was the first time I'd ever called it English. He shook his head. "*Je ne comprends pas*," he shrugged. He finished his cigarette and then lightly twisted it under his shoe. Then he reached into his pocket and unscrolled a parchment. He read it quietly for a while. Then handed it to me.

xxxiv   I could not read a word of it, but mostly it was just a picture of a road. A long road into an open horizon, which matched the view I saw when I looked up. Everyone, a little alone, moving forward with suitcases and bags. Kicking the dirt. Crying. Sometimes reaching out a hand. Hugging. Beyond, the shimmering land, vast and wide and untapped.

xxxv   My friend's daughter will grow up. One day, she will stand in a living room facing her mother, her own face flushed and hot. "You never understand me!" she will yell. She will stomp into her room.

xxxvi   It is the loss of the time when we felt known without effort. It is multiple languages even when we speak the same language. It is beating and beating on that old cracked kettle. But where does it lead?

xxxvii   "To everything."

ויבא אל הגר ותהר ותרא כי הרתה ותקל גברתה בעיניה:

"He cohabited with Hagar and she conceived; and when she saw that she had conceived, her mistress was lowered in her esteem." —Genesis 16:4

LEKH L'KHA ("*Go*")

GENESIS 12:1–17:27

ON THE ROAD: **GOD TELLS ABRAM TO LEAVE** his home and head to a destination that will be revealed. As a reward for leaping into the unknown, God promises that Abram's descendants will spawn a great nation, assuring him he will become known as a great man. In the future, those who bless Abram will be blessed, but those who curse him will be cursed.

At the age of seventy-five, Abram takes to the road, heading for Canaan with his wife, Sarai; his nephew Lot; and their entire caravan. Even though the Canaanites control the region, God informs Abram that his descendants will one day rule the area.

Abram builds an altar to celebrate this encouraging news before continuing his journey.

SHE AIN'T HEAVY, SHE'S MY SISTER
A severe famine grips the land, forcing Abram to head to Egypt. As he approaches the border, he tells his wife to pass herself off as his sister—a deception designed to prevent lusty Egyptians from killing Abram so they can enjoy her for themselves.

Abram's worst-case scenario comes to pass: Sarai is so beguiling, she is soon subsumed into Pharaoh's court harem.

Abram profits from her ascendancy, and is plied with sheep, oxen, asses, slaves, she-asses, and even camels.

God intercedes by unleashing mighty plagues upon the royal household, which causes the Pharaoh to express his frustration that Abram had not disclosed the true nature of his relationship with Sarai. Abram quickly finds himself escorted out of Egypt.

YOU GO YOUR WAY, I'LL GO MINE
Abram's caravan is now weighed down by gold, silver, and cattle. His nephew Lot is also well outfitted. So great is their bounty that the two have to separate to ensure there is enough room for their animals to graze without getting in one another's way. Abram lets his nephew choose his preferred destination, and Lot selects the verdant plains around Sodom, a city that is packed full of sinners.

God appears again to Abram and reminds him that all the land he can see in every direction will soon be his and that it will be filled by his descendants, who will be as difficult to count as the dust of the earth. Abram responds to this news by constructing an altar.

CLASH OF KINGS
War engulfs the area as the region's

kings do battle. Sodom and Gomorrah are invaded by the Mesopotamians, who ransack the city, enslaving its populace, including Lot and his party. Abram rounds up 318 men and sets off in pursuit, managing to defeat the captors and liberate all those who have been taken prisoner, including his nephew. The king of Sodom and King Melchizedek of Salem are among those who welcome him back victorious. Melchizedek, who is also a priest, praises Abram and God for their military success. Abram rewards him with booty. The king of Sodom asks Abram to return his people, but suggests Abram keep all of the possessions he has plundered. Abram replies that he is under strict instructions from God not to keep even a thread or a sandal strap.

THE COVENANT
God reappears to Abram, reminding him that he will be protected and richly rewarded. Abram complains that he has no heir and will have to leave his belongings to his steward. God informs him that he will yet have children and that his offspring will be as numerous as the stars in the sky.

Abram asks God how he will know when to possess the land. God tells him to sacrifice a ram, a dove, and a young bird. Abram falls into a deep sleep as the sun sets, and God reveals that his offspring will be enslaved in a foreign land for centuries, only to have God crush their oppressors and free them with great wealth. Abram is also informed that he will live to a ripe old age.

Later, a smoking oven and a burning torch are visible, and God makes a covenant with Abram, revealing the exact parameters of the land he will inherit.

SARAI AND HAGAR
Because Sarai remains barren, she urges Abram to try to have a child with her Egyptian servant, Hagar. Abram agrees and Hagar becomes pregnant, which makes her act self-important around Sarai. After Sarai complains to Abram, he tells his wife to do whatever she thinks fit to resolve the situation. Sarai elects to treat Hagar so harshly that she feels compelled to flee.

An angel tracks Hagar to a watering hole in the desert. When asked why she's fled, Hagar admits she is scared of Sarai. The angel tells her that if she returns to Sarai and tolerates the abuse, her descendants will become too many to count. She is also advised to name her son Ishmael, and told that he will be a wild man who will live a life of conflict. Hagar follows the advice, and Ishmael is born when Abram is eighty-six years old.

ABRAHAM'S BARGAIN
Twelve years later, God tells Abram, "I am 'El Shaddai.' Walk before Me, and be blameless." Abram is also reminded of the covenant. Abram falls to his face, and God changes his name to Abraham while breaking the news of Abraham's end of the deal: He must circumcise every male in his family, himself included.

There are more changes. Sarai's name is now to be Sarah. And sensationally, she will bear a son whose descendants will be nations and rulers. Abraham's reaction is to laugh. "Can a man aged one hundred have a child?" he asks. "Can Sarah become pregnant at ninety?" Abraham asks God to show favor to Ishmael. God confirms that he too will become the father of a great nation, but that his covenant will be carried through Isaac, who will be born to Sarah the following year.

Abraham circumcises every male in his party—even his slaves. At age ninety-nine, he circumcises himself.

JILL SOLOWAY

o I take a bus or a cab from the station? That is what nobody told me. The agency that sends you thinks that if they give you the name of the people, that is enough. I called and texted the lady, but she keeps writing back to my wrong email account. I got rid of Hotmail a million years ago, but for some reason the agency keeps giving it out. The lady's name is Sarah, I know that, and her husband is Avi, I know that, and they are Jewish people. Avi is a record producer and Sarah is an I'm-not-sure.

* *

Lisa used this agency, as did Sandy, so I trusted it. Lisa got an amazing girl from the Research Triangle, a biology student, and Sandy got a black girl from Texas. They all raved about the kinds of girls the agency sent, so I figured it would work. I picked her name from a list of names, Aggie, because she sounded like a farm girl. It was an old picture. If I had seen a new picture, I wouldn't have picked her. She was from Florida, but not the beachy, sandy part of Florida where people you and I know have been; she was from Sweet Gum Head, Florida, which may as well have been Mississippi.

When I look back, I realize she gave a suspicious email address to the agency. Our communication was so damn spotty, I should have written to the agency and said give me another girl. I had a feeling about her, but I didn't trust my feeling. That is the worst thing about me—I don't know how to trust my feelings. There's my gut, and there's my anxiety that chases me like a pack of dogs. It's seriously hard to know which is which.

* *

So, yeah, from the moment Avi the record producer opened the door, I knew there was going to be trouble. Sarah was out with their kid, so it was weird. My first connection was not with her, which isn't her fault or my fault, it just was.

My first connection was with him. He reminded me of my favorite English teacher at Sweet Gum Head High, John Thomas. Avi had the same soap smell as John Thomas, which John Thomas called sandalwood. Is it wrong is it wrong is it wrong that from the moment I walked into their Manhattan double-story loft, I had to fight some tidal impulse to tell Avi I loved him already, forever? That is okay, I thought to myself, I know how to fight this feeling. My mom and my grandma and every other one laid it out for me before I even turned eleven. Men and boys your whole life will want to have sex with you. It is your job to say no.

Mom and Grandma always left one thing out of the conversation, making it seem like boys come after you, and you bat them off like flies on cheesecake or something. Leaving off what you do if your body begs for something so strong and desirable that you don't even know how to describe it, so you don't even try when you write emails to your best friends about what New York City is like.

* *

AVI: How do you even know, she's only been here a week.

SARAH: It's just a feeling.

AVI: I remember you had these feelings before and they turned out to be wrong. Remember when you wanted to buy the loft downstairs to expand into and it ended up having all that water damage?

SARAH: I guess.

AVI: You kept saying, Avi, I have a feeling.

SARAH: Mmm.

AVI: Izzy loves her.

SARAH: Izzy is just barely getting to know her.

THE
ELLIOTT BAY
BOOK COMPANY

1521 10th Avenue
Seattle, Washington 98122
Telephone (206) 624-6600

Toll-Free (800) 962-5311
Fax (206) 903-1601

www.elliottbaybook.com
Internet: orders@elliottbaybook.com

We ship books anywhere
in the world and
will gift-wrap your purchase
at no additional charge.

Orders can be placed by email,
phone or fax.
orders@elliottbaybook.com
Toll-Free: 1-800-962-5311
Fax: 1-206-903-1601

We have over 150,000 titles
in stock and a knowledgeable
staff ready to assist you.

AVI: That's what's so crazy: It's only been a week, and Izzy already begs to go places with her.

A beat, then—

SARAH: Doesn't her diamond cross drive you bananagrams?

AVI: Of course not, my God, it's a necklace, what is your problem?

SARAH: I don't know, honey.

A beat, then—

* *

When Avi and Aggie got together, I knew. Avi and Aggie got together the same day I was trying to send Aggie on an errand to get my sandal strap fixed at Louie's on 86th and Lex. I promise you I didn't mean to be mean to Aggie when I had to give her the instructions over and over again. My dog chewed into my sandal strap, the other sandal strap is fine, if Louie needs to make two brand-new sandal straps to make the sandals match, then Louie should, but if he can make only one new one to match the one that the dog didn't eat, then that's fine, too. I have been told I have a hostile listening face when people are saying things that I don't like. I think of it as my thinking face. I was deep into my thinking face, staring at Aggie's dumbshit face as she was asking me for what felt like the millionth time, Okay, wait, do I tell the man at the shoe place you need one new sandal strap or two?

Aggie, are you even listening to me?

I wanted Aggie to take the sandals in so I could play with Izzy, I always want to play with Izzy, but then it seems I never have time to play with Izzy unless I make time. This time, this day, 3:30 p.m. on a perfect, crispy November Thursday, I had sketched out two hours to play with Izzy. We were going to go to the park and Aggie was going to take my sandals in, better that than sitting in the living room watching *Buckwild*. She can't cook, so she has to do something.

Then screw it, I said, lemme just take Izzy with me. Izzy and I will go on a subway adventure to the shoe place and we'll be back at six. We can order in, I said, my thinking face saying, because you never offer to cook and I don't know why the agency didn't tell you that if you find yourself with nothing to do for the family, cook for the family. Don't just sit there and watch *Buckwild.*

* *

We husbands have a way of talking about it. If the wives could hear how we talk, they'd be—accch, I dunno how they'd be. Look. There's no point saying what everyone knows, that you can feel it when there's a new young girl around. My buddy Barry did Ayahuasca. He said forget all that gender equality crap, on Ayahuasca he could see that men had green and blue light around them and women had red and orange and pink light. Simple as that.

The wives, maybe they talk about it, what it feels like to have this new young girl around taking care of your kid. If they use the word *jealousy* or not, who knows. The husbands, we talk about it. But the husbands and the wives don't talk about it together.

I came home from work early, and there was Aggie, a name that should go on some ugly fatass, but no, it was put for God knows what reason on this blonde shiksa milkmaid. She shoulda been a Kristen or Kirsten, but she was Aggie, and she was sittin' on our couch, clicking through something.

AGGIE: Hi.

AVI: Hey.

AGGIE: Sarah and Izzy went on errands. They won't be back till six.

AVI: (*It's four fifteen.*) (*Thought not said.*)

AGGIE: You wanna watch TV?

AVI: (*Sits next to her, quiet, too close to her leg.*)

AGGIE: This sucks. You can put anything on.

* *

I never said anything, I just felt that thing that I never found a way to ask my mom and grandma about. I didn't move my bod as I watched *Buckwild*. Nor did I twitch or twist even ever so slightly to give him a clue that I was hot as hell for him. But then his hand was on my leg, his left hand, which was the hand closest to me. Then his other hand, his right hand. Then Avi and everything sandalwood about him filled me up, and we were both wood, a raft on a tide that was bigger than Riverside Avenue and the river out the window and all of New York City.

And there we were, looking at each other, wondering what had happened.

* *

We pay people to take care of our children. I had miscarried right before Aggie came, did I tell you that? I don't know if I told you that. I was pregnant with a son—okay, no one told me, I'm making that up, but when I found out I was pregnant, I knew it was a boy. This was my gut, not my anxiety. I knew the difference. Of course I could have taken care of Izzy while I was pregnant, but I knew that I would be barfy and tired and to hell with it, I just wanted a summer girl. To be with Izzy from four to seven, that stretch where the afternoon demons laugh because you haven't made dinner yet, and they know you just want to hide and die. The afternoon demons make you take a nap so you can wake up and make dinner, and pregnant, I knew it would be worse, so I got Aggie. Does it sound like I'm blaming myself? Well, I am. Even after the miscarriage, Avi gave me an out, he asked me, Do you still want the summer girl from Florida? Yes, I said, I still want the summer girl from Florida. I wanted an out. I could spend the summer afternoons sick in bed pregnant with a boy or sick in bed mourning a baby who was going to be my first boy, a baby the size of a bean when I lost it, so why do I keep crying? Yes, I said, I still want the summer girl.

I don't know why Aggie needed Avi to know that she was giving their baby up for adoption. I don't know why she had to tell both of us that she had gotten pregnant. I don't know why Avi wanted to come clean that they had had sex. All I know is that I called the agency and had her removed less than one month after she got here.

All I know is that she won't think of her baby as a Jew. All I know is that whatever family adopts that baby won't think of that baby as a Jew. All I know is that all I hope is that whoever that baby turns out to be,

Let him not be a boy.

God,

Let this goddamned summer not come back to haunt us.

* *

My mom and dad are asleep.

Aggie is gone—she left three whole months ago.

I am six and I will be six for another three months.

My daddy loves my mommy.

At school today in science we learned about electric tails. They come from pulsing stars, and they live in the sky forever.

ויאמר קח נא את בנך את יחידך אשר אהבת את יצחק ולך לך
אל ארץ המריה והעלהו שם לעלה על אחד ההרים אשר אמר אליך:

"And He said, 'Take your son, your favored one, Isaac, whom you love,
and go to the land of Moriah, and offer him there as a burnt offering on
one of the heights I will point out to you.'" —Genesis 22:2

VAYEARA (*"And he appeared"*)
GENESIS 18:1–22:24

ABRAHAM IS SITTING OUTSIDE HIS TENT in the heat of the day when God approaches him in the form of three men. Abraham runs out to greet them, bows down, and eagerly offers up the customary desert hospitality of water, a footbath, and something to eat.

Abraham sprints around, urging his wife, Sarah, to make some cakes with their best flour, and orders a servant to slaughter a tender calf from his herd so he can serve the guests. One of the visitors informs Abraham that he will return the following year and that Sarah can have a son. Sarah overhears this, and because she and Abraham are well past childbearing age, she cannot suppress a burst of laughter. God asks Abraham why his wife finds this funny, asking him, "Is any deed too astounding for God to perform?" Sarah, suddenly afraid, attempts to lie, suggesting she has not laughed, but God knows what is the truth.

The three men then head toward Sodom with the ever hospitable Abraham accompanying them on their way. On the journey, he discovers that God has become outraged by the Sodomites' behavior and plans to exact punishment.

The three men head off, leaving Abraham to argue with God directly. He wonders whether God will punish the city collectively and risk killing the innocent along with the guilty. The two patiently negotiate the number of innocents God would protect. If ten good people can be found, the Lord agrees to spare the city.

CITY OF WRATH

Two angels arrive in Sodom at night and encounter Lot at the city gates. He offers them hospitality, which they initially refuse, agreeing only after Lot insists. Before they have a chance to retire for the night, an angry mob surrounds Lot's home, demanding that he hand over his visitors so that they can sodomize them. Lot tries to offer up his virgin daughters instead, but this proposal only inflames the mob, who scream that an outsider such as he should not tell them what to do. As they prepare to attack Lot, his guests pull him inside the house and proceed to incapacitate the attackers by blinding them with a bright light.

The angels tell Lot that they have been sent by God to destroy the city

and advise him to round up his family and prepare to evacuate. Lot tells them he will seek refuge in a small town nearby; before he leaves, the angels warn him not to look back. As soon as Lot reaches the neighboring town, God aims a violent fire at Sodom and Gomorrah, obliterating the region. His wife cannot resist sneaking a look at the carnage; she is transformed into a pillar of salt.

Lot finds sanctuary in a cave with his two daughters. The two of them, afraid that no man will impregnate them, hatch a plan to get their father drunk and then commit incest with him. Over the course of two nights, the women turn the idea into a reality, and although the drunken Lot is oblivious, they both become pregnant and bear children.

SHE AIN'T HEAVY, SHE'S MY SISTER, PART II

Journeying once more, Abraham encounters King Abimelech of Gerar and employs his "Sarah is my sister" deceit again. This time, God appears to Abimelech in a dream and threatens to kill him because he has taken up with a married woman. Abimelech defends his behavior, confessing he has not yet touched Sarah and rationalizing that he took her only on the basis of Abraham's misinformation. God gives the king the choice of returning Sarah or facing death.

The king and his followers are terrified. They interrogate Abraham, demanding to know why he misled them in the first place. Abraham admits he has been afraid of being killed by those jealous of his wife's beauty and reveals that he merely stretched the truth: Sarah is actually his father's daughter by another mother.

Abimelech bestows sheep, oxen, and slaves upon Abraham, reunites him with Sarah, and offers him the opportunity to live on his land. Abraham prays to God on behalf of Abimelech. God had initially sewn shut the wombs of the king's wives and slave girls as a punishment. The sentence is quickly revoked.

MOTHER'S DAY

As God has promised, Sarah becomes pregnant and bears a son with her 100-year-old husband. Abraham calls him Isaac. Sarah is sensitive to the fact that anyone who finds out that she has borne and breast-fed a child at her age will laugh. She also asks Abraham to cast out Hagar and her son, Ishmael, so there can be no confusion about Isaac's place as heir. Abraham is uncomfortable with the request; after all, Ishmael is also his son. God advises him to do what Sarah tells him, as Isaac is to be his heir, while reassuring him that Ishmael will also birth a nation, as he is Abraham's seed.

The next morning, Abraham gives Hagar some food and a water bottle and sends them out into the desert. After depleting her water supply, Hagar places Ishmael under a bush; she cannot bear to witness his inevitable death.

God hears the child's sobbing and sends an angel to reveal to Hagar that she should have no fear; her son will in fact be the heir of a nation. Hagar immediately spots a well and satiates Ishmael's thirst. He comes of age in the desert and becomes an archer, ultimately marrying an Egyptian.

Abraham and Abimelech argue over ownership of a well, but are able to solve their problem by trading ewes and signing a pact.

THE TEST

Time passes. God decides to test Abraham's faith by instructing him to take his beloved son Isaac to Moriah and sacrifice him on a mountain as a burnt offering. The next morning, Abraham departs with an ass, two servants, and his son. He prepares the wood for a burnt offering and sets off toward the place God has described. After three days, they approach the destination and Abraham tells his servants to wait, promising that he and his son will return after praying. Placing the wood on his son, he carries burning coal and his knife.

Isaac quizzes his father about why they have all the necessary equipment for a sacrifice, except a sheep to offer up. Abraham dodges the question, explaining that God will provide one. Once they arrive at Moriah, Abraham piles up the wood, binds his son, lays him on top of the altar, and grabs a knife with which to kill him. As he does so, an angel's voice shouts his name. Abraham answers, "Here I am." God instructs him to do no harm; since Abraham was prepared to kill his son on command, his fear of God is considered satisfactory.

Abraham then spies a ram conveniently caught by his horns in a thicket and offers it as a sacrifice in place of his son. The angel blesses Abraham for following God's command and promises that his descendants will be as numerous as the stars in the sky and the sand on the beach. The descendants will conquer their enemies' cities and be a blessing to all the nations of the world.

DAMON LINDELOF

SUBJECT: DESIGNATED A

CASE FILE: 18-1-22-24

FOLLOWING IS TRANSCRIBED FROM RECORDING OF INITIAL OBSERVATION SESSION.

[BEGIN TRANSCRIPT]

Coffee?

. . . Sorry?

Coffee. You want some?

No, thank you.

A soda? Some water?

Yes, all right. Water . . .

We don't have any fancy bottled stuff. Tap okay?

That's fine.

Great. Good. We'll get that for you. So . . . you know why we brought you in?

I think so. Yes.

And you're sure you don't want a lawyer? That's your right.

I'm sure.

Because you could say something that'll get you into a lot of trouble.

Trouble with who?

Heh . . . that's . . . you're joking, right?

Not really.

Oh. Okay. Well . . . then I guess . . . sure, I'll answer your question. You'll get yourself into trouble with the *law*.

All right.

"All right?" As in you understand?

Yes. I understand.

Good. Because there's something I *don't* understand. And maybe you can help me understand it. Do you think you can do that?

I'll try.

Good. You *try*. And let's start with this—and I apologize if I'm kinda just leaping in here . . . My wife says I'm a little . . . y'know, blunt? But here we go. I just want to know . . . I want you to *explain* . . . exactly why you tried to kill your son.

But I didn't.

. . . What?

I didn't kill my son.

You didn't . . . well, crap. Crap, Abe . . . I guess you're right. That's why I said you *tried* to. In fact, it says here . . . it says that you were spotted tying him up—

—Binding.

Huh?

I was binding him.

VAYEARA ("*And he appeared*")

Okay. Wow. Sure. You were *binding* your kid . . . and then—and if any of this sounds wrong to you, Abe, you just speak up—but then you were seen putting your son . . .

Isaac.

Right. Isaac. You were seen putting Isaac on top of a pile of wood.

He was meant to be a burnt offering.

Excuse me?

My son. I was told to make a burnt offering of him.

You were . . . told.

Yes.

By *who*?

God.

. . . God.

Yes.

So . . . *God*. He told you to . . . light your son on fire?

After I had killed him, yes.

Sure . . . because burning him *alive* . . . that would be inhuman.

It's what I was asked to do.

What for?

. . . Sorry?

God tells you to kill a child . . . your *own* child . . . for *what*? Why? What do you *get* in exchange for your "offering"?

Nothing.

Nothing?

He had already given me . . . given *us* . . . something.

And what's that?

My wife—Sarah . . . she was way past the point of being able to get pregnant. But He said He would give us a child. And He did.

This would be . . . God again?

Yes.

He gave you a son. So you could raise him. And love him. Then kill him.

But I didn't kill him.

But you were *willing* to.

Yes.

Why?

Because God asked.

And you just . . . ? You didn't . . . *question* it?

No.

Your wife . . . Sarah . . . what'd she have to say about this?

I didn't tell her.

Of course you didn't. And Isaac . . . I'm guessing you didn't tell him either. You just walked him up that mountain and he had no *idea* what you were gonna do.

That's right. Yes.

So what changed your mind?

Nothing did. He stopped me.

. . . God.

No. An angel.

He didn't come Himself?

No.

Too busy?

Maybe.

And this angel . . . what'd he say?

That I didn't need to kill Isaac.

Why not?

Because now He knew that I feared Him.

The angel?

No. God. He knew I feared God.

But that's not what you told me.

. . . Sorry?

You told me you were willing to kill your son just because He asked. Not because you were afraid of Him.

. . . Oh.

Are you afraid of Him?

Oh.

Oh . . . what?

You're the angel.

What?

On the mountain. I only heard your voice. But now . . . yes, I recognize it. You. You're the angel. Calling to me a second time.

I'm an . . . ? C'mon. You're insane, Abe. You've lost your goddamned mind.

I'm not. And I haven't.

And yet you think . . . I'm an angel.

I *know* you are.

Okay. Fine then. You got me. I'm an angel. And *why* is it . . . I'm "calling to you"? A second time?

Because you want to make sure.

Of what?

That I fear God. That's why you asked me.

Ah . . . so He's *testing* you. Again. Because . . . what? Getting you to stab your kid to death wasn't proof enough?

But I *didn't* stab my—

—Yeah, yeah. I got it, Abe.

He spoke to me, you know. Outside Sodom. Did He tell you that?

Why don't *you* tell me.

He was ready to destroy the whole city . . . and I asked Him if He would spare them. If there were just fifty innocent people inside, wouldn't it be worth letting the rest live? And He said He would. Then I said, What about forty-five? And He said yes, He'd spare the city then, too. We negotiated for a while. I was able to get Him down to ten—if there were just ten innocent people, He agreed not to destroy it.

This is . . . wow . . . this is a *great* story.

But He *did* destroy it. He rained fire down on Sodom. Gomorrah, too. Burned them all. And when I learned of this, I thought to myself . . . Maybe I should have pushed further . . . Maybe I should have asked God to spare the cities if just *one* innocent person could be found. Do you know why I didn't?

Tell me.

Because I knew. I knew He was going to destroy those cities no matter what I said.

And why's that?

Because it was His will.

SUBJECT BEGINS TO AUDIBLY CRY NOW . . . THIS LASTS FOR ALMOST SIX MINUTES, FOLLOWED BY A PERIOD OF SILENCE. AFTER WHICH:

Coffee?

. . . Sorry?

Coffee. You want some?

No, thank you.

A soda? Some water?

Yes, all right. Water . . .

We don't have any fancy bottled stuff. Tap okay?

That's fine.

Great. Good. We'll get that for you. So . . . you know why we brought you in?

I think so. Yes.

[END TRANSCRIPT]

FROM THIS POINT ON THE SEQUENCE BEGINS AGAIN.

SUBJECT WAS OBSERVED FOR A PERIOD OF NINETY MINUTES UNDER WHICH THE ABOVE SEQUENCE WAS REPEATED NINETEEN TIMES.

THE SEQUENCE WAS REPEATED VERBATIM.

SUBSEQUENT OBSERVATIONS DETERMINED SUBJECT SPEAKS ONLY THE WORDS TRANSCRIBED ABOVE AS IF ON A PERPETUAL LOOP.

THOUGH THE TRANSCRIPT SUGGESTS THERE ARE TWO PEOPLE PRESENT, THE SUBJECT WAS ALONE IN HIS CELL FOR THE DURATION OF THE RECORDING.

SLIGHT FLUCTUATIONS IN TONE AND ACCENT WOULD SUGGEST THE CREATION OF THE SECOND CHARACTER, PERHAPS AS A PROXY BY WHICH TO CONFESS AND/OR PROCESS SUBJECT'S ACTIONS.

PRELIMINARY DIAGNOSIS

CYCLOID PSYCHOSIS

RECOMMENDED TREATMENT

10–15 mg. OLANZAPINE, twice daily. Limit interaction with family (particularly the victim), continue observation.

"The maiden was very beautiful, a virgin whom no man had known.
She went down to the spring, filled her jar, and came up." —Genesis 24:16

HAYYEI SARAH ("*The life of Sarah*")
GENESIS 23:1–25:18

 ARAH DIES AT THE AGE OF 127 IN HEBRON. In mourning, Abraham approaches the local tribe of Hittites to buy a burial site from them. The Hittites are well aware of Abraham's special relationship with God, so they offer him the pick of their land. He selects an area known as the Cave of Machpelah, and then he buries his wife.

Aware of his age, Abraham makes his chief servant swear that he will make sure that Isaac does not marry a Canaanite, dispatching the man to the land of his birth to find a suitable bride. The servant asks a practical question: If the woman he finds refuses to relocate to be with Isaac, would he consider moving back to her? Abraham says that Isaac will not go anywhere unless God instructs him to. The servant swears to obey Abraham's command, placing his hand under the thigh of his master, as was the custom.

FINDING LOVE DOWN AT THE WATERING HOLE

The servant heads out with ten of Abraham's camels to Nahor. In the evening, he stops his caravan by a well outside the city at a time when the women come out to draw water. The servant suggests that God send him a sign showing him which one should be Isaac's bride. He decides he will ask all the women for a drink, and the one who also volunteers to give water to his camels will be "the one."

No sooner have these words come out of his mouth than the beautiful Rebekah arrives at the well bearing a jar on her shoulder. He asks for some water, and she draws water for the servant and his camels—the sign the servant had decided should make her Isaac's bride. He presents Rebekah with a gold nose ring and two gold armbands and asks if he can sleep on her father's property overnight. Rebekah consents and introduces the servant to her family. He briefs them on his sacred mission and suggests that their daughter is the chosen one. Her family agrees that if the matter has been decreed by God, then the servant must take Rebekah.

The servant intends to begin the return leg of his journey the next morning, but when he wakes, Rebekah's brother and mother beg for ten days to spend with her before she leaves. The servant says that God is guiding this mission; that means they should not tarry. Rebekah agrees to leave immediately. Before she and her servants leave, however, her family bestows a blessing, hoping that her offspring will be numerous and successful in battle.

SPEED DATING

It is early evening: Isaac has just returned to his home in the Negev when he sees the caravan approaching. The servant tells Isaac what has occurred. Isaac walks Rebekah into his deceased mother's tent and takes her as his wife. He loves her; through her he finds comfort after his mother's death.

Isaac is not alone in taking a new wife. Abraham marries Keturah, who bears him six children. Their descendants are listed. Abraham gives all his possessions to Isaac in his will, having already given his other children gifts. He also dispatches them far away from Isaac to the east.

At the ripe old age of 175, Abraham passes away a happy man. His sons Isaac and Ishmael bury him in the Cave of Machpela near Sarah, his first wife. God blesses Isaac. Ishmael has twelve sons who become chiefs of twelve tribes. He lives until he is 137.

REBECCA DANA

Look, I may be a virgin, but I'm not an idiot.

You don't get to be pushing forty in this town without learning a thing or two about men. First of all: They're helpless. They cannot do anything for themselves. It's really quite sad. You know the expression "You can lead a horse to water, but you can't make him drink"? Actually, you probably don't know it because, if you're reading this, you're probably a man. This is a thing women have been saying for hundreds of years, but it will no doubt be another couple of millennia before (a) it occurs to a man, and (b) he has the wherewithal to write it down.

Anyway, the same is true of men, and also camels. You can lead them to water, but then you will have to beg and cajole them to actually drink it. Like, lift the jar to their desiccated lips and bat your eyes and say, "*Please.*" This literally happened yesterday. And when I say "literally" here, I mean it, well, *literally*, not in the way a lot of men use it, when they really mean "figuratively." This is another thing about men: They can be imprecise in their language. They tend to speak poorly. Sometimes you need to help them say what you know they really want to say.

So last night around sunset, I go out to the well, like I always do. But when I get there, I find this catatonic man and his ten dead-looking camels just staring in at the water, like they're about to collapse from thirst, but not doing anything about it. I give them a weird look because, Why aren't they having a drink? The well is *right here.* But whatever—men!—so I fill up my jar, and the guy asks if he can have a sip. Okay, *moron*, sure, you can have a sip. And while I'm at it, I offer to juice up his camels, too, because somebody has to be a functioning adult around here. When I do this, he looks at me like I have just invented particle physics. And then he takes out a big sack of gold jewelry and starts putting it on me: a nose ring, some bracelets. It's insane. He is obviously some sort of rich lunatic, and if he stays outside overnight, someone will rob and kill him. Before I can explain this, my brother Laban comes out after me because I have been gone so long. The dude asks if he can stay with us, and when my brother sees all the gold, he is more than happy to oblige. I love my brother but what was he thinking inviting this completely bonkers individual, who probably stole all this loot and is being chased down by a gang of murderous thugs, into our home? This is a third thing about men: They are easily distracted by shiny objects.

When we get back, my mother and sisters set about feeding this man's camels and cleaning him up. Meanwhile, he is muttering something about being on "an errand from the Lord," and he refuses to eat until we let him talk, so we go, "Okay, guy, tell us the story." And it's a doozy. He's been sent by my great-uncle Abraham to find a wife for his son Isaac. Abraham is extremely old and extremely loaded. His wife, Sarah, just died, and he went through a whole mess trying to get her buried in some special cave. Now he's tired, and all he wants is for his son to marry a girl from his hometown, which is why he sent his senior servant—this dehydrated man from the well—back here to Nahor to find a beautiful and virtuous girl for him. That beautiful and virtuous girl, apparently, is me.

What I want to say at this point is, Why did you not just *talk* to me? What is the purpose of standing at the well dying of thirst and waiting to see if I'll offer you a drink, when you could have just spoken to me and learned of my virtues? (My beauty, of course, is self-evident.) But I don't say it because he is obviously so pleased with his cleverness in devising this scheme for finding a wife for his master that I don't want to burst his bubble.

When he finishes the story, my father and brother, in their infinite male wisdom, are all, "Sure, take her!" And I'm like, "Um, hello?" But then I think about it, and it occurs to me that this is a great idea. If

Abraham really is as big and powerful as they say he is, then his son Isaac must be, too. You know the saying "Behind every great man . . ."? Of course you don't.

The guy takes out more presents, and everyone is thrilled. We hop on our camels and ride off to Canaan while my family sings:

> *"O sister!*
> *May you grow*
> *Into thousands of myriads;*
> *May your offspring seize*
> *The gates of their foes."*

I look back and smile. Damn straight they will.

"When the boys grew up, Esau became a skillful hunter, a man of the outdoors; but Jacob was a mild man who stayed in camp." —Genesis 25:27

TOL'DOT ("*Generations*")
GENESIS 25:19–28:9

ISAAC IS FORTY YEARS OLD WHEN HE TAKES Rebekah as his bride. She, too, is barren until Isaac prays to God, who makes her pregnant with twins. The pregnancy is a difficult one. It often feels as if the twins are wrestling in her womb. Rebekah suffers such pain that she screams out to God, who informs her that the children will become two nations. They are struggling in the womb because one nation will be more powerful than the other, and the older will ultimately serve the younger.

When Rebekah gives birth, the first twin emerges red and hairy. They decide to name the boy Esau. The second infant comes out grabbing the heel of his brother. They name him Jacob. Isaac is sixty at the time of the boys' birth.

BROTHERLY LOVE

Esau grows up to be a skilled hunter and outdoorsman. Jacob is much more reserved and prefers to stay around the camp. Isaac favors Esau because of his hunting instincts, but Rebekah prefers Jacob. One day, Jacob is cooking a stew when Esau returns, famished, from the field. Esau demands food, but Jacob asks for Esau's birthright—his rightful inheritance as the oldest son—in return. Esau thinks it through before he agrees, reasoning that a birthright will be of no use if he dies of hunger. So he swears to give it over to his younger brother in return for a bowl of stew.

Another famine strikes Canaan. Isaac goes down to the Philistine kingdom of Abimelech in Gerar. (God has told him not to go to Egypt, but to trust that God will bless him, reiterating the covenantal promise with Abraham.) In Gerar, Isaac passes Rebekah off as his sister, but when the king spies the two acting like husband and wife, he demands to know why Isaac lied. Isaac admits he was afraid of being killed by someone enchanted by Rebekah's beauty. The king asks his guest to consider what the ramifications might have been if one of his subjects had seduced Rebekah; he then sends out a decree making it a capital offense to hurt either Isaac or Rebekah.

Isaac's farming skills, aided by God's blessing, lead him to grow a bountiful crop and amass a fortune. He stockpiles so many sheep, cows, and servants that he becomes the envy of the Philistines, who express their jealousy by blocking up his wells. King Abimelech suggests it might be better for everyone if Isaac leaves the area, which he does. But every time he sets up camp and digs wells, local herdsmen dispute his right to own them. Abimelech ultimately rides out to ease the friction. Aware that the Lord is with Isaac, the king wisely brokers a peace pact.

Esau marries Judith at the age of forty; the marriage is a source of unhappiness to Isaac and Rebekah, because their new daughter-in-law is a Hittite.

JACOB'S DECEIT

When Isaac is old and his eyesight is failing, he calls Esau and broaches the possibility of his imminent death. He instructs his son to hunt some game and cook his favorite dish before he bestows his final blessing. Rebekah overhears, and as soon as Esau sets off for the hunt, she conspires with Jacob to deceive her husband. Commanding him to bring two kids back from the flock, she sets about cooking one of Isaac's favorite dishes; her plan is for Jacob to bring it to Isaac and steal the final blessing for himself. Jacob sees an immediate problem: Unlike the hairy Esau, he is smooth-skinned. Isaac will only have to use his sense of touch to recognize the deceit. His mother takes full responsibility for the duplicity and instructs Jacob to follow her advice.

GENESIS

Rebekah cooks the dish and then dresses Jacob in Esau's best clothes, covering his hands and neck with lambskins. Jacob takes the dish to his father and passes himself off as his older brother. Isaac marvels that he has been able to prepare the dish so quickly, and Jacob, playing the role of Esau, credits God. The dying man then asks his son to come close so he can verify his identity by touching him, yet he remains confused: He has felt Esau's hairy hands yet heard the voice of Jacob. Still, he blesses Jacob while asking him if he is really Esau. Jacob claims he is. After they eat, Isaac asks for a kiss; upon smelling Esau's garments, he revels in their outdoors smell.

Isaac's blessing promises abundance, power, and familial leadership. No sooner is it delivered than Esau bursts in, freshly back from the hunt. Esau has prepared his father's favorite dish and upon presenting it, demands his blessing. Unable to see him, Isaac asks who he is; upon realizing his mistake, he says that he can do nothing to reverse the bestowal of the blessing. Esau sobs and begs his father to bless him, too; instead, Isaac informs

him of Jacob's deceit. Esau realizes he has been tricked out of both his blessing and his birthright, and must listen as his father reveals the content of the blessing: Jacob will be his master. As Esau weeps, Isaac attempts to calm him, promising that he, too, will enjoy the fat of the land, even though he will always be a swordsman subservient to Jacob.

A furious Esau decides to murder Jacob once Isaac has died and been mourned. Rebekah learns of this plan and advises Jacob to flee to her brother Laban until Esau calms down and forgets. Rebekah talks to Isaac about her fear that Jacob will marry a local Hittite, so the dying man calls his younger son to him and commands him not to take a foreign wife. Blessing him, he suggests Jacob take a wife from among his uncle Laban's daughters. He then expresses his hope that Jacob will receive the blessing of Abraham and possess the land in which they are living, which was promised by God.

Jacob sets off for Laban's home. When Esau realizes that Canaanite wives upset his father, he marries one, taking Mahalath as his third wife.

JOSHUA FOER

I t is well known that Esau loved hunting, the least Jewish of hobbies. Less well known: He was also a scratch golfer, and not half bad on ice skates. Or that he wore tasseled loafers, and a class ring, and didn't mind the taste of eggnog dripping from his bushy mustache. Everything his Orthodox parents dismissed with the flick of a hand as *goyishe nachas*— pleasures of the goyim—he embraced with the full force of his tanned, gym-conditioned arms. Esau was the first Jew to wish he wasn't.

And when he woke up one morning and realized he was forty, and still a bachelor, and that his parents doted on his doughy, bookish brother more than him, he did what many a Jewish man has fantasized about, and more than a few since Esau have actually done: He went off and married a shiksa. Two, actually.

The new daughters-in-law were, it goes without saying, "a source of bitterness" to Esau's parents. Rebekah, the first Jewish mother to think she'd birthed a perfect son, could hardly swallow her outrage. But Isaac tried to keep his disappointment tucked beneath his velvet yarmulke. After all, there was still a chance, despite the Christmas tree in Esau's living room, that the grandchildren might still have bar mitzvahs. And if it was at the Reform temple with the motorized ark that opened and closed as if at a Broadway show—well, that was still better than nothing.

Esau was the first Jew to leave the fold. The first to not have to worry about *treif*ing up the dishes, or getting up early to go to shul, who no longer had to say, "I do this, even though I'm not sure why."

Over the last two thousand years, while the global population has increased thirtyfold, the Jewish population has merely doubled. If the Cohens had managed to keep pace with the Joneses, there'd be 200 million Jews in the world today—more Jews than Brazilians. Many of the numbers missing from our bottom line were deducted by Hitler, Cossacks, and overzealous popes. But many more of the missing Jews vanished not in pogroms or gas chambers, but—as many a well-heeled Jewish philanthropist will tell you—simply disappeared into the background. They took the path first cut by Esau in *Tol'dot*, married out, and joined the nations.

Isaac was not blind to any of this. In fact, he was not really blind at all. When Jacob came to him, cloaked in his brother's musky cologne, Isaac knew exactly who he was not. He knew that Jacob—forty years old, and still his mother's marionette—had been prepped for duplicity by Rebekah. How could he mistake that nasally voice? Or pretend those hairy arms felt anything like real hairy arms? And yet he played along with the ruse, and blessed the child who had no right. When Esau returned and asked for what was rightfully his, Isaac feigned outrage at Jacob's trickery. But he did not, it should be noted, undo what had been done. He knew he'd made no mistake. Instead, he made clear the one condition for Jacob winning his father's favor: "Thou shalt not take a wife of the daughters of Canaan."

Esau, for his part, sulked off in a huff, and did the one thing he knew could still piss off his parents. He went and took yet another wife. This time an Ishmaelite.

"He came upon a certain place and stopped there for the night,
for the sun had set. Taking one of the stones out of that place, he put it
under his head and lay down in that place." —Genesis 28:11

VA-YETZEI (*"And he left"*)
GENESIS 28:10–32:3

EST DREAM EVER: JACOB SETS OUT FOR HIS uncle Laban's camp in Haran. Once the sun sets, he stops for the night, putting his head on a stone to sleep. In his slumber, he dreams of a staircase reaching up to the sky with angels scurrying up and down it. God appears and declares that Jacob's descendants will be as numerous as the dust of the earth and will ultimately cover the world, savoring the honor of having their name invoked as a blessing. Jacob is also reassured that God will always protect him; his safe return to Canaan is a certainty.

When he wakes up, the realization of the godly interaction shakes Jacob to his core. To commemorate the event, he turns the stone upright and pours oil on it, renaming the spot Bethel ("House of God").

Jacob then swears that if God will stay with him and protect him as he makes his way on the journey, he will dedicate himself to God.

LOVE ON THE ROCK
Jacob journeys until he encounters a well covered by a large rock. The locals inform him that the rock is typically

removed after all of their flocks have arrived and are ready to drink. Once Rachel, Laban's daughter, approaches the well, Jacob ignores local custom and rolls the rock aside to give her flock water himself. He kisses Rachel, weeps, and reveals their family connection. Rachel wastes no time before taking him to meet her father, who hugs and kisses Jacob and brings him home.

BAIT AND SWITCH

A month passes. Jacob has begun working for his uncle, who is eager to legitimize the relationship; he asks his nephew to name his wages. Jacob offers to work for seven years in return for the hand of Rachel, the beauty he first encountered at the well. Laban agrees. Jacob toils for seven years, but the time feels like days because of the depth of his love. Laban prepares the wedding, but then cruelly tricks Jacob by sending his older daughter, Leah, who has "weak eyes," to marry him instead. When Jacob confronts his uncle, Laban points to the local custom of ensuring that an older sister marries before the younger.

BABY WARS

Jacob agrees to work an additional seven years for Rachel's hand. They marry, but Rachel is barren. Leah is not: She bears a son, Reuben, which means both "God has seen my affliction" and "now my husband will love me." She proceeds to produce three more sons: Simeon, Levi, and Judah.

Wracked by envy, Rachel tells Jacob she wants to have children or die, a statement that enrages Jacob, who explains that he does not have God's power and that it is God who has made her barren. Rachel suggests that Jacob have a baby with her servant, Bilhah. The servant becomes pregnant and bears two sons, Dan and Naphtali. Leah and Rachel become locked in competition, using their maids as surrogates to bear children by Jacob. In the meantime, Leah also produces two more sons and a daughter, Dinah.

God finally intervenes, opening Rachel's womb so that she can conceive. Once she gives birth to a son, she admits that God has removed her feeling of disgrace, and names the boy Joseph, which means "May God add another son for me."

THE GREAT ESCAPE

After Joseph's birth, Jacob asks Laban to allow him to leave and return to his homeland, but Laban enjoys having

Jacob around—he feels vicariously blessed by God's fortune and offers to pay his son-in-law any amount to stay. Jacob negotiates the right to take every speckled or spotted animal from his uncle's flock—the animals that are quickly identifiable and easy to separate.

Once they have struck a deal, the crafty Laban removes all his spotted animals and then travels three days away from Jacob. Jacob counters by manipulating the flock's mating patterns, so that many strong yet streaked animals are born, whereas the weaker ones all have solid coats. Laban's flock becomes feeble; Jacob becomes rich.

Laban's sons believe Jacob has taken advantage of their father to build his fortune illegitimately, and Jacob senses a change in Laban's mood. So, when God suggests he return to his homeland, the shepherd asks his wives to leave with him. After he reminds them of how Laban cheated him, and assures them that God will watch over their family, Rachel and Leah agree to follow the Lord's command.

Jacob puts his family on camels and drives his livestock toward Isaac's home in Canaan. (Rachel has cheekily stolen her father's idols before leaving.)

It takes three days for Laban to discover his daughters have fled, but he sets off in pursuit, managing to catch them within a week, even though God appears to him in a dream and warns him off.

Laban demands to know why Jacob has felt the need to flee under the cover of secrecy, claiming he would have celebrated their departure in style. He also admits that God has threatened him in a dream; still, he wants to know why Jacob has stolen his idols.

Jacob reveals his reasons: He cloaked his departure in secrecy because he did not believe Laban would permit Leah and Rachel to leave. Neither man is aware that Rachel stole the idols, and Jacob suggests that Laban is within his right to search for them and to kill whoever possesses them.

Laban undertakes a thorough search, but Rachel has hidden the carvings under her camel saddle and refuses to rise from it. Laban comes up empty-handed. Now it is Jacob's turn to be furious: Why, he asks his father-in-law, has he chosen to pursue them after the twenty hardworking years of service Jacob has provided? And, while he's at it, he tells Laban that he knew about the flock shenanigans; if it hadn't been for God's intervention, Jacob's family could have been left with nothing.

Laban retorts that the women are his daughters, the grandchildren his, and the flocks his, but he offers to make peace. The men make a mound out of stones and have a meal together. Laban agrees to separate and asks God to look over them, warning Jacob not to ill-treat his daughters. Jacob agrees and offers a sacrifice.

The next morning Laban kisses his daughters and grandchildren good-bye and heads home. Jacob continues his journey, encountering angels along the way.

ADAM MANSBACH

28:11 HE CAME TO A CERTAIN PLACE, AND STAYED THERE ALL NIGHT, BECAUSE THE SUN HAD SET. HE TOOK ONE OF THE STONES OF THE PLACE, AND PUT IT UNDER HIS HEAD, AND LAY DOWN IN THAT PLACE TO SLEEP.

Who the f**k uses a stone as a pillow? "Hmm, lemme see, there's gotta be some crap around here I can use to rectify the appalling softness of the ground." I can only conclude that this muf**ker was extremely drunk, which is what I would be nonstop if I lived back in these sheepherding-ass times.

28:19 HE NAMED THE SITE BETHEL; BUT PREVIOUSLY THE CITY HAD BEEN NAMED LUZ.

How come everybody in here is drunkenly renaming everything all the time? I might have to bring that one back. "Yeah, I gotta go to Moozugabaloo tomorrow for this conference. What? Oh, yeah, it used to be called Cleveland. I changed that crap. Act like you know."

29:4 JACOB SAID TO THEM, "MY RELATIVES, WHERE ARE YOU FROM?" THEY SAID, "WE ARE FROM HARAN."

This is really just a matter of syntax, and I hate to be a dick about it, but this reads like homeboy is having a conversation with the sheep, because no human beings are ever introduced. I hope somebody got smote (smited? I'm pretty sure it's not smitten) for this translation right here. Come on, son. Then again, talking sheep would not be the least plausible thing in here, so who the f**k knows?

29:18 JACOB LOVED RACHEL; SO HE RESPONDED, "I WILL SERVE YOU
SEVEN YEARS FOR YOUR YOUNGER DAUGHTER RACHEL."

Yo, I gotta say I lost a little bit of respect for my man Jacob right here.
Dude fell for the okey-doke real hard. I know this is back in the day and
all, but you don't have to be a rocket surgeon to know how the game is
played: First you get the paper, then you use the paper to buy the girl. You
don't just work *for* the girl, on some layaway-plan crap. No doubt in my
mind—as soon as Jacob went for that, Laban was like, *This dude is funny-
style, and I'ma play him like an all-day sucker.*

29:30 HE WENT IN ALSO TO RACHEL, AND HE LOVED ALSO RACHEL
MORE THAN LEAH, AND SERVED WITH HIM YET SEVEN OTHER YEARS.

That said, I still gotta give Laban props for really taking the art of disre-
spect to the next level right here. I mean, come on—you gotta be some
type of diabolical genius to stand in front of a man who just worked for
you for seven long years and explain to him that yeah, he just spent the
night losing his virginity (I assume) to the wack sister of the girl he's in
love with, but it's all good, he can have the other one, too . . . if he puts in
another seven years. Ninety-nine out of a hundred muf**kers would mash
Laban dead in the facepiece at this point, but old man Laban? He *knows*
Jacob is that one percenter. Dude probably didn't even sleep the night
before, just lay there in his bed cackling and rubbing his hands together
in gleeful anticipation. On another note—the f**k is wrong with Leah?
She couldn't have said something?

29:31 THE LORD SAW THAT LEAH WAS UNLOVED AND HE OPENED HER
WOMB; BUT RACHEL WAS BARREN.

On a narrative level, I like how crap speeds up here, and we glide right
over what has got to be a good three years, minimum—and that's if Jacob

has been reimpregnating Leah like five minutes after she gives birth, every time—in fewer words than it took the dude to talk to those sheep earlier. Nonetheless, this chapter is still mad boring.

30:4 SHE GAVE HIM HER MAID BILHAH AS A WIFE, AND JACOB BEDDED HER.

Now we're getting into that ill Margaret Atwood *Handmaid's Tale* territory. This semi-famous actress I know is trying to option the rights to that book and star in it because, and this is an actual quote, "I look really good in a bonnet." Which, to be fair, is a way better reason than most reasons that movies get made these days.

30:6–8 AND RACHEL SAID, "GOD HAS VINDICATED ME; HE HAS HEARD MY PLEA AND GIVEN ME A SON." SO SHE NAMED HIM DAN. RACHEL'S MAID BILHAH CONCEIVED AGAIN AND BORE JACOB A SECOND SON. AND RACHEL SAID, "I WAGED A COMPETITION WITH MY SISTER; YES, AND I HAVE PREVAILED." SO SHE NAMED HIM NAPHTALI.

The notion of having one son named Dan and another named Naphtali reminds me of mad kids I grew up with whose families had, in the seventies, been really Afrocentric, and then, in the eighties, kind of moved on. But continued to have kids. So the kids would be named, like, Chiwale, Rukiya, and Tommy.

30:14–15 AT THE TIME OF THE WHEAT HARVEST, REUBEN CAME UPON SOME MANDRAKES IN THE FIELD AND BROUGHT THEM TO HIS MOTHER, LEAH. RACHEL SAID TO LEAH, "PLEASE GIVE ME SOME OF YOUR SON'S MANDRAKES." BUT SHE SAID TO HER, "WASN'T IT ENOUGH THAT YOU TOOK AWAY MY HUSBAND, THAT YOU WOULD ALSO TAKE MY SON'S MANDRAKES?" RACHEL RESPONDED, "I PROMISE, HE SHALL LIE WITH YOU TONIGHT, IN RETURN FOR YOUR SON'S MANDRAKES."

For the last little while, Jacob has quite likely been feeling himself a lil' bit. He's probably thinking that sure, he might've fallen in shit, but he still came up smelling like roses. Not only does he have two wives, but he's also got f**king various concubines, and there are all types of kids running around, and soon some of them will probably be old enough to hold it down in the fields, and then Jacob can semi-retire. Right here is where Jacob realizes that, as usual, he is very much mistaken. When people are saying stuff to you like "You are to sleep with me, for I have hired you with my son's mandrakes," you can be pretty sure that you're still no goddamn alpha male.

30:34–35 LABAN SAID, "BEHOLD, I DESIRE IT TO BE ACCORDING TO YOUR WORD." THAT DAY, HE REMOVED THE MALE GOATS THAT WERE STREAKED AND SPOTTED, AND ALL THE FEMALE GOATS THAT WERE SPECKLED AND SPOTTED, EVERY ONE THAT HAD WHITE IN IT, AND ALL THE BLACK ONES AMONG THE SHEEP, AND GAVE THEM INTO THE HAND OF HIS SONS.

At some point, you gotta just accept defeat, like, *Okay, this dude is smarter and more devious than me, and every time I do business with him, I get hood-winked into doing years of manual labor, or snookered into marrying some weak-eyed broad, so let me stop trying to match wits with him and just hit him with a rock-pillow or whatever.* But no. Jacob wants some sheep. Laban says sure, take all the spotted ones. Then he (Laban) takes all the spotted ones and bounces. I'm beginning to wonder why this muf**ker isn't a major figure in this religion. Dude is *nice* with his con game.

וּבְנֵי יַעֲקֹב בָּאוּ מִן הַשָּׂדֶה כְּשָׁמְעָם וַיִּתְעַצְּבוּ הָאֲנָשִׁים וַיִּחַר לָהֶם
מְאֹד כִּי נְבָלָה עָשָׂה בְיִשְׂרָאֵל לִשְׁכַּב אֶת בַּת יַעֲקֹב וְכֵן לֹא יֵעָשֶׂה:

"Meanwhile Jacob's sons, having heard the news, came in from the field.
The men were distressed and very angry because he had committed an outrage in
Israel by lying with Jacob's daughter—a thing not to be done." —Genesis 34:7

VA-YISHLAH ("*And he sent*")

GENESIS 32:4–36:43

JACOB DISPATCHES MESSENGERS TO HIS brother, Esau, to gauge his mood. Their report is not good: Esau is headed toward Jacob with an army of four hundred men. Rattled by the news, Jacob divides his household into two camps to make them less vulnerable and begins to pray to God, revealing a fear that his whole household might be killed.

The next day Jacob rounds up select goats, ewes, rams, cows, camels, bulls, and asses to offer as a generous gift to Esau. He instructs his staff to drive them toward Esau in separate groups. When each encounters Esau, he is to be informed that the animals are a present from "his servant Jacob." Jacob's plan is to shower his brother with gifts and calm him with kindness.

While his servants drive the animals toward Esau, Jacob takes his wives and sons across the river with his possessions and returns alone. A "man" suddenly wrestles with him through the night. As dawn approaches, the "man" strains Jacob's hip at its socket and demands to be released from his grip, but Jacob insists on receiving a blessing first. The "man" asks Jacob for his name and upon learning it, informs him that from now on he will be known as Israel. Jacob wants to know his adversary's name, but the "man" tells him not to ask and then disappears. Jacob names the place Peniel, meaning "I have seen a divine force face-to-face and survived."

Looking up, Jacob sees Esau approaching with his posse of four hundred men. He splits up his maids, wives, and children, making sure Rachel and Joseph are at the rear, and then approaches Esau alone, bowing low to the ground as his brother nears. But he should not have worried. Esau runs toward him with hugs and kisses. The two split up and proceed on their journeys at their own pace.

THE RAPE OF DINAH

After Shechem, a local prince, rapes Jacob and Leah's daughter, Dinah, he takes such a liking to her that he asks his father, Hamor, to arrange a marriage. Jacob knows what has happened, but waits to take action until his sons return from herding their cattle. No surprise: They are as furious as their father.

Hamor asks Jacob's family for Dinah's hand; to reciprocate, he will give his daughters for marriage. Additionally, Shechem asks them to name whatever price they want for Dinah. Jacob's family denies the request, saying that Shechem can take Dinah's hand only if he is circumcised. So besotted is he with Dinah that he and his father agree, running to the town square and giddily telling their followers to prepare themselves to undergo the painful procedure. The upside is clear: If Dinah marries the prince, Jacob and all of his riches will become part of their community. All of the males agree and are circumcised.

Three days later, while all the men are still gripped by the pain of recovery, two of Dinah's brothers, Simeon and Levi, walk into the city and murder all the males, including Hamor and Shechem. The other brothers ransack the town, stripping it of flocks, herds, and wealth, and enslaving the women and children. Jacob is not at all pleased about the act of violence—he thinks it will make him a target in the region—but Simeon and Levi explain that they had no choice when their sister had been treated like a prostitute.

God tells Jacob to head to Bethel and build an altar. Jacob commands his servants to give up their idols, which he buries. God then sends a "terror" from the heavens, which falls on the surrounding cities and prevents their inhabitants from pursuing Jacob. God reminds Jacob that his name is now to be Israel, encourages him to reproduce, informs him that kings will descend from his line, and reinforces the promise to Abraham and Isaac about the inheritance of land.

THE DEATH OF RACHEL AND ISAAC

Once they hit the road, Rachel experiences a difficult labor and dies while delivering a baby boy named Benjamin. She is buried on the road, and Jacob builds a pillar on the grave.

Soon after, Jacob returns to his father, Isaac, who passes away at the age of 180. Esau and Jacob bury him together.

Esau's line is described all the way to the ruthless clan of the Amalek. His wives are Canaanite. He moves away from Jacob, because the land can't support both their households.

MICHAELA WATKINS

THE RAPE OF DINAH IF TOLD BY MY MOTHER

EXT. TRADER JOE'S PARKING LOT/INT. MY CAR--DAY

A cell phone rings.

> ME
> Hello?

> MOM (O.C.)
> What's new?

> ME
> Not much. You?

> MOM (O.C.)
> Oy. I can't get dug out here. I just paid a
> Wellesley College student to come move some boxes
> around the basement. I can't lift them. Do you
> need an ice cream maker?

> ME
> No.

> MOM (O.C.)
> Any of these editions of Trivial Pursuit?

> ME
> No.

                    MOM (O.C.)
What about Mom-Mom's gravy boat that goes
with the dishes with the purple flowers from
Berck-Plage?

                        ME
Definitely no.

                    MOM (O.C.)
Oy. She got raped. Or something.

                        ME
WHO? Mom-Mom?!

                    MOM (O.C.)
Fiona.

                        ME
. . . Who is Fiona?

                    MOM (O.C.)
The girl. The Wellesley College girl who moved
the boxes around the basement with me, trying to
get me dug out.

                        ME
Good segue. What the hell happened?

                    MOM (O.C.)
Who knows. Some clod from Mass Bay Community
College. What's his name--Seth, Sean. Something.
One of the Hammer kids.

———

                         ME

What Hammer kids?

                      MOM (O.C.)

. . . Of "Hammer Pool and"--whatsit--"Tile" over
in Lynn. Remember? We were there when you thought
you were dying and it turns out you were. Mono.

                         ME

What a horrible thing! The rape.

                      MOM (O.C.)

When I went to Wellesley, this didn't happen. One
foot on the floor at all times. And we had to
keep the door open.

                         ME

Is she okay?

                      MOM (O.C.)

Meh. She has a baby from it. So much for Akin's
theory. What a nudnick. It turned into a real
mess. It was in all the papers. You don't know
about this? That's the problem with you. You
don't read. How can you know what's going on in
the world if you don't read? It was all anyone
was talking about here. She has two brothers,
Simon and the other one . . . Lewis? Uh--Vinny
. . . Levi. It's Levi. They live in Swampscott,
and they were mad as hell. Oy. My foot, my
peripheral neuropathy is inflamed. I go to the
Fancy Hands place now.

Guess how much they charge for a foot massage.
Guess. Okay--twenty-five dollars for twenty-eight
minutes. She knows just where to push to make me
go "ahhhhhhh." What's new?

                         ME
MOM--what did her brothers do?

                     MOM (O.C.)
They were going to go to court and prosecute him,
Hammer boy stalked her, asked her to marry him,
thought he was in love with her, meshugana, I guess
they thought he would get off on insanity charges,
so they decided to go to his neighborhood--
apparently he was part of a gang. A real loser
pothead. From Lynn, Mass. "Lynn Lynn, City of
Sin, You never go out the way you came in."

                         ME
Mom.

                     MOM (O.C.)
That's what we used to sing. Now it's really
awful. Cambodian gangs and drugs and whatever
else. Uch, it's a real problem. His father is a
big to-do there, but the kid was spoiled. His
father was very successful for an immigrant.
Second generation. Like me. I've done pretty well
for myself, considering. Did you know Pop-Pop
lied about his age and was born in Poland? That
makes me second generation. I need a cat sitter--

                            ME
Mom does this story have an ending?

                         MOM (O.C.)
Stop yelling at me. Fiona's brothers went to Lynn
with a bunch of their Irish buddies and who-
knows-who and they beat the sneakers out of him
and all his friends. They were in some club where
they were drunk and drugged up and couldn't fight
back very well--NEVER mix pills and alcohol, do
you hear me? Never. Did you know you can't eat
grapefruits if you take Lipitor?

                            ME
Mom! I don't take Lipitor. I've never taken
Lipitor. What are you even talking about? What
happened with Sean? Or Seth or whatever??

                         MOM (O.C.)
Nothing. Next thing you know, most of them are in
the hospital and the Hammer kid was in a coma.
They just unplugged him. The others were so out
of it, they couldn't identify who did it, but
anyone who knows anyone will tell you it was
Fiona's brothers. They play football at BC. No
one was going to tattle on them, and the school
is silent about it.

                            ME
This is the woman who helped you move boxes
around your basement??

                         MOM (O.C.)
See? Think I don't know famous people, too?

                    ME
God, what did her parents do?

                   MOM (O.C.)
They sat silent on the whole thing. You know how
it is with some people. You get pregnant, you get
pregnant. That's that. Not me, though. Not with
my daughters. I'd never sit silent--

                    ME
No. I don't see that happening. Ever.

[Beat.]

                 ME (CONT'D)
I will take the gravy boat. That was a good
summer in Berck-Plage. I was only eight, but I
remember Mom-Mom putting the chocolate inside the
baguette and handing the pieces out as snacks.

                   MOM (O.C.)
I knew you'd want it. This is why I don't throw
anything away. I hold on to everything.

"About three months later, Judah was told, 'Your daughter-in-law Tamar has played the harlot; in fact, she is with child by harlotry.'" —Genesis 38:24

VA-YEISHEV (*"And he dwelt"*)
GENESIS 37:1–40:23

ENVY IS A KILLER: **AFTER JACOB RETURNS TO** the land of Canaan, he makes no attempt to conceal the fact that Joseph, his seventeen-year-old firstborn son with his favorite wife, Rachel, is his favorite child. This reality doesn't sit well with his eleven other sons, who are further irritated when Joseph tattles to their father about their sloppy shepherding work ethic.

Familial relations are further frayed by Jacob's decision to give Joseph an extravagantly colored robe. Stung by this visible snub, the brothers find it almost impossible to share a kind word with him.

Joseph worsens matters by deciding to share two dreams with the entire family. In the first, the brothers are in the fields binding sheaths of wheat. Joseph's sheath suddenly stands tall, and those of his brothers bow down to it. In the second, the moon, sun, and stars kowtow to him. Unsurprisingly, these images are not well received within the family. The brothers are repulsed and infuriated by the suggestion that they will one day be subservient to their younger brother; even Jacob is disappointed enough to rebuke Joseph.

The family friction boils over when Joseph journeys down to check in on his brothers, who are shepherding their flocks in the pasture. As he approaches, the jealous bunch hatches an impulsive plan to murder him, believing they can dispose of their brother's body in a nearby pit and cover over their crime by claiming a wild animal has killed him.

One of the brothers, Reuben, suggests they can avoid killing Joseph and simply toss him into a pit. He has a vague hope that he might somehow rescue Joseph later. The brothers agree, but once Joseph is in the pit, Judah broaches the notion of selling him to some Egypt-bound Ishmaelite traders they encounter. But before they can act on this plan, a group of wandering Midianites yank Joseph out of the hole and sell him to the Ishmaelites themselves.

The brothers panic and execute a cover-up. After ripping the colored tunic they stripped from Joseph and dipping it in animal blood, they present it to their father. Jacob concludes that an animal has devoured his favorite son, and begins to wail inconsolably in mourning.

As his father grieves, Joseph arrives in Egypt, where he is sold as a slave to Potiphar, a captain serving in the Pharaoh's palace guard.

TWO WEDDINGS AND TWO FUNERALS

The tale shifts back to Judah in Canaan. He fathers three sons with a Canaanite wife, and names them Er, Onan, and Shelah. Er is married off to a young woman named Tamar, but he annoys God, who takes his life. Judah instructs Onan to follow the local custom of marrying his brother's widow. However, Onan does not fulfill his duties as a husband, aware that any children the two produce will be perceived by local custom as his deceased brother's and not his own. God is again displeased and kills Onan, too.

Having mourned for two of his children, Judah attempts to protect the third by telling Tamar that she should let Shelah mature before marrying him. Sensing a diversionary tactic, Tamar goes to extraordinary lengths to take control of the issue. After disguising herself as a prostitute, she ensnares Judah, who trades his staff, cord, and seal for sex and unwittingly impregnates her.

Back at the homestead, Judah learns that Tamar is pregnant and assumes she has committed adultery; he threatens to apply the standard punishment for such a sin: death by burning. Tamar saves herself by producing the staff, cord, and seal that prove Judah is the father of her child, causing him to recognize that his actions are to blame for her whole predicament. Tamar proceeds to bear twins.

JOSEPH IN THE BIG HOUSE

Back in Egypt, where God definitely has his back, Joseph's career is blossoming. His work is peerless among the servants. An impressed Potiphar promotes Joseph to run his entire household. Despite his professional success, interpersonal challenges continue to pose problems for Joseph. Potiphar's wife is attracted to his build and repeatedly attempts to seduce him. Joseph resists her advances out of respect for Potiphar and because he is a godly man.

Matters come to a head when the eager woman attempts to grab Joseph. The servant manages to extricate himself from her clutches and effects a hasty escape, only to leave his clothing in her grasp. Potiphar's cunning wife uses the clothing as proof that Joseph was the aggressor, claiming he tried to rape her. A furious Potiphar throws his servant into prison. Luckily for Joseph, God is with him and he quickly rises to the pinnacle of the prison hierarchy, gaining the favor of the chief jailer.

Joseph's uncanny ability to decipher dreams comes to the fore once more when he encounters Pharaoh's cupbearer and baker, who have been imprisoned after falling afoul of the king. Both men experience visions that Joseph proceeds to explain. He tells the cupbearer he will be restored to his former glory within three days, but the baker's fortune is bleaker. Joseph believes he will be executed and left to rot on a spike as birds peck away his flesh. Both predictions come true. And while Joseph hopes the cupbearer will remember his favor once he is freed, his hopes are dashed as the servant quickly puts him out of mind.

DAVID AUBURN

TAMAR stands before JUDAH. Her wrists are bound.
They are surrounded by members of JUDAH'S
HOUSEHOLD. The effect is of a trial or hearing.

JUDAH

Do you know the reason you are here?

TAMAR

You sent for me.

JUDAH

Do you know why?

TAMAR

Yes.

[Beat.]

JUDAH

Do you know what must happen to you?

TAMAR

I know what will happen.

JUDAH

Say it, then.

                    TAMAR
I am to be killed.

                    JUDAH
Yes. Say as well how.

                    TAMAR
By burning.

                    JUDAH
And say why this must be.

                    TAMAR
I cannot say why it MUST be. Only what you will
say is the reason.

                    JUDAH
Do you dispute this reason?

                    TAMAR
I cannot.

                    JUDAH
Then say it now.

                    TAMAR
The reason is my pregnancy.

[Beat.]

                    JUDAH
How many months?

TAMAR

Three.

JUDAH

Do you have a husband?

TAMAR

You know I do not.

JUDAH

Everyone must hear. Do you have a husband?

TAMAR

No.

JUDAH

How did you come to be with child?

TAMAR

I put on a veil and stood by the side of the
road.

JUDAH

By harlotry, then.

TAMAR

Yes, by harlotry.

JUDAH

This is what I was told. I hoped with all my
heart the reports were false.

                    TAMAR
They were not false.

[Beat.]

                    JUDAH
You married my son.

                    TAMAR
Yes.

                    JUDAH
He died.

                    TAMAR
He was killed, yes.

                    JUDAH
He died by fever.

                    TAMAR
The Lord saw that he was evil and killed him.

                    JUDAH
This is what you have always said. I won't
dispute it again with you now.

                    TAMAR
You did not want to see it. But it was so. You
took me into your household for your son and
never saw what he was. But the Lord saw, and I
saw.

JUDAH

This is not why we are here. To resume. One son
being dead, I gave you to my second son.

TAMAR

Now we come to him.

JUDAH

He too died.

TAMAR

Was killed.

JUDAH

Oh? And was my second son also evil?

TAMAR

No. But there were other issues with Onan.

JUDAH

Tell us, please. What were they?

TAMAR

I don't think this is the place.

JUDAH

What better place? We're all listening.

TAMAR

Let us just say there were issues and leave it at
that. Or rather, the issues were the issues. The
Lord, let us just say, was not pleased.

                    JUDAH
Two marriages leaving you twice a widow. Two
brothers dead. No children.

                    TAMAR
That would appear to be the tally.

                    JUDAH
What are we to think?

                    TAMAR
Whatever you choose.

                    JUDAH
No children; two of my sons dead. Still, did I
blame you? No. I did not. I sent you to your
father's house. Did you stay there? No. The next
we learn, you are veiled by the side of the road.

                    TAMAR
I do not deny it.

                    JUDAH
And now everyone has heard.

                    TAMAR
Yes. Everyone has heard.

[Beat.]

But there is something you have not said.

JUDAH

Say it now.

TAMAR

Your third son.

JUDAH

Yes.

TAMAR

Promised to me when he came of age. Did you make
this promise?

JUDAH

I did.

TAMAR

Yet I stayed in my father's house. I was not
given to your third son. Do you deny it?

JUDAH

I cannot.

TAMAR

Did you fulfill this obligation to me?

JUDAH

I did not.

TAMAR

Now everyone has heard.

                         JUDAH
Two brothers married to you, leaving you twice a
widow. No children. Two of my sons dead. Who here
would condemn me for sparing a third?

[Silence.]

So. We are left only with the question of your
conceiving a child by harlotry. Which you do not
deny.

                         TAMAR
I cannot.

                         JUDAH
Then what else can be said?

                         TAMAR
Only this.

[To a HOUSEHOLD MEMBER]

Bring me the things that I gave to you to keep.

                         JUDAH
What is this?

                         TAMAR
You will see. Everyone will see.

[The HOUSEHOLD MEMBER brings Tamar a staff, a
cord, and a seal. She puts them on the ground in
front of Judah.]

Whose things are these?

[Beat.]

                    JUDAH
They are mine.

                    TAMAR
You do not deny it.

                    JUDAH
I cannot.

                    TAMAR
They are your cord, your seal, and your staff.

                    JUDAH
Where did you get them?

                    TAMAR
Where did you give them up?

[Beat.]

                    JUDAH
I gave them to a woman.

                    TAMAR
Who?

                    JUDAH
A woman I met on the road. I do not know her name.

                    TAMAR
What did she look like, then?

                    JUDAH
I did not see her face.

                    TAMAR
Tell us why.

                    JUDAH
She was veiled.

                    TAMAR
A harlot, then.

                    JUDAH
Yes.

[Beat.]

                    TAMAR
When did you meet her?

                    JUDAH
Three months ago.

                    TAMAR
Why did you give her these things?

                    JUDAH
I promised her a kid from my flock.

                    TAMAR
Why?

                    JUDAH
As payment.

                    TAMAR
Payment for what?

                    JUDAH
She was a harlot. What else?

                    TAMAR
And?

                    JUDAH
I had to send for the kid. Until it was received,
she asked for these things as a pledge.

                    TAMAR
Did you send her the kid from your flock?

                    JUDAH
I did.

                    TAMAR
But she didn't receive it?

                    JUDAH
The person I sent went back to the road but could
not find the woman. They said there was never a
harlot there.

———

TAMAR

So she kept your cord, your seal, and your staff.

JUDAH

So it would seem.

TAMAR

"There was never a harlot there" is what they
said?

JUDAH

Yes.

TAMAR

So.

[Beat.]

JUDAH

I do not understand. How did you come by these
things?

TAMAR

I received them. As a pledge. For I am with child
by the man to whom these things belong.

[Reaction from the HOUSEHOLD. JUDAH picks up the
staff, cord, and seal. He looks at Tamar. A long
moment.]

JUDAH

She is more righteous than I am.

[The HOUSEHOLD moves in and surrounds them,
unties Tamar, and helps her offstage. Judah is
alone. He speaks directly to us. His tone becomes
contemporary, conversational.]

JUDAH
Years ago I had a brother. I had a lot of
brothers, actually, brothers and half brothers,
it was a big family, but this one I'm talking
about, Joseph, stood out because he was my
father's favorite: Dad just doted on the kid; to
hear him tell it, he could do no wrong and the
sun more or less shone out of his ass, you'll
pardon the expression.

And whether it was because Joseph really was all
that wonderful or just because on some level--and
I'm not even saying he was necessarily conscious
of this--he enjoyed the envy all that favor
inevitably aroused in others--or some combination
of the two--Joseph, I felt (and I wasn't alone in
this), went out of his way to sort of emphasize
his righteousness to the rest of us and make us
feel bad for getting up to the kinds of things
young unmarried men have always gotten up to
since the beginning of time: I mean a certain
amount of drinking, brawling, and fooling around
with girls, some of them tarts.

Don't misunderstand me: If Joseph had simply
chosen not to participate, that would have
been one thing, and we probably wouldn't even
be discussing it now. It was his bizarre and
infuriating eagerness to proclaim his superiority

that really rankled. It was aggressive. Example:
The group of us would be up at dawn with the
flocks, cranky and exhausted after a chilly
night spent sleeping rough in some rocky pasture
somewhere, no breakfast, and Joseph would come
running up, bright-eyed, just dying to tell us
about some dream he'd had the night before.
You know how annoying it is when someone wants
to tell you their dreams. And Joseph's dreams,
according to him--who knows if he was making
it up or not, it doesn't matter--would always
be something like he's a sheaf of wheat in the
field, and the rest of us are all sheaves of
wheat, too, only he's the largest sheaf, and
we're all bowing down to him. Subtle, Joseph.

So given all that, it was probably inevitable
that some of the more hotheaded among us started
talking about getting Joseph out of our hair more
or less permanently. I'm not going to take you
through all the arguments and all the plotting
that went on. That's ancient history. Suffice
it to say that at a certain point we're out in
the middle of nowhere standing over a pit, and
Joseph's down in it. And there's a faction--a
sizable majority of the brothers--that's all for
cutting his throat and filling in the pit and
calling it a day.

I'm not going to stand here and tell you that in
the moment I was appalled or shocked at what we
were contemplating, or even that I argued against
it very forcefully. I was part of it; I had let
it get that far, and it wasn't just passivity

or cowardice that had prevented my stepping in
earlier, before we were actually at the point of
murdering a brother. I carried no brief for Joseph
and had fresh memories of mornings when, hungover
and sore-balled after a night of degeneracy in some
fetid one-whore fleshpot, I had staggered out to
the fields and met the eye of my youngest brother,
virtuous, virginal, and smug, watering the flocks
by a wincingly sun-dappled stream, and hated the
little shit.

Still, somehow I managed to propose what I guess
you could call a compromise: Don't kill him; fake
his death and sell him into slavery instead.
Even that was a tough sell with my brothers, but
eventually I did win that one, and now it was my
turn to feel righteous and noble as we dipped his
cloak in goat's blood--sorry: I forgot to mention
that he had this ridiculously fancy and expensive
cloak my father had given him (and, needless
to say, only him), which Joseph practically
slept in, he was so proud of it--and sent the
thing home to poor Dad, who promptly went into
protracted and inconsolable mourning. Joseph we
sold to some traders.

Why am I telling you all this? I don't know. I
guess when Tamar . . . You probably wondered why
I folded so fast when she turned the tables on me
back there. I mean, couldn't I have put up more
of a fight? "She is more righteous than I am,"
I said. I didn't think about it, it just popped
out, and boom, that was the end of it. I'm not
even sure I believe that. Yes, I had slept with

a prostitute and failed to recognize her as my
daughter-in-law (embarrassing), and yes, I had
broken the pledge I made--not the goat one, which
I did try to fulfill, but couldn't, because you
heard why, but the one about my third son--and
she was probably right about that: She deserved
a child by him, that's the way we do things. But
on the other hand: The deception! The disguise!
The sheer brazen manipulation! Not to mention the
sexual exploitation--it's outrageous, disgusting.
I could have made that case. It would have been
easy. Why didn't I?

I don't know. I couldn't. I was standing there and
the spirit just went out of me. I was looking at
her, thinking, SHE'S PREGNANT WITH MY CHILD. Or
children--the midwives say it could be twins. And
that phrase: leaping into my head, onto my lips,
heard by everyone before I was even aware I'd
spoken it. "She is more righteous than I am . . ."

[Beat.]

What were we talking about? Oh yes. Joseph, my
little brother. We never heard from him again. No
idea where he is today.

I dream of him most nights.

END

"And Pharaoh said to Joseph, 'I have had a dream, but no one can interpret it.
Now I have heard it said of you that for you to hear a dream is to tell its
meaning.'" —Genesis 41:15

MI-KETZ (*"At the end"*)

GENESIS 41:1–44:17

THE DREAM TEAM: **TWO YEARS LATER,** Pharaoh dreams he is standing alongside the Nile when seven healthy cows emerge to graze in the reeds. They are quickly followed by seven feeble, sickly cows, who proceed to devour their more vigorous counterparts. The dream momentarily shocks Pharaoh awake, but once he returns to sleep, a second vision appears: seven ears of grain growing off a single stalk. But a neighboring stalk, scalded by the hot wind, bears seven shriveled ears, which gulp up the perfect ones.

The next morning, Pharaoh commands all his magicians and wise men to decode the dreams. When none is able, the chief cupbearer remembers the young Hebrew he encountered in jail, and Joseph is quickly rushed from prison, cleaned up, and brought before the court.

Pharaoh begs Joseph to divine his dreams, but Joseph modestly admits that the interpretation skills are God's. Pharaoh recounts both dreams, and Joseph says that the visions amount to the same prediction. God is telling Pharaoh that seven healthy years will be followed by seven years of famine.

HOMELAND SECURITY

Joseph advises Pharaoh to prepare for the oncoming crisis by appointing a wise man to oversee the land and organize the nation during the time of abundance. A food surplus should be reserved and grain stocks built up. Pharaoh announces that because God has revealed this through Joseph, he should be the crisis manager, a position second in authority only to the Egyptian king. He then removes his own signet ring and places it on Joseph's hand, clothing him in finery and gold, before renaming him Zaphenath-paneah and giving him a priest's daughter to be his wife.

Though only thirty, Joseph journeys across the Egyptian kingdom organizing grain reserve silos as vast as the ocean. He and his wife also bear two sons, Manasseh ("God has made me forget adversity and my homeland") and Ephraim ("God has made me fertile in the country of my suffering").

BROTHERS GRIM

The seven years of feast and famine occur just as Joseph has predicted, but there is still bread to eat, because of his preparation and rationing. Neighboring countries that have not stockpiled food are not so lucky, and starving foreigners cross into Egypt in search of sustenance. Jacob dispatches ten of his sons to bring back supplies. Only Benjamin, Joseph's youngest brother, remains behind; Jacob is determined to keep him out of harm's way.

In his ministerial role as vizier, Joseph dispenses rations himself; he recognizes his brothers the moment they bow deeply before him. Joseph chooses not to reveal his true identity, electing to interrogate his brothers and accuse them of spying on Egypt while it is in a weakened state. They assure him they are not spies, referring to themselves as his "servants," and echoing the dreams he envisioned as a child. Joseph grills his brothers. They tell him they had been twelve brothers, but that one of them was lost and one remained at home. He demands they prove that fact: I will imprison one of you as a hostage, he says, while the rest of you return for the other brother and bring him back to Egypt. The brothers immediately guess they are being punished for their treatment of Joseph. Reuben blames the others for failing to listen to him when they dispatched their brother into the pit, and suggests they are about to receive a reckoning for their actions.

Joseph has used an interpreter to speak Egyptian to his brothers, so they are unaware that he can understand their bickering. As he listens to their heated arguments, he cannot help but turn away and weep. Once he has recovered his emotions, he has Simeon tied up and tells the rest to load their asses with grain and begin their journey. He also orders his men to return the money they have paid for the provisions.

On the journey home, the brothers discover that their money has been reimbursed and fearfully take it as a sign that God has done something terrible to them.

Once they have briefed their father, he admonishes them, blaming them for the loss of Joseph, Simeon, and now, potentially Benjamin. Reuben vows that his father can kill him if he fails to protect Benjamin, but Israel (Jacob) cannot cope with the possible loss of Benjamin and refuses to send him.

The ongoing famine forces his hand. Once their grain runs out, Israel orders his sons to acquire more in Egypt, but Judah reminds him that they can return only with Benjamin in tow. Israel screams at them for telling the Egyptians about their youngest brother

in the first place, but the brothers defend themselves by reminding their father how brutally the vizier interrogated them.

Judah tells his father he will take full responsibility for Benjamin's safety, suggesting the family has no choice: They will die of hunger if they tarry. Israel instructs him to load up with gifts for the vizier—balm, pistachio nuts, and almonds—and to take double the money they carried on the original visit. He begs God to be merciful and prepares himself for the worst.

THE TRAP IS SET

The brothers arrive in Egypt and appear before Joseph. He sees Benjamin and orders his servants to prepare a feast in his home. The brothers are afraid that Joseph plans to enslave them. They try to explain themselves to Joseph's servant, but he tells them not to worry and that the God of their fathers is watching over them.

The brothers are treated like guests in Joseph's household. Their feet are bathed. Their asses are fed. Once Joseph arrives, they present him with their gifts. He inquires about their father's well-being, but when introduced to Benjamin, he becomes overwhelmed by emotion and has to excuse himself. When dinner is served, the rest of the Egyptian company sits separately, as it is not socially acceptable for them to sit with Hebrews, but Joseph sits with his astonished guests. When Benjamin is served, his portion is huge in comparison with all others.

Joseph then instructs his servants to load up his brothers' bags with as much food as they can carry and to return their money. He also commands them to secrete a silver goblet among Benjamin's possessions. Once his family departs the following day, Joseph orders his stewards to pursue and catch them, then accuse them of repaying good with evil by stealing the goblet.

The brothers, nonplussed by the allegation, suggest that if it is true, the thief should be killed, and the rest of them turned into slaves. The servant counters by proclaiming that only the thief will become enslaved. Each of the brothers opens his bags; the goblet is discovered in Benjamin's possession. The panicked brothers ride back to the city and find Joseph. He asks them why they have committed a robbery they knew he would detect. Judah begs him to reveal how they can prove their innocence and urges him to inflict a collective punishment. Joseph refuses this request, explaining that only Benjamin was found with the goblet, so only he will be enslaved. The rest are ordered to return to their father.

TODD ROSENBERG

B eing an artist before having my talent recognized often felt like living in a jail cell.

I worked for a large company, sitting in a cubicle selling products. Technically, I was called a "salesperson" or "account executive," but for the most part my job was answering calls and writing down orders. I wasn't ambitious, or a go-getter, or a ladder climber, or a morning person, or a schmoozer.

My work ethic was maintained at an extraordinarily low level. Ankle height. Just enough to keep me anonymous but still somewhat profitable. I exploited my lack of upward mobility by using all my free time at work to pursue artistic goals on their clock. I'd doodle furiously. Make flipbooks on Post-it notes. I'd write a short story about being in a meeting during the meeting I was in. I'd illustrate a blood-soaked battle scene on the back of an agenda.

The company had one division that was reserved for artists and creators. *The Creative Dept.* I wanted to be a part of that world. But the jobs that existed there weren't applied for. There were no help-wanted signs posted. To become a part of the Creative Dept., you needed to be chosen.

I suspected I was a writer. And an edgy, funny cartoonist. And a fantastic illustrator. A triple threat of artistic potential. Evidence of my artistic value was a pile of scribbled paper and rant-crammed notebooks that filled a large

wooden box I kept under my desk. I saw my creative work as practice. A grand exercise. Preparation for the day I would escape my cubicle world and finally be acknowledged as a talent worthy of promotion.

My cubicle row was filled with others like me. Artists. Musicians. Painters. Sculptors. All snared by the need to make a simple living. All trapped in occupations far removed from the Creative Dept. We all hoped to one day be recognized and freed. Until then we were a family together. Unified in our struggle to be chosen. Supporting one another's passions and attempts to spotlight ourselves as genuinely inspired.

Now and then, the Pharaoh of the Creative Dept. would stroll among our cubicles unannounced. He'd walk with his hands behind his back, trailing behind him a wake of hope. We knew that when Pharaoh visited, he was looking for something new. *Someone new.* He wandered casually, yet emanated the immense power of life-changing potential based on a whim or mood. He'd listen to a song and squint his eyes. He'd look at a painting and nod cryptically. We'd all pray and hope he would find what he was looking for in our work.

On rare occasions, I watched with immense jealousy as a lucky one, a fortunate one, was freed from his cubicle. Pharaoh would see a spark and tap someone. This person would leave his desk glowingly and rush straight into the embrace of Pharaoh's robes. I'd hear Pharaoh whisper to him promises of wealth and fame. I'd squeeze my pencils till my knuckles turned white as they headed off together. I'd mark the person's age in comparison to my own—then I'd go back to work. Selling for others.

When I'd see him coming, I'd cover my desk with sketches, journals, and doodles, so he'd know I was a hard worker with history. I'd wave sketches in the air with proudly ink-stained fingers. But year after year, Pharaoh refused to shine a light on me. He'd reject my work with a wave or ignore it altogether. After he'd leave, I'd grumpily clear my desk and put everything back in the box under my desk. Time after time, start anew.

At times of discouragement, it was good to have my workmates or "family" around me. We were all in the same place with the same hopes. Suffering through the same sadly defaulted careers. We were brothers and sisters both blessed and cursed with the same hesitant, tortured surname. *Creative types.* We'd share our creative energy. Inspire one another. Exchange ideas. Weather failure together. Interpret one another's dreams.

The most discouraging times were the occasions when Pharaoh would favor the talents of a newcomer. Someone would be in a cubicle all of two months and snag the attention of Pharaoh based on a single piece of work. The person would instantly strike a chord and off they'd go, leaving behind a gnawing sense in my family that we were all doing something

wrong. We'd all sit in silence and digest the fear that we were not simply being misunderstood, more that our creations were worthless.

Over time, I started to believe I didn't have it in me anymore. I began to take my salesman job more seriously. I considered sealing my wooden box and accepting the idea that my permanent career was already thrust upon me. Only then, *only* at my very lowest point, did Pharaoh stop at my desk and flip through an old sketchbook that was sitting on a shelf. He flipped pages and nodded. There was a long pause on a particular image. Silence in the room.

He shut the book and announced he had a job for me in the Creative Dept. My family gasped. I gasped. He was indeed freeing me from my cubby, as if unlocking a prison cell door! He put his hand on my shoulder and told me to bring my wooden box, my colored pencils, my sketches and journals. He insisted I bring everything I had.

I had been chosen.

As I felt the warm robes of Pharaoh surround me, I was instantly filled with doubt. Although I had always fantasized about being promoted and freed, I felt at home with my family. But I was welcomed into this new world by the other artists. The old and young. Some familiar. Some not. Some with immense wealth. Some not. I knew my life from that point forward would be different. Regardless of what I would do for Pharaoh, one thing was clear . . . I was no longer a salesman for the company. I was an artist.

My assignment? Pharaoh needed me to interpret his dreams and find a way to exploit the visions for profit. Pharaoh was obsessed with his dreams. He loved to sleep, and his dreams were stunningly lucid. He felt they were gifts from the gods. His ego declared that the images they contained could be turned into gold if interpreted correctly. It would be my job to do so. Entry-level stuff in this department. To prove my worth.

I started work that day and immediately came through for Pharaoh. I interpreted his dreams exactly how he wanted to hear them. Using my artistic abilities, I prophesied crops lush and lucrative. For the first time in my life my creations were seen as valuable.

I would sit by his bedside and watch him dream. And when Pharaoh woke, he would tell me a dream of winged beavers making dams out of rain clouds. (I would find a way to improve irrigation in his fields.) He would nervously tell me a nightmare involving a dead man with a beak on his face. (This would become a highly effective new scarecrow product.) A dream of a volcano with golden lava. (A new smelting method for our blacksmith.) I'd sketch and interpret. And gloriously, find ways to translate his visions into profit. I had become known. Accepted.

But I didn't want to abandon my family. I would often walk down to the old row of cubicles and visit my old family. They were eager to hear stories of my work in the Creative Dept. Compliment me on a newfound confidence that had never been present before. They saw me as different. I

wore stubble with pride while my family was still obligated to shave daily. I no longer wore a tie to work—I wore a blue robe. Distinctive attire for someone who had been tapped by the Pharaoh.

For a while, life was actually a dream. I worked hard to listen and interpret. And products went to market based on my interpretations. Some made profit. Some did not. But over time, I found it more and more difficult to find the hidden meanings in Pharaoh's dreams. I couldn't focus on his descriptions. They seemed scattered. I wouldn't be able to connect a vision to profit or product. I became discouraged, as did he.

I soon resented how hard I was working for him. I'd listen to a thorough retelling of a unicorn stampede and desperately try to link it to a new way to herd cattle. What he wanted didn't make sense. I soon realized I was just pretending to know what I was doing. My frustrations led me to believe that Pharaoh was just a lazy dreamer who had persuaded himself that he did his most brilliant work while dead asleep. I doubted I needed his daydreams to find profit for him.

Soon my mind fought for my attention. It pulled me away from Pharaoh's visions, and I found myself writing my own stories on the side and making flipbooks at night. I had a growing interest in my family's work as well. We would happily collaborate and share ideas. The work was more interesting and better than the lazy dream interpretations I cranked out for Pharaoh, which admittedly were getting repetitive and stale.

One afternoon, while Pharaoh was enthusiastically telling me one of his daydreams (it involved him standing on a ladder wearing only a wolf's mask with a large yellow crab on his head—don't ask) . . . I shamelessly *yawned*.

Pharaoh sat back and asked if I was tired of my job in the Creative Dept. Instead of denying it, I leapt at the opportunity to change our relationship. I asked if we could move away from his dream world and try imagining things in reality. I suggested we try to work together while he was actually awake. Walk the farms for inspiration. Talk to villagers. Gather ideas from common cubicle dwellers. I let him know that my previous family was overflowing with fresh ideas. I suggested we work with all divisions of the company to identify new revenue lines.

Pharaoh reminded me that for the last quarter, profitability in my dream interpretations had been sliding downward. He was not concerned with inspiration. He didn't want distractions. He was concerned only with profit.

I insisted we could surprise the world together by providing something truly unique and new. Reconfigure the Creative Dept. altogether. If we took on a new direction, I insisted, profits would pour in. Pharaoh sat back in his chair and nodded. He told me he appreciated my bravery and confidence. He told me he was excited to see what else I had in store for him. Pharaoh asked me to gather my thoughts with my family. I was excited. It was a breakthrough!

When I arrived downstairs, I noticed my old cubicle had been restored. My sales log had returned. A fresh stack of business cards with my position declared. *Account executive.* I wasn't returning to my cubicle for "inspiration." I had been officially demoted. Dismissed.

My family somberly welcomed me back, but most seemed happy just to have me around full-time once more. Although I was embarrassed to be sitting back on cubicle row again in my old department, I felt inspired. Reenergized. I embraced my newfound freedom from Pharaoh's wants and babbling dreams.

I found I was far more nourished by the lives of my immediate family than by the dreams in Pharaoh's head. The range of personalities. The variety of dreamers. The struggles. The weathered souls. The close calls. I started writing their stories. Doodling their adventures. Pharaoh's dreams were simple and repetitive by comparison. And for the first time, I felt like a *true* artist. There would be no distraction with profit. I was also free from rejection and doubt! Free to love my art!

Years later, here I am. I still sit in a cubicle. Recently promoted to *sales manager*. My bar has been raised from ankle height to knee. I've noticed my family is more career-focused as well. We have to be. Age eventually takes a toll, and we all know that Pharaoh favors youth. But there is a certain pride in not flailing around when Pharaoh strolls the cubicles. Although I still doodle and write, I'm no longer desperate to be a part of the Creative Dept. I doubt I will ever be chosen again, as I never produced the profits that were expected.

But in between sales calls, I often wonder if I sabotaged my true potential by attempting to change Pharaoh. Whether my ego rose above Pharaoh's prematurely. Perhaps I never felt at home in the Creative Dept. and am better off on my own. Free of direction and expectation. But there also is the fear that what keeps Pharaoh from choosing me again isn't based on spite for profits lost but a nagging suspicion of a potential truth: that I was never quite worthy of his promotion in the first place.

"So Joseph settled his father and his brothers, giving them holdings
in the choicest part of the land of Egypt in the region of Rameses,
as Pharaoh had commanded." —Genesis 47:11

VA-YIGGASH (*"Then he drew near"*)
GENESIS 44:18–47:27

ERCY, MERCY ME: **AS THE STORY OF** Joseph picks up, Judah, unaware that he is speaking to his brother, approaches the Egyptian vizier and begs for mercy, as Benjamin, the youngest brother, who is about to become enslaved, is their elderly father's favorite. He then relates his version of Joseph's "death" at the hands of wild animals and asks to be enslaved in place of Benjamin, saying that his father will die if his youngest son does not return.

Joseph, unable to contain his emotions, orders all of his attendants to leave the room. He then reveals himself to his brothers, sobbing so loudly that rumors of the scene soon reach Pharaoh.

Joseph wants to know more about his father's health, but his brothers have been stunned into silence. Acknowledging himself as the brother they sold into slavery, he absolves them of blame, suggesting that God dispatched him to Egypt as part of a divine plan: Only by becoming Pharaoh's counsel was he able to save so many lives.

He commands his brothers to return to their father and bring him and their entire household down toward Joseph in an area named Goshen. Joseph intends to use his political power to save them; he knows there are still five more years of famine to survive. He then embraces Benjamin around the neck, weeps, and kisses all his brothers.

FATHER AND SON REUNION

Back at the Egyptian court, Pharaoh is delighted by the news of Joseph's brothers' arrival. He encourages Joseph to have his family move down to enjoy everything Egypt can offer them, even providing transport to aid in the relocation process.

Joseph follows Pharaoh's advice, equipping his brothers with wagons and provisions for the journey, taking extra care of Benjamin. When they return home and relay the story of Joseph's fortune to their father, the old man is so shocked that he does not believe them until he sees the Egyptian wagons. He immediately expresses his desire to see Joseph again before he dies.

Sixty-six members of the family travel down to Egypt. On their journey, God appears to Israel in a dream, calling him Jacob, making it clear that no hardship will befall them in Egypt: His heirs will become a great nation.

He also reassures him with the news that Joseph will be beside him when he dies.

Joseph rides by chariot to meet them in Goshen, and weeps as he embraces his father. Israel says that now that he has seen his son alive, he is ready to die. Joseph prepares his family to meet Pharaoh, instructing them to tell anyone who asks that they breed cattle; Egyptians abhor shepherds.

Joseph takes some of his brothers to meet Pharaoh, who asks them what they do for a living. The brothers say they are shepherds driven to Egypt by the famine. Pharaoh directs Joseph to settle his family in the most fertile region of his kingdom and suggests that the most capable brothers look after the royal livestock.

Joseph then introduces his father to Pharaoh. When asked his age, Israel says he is 130 years old. His life has been hard, he says, even though he is not as old as his ancestors. Joseph then settles and provides for his family in Rameses, the most fertile region in all of Egypt.

As the famine worsens, Joseph sells the rations to raise money for Pharaoh. When the Egyptian subjects run out of money, he takes their livestock in exchange. When the livestock are gone, he takes possession of their land on behalf of Pharaoh, giving out seed that can be planted; the king will take a fifth of the harvest and the serfs, four-fifths. Joseph is widely praised for the ingenuity with which he saves the lives of the Egyptian people.

SAKI KNAFO

T he morning of the reunion, Joseph put on his best tunic and looked at himself in the mirror. A lot had happened in the past twenty-two years. His brothers had sold him out. He'd been to jail. He'd made a lot of money. He'd married a beautiful woman. Looking at himself in his gold-fringed tunic, he thought about how happy he'd become since he'd last seen his father. He never could have imagined that he'd be so content, so successful, so rich. He straightened the fringes of his tunic, because he'd learned that that's what wealthy people do when they look at themselves before an important moment, and then he went out into the court, where an old man with a walking stick was standing next to a soldier. "Dad," he said. "Why did you come?"

His father shrugged. "I heard that there was some lucky bastard from Canaan who managed to get laid by an Egyptian princess. I thought, *Yep, that's my boy*."

Joseph stared at him for a moment, and then laughed one of those short, sarcastic laughs. They embraced, and Joseph looked his father in the eyes. "I can't believe I actually missed you," he said.

"You're such a liar," his father replied.

Joseph and his father had never really liked each other. When Joseph was a teenager, his father had dragged him to all kinds of family meetings, festivals, and fights, always introducing him as the future of Israel.

"But I don't want to be the future of Israel," Joseph would say.

His father would smile lightly and turn to the rich couple next to them and ask about their children, their children's spouses, and their livestock.

Joseph thought of his father as a huckster, and he refused to believe that he'd inherit his father's lust for power or his talent for manipulating people. Then he ended up in Egypt, where manipulating people meant the difference between life and death. He played a part—the part of a powerful man like his father—but he knew deep down that he was doing it only to survive, and that if he wanted to, he could give it all away. The money, the servants, the wife. He could ride off to another city and start all over again. He'd be fine. He had a talent for survival, and he would have thanked his father for that if his father hadn't been such a lying, shallow prick.

In Egypt, Joseph's father wasted no time making himself comfortable. By the end of the first day, he and Pharaoh were drinking buddies. By day two, they were business partners. By the following Sabbath, Pharaoh had appointed Joseph's father to the top post in the new tax collection agency. As Joseph watched his father ingratiate himself with his powerful friends, he realized for the first time that he couldn't ride away after all. He'd worked hard for his success, he'd risked his life for it, and now his father was claiming it for his own. It had taken years of danger and hardship, but he'd finally built his own world, and now his father wanted it for himself.

After a year, Joseph's father married an Egyptian woman of his own, his third wife altogether, and nine months after that, he had his first Egyptian kid. Joseph watched with the usual boredom. He grinned his way through the promotion ceremonies, the wedding, the bris, the second bris, and then his father's fourth wedding, the third bris, and the first bar mitzvah. At the age of 147, Joseph's father finally died. The family, including the Egyptians, mourned him for seventy days. Joseph had his father embalmed, a traditional process that took another forty days. Then he prepared a ceremonial journey back to Israel, leading twenty of Pharaoh's servants and many of his closest associates over the Jordan River. They stopped at a small village where they mourned Joseph's father for yet another seven days. Here, according to the historical record, their cries caught the attention of the surrounding Canaanites, who remarked that Joseph must have loved his father deeply.

המלאך הגאל אתי מכל רע יברך את הנערים
ויקרא בהם שמי ושם אבתי אברהם ויצחק וידגו לרב בקרב הארץ:

"Bless the lads. In them may my name be recalled, and the names
of my fathers Abraham and Isaac. And may they be teeming multitudes
upon the earth." —Genesis 48:16

VA-Y'HI (*"And he lived"*)
GENESIS 47:28–50:26

ACOB'S END: **JACOB LIVES IN EGYPT FOR** seventeen more years. As he approaches his death at the age of 147, he makes Joseph promise to bury him in his ancestral homeland rather than Egypt.

Jacob soon falls ill, and Joseph takes his sons, Manasseh and Ephraim, to his bedside. Jacob adopts the boys as his own and brings them close to bless them, favoring the younger over the older with his right hand. Joseph goes to correct this, thinking his aged father is making an absentminded mistake, but Jacob says no: Although both boys will birth nations, the younger, Ephraim, will be the greater. Israel (aka Jacob) then tells Joseph that he is close to death, that God will bring him back to Canaan, and that he has saved him an extra inheritance over and above that of his brothers.

Jacob then calls all of his sons together and predicts their fortunes. Unstable as water, Reuben, the firstborn, once a force, is doomed to mediocrity because he seduced his father's concubine, Bilhah. Simeon and Levi share a temperament—they are both angry and violent—and a fate: Their descendants will be scattered across Israel. Judah will dominate his enemies; ultimately, his brothers will bow before him. He will wash his clothing in wine and have teeth whiter than milk.

Zebulun will dwell by the sea and work with ships. Issachar will be as strong as an ass and live in a beautiful region. Dan will rule but remain as treacherous as a serpent. Gad will live a tumultuous existence: His ancestors will raid and be raided. Asher will be the richest. Naphtali will be like a liberated deer that bears beautiful offspring. Joseph will be a spiritual man: Archers will shoot at him, yet his own bow will stay taut, strengthened by God, who blesses him as he did Jacob. Finally, Benjamin's life is foreseen as that of a hungry wolf who hunts in the morning and divides the spoils by night.

Having defined the futures of the Twelve Tribes of Israel, Jacob says farewell to each of his sons. He then instructs them to bury him in the Cave of Machpela, where Abraham and Sarah, Isaac and Rebekah, and Leah are entombed, and breathes his last.

Joseph flings himself onto his father's body, weeping and kissing his face. Then, gathering his senses, he commands his physicians to embalm the corpse, a task that takes forty days.

The Egyptians mourn for seventy days; once the period comes to an end, Joseph asks Pharaoh for leave so he can fulfill his promise and bury his father in Canaan. Pharaoh grants permission and orders senior members of his court to escort Joseph on the journey and witness the funeral at the Cave of Machpelah.

FAMILY TRUMPS ALL

The entire party returns to Egypt, but the brothers are afraid that Joseph will exact his revenge now that their father is dead. They test the waters by sending Joseph a message suggesting that Jacob has left him instruction to forgive his brothers. Joseph weeps as he hears this, and his brothers fling themselves at his mercy and offer to be his slaves. Joseph assures them he is no god and reiterates that although they may once have wished him harm, the outcome of their action has been good, thanks to God. He reassures them that he will look after his entire family.

Joseph lives to be 110. Before he dies, he makes his brothers swear that they will take his bones back to the land promised to Abraham, Isaac, and Jacob. Once he dies, he is embalmed and placed in a coffin in Egypt.

DENNIS BERMAN

A LETTER TO MY UNBORN SON

* * *

You are coming soon. And when you arrive, we will bless you. But for whom is this blessing? Is it for you? Or is it for us?

I can already feel the moment. It's January, and the wind is leaking through the window. Your mother will be spent, and in the drafty night, crankily demand that I try to soothe you.

You will be at my shoulder, both of us stuck between sleep and alertness, barely able to see.

And then will come my blessing for you, remembering how my father and I recited the *Shema* together before bed. We would name each aunt, each uncle, each cousin, and then finish with a patriotic flourish that invited God to look after "all the Jewish people, the United States, and all Earth."

Jacob to Manasseh and Ephraim. All the way down, from me to you.

I can already feel that sensation of your tired lungs on my chest. I will find your head with my hands, issuing a directive into the darkness:

**GOD BLESS AND KEEP THIS CHILD. SEND HIM ON THE RIGHT PATH.
ABOVE ALL, BESTOW ON HIM A PERFECT JUMP SHOT.
KEEP HIS FEET SQUARE TO THE BASKET. MAKE SURE THE ELBOW IS
TUCKED AT NINETY DEGREES BENEATH HIS SHOOTING HAND.**

Is there a difference between a prayer and a blessing, especially a blessing lost on an unknowing infant? We use the terms interchangeably, but there seems to be an abiding difference.

To pray seems suitably humble. It is a beseechment.

To bless a child suggests I have some power, some priestly redirection, to channel God's wishes. God, show my son Your favor! And right now!

Here I must level with you, son: I've got no pull. My blessing will rise from the earth like all the others, a moisture for clouds. But it is really up to God or whatever forces you may one day understand: luck, genetics, parenting, economics, evolution.

On this night, son, the blessing will not soothe you or cheer you. The blessing is to soothe and cheer me.

* * *

And before long, you will understand words. And you will watch your father fret about this world and your role in it.

It will be hard to resist assigning you a path. Maybe I will regard you as a Reuben, too intemperate for your own good.

Or you will be lavished with expectation, a Judah in your parents' eyes.

Prophesy is dangerous stuff, son. Not that saying it will directly make it so. But that slowly, unconsciously, I will try to shape your adult self to some vision erected when you were a child.

I will teach you all that I know. But we must remember: This is your gig.

* * *

The years move on, and I can see you again. Your tired lungs have grown strong. You are nearly a man yourself, and far from home, angry with me. In the dark, I will say a prayer for you, thinking of myself no more.

* * *

And then the moment further off, perhaps, when the blessings lost on you as an infant are finally made whole.

You are in the dark with your own son, my grandson. You are tired, and not sure how things will go. And then you will discover your own words, left like a cask of bourbon biding its time.

SQUARE TO THE BASKET. FEET SET. ELBOW. PLEASE, GOD.

PART TWO

EXO

DUS

THE NARRATIVE HURTLES FOUR
hundred years on, and the story turns to that
of nation building and the moment when the
covenant that had first been revealed to Abraham
is made manifest.

Exodus begins with a listing of the sons of Jacob,
the man who became known as Israel. His descendants, the Israelites, have become a slave people;
the book tells the story of their liberation. And since
every freedom story needs a hero, Moses—a man
with a mysterious orphan-turned-prince upbring-
ing and a personality that can be both stubborn and
insecure—is introduced as God's chosen leader.

God and Moses meet at a burning bush and
quickly become a mutually enabling partnership.
Both appear able to manipulate the other as the
Israelites wander through the wilderness, suspended
between the suffering of the past, the indignity of
the present, and the promise of the future. They are
not an attractive people: fickle, weak, ungrateful,
and undermining. But their adventures are made for
Cecil B. DeMille: They career from one visual spectacle to another—the Ten Plagues, the parting of
the Red Sea, the fury at Mount Sinai, and the desert wonder of the Tabernacle.

SUSAN DOMINUS
SH'MOT (*"Names"*) Exodus 1:1–6:1

SLOANE CROSLEY
VA-ERA (*"And I appeared"*) Exodus 6:2–9:35

STEVE BODOW
BO (*"Go"*) Exodus 10:1–13:16

JOEL STEIN
B'SHALLAH (*"When he let go"*) Exodus 13:17–17:16

REBECCA ODES & SAM LIPSYTE
YITRO (*"Jethro"*) Exodus 18:1–20:23

BEN GREENMAN
MISHPATIM (*"Laws"*) Exodus 21:1—24:18

MARC KUSHNER
T'RUMAH (*"Offering"*) Exodus 25:1–27:19

MARK LAMSTER
T'TZAVVEH (*"You command"*) Exodus 27:20–30:10

RICH COHEN
KI TISSA (*"When you take"*) Exodus 30:11–34:35

ROSS MARTIN
VA-YAK·HEL (*"And he assembled"*) Exodus 35:1–38:20

JOSH KUN
P'KUDEI (*"Amounts of"*) Exodus 38:21–40:38

"The daughter of Pharaoh came down to bathe in the Nile,
while her maidens walked along the Nile. She spied the basket among
the reeds and sent her slave girl to fetch it." —Exodus 2:5

SH'MOT ("*Names*")
EXODUS 1:1–6:1

JOSEPH'S FAMILY NUMBERS ONLY SEVENTY when they first come down to Egypt, but they breed prolifically, and soon fill the region. And so, when a new king, with no memory of Joseph and the heroic role he has played, arises, he views the number of Hebrews as both a security risk and a potential fifth column in a time of war. He has them rounded up and forces them to work as slave laborers, but despite the brutality of their work, the Hebrews still multiply, and the Egyptians begin to despise their presence.

In the name of population control, the king of Egypt commands every Hebrew midwife to kill newborn boys at birth. The midwives, fearing God more than Pharaoh, disobey the order; he counters by commanding his people to throw every newborn Hebrew boy into the Nile.

A Levite man and wife conceive a son. Entranced by his beauty, the mother hides him for his first three months. Once he has grown too large to conceal, she places him in a carefully constructed wicker basket and floats him on the Nile, telling his sister to watch over him from close by.

When Pharaoh's daughter comes down to the Nile to bathe, she spots the basket in the reeds and orders her servant to fetch it. Discovering a crying boy, she guesses that the infant must be a Hebrew. His sister approaches Pharaoh's daughter and offers to find a Hebrew who can nurse him. The baby's mother is fetched, and Pharaoh's daughter retains her as a nurse. When the boy grows up, the princess adopts the boy and names him Moses, which means "I pulled him out of the water."

COMING OF AGE

Moses sees the Hebrews hard at labor and witnesses an Egyptian guard beating a slave. After looking around to check that no one is watching, he strikes and kills the guard; he then buries him in the sand. The next day he encounters two Hebrews brawling and intercedes to try to calm them down. One of the Hebrews sarcastically asks if Moses intends to murder him as he did the guard, and a panicked Moses realizes that his violent act was witnessed. Pharaoh soon finds out about the matter and issues the death penalty, so Moses flees deep into the desert to a well in Midian.

Moses watches the seven daughters of a local priest drive their flocks to this well, but before they can water their animals, local shepherds chase them away. Moses leaps in to defend the women and to make sure they can get the water. The priest cannot believe that his daughters have accomplished their task so quickly, so they tell him about the Egyptian who came to their aid. The priest invites Moses to be their guest and ends up giving him one of his daughters, Zipporah, as a wife. The two give birth to a son, Gershom, which means "I've been a stranger in a foreign land."

Time passes. The king of Egypt dies, yet the Israelites' suffering only increases. God hears their cries for help and recalls the covenant made with Abraham, Isaac, and Jacob.

BURNING MAN

An angel of the Lord appears to Moses in a blazing bush, which he encounters while driving his father-in-law's flock. The bush burns without ever being consumed. When Moses wonders aloud how that is happening, God calls out to him by name, instructing him to take off his shoes and respect the holiness of the ground. Moses hides his face out of fear, as he instantly connects God to the stories of Abraham, Isaac, and Jacob.

The Lord reveals the plan. It is time to rescue the Hebrews from their suffering and to bring them out to a land, flowing with milk and honey, that is currently populated by a number of tribes, including the Canaanites. Moses' job is to go to Pharaoh as God's intermediary, so the Israelites can be liberated from Egypt.

Moses questions whether he has the right credentials for the task, but God reassures him that the Lord's presence will be all that he needs to succeed. He is then commanded to ensure that the newly liberated Israelites will travel to this mountain and worship the Lord.

Moses asks how he should describe God to the Israelites, so they will know to take his story seriously. God uses the name Ehyeh-Asher-Ehyeh ("I will be what I will be"), and offers specific advice about how Moses should address the Israelite elders, reminding them of the covenant with Abraham, Isaac, and Jacob and the promise of land. God is aware that Pharaoh will agree to liberate the Israelites only if he is exposed to a greater power; the plan is to batter the Egyptians with a series of wonders.

Moses remains apprehensive, worrying that the Israelites will not believe his story, so God performs a pair of miracles to strengthen his courage: First, Moses' rod is turned into a serpent and back again, and then Moses' hand is frozen. God believes these visual wonders will convince the Israelites, but if they both fail, Moses should pour Nile water onto dry ground and watch as it is converted into blood. The next concern Moses raises is about his speech impediment. God dismisses his anxiety, asking him to remember who it is that gives humans the power to speak and who makes them deaf, dumb, or blind. Moses continues to express his doubt, and God begins to lose patience, suggesting Moses employ his brother, Aaron, as a spokesman.

God instructs Moses to return to Egypt, reminding him that all those who wanted to kill him are themselves dead. So Moses takes his wife and sons on an ass and heads to Egypt.

LEADING IN TROUBLING TIMES
On the journey, God prepares Moses for the wonders that will be performed before Pharaoh, briefing him on the plan to harden Pharaoh's heart so the king will be humanly unable to let

the Israelites go until the life of his oldest son is threatened.

A mysterious incident follows, where God suddenly sweeps down and attempts to kill Moses' son at night. Zipporah responds by circumcising her son with a flint.

Meanwhile, God directs Aaron to meet Moses in the desert. Moses briefs him, and the pair assemble the elders of Israel. Aaron handles the talking and performs the miracles God has prepared. The elders respond immediately, bowing down in relief that the Lord has recognized their suffering at last.

LIBERATION BEGINS

The duo confront Pharaoh, demanding in God's name to be allowed to take the Israelites into the desert to worship. Pharaoh rejects the request: He has not heard of God, and is frustrated that Moses and Aaron are distracting the Israelites from their slave labor. The Egyptian king orders his slave masters to worsen the Israelites' conditions, hoping added punishment will encourage them to forget about God.

The Israelite foremen beg Pharaoh to relent, but he shows them no mercy, calling them shirkers. Returning to work, the foremen encounter Moses and Aaron and berate them for worsening their conditions. Moses turns to God and begs to know why their plan appears to be backfiring. God tells Moses to wait and see. Before long, Pharaoh will be exposed to a force so superior, he will not just let the Israelites go, but will drive them from his land.

SUSAN DOMINUS

I knew who she was right away. Before I could even see her face, I could see the embroidery around her neckline, and then I knew. Everyone in town was wearing a similar but simpler version, a stitch anyone's little sister could make in a quarter of the time, but I knew the original when I saw it, because my friend Tamar had designed it, the crazy shimmering stream of tiny triangles in gold and yellow, so many in that infinite line of pattern that it made my head ache just watching my friend bend her head over that precious piece of cloth, hour after hour, stitching loop after loop. I would have been seeing triangles in my nightmares, but Tamar saw them in her dreams, like revelations; Tamar was an artist, which made her different. She was also a slave, which made us the same. "It's for his daughter," she whispered to me. No one ever mentioned him by name, out of fear, out of loathing. His name was cruel. His name was dirt in our mouths.

And so I knew who that was, that girl on the shore, the one staring out onto the water. On any other day, I would have run, run like my life depended on it, breathless with the news of my sighting, electrified by my close brush with power. On any other day, it would have been a short story I told my friends, maybe even my children, although at that time I did not let myself think I might have children of my own: the time I saw the princess, alone, across the Nile.

I had no intention of running away this time. I was there for a reason, even if I could not say what it was. I had already run away that morning, escaping the sight of my mother, collapsed on the floor. For three months, my brother, a life banned by edict, had cried out for food, for love, for life. Every time he did, he endangered our own. I could live with that cold, crawling feeling of imminent disaster, ignoring the ceaseless throb of terror as I carefully tended his bath, beating his cloth swaddlings until they were softer than his own skin—I had no responsibilities other than to this child, this princeling in our midst, my baby brother, a creature whose head touched my hands before any other's as I ushered him out of the same woman who had given me life. I had no other loyalty: He was my world. But my mother had another child to protect. That child was me. And she had chosen. She had sent my brother on his way, sending him floating away. She could not protect him any longer; maybe the perch and the catfish, the crocodiles and the water lilies could.

As children, my friends and I had taken stalks and husks and tied them into miniature boats like the real ones we saw on the river, creating our own mini fleets, pitching them downstream, then racing for miles to see whose had gone the farthest. I knew the banks of the river, I knew its pacing, where the boats got stuck in the banks at a curve and had to be poked out with a long branch, where the current picked up and boats might go out too far to be retrieved. I ran to find my brother, and when I finally spied him, sleepy and silent, lulled or stunned by sun, I looked up and saw her, too. Later, the stories would all say she was with her handmaids, but that was royal editing. I know the truth; she was alone. And she was crying, for what reason, I never found out: A lost treasure? Heartbreak? Shame?

Maybe I was blindly guessing, or maybe I was distilling, in the compressed urgency of the moment, something essentially true about the person I saw. I took a chance; I flung a rock, not at her, but into the river. I made a splash. I saw her look up, I saw her see, and comprehend, immediately, what should not have been comprehensible: a baby, three months old, floating down the river in a basket that should have been dry, in someone's larder, packed with food from the market. And then I saw her reach, reach out to grab my brother, reaching so far that I thought she would almost certainly fall in. Her arm seemed to stretch, so that she seemed not just royal in that moment but almost divine, sure of having whatever she wished, whatever its cost.

And then Moses was on land and in her arms. He awoke, sobbing with hunger, with thirst—to her, the sound of any baby crying; to me, the sound of my brother in pain. I gave her a moment to register the situation, how unequipped she was to offer him solace, how badly he needed it. I waited, biding my time until I saw her awe turn to uncertainty, and then:

"I know a Hebrew nurse," I called out across the river. I was loud, and my voice sounded ragged to my ears. She looked up from my brother and saw me. What did she see? I had no time to compose myself; I am sure she saw it all. Desperation. Fear. How starved I was for an answer to my offer. And then she nodded.

"I'll be back," I said, already running.

"What is your name?" she shouted.

I did not hesitate. "Teshubah," I called out, and then I ran as I had never run before, already thinking about what I would tell my mother, my broken mother, how I could coax her to believe, to come with me back down the banks of the Nile, where she would find her son, starving and screaming and desperately hungry for her milk. Could I carry her if I had to? I could. I would. I am Miriam, star of the sea, star of the river, and I delivered my brother not once but twice.

ויקרא גם פרעה לחכמים ולמכשפים ויעשו גם הם חרטמי מצרים בלהטיהם כן:

"Then Pharaoh, for his part, summoned the wise men and the sorcerers; and the Egyptian magicians, in turn, did the same with their spells." —Exodus 7:11

VA-ERA (*"And I appeared"*)
EXODUS 6:2–9:35

T HE PLAN IS REVEALED: **GOD TELLS MOSES** that Abraham, Isaac, and Jacob knew the Lord by the name *El Shaddai*, but that the real name of God is YHVH (pronounced Yah-weh). The Lord then repeats the covenant and declares that slavery will soon be ended after a series of extraordinary punishments have been inflicted on the Egyptians. Moses relays this news to the Israelites, but they refuse to believe it: The slave experience has crushed their hopes.

Undeterred, God instructs Moses to go to Pharaoh and demand the Israelites' release, but Moses questions God, wondering why Pharaoh will believe a man with a speech impediment when even his own people have ignored him. God attempts to compensate for this speech problem by instructing Aaron to accompany Moses on his way.

The Lord informs Moses that he will play the role of God before Pharaoh, and Aaron will act as a prophet. Moses will repeat God's words; Aaron will handle the small talk and demand that Pharaoh liberate the Israelites. But Moses is also warned that God will harden Pharaoh's heart, preventing the

Egyptian from freeing the Israelites, so the Lord will have the opportunity to perform multiple miracles and leave no doubt which deity forced the Egyptians' hands. Moses is eighty years old and Aaron eighty-three when they assume this task.

The Lord sets out the plan: When Pharaoh asks to see a sign of God's power, Moses is to instruct Aaron to perform the "rod into a serpent" trick. They do as directed. Pharaoh reacts by ordering his sorcerers to do the same; they meet his challenge. But no sooner have their rods become serpents than Aaron's rod swallows them all. Despite this, Pharaoh's heart hardens, exactly as God promised.

BLOODY HELL

God commands Moses to intercept Pharaoh as he takes a morning bath in the Nile and ask that he release the Israelites. To reinforce the point, Moses is to threaten Pharaoh. If he does not accede, the Nile water will be turned into blood and instantly made undrinkable on account of the dead fish it will contain.

Aaron is then to hold his rod over the Nile, and all the water in Egypt—even that borne in water jugs—will turn into blood. The plan is executed: The Nile stinks and blood flows across Egypt. But once the Egyptian sorcerers work out how to replicate the spell, Pharaoh's resolve stiffens and he will not free the Israelites, even as his people dig into the ground in search of water to drink.

FROG ATTACK

A plague of frogs is next to be unleashed. God tells Moses to threaten Pharaoh with the prospect of having amphibians cover the Nile, the royal palace, and even Pharaoh's bed. Aaron triggers the plague with his rod, but again the Egyptian sorcerers are able to replicate the feat. Pharaoh asks Moses to intercede with God; the Lord makes all the frogs die, leaving them to rot in stinking piles. But once Pharaoh sees the threat has been removed, he changes his mind as God predicted.

LET THERE BE LICE . . . AND OTHER GHASTLY STUFF

Aaron's rod then produces a plague of lice, which smothers man and beast across Egypt. This time, Pharaoh's magicians cannot reproduce the trick. All they can manage is to express their admiration for God's work. But Pharaoh remains unmoved. Insects are then unleashed across the land—swarming amid Egyptians yet avoiding Israelites. Pharaoh encourages Moses to make a sacrifice to his God in the hope that the insects will be removed. Moses agrees, warning Pharaoh not to change his mind again. But once God withdraws the insects, Pharaoh says he will not let the people go. The Lord tells Moses to threaten Pharaoh with an epidemic that will destroy the country's livestock. The next day, all the Egyptian farm animals are struck down, but still Pharaoh remains stubborn.

Moses and Aaron receive instruction to take soot from an oven and throw it in the air in front of Pharaoh. The gesture will make a dust to cover the region and cause boils to break out on humans and animals everywhere. The Egyptian magicians are among those struck down and so are prevented from reversing the plague, but God

has hardened Pharaoh's heart, and he remains unmoved.

The next morning, God dispatches Moses once more to implore Pharaoh to let the Lord's people go and to threaten that worse will befall him; God can wipe him out, but has spared the king as a demonstration of power and to spread renown throughout the world. A hail shower is threatened—one so powerful, it will kill animals and humans alike.

Moses is told to hold his arms to the sky so the hail will fall. He does, and thunder, hail, and fire rain down on Egypt, striking down humans and animals and shredding trees.

Pharaoh summons Moses, admits his guilt, and promises to let the Israelites go if he can make the hail stop. Moses promises to do so. But once the hail and thunder stop, Pharaoh reneges on his deal, just as God has predicted.

SLOANE CROSLEY

www.webmd.com [ENTER]

| Search | 🔍 |

| Health A–Z | Drugs & Supplements | Living Healthy | Family & Pregnancy |

Sign in or sign up? [SIGN UP]

Registering with WebMD is quick and easy . . . and free! Fill out the information below, and you're on your way to enjoying better information and better health.

First Name: Pharaoh
Last Name: Pharaoh
Email: @
Confirm Email: @
Password: FingerofGod8
Gender: Male
Zip Code: Red Sea 84511, 84515, 84712, 84715, 84722

Screen Name: Lice_All_Up_In_My_Grill

Sign up for free WebMD newsletters: (OPTIONAL)
Check Those That Apply:
WebMD the Magazine - Digital Edition (Irregular)
Depression (Bi-Weekly) [X]
Living Better (Weekly) [X]
Men's Health (Weekly) [X]
Weight Loss Wisdom (Weekly) [X]
Chronic Pain (Weekly) [X]

Welcome, Lice_All_Up_In_My_Grill! Continue to search?

[YES]

Search:	Bloo_ 🔍

Automated Guesses:	**Bloo**d Blister
	Blood Cancer
	Blood Clot

Search:	Blood in_ 🔍

Automated Guesses:	**Blood** clot **in** leg
	Blood clot **in** lung
	Blood clot **in** lungs
	Blood clot **in** legs

Search:	Blood in the 🔍

Automated Guesses:	**Blood in the** eye
	Blood in the stool
	Blood in the urine

Search:	Blood in the water 🔍

No Guesses.

[ENTER]

High **Blood** Pressure and Diuretics (**Water** Pills)

Diuretics can help treat high **blood** pressure. Learn more about these drugs commonly known as **water** . . . For high **blood** pressure, diuretics, commonly known as "**water** pills," help your body get rid of . . .
WebMD Medical Reference

Childbirth: Laboring in **Water** and **Water** Delivery - Topic Overview

Laboring **in water** Some hospitals and birthing centers offer tubs or whirlpools for laboring. If yours does, talk to your health . . . body and helps you to relax. For many women, laboring **in water** has been . . .
WebMD Medical Reference from Healthwise

Search: Blood, rivers, OVERFLOWING   🔍

Re-routing **Blood** to the Heart

Surgeons borrow veins and arteries from non-critical areas of the body to get around blockages in the heart.

Search: Foul fish. FOUL   🔍

If You Have Body Odor, It May Be in Your Genes!

A genetic condition called **fish** odor syndrome may be responsible for more cases of body odor than . . . diet can all but eliminate this **foul**, fishy odor. TMAU is a genetic disease.

Search: Holy Moses   🔍

We're Sorry.

We found no results matching your search. Try broadening your keywords.

[*Broader than Moses? Whatever.*]

Search: | Fro | 🔍

Automated Guesses: **Fro**ntal lobe
Frostbite

Search: [*Screw it...*] | LICE | 🔍

Lice Overview:

A **lice** infestation can be caused by head **lice**, pubic **lice**, or body **lice**. Get information on the symptoms and treatment of **lice**, as well as how **lice** spread from person to person.

Medications: Over-the-counter or prescription? **Prescription:**

Prescription products for head or pubic lice

- **Permethrin cream 5% (Elimite)** is used to treat head lice or pubic lice. It is applied to the skin or scalp, left on for 8 to 14 hours, and then rinsed off.

- **Malathion lotion (Ovide)** is used to treat head lice. It is applied to hair on the head, left on for 8 to 12 hours, then rinsed off. If lice are still present 7 to 9 days later, a second treatment must be done.

- **Benzyl alcohol 5% (Ulesfia)** is used to treat head lice. It is applied to the hair on the head, left on for 10 minutes, and then rinsed off.

- **Spinosad (Natroba)** is used to treat head lice. It is applied to the hair on the head, left on for 10 minutes, and then rinsed off.

- **Lindane** shampoo is used to treat head lice or pubic lice. It should only be used when other products fail to get rid of lice or when a person cannot use any of the other products.

[NEW WINDOW]

GOOGLE SEARCH: | Lindane | 🔍

GOOGLE SEARCH: | Lindane BULK | 🔍

YouTube Video Copy:
"In 2003, FDA issued an advisory on the potential neurologic toxicity of lindane, a topical second-line treatment for scabies and lice. The advisory noted the importance of limiting the use of lindane to just one application and specified that lindane must be dispensed only in single-use containers of one or two ounces. This was intended to reduce the possibility that patients would apply an excess amount of the product, or that they'd re-apply it. A recent article in MMWR cautions about a different problem related to lindane. The article reported on 870 cases of illness from 1998 to 2003 that were caused by the unintentional ingestion of lindane. In a number of these cases, lindane was mistaken for a liquid oral medication, such as cough syrup."

[*Great.*]

[NEW WINDOW]

GOOGLE SEARCH: | Aaron's Rod | 🔍

PORN [click closed] **PORN** [click closed] **PORN** [click closed] **PORN** [click closed] **PORN** [click closed] **PORN PORN PORN PORN PORN PORN PORN PORN PORN PORN PORN PORN** [click closed] **PORN PORN PORN PORN PORN PORN PORN PORN PORN PORN PORN PORN PORN PORN PORN PORN PORN PORN PORN**

CTRL + ALT + DELETE

Would you like to restart your computer?

[YES.]

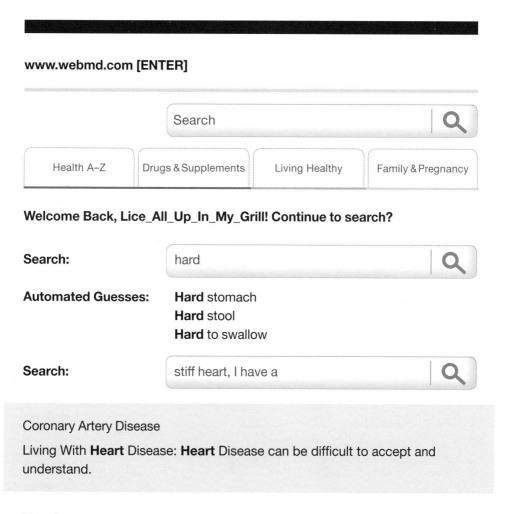

www.webmd.com [ENTER]

Search 🔍

| Health A–Z | Drugs & Supplements | Living Healthy | Family & Pregnancy |

Welcome Back, Lice_All_Up_In_My_Grill! Continue to search?

Search: hard 🔍

Automated Guesses:
 Hard stomach
 Hard stool
 Hard to swallow

Search: stiff heart, I have a 🔍

Coronary Artery Disease

Living With **Heart** Disease: **Heart** Disease can be difficult to accept and understand.

[*Sigh.*]

[NEW WINDOW]

GOOGLE SEARCH: | swarms of | 🔍

Automated Guesses: **Swarms of** dragonflies
                     Swarms of butterflies

GOOGLE SEARCH: | swarms of flies, grievous | 🔍

GOOGLE IMAGES:

[Not it.]

GOOGLE SEARCH: | Pest Control? | 🔍

GOOGLE SEARCH: | Pest Control, open early hours | 🔍

GOOGLE SEARCH: | Exterminator | 🔍

GOOGLE SEARCH: | Exterminator, 24:7 | 🔍

GOOGLE SEARCH: | Exterminator (not bed bugs) | 🔍

GOOGLE SEARCH: | Pest Exterminator Open Fridays? | 🔍

[NEW WINDOW]

Egyptian Craigslist>for sale/wanted>horses, asses, camels, flocks, cattle>farm&garden>by owner

Various animals for sale cheap. Slightly afflicted by grievous murrain.

Photos do NOT do them justice. Nile views!

Date: 1450 B.C., 6:04PM EET

Reply to: qtt8t-3205874622@sale.craigslist.org

----

www.webmd.com [ENTER]

Search: | Boils | 🔍

Automated Guesses: Skin **boils**
What causes **boils**

What are **boils**?

A **boil** is a red, swollen, painful bump under the skin. It often looks like an overgrown pimple. **Boils** are often caused by infected hair follicles. Bacteria from the infection form an abscess, or pocket of pus. A **boil** can become large and cause severe pain.

Search: | CAUSE of boils | 🔍

How can you prevent **boils**?

If you often get **boils** in the same spot, gently wash the area well with soapy water every day. Antibacterial soap may help prevent **boils**. Always dry the area well. Do not wear tight clothing over the area.

Search: | Boils, F**KING BOILS!! CAUSE. CAUSE of boils

When should you call a doctor?
Call your doctor if:

- The boil is on your face, near your spine, or near your anus.
- A boil is getting larger.
- You have any other lumps near the boil, especially if they hurt.
- You are in a lot of pain.
- You have a fever.
- The area around the boil is red or has red streaks leading from it.
- You have diabetes and you get a boil.
- The boil is as large as a ping-pong ball.
- The boil has not improved after 5 to 7 days of home treatment.

GOOGLE SEARCH: | What is "ping-pong"?

[*Oh. Cool.*]

GOOGLE SEARCH: | furnace? Boils, CAUSE. Something about a furnace maybe?

#1 Search Answer:

"And the LORD said unto Moses and unto Aaron: 'Take to you handfuls of soot of the furnace, and let Moses throw it heavenward in the sight of Pharaoh. And it shall become small dust over all the land of Egypt, and shall be a boil breaking forth with blains upon man and upon beast, throughout all the land of Egypt.' And they took soot of the furnace, and stood before Pharaoh; and Moses threw it up heavenward; and it became a boil breaking forth with blains upon man and upon beast."

GOOGLE SEARCH:	Getting rid of soot	🔍

GOOGLE SEARCH:	How To Sweep Your Own Chimney	🔍

Answer:

Yahoo! Results: Five Tips on How to Sweep Your Own Chimney

[Scroll to Bottom]

You should always use a vacuum to control the soot, or at least cover your floor and furniture with a tarp. When you sweep your own chimney, you should also choose a brush depending on how dirty your chimney is.

[*Dirty. Very dirty.*]

GOOGLE SEARCH:	Hail! Locusts! Darkness!	🔍

GOOGLE SEARCH:	Camping supplies . . . urgent	🔍

[NEW WINDOW]

http://www.rei.com/

Search: | Pon | ▶ SEARCH |

Automated Guesses: **Pon**chos
Bicycle Com**pon**ents
Men's Rain **Pon**chos

Men's Rain Ponchos:

The great backpacker's standby, this Outdoor Products Packframe poncho is easy to pull out of your pack and throw on for quick weather protection for you and your backpack.

[ADD TO CART]

Search: | Mos | ▶ SEARCH |

Automated Guesses: **Mos**quito Bed Nets
Mosquito Repellent
Mosquito Nets
Coffee Ther**mos**

Mosquito Netting:

Don't let the bugs get you down! The REI Screen House is a floorless shelter that offers bug and shade protection, great ventilation, and a 360° view.

[ADD TO CART]

Search: | Afraid of the_ ... *never mind.* | ▶ SEARCH

Search: | Flas | ▶ SEARCH

Automated Guesses: **Flas**hlight
Flashlight accessories
Flasks

Fenix LD22 Flashlight:

For road trips and treks into the mountains, the bright Fenix LD22 flashlight turns night into day. High-quality Cree XP-G LED operates in 6 lighting modes (4 brightness levels and 2 strobes) to meet your everyday and emergency needs.

[ADD TO CART]

[NEW WINDOW]

http://www.paperlesspost.com/ [ENTER]

PLEASE JOIN US FOR A BABY SHOWER HONORING OUR FIRST BORN!

COCKTAIL ATTIRE, WINE SERVED.

Will you attend? **[NO.]**

Would you like to be notified when others respond?

[SURE, WHY NOT.]

"Then the Lord said to Moses, 'Go to Pharaoh. For I have hardened
his heart and the hearts of his courtiers, in order that I may display
these My signs among them.'"—Exodus 10:1

BO ("Go")

EXODUS 10:1–13:16

NEGOTIATIONS BEGIN . . . AND FAIL. GOD
tells Moses to return to Pharaoh and threaten him
with an attack of locusts that will devour whatever
is still standing after the hailstorm. Pharaoh's advis-
ers beg their leader to let the Israelites go, but he dismisses the
notion, debating the possibility of liberating only the menfolk.

Moses raises his arm on God's command, and an easterly wind propels a
swarm of locusts, so numerous they
hide the land from view and make the
sunlight disappear. When Pharaoh
begs Moses to end the plague and
asks for forgiveness, God dispatches a
westerly wind, which drives the locusts
into the sea. But the Lord has stiffened
Pharaoh's heart, and he will not let the
Israelites go.

Moses raises his arm once more,
and absolute darkness descends upon
the land. In the three days it reigns, no
Egyptian can move as only the Israelites
enjoy light in their own homes.

At last, Pharaoh offers to let the
Israelites go, but demands that they
leave their livestock behind. Moses
declines, knowing that without livestock, they cannot offer sacrifices to
the Lord.

THE BITTER CLIMAX

The Lord fills Moses in on the plan to execute one final, deadly plague that will enable the Israelites to grab the gold and silver from their Egyptian neighbors and then flee. At midnight every one of the Egyptians' firstborn sons will die, including even farm animals. The chaos of death will trigger a scream the likes of which will never be heard again.

Moses warns Pharaoh, but God hardens the Egyptian's heart so he will not heed him. God also makes sure the Israelites mark their doorposts with lamb's blood as a symbol of recognition, so God can "pass over" the Israelites when the land is swept of its firstborn. As the murders occur, the Israelites are to prepare to leave. From that night on, the day shall be commemorated as Passover, in which unleavened bread will be eaten for seven days to remember the Lord's ability to liberate the Israelites from slavery. Moses briefs the Israelites' elders, giving careful instructions about the blood on the doorpost.

In the middle of the night, the killing takes place. A scream arises, waking Pharaoh from his slumber, as there is not an Egyptian home in which death has not struck. Pharaoh summons Moses and tells him to take his people and their flocks and be gone. The Egyptian people urge the Israelites to leave before the entire nation is killed, allowing the Israelites to take their gold and silver from them as they do so. Six hundred thousand men (this being the Bible, women are not mentioned, only assumed), accompanied by children and herds, leave in such a hurry that their bread does not have time to rise.

On this night, 430 years of Israelite slavery comes to an end. God explains the laws of the Passover offering of lamb, which is not to be eaten by foreigners or the uncircumcised, to Moses and Aaron. As the Israelites troop out of Egypt, Moses addresses them, making it clear that the Lord has plans for them to go to the land promised in the covenant, which will flow with milk and honey. A number of rituals are instituted to help the Israelites remember the day the Lord freed them from Egypt with a mighty hand. The festival of Passover is inaugurated. The Israelites are also commanded to wear a sign on their hands and foreheads to help them remember the Lord's power. And firstborn sons are to be "redeemed"—or celebrated—with a gift of silver to the priests.

STEVE BODOW

[THINK COFFEE, BOWERY, NYC, EARLY 2012]

[Begin transcript section.]

RB: The Bodow. Loving that. Want more of that. Listen, little project. Will move mountains to have you take a bit.

SB: Sure, Roger. What is it?

RB: Aces. Thrilled. Beyond thrilled actually. The Bodes. So, against all wisdom and sense I'm organizing a group to rewrite the Bible. The five books. Definitely, definitely wanting you in it. Little riffs on whatever interests. Looking at it fresh, no off-limits. Having a dialogue with this very rich stuff. Some tasty parashat I've held back for the Bodow.

SB: Sure, Roger.

RB: Fantastic. Toppers. You gorgeous man. Here's one: back half of the Ten Plagues.

SB: Okay, Roger.

[End transcript section.]

[V.O.]

Previously on
BOOK OF EXODUS:

God (יהוה) conspired with Moses (BEN AFFLECK) to
get Pharaoh (F. MURRAY ABRAHAM) to free 600,000
Jewish slaves (ZOSIA MAMET, RAY ROMANO, ETC.)
and let them go back to Israel. When Pharaoh
refuses, God visits a series of increasingly
severe punishments on Egypt, including turning
the Nile to blood and propagating cow flu. Then
God prepares to send the next plague.

[9:20 p.m. Sunday night, Apartment #41, NYC, late
2012]

                     SB
Kathy, you are my wife.

                     KP
That is correct.

                     SB
I just wanted to establish that. And you are both
game for and tolerant of this conceit.

                     KP
Yes I am.

                              SB

Now we're going to conduct a dialogue. You be the
Bible and I'll be me, reacting naturally, in real
time.

                              KP

You are the best husband. Okay, here we go.
Chapter ten. "Then the Lord said to Moses,
'Go to Pharaoh. For I have hardened his heart
in order that I may display these My signs
among them . . .'"

                              SB

Hang on. Sorry.

                              KP

Yes . . .

                              SB

Not to interrupt, but--"I've hardened his heart"?

                              KP

Yeah.

                              SB

Pharaoh's heart wasn't already hard?

                              KP

I guess that's what it's implying.

                              SB

He went out of His way to harden it? Because I
always thought it was "Evil, intransigent Pharaoh

just wouldn't learn his lesson." That he was so
stubborn or dumb that to get the Jews out of
Egypt, God had to keep raising the stakes. But
now it's "God MADE the Egyptians stubborn so
He'd have an excuse to bring more hurt"? That's
mental. There had to be some other reason.

KP

". . . And that you may recount in the hearing
of your sons and of your sons' sons how I made a
mockery of the Egyptians and how I displayed My
signs among them--"

SB

Oh boy . . .

KP

"--in order that you may know that I am the
Lord."

SB

Wow. So we could have been out of there sooner,
with way fewer plagues--but us getting free was
actually less important to Him than Him being
seen as He wanted to be seen by the all-important
Jewish demographic?

KP

I think God hadn't been having such an easy time
with the Jews.

SB

Let me guess: We were being argumentative.

                              KP
Or forgetful. I mean, understandably. Four
centuries in bondage, even a faithful people
might get skeptical. So He had a problem.

                              SB
And now helicopter-parent Yahweh has decided
that to win back the kids, He has to make an
amaaaazing impression.

                              KP
You have a crap attitude on this, don't you?

                              SB
[Silence.]

                              KP
[Clears throat.] "So Moses and Aaron went to
Phar--"

                              SB
I mean, I'm trying. Me doing this Bible chapter
is--you know, I'm trying to engage, or maybe find
a way through the skepticism.

                              KP
[Silence.]

                              SB
Sorry. You were saying.

                              KP
". . . and said to him, 'Thus says the Lord, the
God of the Hebrews, "How long will you refuse to

humble yourself before Me? Let My people go that they may worship Me."'"

SB
So Moses says that instead of doing unpaid construction work in South Cairo, the Jews want to worship the Lord. So far so good.

KP
"For if you refuse to let My people go, tomorrow I will bring locusts on your territory. They shall cover the surface of the land, so that no one will be able to see the land . . . and they shall eat away all your trees that grow in the field."

SB
A rough punishment, but not inappropriate. Pharaoh's no saint. You don't get to run a dynasty if you cave to every menacing portent.

KP
"Moreover, they shall fill your palaces and the houses of all your courtiers and of all the Egyptians--something that neither your fathers nor fathers' fathers have seen from the day they appeared on earth to this day."

SB
Gothic.

KP
"With that he turned and left Pharaoh's presence."

SB

Moses throws down mic, bounds offstage.

KP

"Locusts invaded all the land of Egypt . . . They
hid all the land from view, and the land was
darkened; and they ate up all the grasses of the
field and all the fruit of the trees which the
hail had left, so that nothing green was left, in
all the land of Egypt."

SB

Very persuasive. I mean, that is a DAMN PLAGUE.
No way Pharaoh wouldn't relent at this point. Not
even he would let his own people--many innocent
people--suffer so deeply.

KP

"But the Lord stiffened Pharaoh's heart, and he
would not let the Israelites go."

SB

And we're back here again! Your honor, this
clearly constitutes entrapment.

KP

Go on, counselor.

SB

Plaintiff, who is omnipotent, coaxed my client
into a pantomime of disobedience simply so
plaintiff could show off His almightiness and

hurt-bringing abilities. Your honor, I submit
that there is nothing more dangerous than an all-
powerful being with an inferiority complex.

                    KP
"Then the Lord said to Moses, 'Hold out your arm
toward the sky that there may be darkness upon
the land of Egypt . . .' People could not see one
another, and for three days no one could get up
from where he was; but all the Israelites enjoyed
light in their dwellings."

                    SB
Completely terrifying. A miracle in every sense.
No question, everyone gets it now, Egyptians and
Jews alike, this Yahweh is the One.

                    KP
"But the Lord stiffened Pharaoh's heart and he
would not agree to let them go."

                    SB

Grrrrrr . . .

                    KP
And then, a little later, "Moses and Aaron had
performed all these marvels before Pharaoh, but the
Lord had stiffened the heart of Pharaoh so that he
would not let the Israelites go from his land."

                    SB
Because He had His big finale.

KP

I'll grant you, it's a bit creepy how bent He was
on getting to that tenth plague. By the way, I'm
going to stop now.

SB

That's fine. I'll just lose the "actual dialogue"
pretense.

Chapter eleven: MOSES SAID, "Thus says the
Lord: Toward midnight I will go forth among the
Egyptians, and every firstborn in the land of
Egypt shall die, from the firstborn of Pharaoh
who sits on his throne to the firstborn of the
slave girl who is behind the millstones."

Here's the nub of it: Across all the seders and
schooling, I must have heard or read versions
of the "final plague" story--what, two hundred,
three hundred times? And I still can't believe
THIS is the God who my people, whom I'm generally
very proud of, have organized their culture
around for the last fifty-eight-hundred years.

". . . Moses then summoned all the elders of
Israel and said to them, '. . . And when your
children ask you, "What do you mean by this
rite?" you shall say, "It is the Passover
sacrifice to the Lord, because He passed over the
houses of the Israelites in Egypt when He smote
the Egyptians."'"

". . . And you shall not say, 'Though technically
He didn't have to do any of that smiting; it

was actually this purely optional thing He did because He wanted to make sure we would have something to talk about.'"

"In the middle of the night the Lord struck down all the firstborn in the land of Egypt, from the firstborn of Pharaoh who sat on the throne to the firstborn of the captive who was in the dungeon . . ."

Wow. Just wow.

". . . and all the firstborn of the cattle."

And I thought it was pigs He hated.

"And Pharaoh arose in the night, with all the Egyptians--because there was a loud cry in Egypt; for there was no house where there was not someone dead."

What's the opposite of DAYENU?

Look, יהוה, thanks for getting us out of Egypt. Sincerely. It was awful there. And I know the Bronze Age desert was a brutal place, and Your ghostwriters were writing for that scene. And I suppose if the programmatic killing of children had been the only way to get us slaves freed, You'd at least have an argument. But this was not that. This was premeditated heart-hardening so we could see You in terrible, terrible action. You didn't care about the murder; You cared that we Jews saw the murder. So this looks less like

"win back the loyalty of your chosen tribe" than
"gratuitous child killing."

                         KP
I've got to come back in here. You know, there
are other ways to take this in. At least for
non-adolescents.

                         SB
Ouch.

                         KP
Why not take--not just this story, but this
entire conception of God--take it maybe as
an allegory. The universe is capricious and
sometimes cruel. It just is. And being aware that
there are forces at play, or just chaos--the
point being that we can't control or appeal to or
make sense of it, but since that's reality, then
living in regular acknowledgment of that could be
a kind of spiritual practice.

                         SB
Well, aren't you sophisticated?

                         KP
You're just jealous.

                         SB
Actually, I am. Because for me, right now,
it's still: God of love, I'm good with. God of
justice--I get it. But God of unnecessary baby-
and-cow-killing plague number ten? Sorry. I'm
never going to feel it.

B'SHALLAH (*"When he let go"*)
EXODUS 13:17–17:16

ONCE THE ISRAELITES HAVE BEEN FREED, God leads them on a roundabout journey through the wasteland of the Sea of Reeds, selecting an indirect route to prevent them from wishing for a return to slavery as soon as they are attacked.

The Israelites, who are both armed and bearing Joseph's bones, know where to go because the Lord travels before them in the form of a pillar of cloud by day and a pillar of fire by night. God reveals to Moses that Pharaoh's heart has been hardened once more, compelling him to send his armies in pursuit of the Israelites.

Back in Pharaoh's court, the Egyptian king calls up six hundred of his finest charioteers to give chase. No sooner do the Israelites glimpse the approaching Egyptian column than they become gripped by fear, begging the Lord to tell them why they have been liberated from Egypt just to die in the wilderness. Moses preaches calm, promising that the Lord will protect them from the Egyptians, whom they will never see again.

Again, the Lord tells Moses the plan of action. He is to hold his rod over the sea so it will split, allowing the

Israelites to march through on to dry ground. The Egyptians will pursue to their peril—God will see to that. Just then, the pillar of cloud shifts from the lead of the Israelites to the rear, acting as a buffer between them and their Egyptian pursuers, who cannot pass through.

Once Moses holds his arm out over the water, a strong east wind blows back the sea and turns it into dry ground. The Israelites march through with the water stacked up like a wall to their right and left. The Egyptians charge after them, but the Lord creates panic by locking the wheels of their chariots. On God's instruction, Moses holds his arm over the sea once more, closing the waters upon the Egyptians, who try to flee, but the Lord hurls them into the sea, drowning every last man.

The Israelites have made it on to dry land; witnessing the scene of destruction, they sense the power of God and Moses. They sing a song of triumph in tribute to God's power.

IN NEED OF SUSTENANCE

The Israelites travel into the desert and are without water for three days. The people begin to grumble; Moses follows God's lead and throws some wood into bitter water, instantly rendering it drinkable. God issues a nonnegotiable rule: The Israelites will be protected if they keep the commandments.

The Israelites are having a hard time adjusting to wilderness living and complain constantly, romanticizing the slave experience and wondering if Moses and Aaron will lead them only to their deaths. Meanwhile, God tells Moses that bread will rain down from the sky on a daily basis. Before Sabbath, a double portion will be provided. Moses shares this news with the Israelites and lets them know that their grumbling has not been well received by God.

At night, quail descend in great volume upon the camp. In the morning a flaky substance like dew covers the ground, and the Israelites discover it is bread dispatched by God. Moses instructs them to gather up only what they need, but many greedily stock up extra only to discover it rots quickly and becomes infested with maggots. Moses advises them to take a double portion on the sixth day ahead of the Sabbath. The extra portion they gather miraculously stays fresh.

However, on the Sabbath, some of

the Israelites still set out from camp to gather a portion, and the Lord becomes irate, demanding to know from Moses how long it will take for the Israelites to follow instructions.

The Israelites call the bread, which tastes like honey-coated wafers, "manna," a foodstuff that will sustain them for forty years. Water continues to be a problem, however, and the Israelites are quick to complain. Moses expresses his frustration to the Lord, asking what he should do with his followers and suggesting that he will not be surprised if they stone him before long. The Lord specifies a rock for Moses to strike, promising it will gush forth water. The plan works to perfection.

WIPING OUT THE AMALEK

A tribe known as the Amalek clash with the Israelites. Moses deputizes Joshua to lead men into battle while he retires to a nearby hill and stands with his hands raised. As long as Moses keeps his arms in the air, Israel will triumph in battle. When he tires, Israel will falter. Moses grows weary, and he sits on a stone while Aaron and an assistant support his arms, allowing Joshua and his force to prevail. God vows to battle with the Amalek throughout time, until the tribe is blotted from historical memory.

JOEL STEIN

I shouldn't let it bother me. He's a good man, a godly man, a man who—and this is his best trait compared with all the other Jewish men—doesn't talk too much. But it's just so annoying. Because I didn't marry an idiot. And on battle days, Moses acts like an idiot.

Every battle morning he puts on his Lucky "Israelites" tunic with Joshua's name on the back. Which I'm not allowed to wash. I personally believe it's unlucky to smell like the end of a day of pyramid building in the middle of Av. Then he has to eat his manna from his Lucky Bowl since the Red Sea opened the afternoon after he happened to eat from it. That bowl is disgusting, with caked-on manna that is never going to come out. Also, he—I swear to the Lord our God, King of the Universe—looks into the bag with Joseph's bones, which I keep telling him to throw away because, well, THEY'RE JOSEPH'S BONES. I can't tell you how many places we've lived in where we lugged those gross bones. It's like a game: I hide Joseph's bones; he finds Joseph's bones. The man is like a Joseph's bones dog.

If, Lord our God, King of the Universe forbid, in the middle of a battle, I interrupt Moses with a question, even during a lull, he freaks out at me and has to walk in three circles around his Lucky Rod of God, chanting, "We will! We will! Smite you! Smite you!" Guess what, honey? You're not part of Joshua's army! You're a spectator! What you do does not affect the battle. Go out and do something useful, like sacrificing something. Other than your dignity. Or help me cook. Manna doesn't make itself. Actually, it does, but someone still has to gather it, and you're too busy making an ass of yourself. I think Miriam is starting to notice that on battle days I keep insisting we do timbrel practice at her house.

Moses' dumbest pre-battle superstition started at Rephidim when the Israelites took on the Amalek, which was like a title battle or something. Moses got in his Lucky Seat on top of the hill, with Aaron on the left (not the right!) and Hur on the right (not the left!). He held his Lucky Rod of God in his hand, looking like a moron. He must have scratched his head at some point when one of the Israelites took a sword to the head, because he became convinced that if he lowered his hand, Israel would start to lose. Wait: It gets crazier. At some point in the battle, Moses figured if one raised hand was good, two would be better. But since he's more of a battle-watcher than a battler-doer, he's got the arm muscles of an amateur timbreler. So he sits on a stone and makes Aaron and Hur hold his hands up until the sun sets. Which doesn't even make sense within his idiot superstition logic. God doesn't care about the effort, just that your hands are above your head? God is just interested in reducing blood flow to your fingers? Can you lie down as long as your hands are above your head? And you can stop at sunset because God can't see your hands in the dark? Do you know what OMNISCIENT means? It means "can see in the dark." The only way any of this makes sense, honey, is if the Amaleks saw you and were distracted by the guy with the lisp who was holding hands with two men.

After the battle, Moses made everyone—who were, as you can imagine, tired from all the killing and maiming—make this ridiculous trophy called the Adonai-Nissi Altar, which he inscribed with—get this: "Hand upon the throne of the Lord." Seriously. Like he did all the killing and maiming with the hands that he didn't even raise himself. He also wrote on it, "The Lord will be at war with the Amalek throughout the ages." I'm sure He will, sweetheart. People will be wanting to see Amalek rematches every year. More likely, you'll be talking about it with your battle-watching *altacockers* late into the night until I get so bored, I have to excuse myself to go to timbrel practice.

Here's a secret: I don't even like the timbrel.

Think about that while you enjoy your battle.

ויבא יתרו חתן משה ובניו ואשתו אל משה
אל המדבר אשר הוא חנה שם הר האלהים:

"Jethro, Moses' father-in-law, brought Moses' sons and wife
to him in the wilderness, where he was encamped at the
mountain of God." —Exodus 18:5

YITRO *("Jethro")*
EXODUS 18:1–20:23

MOSES LEARNS TO DELEGATE: **MOSES'** father-in-law, Jethro, the priest from Midian, hears about the wonders God has performed for the Israelites. He travels out into the wilderness to meet him, accompanied by Moses' wife, Zipporah, and their two sons, who have returned home. Moses welcomes him into his tent and gives a blow-by-blow account of Israel's liberation. Jethro is thrilled and proclaims that God is clearly greater than all other gods.

Moses spends the following day performing magisterial duties, ruling on disputes among his followers. Jethro cannot believe the amount of time Moses devotes to this task. Moses explains that he has to do it all, because only he is privy to God's rulings. Jethro is concerned that Moses will burn out and suggests he learn to delegate. The Midian priest thinks they should find reputable God-fearing men to learn the law, oversee the caseload, and share the burden so that only the truly major cases are left in Moses' hands.

Moses executes this idea and creates a legal system to judge matters both major and minor.

THE BIG REVEAL

When three new moons have passed since their liberation, the Israelites enter the desert around Mount Sinai. Moses ascends to confer with God, who instructs him to remind the people of what has been done for them, and how if they keep the covenant, they will become a kingdom of priests and holy people. When Moses relays the message, the people proclaim their agreement as one.

God then reveals the next steps to Moses. In three days God plans to appear in a thick cloud so the people can hear the two of them confer and trust Moses from that point on. The Israelites are to prepare for the moment by staying pure and washing their clothes. God wants the mountain itself to be set off-limits. Trespassers will be put to death.

On the morning of the third day, thunder and lightning crackle around the mountain, and a thick cloud covers the peak. As the Israelites take their place at the foot of the mountain, a ram's horn blasts loudly, filling the air with fear.

The mountain is cloaked in smoke as the Lord descends in fire. The ram's horn sounds louder, and the whole mountain appears to quake. When Moses speaks, God responds in thunder, warning Moses to prevent his people from approaching, as they will die. Moses is then dispatched back down the mountain to invite Aaron to return with him.

God speaks these words:

I am your God who liberated you from Egypt. You shall have no other gods than me.

You shall make no idols to bow down to or serve, for I, God, will take revenge on the third and fourth generations of those who reject Me.

You shall not swear falsely by using My name.

Remember the Sabbath and keep it holy. No work will be done on the seventh day to remember the way God rested and blessed the seventh day when creating the world.

Honor your father and mother.

Do not murder.

Do not commit adultery.

Do not steal.

Do not make false allegations against your neighbor.

Do not covet your neighbor's house, wife, slaves, livestock, or possessions.

All the people glimpse the thunder and lightning, the blaring horn, and the smoking mountain, and keep their distance. They agree to follow Moses' instructions, aware that they will die if God speaks directly to them. Moses advises them not to be fearful, but to understand what will happen to them if they ever stray from God's commandments. He then returns up the mountain.

God tells Moses the Israelites are forbidden to make any idols of silver or gold and directs him to build an altar made of earth on which to sacrifice animals.

REBECCA ODES
& SAM LIPSYTE

SO I SCHLEP THE KIDS OVER TO WHERE MOSES IS CAMPED OUT, MY DAD JETHRO LEADING THE WAY. I DON'T EVEN WANT TO SEE THE DEADBEAT, BUT DAD SAYS IT WILL BE OKAY, AND MOSES SHOULD SEE HIS SONS, FOR HIS OLD BUDDY YAHWEH'S SAKE.

ARE WE THERE YET?

IT'S BEEN A WHILE SINCE MOSES LEFT ME, HIS WIFE OF MANY YEARS, TO RETURN TO EGYPT AND LEAD HIS JEWS OUT, AND I DON'T REALLY KNOW WHAT THE ~~FUCK~~ FALAFEL IS OKAY ABOUT GOING TO SEE THE MO-MAN NOW AFTER BEING DUMPED LIKE THAT, BUT HEY, I'M JUST ZIPPORAH, A MIDIAN, A CHICK AND LET'S REMEMBER, WHEN IT CAME TO MOSES'S PRIORITIES IT WAS NEVER THE 10 WISHES, OR THE 10 IMPORTANT PERSONAL ISSUES TO CONFRONT, OR THE 10 DIFFICULT BUT NECESSARY CONVERSATIONS TO INCREASE INTIMACY AND GROWTH IN THE RELATIONSHIP, WAS IT? IT WAS THE TEN COMMANDMENTS. YOU BET YOUR HAIRY ESAU ASS IT WAS.

my husband saw God's back parts and all I got was this lousy t shirt

SO I'M PISSED, BUT THE THING IS, WITH MOSES, HE HAS THIS WAY OF LOOKING AT YOU, OR AT LEAST OF LOOKING AT ME: TOTAL MELT-O-RAMA. I GO UP TO WHERE HE SITS OUTSIDE HIS TENT-FLAP, AND EVEN BEFORE HE LOOKS AT HIS SONS, HE SHOOTS ME THAT LOOK, THE ONE THAT SAYS,

I KNOW I HAVE A MISSION OF NEAR-BIBLICAL PROPORTIONS, BABY, BUT I'D GIVE ANYTHING TO JUST CURL UP WITH YOU IN SOME DRY CULVERT SOMEWHERE. TALK ABOUT BURNING BUSHES.

AND THEN HE FLASHES ME THAT KILLER SMILE AND SAYS,

SCRAM, ZIPPY, IT'S GUY TIME.

HE CLAPS HIS SONS ON THE SHOULDERS AND SHOVES THEM TOWARD ME, THEN PULLS JETHRO AND ALL THE ROBED BROS INTO THE TENT.

JUST BECAUSE DADDY DOESN'T GIVE A CRAP ABOUT YOU DOESN'T MEAN HE DOESN'T LOVE YOU BOTH VERY MUCH.

OF COURSE, I EAVESDROP. WHAT THE HELL ELSE AM I GOING TO DO? I FIGURE MAYBE THEY'LL TALK ABOUT ME, THAT I'LL GET SOME INTEL ON MY FUTURE AS A SINGLE MOM, BUT NO SUCH LUCK. THEY YACK ABOUT ORGANIZATIONAL MATTERS. EVERYONE'S CONGRATULATING MOSES ON ALL THE GREAT WORK HE'S DONE FOR THE REGION LATELY, SETTLING LOCAL DISPUTES, ADVISING VILLAGE ELDERS, ADJUDICATING PETTY CRIMINAL CASES.

YOU'RE A HERO, MO.

WELL, ALL POLITICS IS LOCAL.

WHEREUPON A THUNDERING PRIEST-LIKE VOICE SHOUTS,

BULLSHIT!

IT'S MY OLD MAN.

I SAY THIS AS A FRIEND AND FATHER-IN-LAW. YOU'VE GOT TO STOP WASTING YOUR TIME WITH SMALL-TIME CRAP. DELEGATE! DELEGATE! YOU'VE GOT TO RUN THIS SHIT LIKE A BUSINESS. YOU NEED REGIONAL MANAGERS, LOCAL MAGISTRATES, WHATEVER IT TAKES. TCB, SON.

WHAT HAPPENS IN THE MAN CAVE STAYS IN THE MAN CAVE

But everyone, you know, totally kneweth that Jethro was right. And Moses learned to delegate. He even let Aaron white-board an org chart. There were no computers then, or there were, but they were slow and clunky and took up an entire tent.

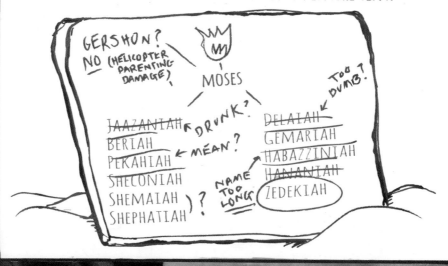

NOT LONG AFTER THIS MR. I'M-NUMBER-ONE HOOKED MOSES UP WITH THE TEN (OR SO) COMMANDMENTS. YOU'VE PROBABLY HEARD OF THESE RIGHT? THE RULES?

NO KILLING, EXCEPT YOU KNOW, IF YOU'VE GOT TO STONE A GAY DUDE OR SOMETHING,

NO COVETING YOUR NEIGHBOR'S OX OR WIFE,

NO ADULTERY WITH YOUR NEIGHBOR'S OX,

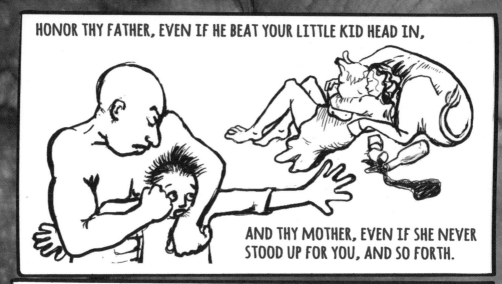

HONOR THY FATHER, EVEN IF HE BEAT YOUR LITTLE KID HEAD IN,

AND THY MOTHER, EVEN IF SHE NEVER STOOD UP FOR YOU, AND SO FORTH.

FACT IS, I WAS SURPRISED IT ALL CAUGHT ON. I THINK EVEN MOSES THOUGHT THEY WERE A LITTLE EXCESSIVE, ESPECIALLY THOSE FIRST ONES, THE BITS ABOUT NO OTHER GOD AND NO GRAVEN IMAGES. I TOLD HIM MR. OMNIPOTENCE WAS A LITTLE SENSITIVE. MOSES DIDN'T EVEN BOTHER TO SMILE.

WHEN WE WERE YOUNG HE USED TO SAY THE ONLY RULE THAT MATTERED WAS HONESTY. HE SAID HE WOULD NEVER TELL SOMEBODY HE MET THAT HE HAD AN OPEN MARRIAGE UNLESS HE REALLY DID. "SO DO WE?" HE ASKED. BUT ANYWAY, EVERYBODY WENT NUTS FOR THE COMMANDMENTS. I COULDN'T TELL YOU WHY. NOBODY'S GOING TO COMMAND ZIPPY'S SHIT.

the end.

ויבא משה בתוך הענן ויעל אל ההר ויהי משה בהר ארבעים יום וארבעים לילה:

"Moses went inside the cloud and ascended the mountain;
and Moses remained on the mountain forty days
and forty nights."—Exodus 24:18

MISHPATIM (*"Laws"*)
EXODUS 21:1–24:18

CRIME AND PUNISHMENT: **A MULTITUDE OF** laws are detailed, including rules about issues as diverse as slavery and murder. The death penalty is prescribed for those who strike or insult their parents. Compensation is set for victims of violent attack, and rules of vengeance are rigidly defined.

Physical damage is to be punished with a like-for-like approach—an eye for an eye, a tooth for a tooth—unless the injury involves a slave-master relationship, in which case freedom can be exchanged. Remedies for injuries caused by livestock are clarified, as is the punishment for seducing a virgin without paying the bride-price. Sorcery is prohibited, as is sleeping with animals. Ill-treatment of strangers, widows, and orphans is prohibited. The Israelites are reminded that they are to be a holy people.

RITUAL TIME

The land can be farmed for six years, but in the seventh it should be left to lie fallow, so the needy can take from it. The notion of the Sabbath as a day of rest is reinforced; the day is to be observed, even by livestock.

A rudimentary cycle of festivals is prescribed: the seven days of Passover to remember the liberation from Egypt, the harvest festival to celebrate the sowing of the field, and the Feast of Ingathering at the end of the year to celebrate reaping. At those times, all males are to gather together before the Lord. A clutter of rules about food and sacrifice are also outlined. The best first fruits are to be offered to God. A kid is not to be boiled in its mother's milk.

An angel is dispatched to guard the Israelites as a symbol of God's authority. Led by the angel, the Israelites will annihilate every tribe they encounter and shall tear down their idols. Sickness will be removed from the Israelites' midst, and no woman shall miscarry. Everyone will live till the end of their days.

God's terror will proceed ahead of the Israelites. All those who live around them shall be thrown into panic and will flee. A plague will destroy many, but these enemies will be overthrown gradually to prevent the land from becoming overpopulated by wild animals, who will pose a danger.

God describes the borders of the land promised in the covenant: It will stretch from the Sea of Reeds to the Sea of Philistia, and from the desert to the Euphrates.

GAME ON!

Then the Lord instructs Moses to climb back up Mount Sinai, accompanied by Aaron and the seventy elders of Israel, who are to bow from afar, for only Moses is allowed to approach God. Before setting out, Moses repeats God's commandments and rules. With one enthusiastic voice, the Israelites agree to comply. Moses then builds an altar and offers up a series of sacrifices to the Lord, dabbing the people with blood as a sign of the covenant.

Moses, Aaron, and the elders then scale the mountain. They see God and are not struck down. Instead they feast together. Moses is instructed to come closer and receive stone tablets on which God has already inscribed the commandments. Moses and his assistant, Joshua, advance to receive them as a cloud covers the top of the mountain. After seven days, God calls to Moses from within the cloud. From the perspective of the Israelites at the base of the mountain, the Lord's presence appears like a burning fire. Moses ventures into the cloud, remaining there for forty days and nights.

BEN GREENMAN

S o he said he was going to Mount Sinai, and someone in the room,
maybe Lou, said, "You mean the hospital?" and the rest of us
snickered.

We knew him, so we knew he'd do exactly what he did, which was
to turn his back on us as if hurt, take a few steps, and then turn around
again, eyes blazing, and say, in a deliberately resonant voice, "The Mount!"

He needed those few steps to get his eyes and his voice that way, trust
me. He's an actor if I've ever seen one.

We went on playing cards. Mikey won that hand and Nicky won the
next one, and then Lou said he had to be up early the next morning for
work and the night broke up.

The next week, we met again, this time at Nicky's house, and after we
had dealt out the first two hands, Donald squared his cards on the table
and asked if anyone had seen Moses.

I shook my head, and then I noticed that everyone else's head was
shaking, too. "What gives?" Donald said. "He hasn't missed card night
in years."

"The Mount!" Lou said, his eyes on fire like Moses' had been the week
before, and we all bagged up.

That night I did a little better, not at cards, but in general, because
Mikey brought his daughter Jane to the game. I don't want to give anyone
the wrong idea: Mikey's about twenty years older than the rest of the guys,
so his daughter is only a little bit younger than we are. We've all known
Jane since she was a teenager, and all of us shed a tear when she told Mikey
she was moving in with her boyfriend, but that didn't pan out, and we all
wiped the tear away. At least I did. I can't speak for the other guys. All I
can say is that I've had a thing for her since before it was allowed.

Nicky was on a serious winning streak, to the point where Donald accused him of putting mirrors or cameras up so he could see the rest of our cards. When he had most of our money and most of our pride, I decided to sit out a hand and talk to Jane.

She was sitting in a chair in the corner, wearing a short dress that was made from a material that looked like curtains in an expensive house, and I was pretty sure that if I got her into the light, I'd be able to see through it, but I was happy to talk to her in the dark, too.

She told me about a business she was starting, something about arranging for house sitters who were also maids, so you could go away on a trip and come back to find it in perfect shape. "That sounds like a good idea," I said. "It's the kind of thing I have never considered before, but now that I hear it, it makes sense."

Just at that moment, Moses burst in. His eyes were as wild as when he had left, but this time it didn't seem like acting. "The courts must execute by strangulation those who deserve it," he shouted.

"And it's nice to see you, too," said Lou.

Moses went on like he hadn't even heard. "Assess the damages incurred by fire," "Do not eat the meat of an animal that was mortally wounded," "Do not afflict any widow or orphan."

"Just calm down," Donald said. "We're trying to derail the Nicky Express here."

But Moses wouldn't calm down. He flailed his arms and moved his head from side to side so that his hair flew out. "Transgressors must not testify," he said. "Transgressors must not testify." Then he fell, just dropping like a rock to the floor. His head bounced off a chair on the way down, and he lay still on the hardwood.

"Crap," Nicky said. "You okay?" He sprang up to tend to Moses. He brought him a pillow from the couch and also some water and then some scotch and something else that came out of a flask he took out of his pocket.

Moses was murmuring now. "There are rules," he said.

Mikey banged his hand on the table. He was into Nicky for more than two hundred, and he was furious. "We know about rules," Mikey said, sweeping his hands over the table. "This whole bloody game is rules."

And then he looked a little embarrassed that he had talked that way in front of his daughter, and he stood roughly and went outside to have a cigarette.

Jane wouldn't come out of the chair in the corner. "What's wrong?" I said. "You're not mad at your father, are you? Cut him some slack."

"It's not him," she said. "It's him." She pointed at Moses. Nicky had gotten enough water and whatever else into him that he was calmed down, or at least silent, though his eyes were still burning. "I had a little thing with him once."

"You did?" I was suddenly furious. I could have strangled him right there and then.

"He wasn't like this then. He was much more of a live-and-let-live kind of guy. He's changed."

Moses was our age, maybe a few years older, but stretched out there on the floor he looked ancient, like the next change wouldn't be for the better, like he was maybe already being returned to the earth.

Jane came to her feet as abruptly as her father had. "I think a cigarette's a good idea," she said. "But not with my dad. I don't want him to see. Want to go out back with me?"

"I don't smoke," I said. "But you know me: Live and let live."

She let me get her shirt half off there in the backyard, the sound of the TV coming from the house, the peak of the Mount looming a ways off in the moonlight. But when I heard crying from the house, one that started human and ended animal, I buttoned her shirt back up and told her we had to go back in to help.

ככל אשר אני מראה אותך את תבנית המשכן ואת תבנית כל כליו וכן תעשו:

"Exactly as I show you—the pattern of the Tabernacle and the pattern of all its furnishings—so you shall make it."—Exodus 25:9

T'RUMAH ("*Offering*")
EXODUS 25:1–27:19

THE LORD COMMANDS MOSES TO INSTRUCT the Israelites to offer up gifts of gold, silver, and copper, plus other, more exotic fineries like tanned ram skins and goats' hair. Instructions are then provided for the building of a dazzling Tabernacle—a house of the Lord that will allow God to dwell among the Israelites.

The Tabernacle is to be covered with a fine linen curtain, blue, purple, and crimson in color.

The Lord then dictates exact specifications: the raw materials (acacia wood), ornamentation (including cherubim and dolphin skins), and detailed dimensions. The Tabernacle will also house the Ark of the Covenant, containing the stone commandments God has carved. It will also provide God and Moses with a meeting place, where they can discuss the governance of the Israelites.

MARC KUSHNER

Parshat T'rumah

HWKN (Hollwich Kushner) makes one minor tweak to the detailed architectural plans in **T'rumah**. It's the only way to squeeze the Tabernacle into the world's biggest Jewish city.

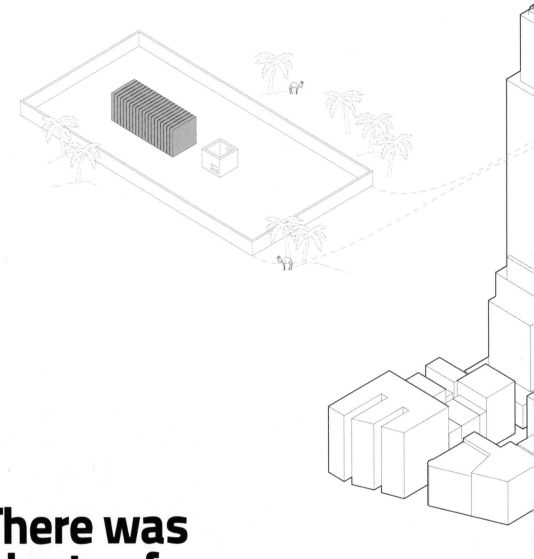

There was
plenty of room
in the desert . . .

...but 120x60 cubits is a lot of Manhattan real estate.

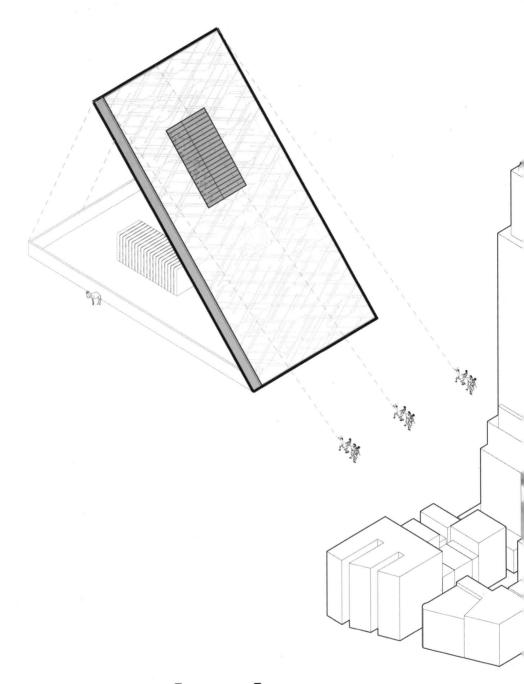

Just one simple
adjustment . . .

...and the tabernacle finds a permanent home.

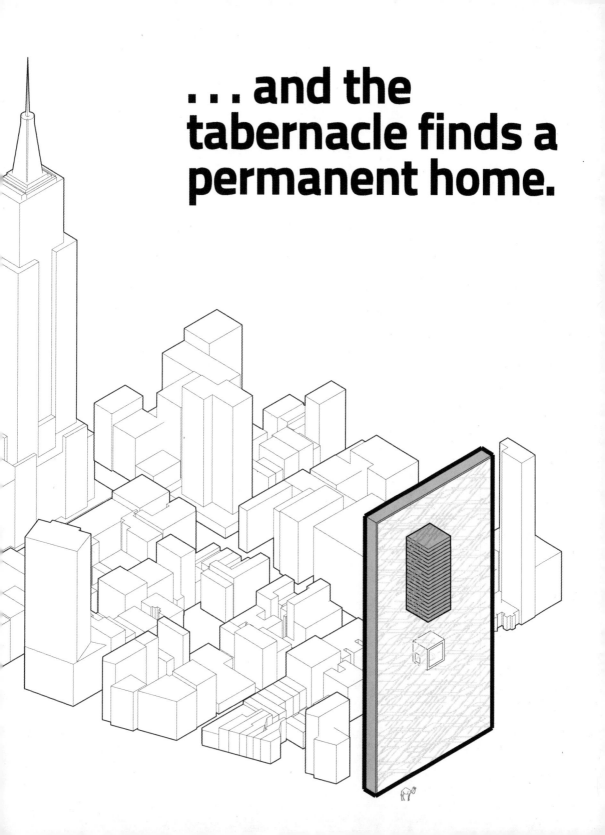

T'TZAVVEH ("*You command*")
EXODUS 27:20–30:10

RIESTLY STYLE: MOSES' MOUNTAINTOP encounter with God continues as the Tabernacle design is further detailed. The Lord reveals specifications for the lights, which Aaron and his sons are to ensure burn night and day. Their priestly uniforms are also described. Aprons made of blue, purple, and crimson linen yarns will be worn with breastplates engraved with twelve gemstones for the twelve tribes, plus tunics, sashes, and headdresses.

Aaron's breastplate will also contain "Urim and Thummim," two mysterious objects that are thought to be "light and perfection." But his robe is functional as well as ornamental: Bells woven into it will ring out before him and warn off harm, serving as a reminder that the Tabernacle is a place rife with danger.

THE CONSECRATION
Aaron's sons are to be clothed, given turbans, and anointed as priests. Their consecration ceremony will include the offering of a young bull, two unblemished rams, and some unleavened bread and cakes. After Aaron and his sons are washed in front of the Tent

of Meeting and then dressed, the bull will be slaughtered at the entrance and its blood poured on the altar while its organs are burned. One ram will suffer the same fate. The blood of the second is to be dabbed on the priests' right ears, right thumbs, and right big toes, and then poured against the altar. Afterward, the altar blood is to be splashed on the priests' clothing, making them holy.

The fat parts of the ram are then to be put onto the palms of the priests, along with the bread and cakes, before being burned as a gift to the Lord. The entire ordination will take seven days.

The daily sacrifice cycle is also outlined: two lambs a day—one in the morning, one at twilight—alongside an altar for burning aromatic incense.

MARK LAMSTER

ON THE LINE WITH GOD'S TAILOR

"If we're telling client horror stories, I've got an all-time classic for you."

"Spill."

"Okay. So it's a cold January morning, totally forgettable day, and some guy in a cape and sandals bursts through the door and starts barking at Sheila—he's got a voice like a thunderclap—and it's her first week and she's already in tears before I can get my fabric guy from Hong Kong off the line."

"Oy."

"Oy is right. So I rush over and I'm like, 'Welcome to Murray's Wholesale Fashions, how may I help you?' And the guy looks at me like I'm some kind of cockroach and says, 'I come with an order from the Lord.'"

"No."

"Yes. Now ordinarily I kick a guy like this right out on his *tuchas,* but this one . . . Something seems different. That cape has gold thread running through it, and not the imitation stuff. So somehow I keep it together. 'Okay,' I tell him. 'We're used to demanding clients here at Murray's. But maybe you could start by telling me your name?' And he says, 'Moses.' And I'm like, 'Okay, Moses, what exactly is your Lord looking for?' And it turns out they need to outfit all the priests for their spectacular new temple."

"Gold mine."

"Exactly what I'm thinking. But then he starts telling me about these priestly vestments, which have some very, shall we say, esoteric instructions. Crazy ostentatious. The taste level, if I may be frank, is fresh off the boat."

"Go on."

"Do you know what an ephod is? No? I didn't either. Turns out it's kind of like a smock, but a holy version. So he tells me he needs an ephod, and he needs it to be in linen, and it needs to be gold, blue, purple, and scarlet, with gold-braid shoulder straps, a blue cape, and a pair of onyx stones in gold settings engraved with the tribes of Israel. Oh, and there's jewels everywhere. Emeralds, sapphires, beryl, agate, jasper, carnelian—and on and on."

"Oh my God."

"Exactly. It's waaaaay too much. So I wonder suggestively if maybe he'd like something a bit more . . . restrained? A more subtle palette? Some cool tones to set off the bling?"

"And?"

"Big mistake. He just gives me a death glare and continues. You can't imagine. The whole getup is like something drawn from the mind of a six-year-old girl: a train wreck of colors and jewels and every gaudy thing you can imagine. The only thing missing is a pink pony, and he probably has one of those on order. Flat-out bonkers."

"Maybe someone slipped something into his manna."

"Who knows? But what can you do? The customer is always right, and we'd make a few extra shekels, so why argue? So I don't. Then, when he's finished giving me the whole order, I add up the figures and, let me tell you, it's a big number. I read it to him and he nods approvingly, looks me straight in the eye, and says, 'This is for the Lord, so of course there will be no charge.' Just like that. Matter-of-fact."

"And what did you do?"

"What am I, *meshugenah*? I told him I'd knock off twenty percent and he can either take it or go wander the desert for another forty years, his choice. So we made the sale. And that's how I got my place in Boca."

"When the people saw that Moses was so long in coming down from the mountain, the people gathered against Aaron and said to him, 'Come, make us a god who shall go before us, for that man Moses, who brought us from the land of Egypt—we do not know what has happened to him.'" —Exodus 32:1

KI TISSA (*"When you take"*)
EXODUS 30:11–34:35

THE LORD TELLS MOSES TO TAKE A CENSUS of his people, so that each person over the age of twenty can pay a half-shekel offering to the Lord—a gift that will defend them against disease while providing funds for the maintenance and operation of the sanctuary. The priestly rules for washing before approaching the Tabernacle are detailed, along with the correct recipe for the aromatic oil that should be burned (it's a complex creation of myrrh, fragrant cinnamon, aromatic cane, cassia, and olive oil). The composition of the priestly incense is also spelled out; it shall consist of herbs and frankincense.

GOD'S ARTIST
Then God reveals that Bezalel, of the tribe of Judah, has been selected to be endowed with divinely inspired artistic skill. Working with gold, silver, copper, stone, and wood, Bezalel is to execute the designs for the Tabernacle, its furnishings, and the priestly clothing.

The Lord then orders Moses to reinforce the centrality of the Sabbath: Anyone breaking it is to be put to death. The covenant is then proffered, written on two tablets by the finger of God.

IDLE IDOL

Back down at the foot of the mountain, the people have become concerned about Moses' extended absence. Fearing him lost, they surround Aaron and pressure him to construct a god they can worship. Aaron orders them to gather up their gold jewelry. He then casts the collection in a mold and forges it into a calf. The people begin to worship the idol as if it is the force that delivered them from Egypt, feasting and dancing around it in celebration.

A disgruntled God monitors the situation and commands Moses to hurry down the mountain, lambasting the Israelites as "stiff-necked" or stubborn. The Lord's immediate impulse is to destroy them, but Moses counsels caution, urging God to think what pleasure the annihilation of the Israelites will bring the Egyptians. He reinforces this message by reminding God of the covenant made with Abraham, Isaac, and Jacob.

As Moses descends, Joshua wonders if they are hearing the sounds of war emanating from the Israelites' camp. Moses knows better, suggesting it is neither triumph nor defeat they hear, but more the sound of song. But once they come closer and Moses glimpses the celebration and dancing, he is unable to contain his fury, hurling down the tablets and shattering them before burning down the calf, grinding it into powder, mixing it with water, and forcing the people to drink it.

Moses confronts Aaron, demanding to know what has clouded his brother's judgment. Aaron defends himself by blaming humanity's predilection for doing evil. Recognizing the extent to which the Israelites are out of control and the extent of the physical threat they pose, Moses stands by the camp's gate and asks anyone who remains on God's side to rally to him. The Levites walk over, and he orders them to pull out their short swords and take revenge on the ringleaders. Their response is immediate: Three thousand of their fellows are massacred.

FORGIVE AND FORGET?

With order now restored, Moses addresses the people the following day, outlining the process through which they can gain forgiveness. He then approaches the Lord and says that the people will be forgiven or he will quit the entire divine project. God decides that Moses will continue leading the people, but he should let them know that sinners will receive their punishment in due time. Indeed, a plague soon descends on the people as retribution for their calf-worshipping ways.

Then the Lord tells Moses to continue the journey, restating the covenant; however, God will no longer travel in the people's midst, not wanting to be tempted to destroy them if provoked by their stubborn behavior. An angel will now lead them as they begin to drive enemy tribes out of the land.

The people are upset by this news, so Moses asks God how he will be guided through the wilderness. He demands to learn more about the Lord's true nature, suggesting it would be better not to set foot on the journey than to be left without God's leadership. Moses then asks God to offer a full-frontal revelation, to which the Lord agrees.

Because a human cannot survive seeing God's face, the Lord instructs Moses to place himself on a rock so he will be shielded in a crevice as the flyby occurs. Moses carves the covenant onto two replacement stones and ascends the mountain. The Lord descends in a cloud. Moses proclaims God's name, and as the Lord passes by him, exclaims, "The Lord, The Lord,

compassionate and gracious, slow to anger, abounding in kindness and good faith, kind to the thousandth generation, forgiving crime, transgression, and sin, yet willing to visit punishment of parents upon their children and descendants up to the third and fourth generation."

Once Moses has begged for forgiveness on behalf of the Israelites, God restates the covenant and promises to work wonders on their behalf. The Israelites will destroy every tribe that confronts them, because God is a jealous force. The Israelites are reminded that they cannot craft idols of their own, and are commanded to maintain the Festival of Unleavened Bread, dedicate their firstborn to God, keep the Sabbath, and maintain the Harvest Festival and the Festival of Ingathering.

Moses is on the mountaintop for forty days and nights, during which he does not eat or drink. He descends with the commandments on the tablets, unaware that God's presence has made his skin glow. The radiance makes Aaron and the leadership afraid to come near him, but Moses calls them back and tells them all that God has instructed. After that, he begins to wear a veil, taking it off only to consult with the Lord.

RICH COHEN

Everything you've heard about the golden calf is wrong. For starters, it was not a calf. It was more like a pig, with a snout nose and fiery eyes, like a god of yore, but then, later, swine were made verboten. But not yet; remember, this happened long before Deuteronomy had been written. Second, this idea that in making the thing I was transgressing or violating, behaving like a moron who did not understand that it was He of the unsayable name, He who wrestled Jacob in the desert as the moon wept, who freed us, well, that is another untruth. I knew and loved God, but I did what I did because my brother left me in the desert with about 600,000 newly freed, utterly psychotic slaves while he went into the mountains to "figure a few things out."

When you go away like that, how long are you usually gone? For me, it's hours. If I'm gone more than a day, my wife calls the cops and the neighbors start combing the weeds along the running path to see if I've dropped dead of a heart attack or cut my own throat. Moses was gone three weeks before the people boiled over and started demanding an answer, a plan, a way to relieve all that accumulated suffering. And remember who I was dealing with! This was a mob! At first, I said, "No, no, Moses will be back." But finally, when it was do something or let them riot and kill one another, I decided to act. What the hell? Let's make an idol, as of old. A calf? No, a swine, which was my way of adding a subtext.

On one level, it's a tchotchke like back in Egypt, whereas on another it's an admonition. It tells the people, You're behaving like pigs. And this notion, written into the book of Exodus thousands of years later by people with their own agendas, that the Israelites bowed before it as if it were God? Not true! The golden calf—I will call it that, as that's how it's become known—was a symbol, a way of concentrating the brain, giving the people something to look at as they worshipped the pillar of smoke or fire they followed in the desert. (And what is a pillar of smoke or fire if not another kind of symbol?) Why? Because they needed it. Moses had left, God was talking to someone else, and they needed a rail to hold.

That's what I gave them. So I reject the notion that we were worshipping a foreign god. We were worshipping the One God via One Calf. The real issue was the matter of creating idols. We did do that. We were worshipping with the aid of an icon, and it's a sin. It's also about the hardest demand of our faith. Cleanse your mind of images, leave it open to nothing, thus everything. Nearly impossible! Just look how image-filled the Jewish and Christian world is even today! And these were the first people told to do it. But here's the key: They had not been told yet. You've got me in your books for violating a law that had yet to be written! I think, in your country, you're protected by an ex post facto law. You can't be charged for breaking a rule if that rule did not exist when you broke it. When I built the calf, Moses was still up the mountain. There were no commandments, no law forbidding what I was doing. So condemn me, but please notice how God never did so. The priests come from me; I was the first of the line, the father of vestments. If you don't believe it, check your New York phone book and count the number of Cohens. So add me to that list of those Jews condemned for doing what had to be done. And, by the way, and this is the last thing, I neither looked nor talked anything like Edward G. Robinson. I was in fact a very decent-looking man.

ויאמר משה אל בני ישראל ראו קרא יהוה
בשם בצלאל בן אורי בן חור למטה יהודה:

"And Moses said to the Israelites: See, the Lord has singled out by name
Bezalel, son of Uri, son of Hur, of the tribe of Judah." —Exodus 35:30

VA-YAK·HEL (*"And he assembled"*)
EXODUS 35:1–38:20

UILDING BY COMMITTEE: **MOSES ASSEMBLES**
the entire Israelite community, and lectures them as
God has commanded. He demands they keep the
Sabbath, describes the gifts—from gold to dolphin
skins—that God desires, and invites skilled craftsmen to volunteer to build the Tabernacle.

The Israelites donate their finery, making a collection of the gold, earrings, pendants, yarns, linens, and even dolphin skins. Moses then announces the elevation of Bezalel, who has been endowed with a divine mastery of every craft. He is to oversee every Tabernacle detail, from construction to clothing design.

The Tabernacle begins as a tent covered with ram and dolphin skins; then acacia-wood planks are crafted to form the Tabernacle, which is overlaid with gold.

Curtains of blue, purple, and crimson yarns are cut and hooked onto gold and silver sockets.

Bezalel is at the center of it all: carving tables; forging lamp stands; shaping cups, moldings, and altars; and constructing a huge enclosure cloaked in ornate hanging.

ROSS MARTIN

EARLY REPORT CARD OFFERS INSIGHTS INTO ARTISTIC INSPIRATION

ST. LOUIS, Missouri (AP) A professor of archaeology at Washington University yesterday announced the discovery of a small stone tablet that he says originates from 1440 B.C. If his claim is true, the tablet dates from a time when biblical tradition says Moses received the Ten Commandments from Mount Sinai, in Egypt.

According to Stuart Newman, Ph.D., whose team of students made the discovery, the stone block contains text that may cast light on early Jewish attitudes toward artistic creation.

The size of a notebook, it has an inscription chiseled in a dialect of ancient Hebrew. Although some of the inscription has been obscured by the passage of millennia, the majority of the text is still visible, preserved by the Sinai desert. According to Dr. Newman, the text appears to be an academic review of a craftsman named Bezalel. It is an ancient version of a contemporary report card.

If authenticated, the tablet may be the first physical evidence ever of a character mentioned in the Bible. In Exodus, God selects Bezalel—along with another laborer, Oholiab—to create the first Tabernacle, to house the Ark of the Covenant. The text follows: "I have endowed him with a divine spirit of skill, ability, and knowledge in every kind of craft." After his selection, Bezalel came to represent the prototypical artist in Jewish tradition (a popular school of art in Israel now bears his name).

According to Dr. Newman, the tablet proves that Bezalel was a poor student who was given his talent by the Lord. "Bezalel was marked as a 'goat' in every single subject, signifying his unimpressive academic performance, yet God hired him for the job anyway," Dr. Newman said. "God can endow even the least talented person with divine skill."

However, Professor Herman Fleur of Brandeis University, author of the book *Bob Dylan & Jonah Lehrer: The Origin of Poetic*

License, disagrees with Dr. Newman's interpretation. "In biblical times, the goat was the preferred form of sacrifice to God," Professor Fleur said. "To be marked as a 'goat' shows Bezalel was already a gifted student. God was making a choice that any employer today would make: hiring the best for his construction crew."

The disagreement raises serious questions about the nature of artistic inspiration. Does artistic ability come from within? Or is it divinely bestowed?

It's a question that scholars, artists, and, for that matter, scientists may never answer.

In ancient Rome, a *genius* was regarded as an external, guiding spirit. By the time of Augustus, however, the word had come to be associated with the creative vision of talented artists themselves.

That debate has continued through modern times. Romantic poets imagined their inspiration coming from outside. Their model was the aeolian harp—a musical instrument that is played by the wind. Conversely, Sigmund Freud and the psychoanalysts believed artistic ability was derived from the subconscious.

"If we accept that the goat image is a sign of success, we know that artistic ability is innate, and not external," said Professor Fleur. "It allows us to begin to understand and quantify ability."

Dr. Newman disagrees. "Culture holds that a goat is a sign of failure," he said. "Bezalel's abilities were clearly God given. Now that we know artistic creation comes from God, we can treat that divine gift with the humility and respect it deserves."

Other experts disagree that the image is of a goat at all. "It looks like a man with large ears," Roger Butterfield, director of the Institute for Judaic Art, wrote in an email. "Maybe Bezalel was just a really good listener?"

Controversy surrounding the selection of Bezalel and Oholiab has plagued the two for centuries. Talmudic scholars have long debated whether or not God's hiring decisions for the Tabernacle accord with best practices for contemporary human resources. It's widely believed, for example, that artists and craftsmen of the time who were *not* chosen challenged Moses, arguing that no craftsmen of their impoverished backgrounds could possibly be expert in materials as diverse as wood, gold, and copper.

Allegations of cronyism persist. Bezalel, critics claim, was chosen as a way of rewarding his grandfather Hur, who laid down his life to sanctify the name of the Lord, rather than join in worshipping a golden calf.

Others have wondered why two craftsmen of such diverse backgrounds—Oholiab is said to be the descendant of prostitutes—could be expected to collaborate.

Although Dr. Newman's discovery holds out tantalizing possibilities for understanding our most inscrutable skills, scholarly agreement seems unlikely.

"Think about it. The Tabernacle wasn't designed or built by either of these guys," added Mr. Butterfield, a former Judaica fabricator. "Given what we know about the social culture of the Israelites, this was a community effort. The Tabernacle was crowd-sourced."

P'KUDEI ("*Amounts of*")
EXODUS 38:21–40:38

ONSTRUCTION COMPLETE: BEZALEL'S achievement as project chief is celebrated, alongside that of Oholiab, son of Ahisamach, of the tribe of Dan, his carver, designer, and embroiderer. Working backward from the half-shekel levy, the census determines that the Israelites number 603,550 men over the age of twenty.

Upon completion, the Tabernacle, with its tent and full complement of furnishings, is presented to Moses. He inspects the new construction; after determining that it has been built to the Lord's exacting specifications, he blesses those who created it.

The Lord runs through the Tabernacle's day-to-day operations with Moses, teaching him how to make it holy, and how to purify Aaron and his sons. Moses follows every detail.

When Moses finishes his task list, God's cloud descends on the Tent of Meeting, and the Lord's presence fills the Tabernacle. Whenever the cloud rises, the Israelites know it is time to set out on their journey, and they will follow God's presence in cloud form by day, and as a pillar of fire by night.

JOSH KUN

The MLS. Your #1 Real Estate Choice

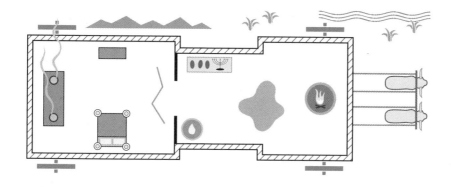

No Address
The Wilderness, Sinai Desert
Price: $59,999,000

Listing Agent: Sotheby's Tanakh

MLS#: 2-38214038

Status: Active

Lot Size: Variable

Sq Ft: 11,700

Beds: N/A

Baths: 1

Style: Mobile/Live-Work/Desert Ancient/Tabernacle

Year Built: 1250 B.C.

Roof: N/A

View: Sky, treetop

Amenities: Gold inlays, animal skins, fine yarns, incense station, bread table, indoor fire pit

Sewage: N/A

Spa: 1

Parking: Outdoor, attached

Security: N/A

Tennis: N/A

Laundry: Washer inside; dryer outside

Heat: No

Air: Swamp cooler

Open House: Sundays 10–5

Property Type: Single family

Sale Type: In foreclosure, notice of default, short pay

School: Wilderness Elementary, Canaan High. Check API ratings—excellent!

REMARKS

Your dream home awaits. This turnkey, unparalleled, LEED-certified, green architectural mobile home was designed by Moses, Aaron & Sons Architects and built by Bezalel & Oholiab Construction, both veterans of creating unique environmental mobile home properties. Ideal for families looking to relocate regularly, retirees searching for the ultimate way to tour the desert from the privacy of their own home, or artists/musicians ready to settle in a secluded, private desert live/work compound.

FEATURES AND MATERIALS

Includes features not typically found in mobile home properties in this region. The spacious one-story, loft-like floor plan illuminates the seamless transition between the home's lavish interior and exterior, offering endless possibilities and versatility, especially for families looking for one-of-a-kind amenities and classic materials. Primary construction materials include 2,204 pounds of gold, 7,584 pounds of silver, and 5,338 pounds of copper. All hinges and sockets are the original silver and copper, as are the fixtures of the exterior, storm-resistant wood walling. The nearly 100 boards of original endangered acacia wood have been meticulously restored and refurbished and weather treated with a century's guarantee.

LUSH MASTER LIVING SPACE

The interior space consists of three principal live/work modules. The master living space comes complete with a four-pillar (gold-overlay) bed; a room divider made of an angel-embroidered veil of fine linen, and blue, purple, and scarlet yarn; a built-in ark to hold and display that collection of valuable books, documents, and artifacts; a gold altar with antique gold incense holders; a gold Hollywood Regency floor lamp; and a table designed to showcase artisanal sunbaked breads. The house also comes furnished with the treated skins of dolphins and rams that can be used for the construction of a tent (original design plans had the tent assembled inside the house for meetings, but the tent can certainly be used outside for camping expeditions, sleepovers, or birthday parties).

MULTIPURPOSE WATER SYSTEM
The middle space is an unconventional bathroom/kitchen/washer hybrid that is centered on a majestic multipurpose water treatment, a bronze basin of purified water that functions as a bathing area, kitchen sink, and water-conserving clothes-washer.

BEAUTIFUL FOYER
The final space—the main entry foyer—is an indoor/outdoor showstopper centered on a bronze overlay fire pit/barbecue pit built with a bronze grating, ram's-horn grill brackets, and acacia-wood sidings.

ADDITIONAL AMENITIES
House includes a walk-in closet and a rare collection of vintage clothing: robes, breast-pieces, tunics, and a spectacular linen apron embroidered with lazuli stones. Floors are dirt and gravel. Roofing is original, opening to the sky, so bring your telescope to stargaze from bed. *Note*: The roof is occasionally covered by a storm canopy of wind, clouds, and debris that follows the house wherever it goes, but with a little TLC and imagination, the possibilities for a privately controlled climate system are endless. This is a one-of-a-kind, solar-powered home. Walk to shopping, golf course, and local parks (depending on where you are). Incredible curb appeal! This is a must-see! It's your ticket to the promised land!

PART THREE

LEVIT

ICUS

I F YOU LIKE RITUAL, THIS IS THE BOOK
for you.

Beginning with detailed breakdowns of altar offerings, ranging from rams and he-goats to oxen, this is a volume in which the blood, organs, and smoke of sacrifices always linger.

No need for narrative here! The text reads like a crash course in Israelite legislation, concerning matters of purity, priestly probity, genital infections, and bestiality. The prescribed dose of fire, water, oil, or blood appears able to correct most things. It also makes this book tough going for most first-time readers.

והקריב מזבח השלמים אשה ליהוה חלבו האליה תמימה לעמת העצה
יסירנה ואת החלב המכסה את הקרב ואת כל החלב אשר על הקרב:

"He shall then present, as an offering by fire to the Lord, the fat from a sacrifice of well-being: the whole broad tail, which shall be removed close to the backbone; the fat that covers the entrails and all the fat that is about the entrails." —Leviticus 3:9

VA-YIKRA (*"And he called"*)
LEVITICUS 1:1–5:26

THE MYSTERY OF OFFERINGS IS REVEALED. The Lord breaks down the specific categories of altar offerings so that Moses can explain the technical mechanics of sacrifice to the Israelites:

"Burnt offerings" require male bulls free of blemish. Aaron and his sons are to splash the blood against the altar before burning the flayed sections on a wood fire. A similar procedure is outlined for sheep or goats. If birds are brought for sacrificial purposes, only turtledoves or pigeons will suffice.

The recipe for "meal offerings" is spelled out: flour mixed with oil and frankincense. Unleavened cakes, wafers, grain, or fruit can also serve. The priests are to burn a token amount, but should feel free to eat the remainder.

"Sacrifices of well-being" are male or female livestock free of blemish.

"Sin offerings" for inadvertent transgressions require an unblemished bull, unless the sin is performed by a tribal chief, in which case a goat will be needed.

A "guilt offering," necessary in the case of an unwitting transgression of a sacred commandment, can take the form of a female goat or sheep.

A person guilty of failing to testify when in a position to do so, of touching an unclean object like a carcass, or of breaking a forgotten oath can rectify the situation by offering a sheep or goat, two turtledoves or two pigeons—one for a sin offering and the other for a burnt offering—or, if the lawbreaker is impoverished, choice flour and oil.

If a person has been sacrilegious, a ram or its equivalent worth in silver shekels is required. A ram is also needed for someone guilty of deceitful dealings with other humans, be it through broken pledges, robbery, or fraud. A restitution payment of the principal amount plus 20 percent is also demanded.

MICHELLE QUINT

THE TENT OF MEETING: AN OFFERINGS GUIDEBOOK FOR YOUR KITCHEN

. . . .

Tony's Bloody Guilt Roast

. . . .

Ingredients

1   bull of the herd

7   bunches aromatic incense, such as bay leaf, frankincense, or hyssop

40 pounds hickory wood chips for the altar

Salt and pepper, to taste

W hen we first put this dish on the altar, it brought a lot of guilty Israelites into the Tent. So we heard a lot of opinions. Some folks prefer to do the slaughter inside or flash fry smaller strips of fat. But at the Tent, we like to keep our floor clean and our cuts large.

Big cuts of meat—like you're going to have with a bull—are some of our favorite offerings to burn at the Tent, because they're so easy to do well. The Lord might disagree, but we think that, at the end of the day, it doesn't really matter if you do entrails first or last, because that liver/kidney/loins combo is impossible to beat.

Throw a hunk on your altar and let it rest a good, long while. You might notice the meat shrinking and be tempted to jump in there. Don't do it. Meat is a muscle, so it's going to contract as it burns. If you're doing it right, that bull is going to get nice and smoky. Just relax. You can't rush a good guilt offering.

VARIATION: If you can't get a bull, you can sub in a sheep or an ox (just make sure it's blemish-free).

ACTIVE PREP TIME: 6 hours

TOTAL COOK TIME: Three days/three nights

SERVINGS: One for the Eternal, blessed be He, or 40 appetizer portions

SERVING SUGGESTIONS: Alongside a shame offering, or with panzanella salad (p. 32)

1 Preheat a wood fire on a clean ash heap outside.

2 Slaughter bull (at any entrance to the altar) by slitting throat, keeping hand on bull's head in the presence of the Lord. Collect blood in a large bowl.

3 After bringing bowl into your kitchen, dip two fingers into blood and sprinkle the ground seven times, taking care not to splash the curtain of your shrine.

4 Apply a thin coat of blood to the altar (blood should coat the surface but not pool).

5 Pour remaining blood at the base of the altar of burnt offering, or reserve for later use.

6 Remove all fat from the bull, taking special care to remove fat surrounding the entrails, the loins, the kidneys, and the protuberance of the liver (removal of the entire kidneys is also fine). Burn fat on the altar as an offering, taking care to waft smoke upward toward heaven (guilt should begin to lift, too).

7 Take the hide, the flesh, the head, the legs, the entrails, and the dung of the bull to the ash heap outside of camp. Burn it all in the wood fire until only ash is left.

ויקח משה משמן המשחה ומן הדם אשר על המזבח ויז על אהרן על בגדיו
ועל בניו ועל בגדי בניו אתו ויקדש את אהרן את בגדיו ואת בניו ואת בגדי בניו אתו:

"And Moses took some of the anointing oil and some of the blood that was on the altar and sprinkled it upon Aaron and upon his vestments, and also upon his sons and upon their vestments. Thus he consecrated Aaron and his vestments, and also his sons and their vestments."—Leviticus 8:30

TZAV ("*Command*")
LEVITICUS 6:1–8:36

MAKING SACRIFICES: **THE LORD BREAKS** down the details of sacrificial procedures for Moses to relay to Aaron and the priests. The critical issues of how long a burnt offering should last, what the priest should wear, and where the waste should be disposed of are explored. Moses is also instructed to ensure that the altar fire burns perpetually.

Procedures for sin offerings, guilt offerings, sacrifices of well-being, and meal offerings are also clarified, including exactly how much the priests can keep to eat themselves.

THE ORDINATION OF THE PRIESTS
Moses invites the entire community to assemble at the entrance of the Tent of Meeting with the priests, their clothing, anointing oil, a bull for sin offering, two rams, and a basket of unleavened bread.

During the ceremony Moses motions Aaron to step forward, then washes and dresses him as the Lord commanded. He takes the oil and uses it to consecrate the Tabernacle by sprinkling it on the altar before pouring some on Aaron's head. After that, he dresses Aaron's sons, who then help Moses pull the bull and rams to slaughter to consecrate the altar. Moses pours oil and blood on the priests' clothing and concludes the ceremony by ordering them to remain in the Tent for seven days to complete their ordination.

RACHEL LEVIN

I am only a few lines into the Torah portion that is *Tzav* and my eyes have already glazed over. Burnt offerings, linen raiment with linen breeches, ashes, vestments, smoke, fat, flour, fire. The details are exhausting, and I have yet to reach verse seven.

I think of stopping, but I have been assigned to write about this passage, and I am at my core the dutiful oldest daughter of a rabbi, a follower of directions. So I begin again, and that is when I notice him—a kindred responsible older sibling. It is Aaron, the brother called in to speak to Pharaoh for Moses, the one left to deal with a bunch of complaining Israelites when his younger sibling climbed up a mountain for forty days.

Here he is being given a new task; he is to become a priest. *Tzav,* I now see, is Aaron's instruction manual, a ninety-seven-verse "to do" list dictated by God via Moses: Prepare flour on a griddle, divide meals into morning and evening portions, eat the leftovers of a sin offering. The directives are endless, the prescriptions exact. Yet Aaron does not complain once. In fact, throughout the entire Torah portion, Aaron does not utter a single word.

I am irritated for him.

As kids, my sisters and I promised one another that we would never become rabbis. Being a rabbi's daughters had taken its toll on us—the seemingly endless "short" stops at the hospital on our way to dinner; comments of praise or derision about our father, which somehow seemed equally appropriate to share with his children; couches re-covered with a mistaken fabric but not able to be returned because they were done as a favor by a congregant. Yes I complained, but I also understood that this job of modern priest required offerings to be made morning *and* evening— that when our portion was the leftovers, we could not be picky.

My father, who shares his Hebrew name with Moses, not Aaron, was bound to his duties, but not so easily compliant. He chafed at being told what to do. He had his own creative approach to the rabbinate and saw his job as interpreting tradition in a way that was relevant and less about how things should be done. This meant that at a young age, I already knew about disgruntled synagogue presidents, split board votes, and what it meant to leave a synagogue with half the congregation to start one of your own. Around that time my mother moved to Arizona. Being the rabbi's wife had taken its toll on her as well.

These old memories return as I read Aaron's new job description, and I feel suddenly that this time, someone must speak for Aaron, must say what he himself does not, cannot, say. "Wait, God," I call out. "I OBJECT. This new duty may be what is needed for the people, but what about Aaron? What of his children, his sons, who will also be forced to be priests?"

I have read ahead and know how the story will end: Two of Aaron's sons will get too close to the fire when making an offering and will be consumed by flames. The sacrificers will become the sacrificed.

And yet, years later I am in Jerusalem at a dinner party, sitting on one end of a meticulously set table with thirty other guests. I suddenly notice a woman staring at me. She calls out, "Are you Martin Levin's daughter?" Yes, I nod. Knife to wineglass, she silences the other conversations. "Listen," she says. "I have a story to tell." The story is of her son who is mentally disabled and how one morning, many years ago in synagogue, a rabbi gave her son a spur-of-the-moment bar mitzvah, something she had never thought possible. The rabbi called him up to the Torah and then led the entire congregation in dancing so joyous that it spilled out into the street. The congregation was celebrating her son, welcoming him as a full member of the community. "I will never forget what your father did for my family," she says. Suddenly, she is crying and I am crying, too.

I have seen through the years how rabbis have special access to people because they are present when people are at their most joyous, most vulnerable, most pained, most in need of hope. My father knows that in these moments, there is possibility, and that has always been more than enough for him.

I whisper through the letters of the text, "Was that enough for you, Aaron?" And I wait.

SH'MINI ("*Eighth*")
LEVITICUS 9:1–11:47

I T'S A DRAMATIC APPEARANCE. **EIGHT DAYS** later, Moses convenes Aaron, his sons, and Israel's elders, and commands them to arrange a complicated series of sacrifices involving a ram, a he-goat, an ox, some calves, and a meal offering.

The entire Israelite tribe assembles as Aaron goes to work amid the blood, organs, and smoke of the sacrifices. As he raises his arms to bless the people, the Lord appears in the form of fire, which bursts forth to consume the burnt offering. At the sight of this spectacle, the Israelites scream, fall forward, and bow down to the ground.

Aaron's sons Nadab and Abihu set a fire and load it with incense to make an offering that God has not commanded. The Lord sets them on fire, burning them to death in an instant. Moses has to explain to Aaron that God meant it when speaking these words:

"Through those near to Me I show Myself holy,
And gain glory before all the people."
Aaron remains silent.

Moses instructs Aaron's cousins Mishael and Elzaphan to dispose of the burned bodies and warns Aaron and his family against following the traditional mourning ritual; if they tear their clothes or bare their heads, they will be struck down. The Lord takes a moment to prohibit Aaron and the priests from drinking alcohol before they enter the Tent of Meeting; they must be able to distinguish between the holy and the profane. The sacrifices then continue.

THE BIRTH OF KOSHER

God fills Moses and Aaron in on the details of kosher food. The Israelites are allowed to eat any animal that has real hooves, and that chews the cud. Camels, a hare-like animal called daman, and swine are expressly prohibited. Any fish can be eaten if it has fins and scales.

Birds of prey, including the eagle, vulture, black vulture, hawks, and falcons, are off-limits. Ravens, nighthawks, ostriches, seagulls, little owls, great owls, white owls, cormorants, pelicans, bustards, storks, herons, hoopoes, and bats are prohibited.

All winged insects that walk are considered an abomination, though locusts, crickets, and grasshoppers are permitted.

A detailed list of animals deemed unclean is offered; it includes every beast that does not chew the cud or walk on paws. Anyone who carries the carcasses remains unclean until the evening and will have to wash their clothing.

God wraps up the legislation by reminding them of the intention behind the laws, declaring, "You shall be holy, for I am holy." It becomes the Israelites' task to distinguish between living things that can be eaten and those that cannot.

DAVID SAX

O kay, this all seems pretty straightforward.

No pigs, shrimp, oysters, or mussels. Steer clear of the baby goats boiled in their mother's milk, not to mention eels and sharks, crocodiles and geckos, hawks and vultures, and the rock badger (and I'm guessing that You're also implying all other badgers as well).

Now, here's a genuine product that's clearly on Your hit list: Baconnaise, a spreadable mayonnaise, touted as a condiment and dressing, that tastes like the salted belly fat of the cloven-footed, hoof-parted, non-cud-chewing swine that are clearly verboten (right there in clause seven). It's made by J&D's, a food company based in Seattle whose slogan proclaims, "Everything Should Taste Like Bacon," and it works to fulfill that commandment with products like bacon salt, bacon popcorn, bacon gravy, bacon lip balm, and bacon-flavored envelopes (called MMMMMMvelopes).

Sounds like *treif* city to me. Cue the fire, bring on the brimstone.

Wait, it's kosher? Certified by the Orthodox Union to be consumed with meat, dairy, and parve foods? Seriously?

Okay, but how about the belly-crawling shellfish buffet offered by the idolaters at Dyna-Sea: crab salad and lobster rolls fit for a Kennebunkport summer's lunch, and pink shrimp curled around a martini glass, mocking You from their horseradish-spiked red cocktail sauce, colored the very fire of hell they're surely destined for.

Kosher, too? Certified by Kof-K for consumption with all foods. Oh, come on!

For close to three thousand years, Your chosen people have largely followed the dietary laws, avoiding the unclean creatures, making delicious brisket out of the clean ones, all while pretending You never really mentioned the whole edible-insects thing (locusts, crickets, and grasshoppers are perfectly kosher, because they have jointed legs, though the fried-cricket market of Crown Heights, Brooklyn, has yet to take off).

Then, in the mid-twentieth century, some among Your faithful realized that the devout were deprived, and, like Soviets trading a month's supply of toilet paper for a pair of Levi's, they would pay handsomely for the illusion of transgression wrapped in the legal safe ground of kosher certification.

"Look," these people say, "it's certified, within the letter of the law, kosher as a matzo. What's the harm in eating a Whopper at the kosher Burger King in Costa Rica, or McNuggets at one of several kosher McDonald's in Israel? If eating a Reuben sandwich with kosher corned beef and a slice of soy-based cheese was a sin, wouldn't that be there in the *Sh'mini*? Wouldn't there be a clause saying that we shall not eat foods that *pretend* to be unclean, even though they aren't?"

Decades from now, a bar mitzvah buffet at a kosher banquet hall will resemble a Roman feast, once the tempeh tipping point is breached and test-tube experiments with embryonic protein cultures yield remarkably tasty kosher animal flesh. We'll bypass the mock shrimp scampi wrapped in mock bacon, and head straight for the mock alligator jambalaya, mock eagle-egg sliders, and the pièce de résistance, an entire roast mock suckling pig, apple and all, carved with great flourish, in an act of legally certified, morally questionable mockery that the devout will eat with a greedy ferocity, grease painting their lips, as they turn to a shocked-looking elderly relative and say:

"Don't worry, it's perfectly kosher."

אדם כי יהיה בעור בשרו שאת או ספחת או בהרת והיה בעור בשרו
לנגע צרעת והובא אל אהרן הכהן או אל אחד מבניו הכהנים:

"When a person has on the skin of his body a swelling, a rash, or a discoloration,
and it develops into a scaly affection on the skin of his body, it shall be reported
to Aaron, the priest, or to one of his sons, the priests." —Leviticus 13:2

TAZRI·A ("*She conceives*")

LEVITICUS 12:1–13:59

THE LORD'S NEXT BRIEFING REVOLVES around the rules of purity. Moses learns that a woman is considered unclean for seven days after birthing a male, remaining in a state of "blood purification" for thirty-three days, during which time she cannot touch anything holy or enter the sanctuary. In the case of the birth of a daughter, however, the blood purification period is much longer, stretching to sixty-six days.

Upon concluding this blood purification process, the mother has to present the priest with a young lamb for a burnt offering and a pigeon or turtledove for a sin offering. Once the priest makes these two offerings on her behalf, the mother will be considered clean.

MONITORING THE SWOLLEN

The Lord shows Moses and Aaron how to cope with bodily swellings and rashes. Priests are to perform an examination of the offending area and follow God's detailed procedures to determine whether the patient is merely unclean or in need of isolation.

When a burn victim is examined, the priest has to inspect the depth of the wound and its coloring to determine whether the scarring is unclean. The same procedure has to be followed by those suffering from a disease of the head or beard.

Anyone found to be suffering from skin infections is to dwell outside the camp and have his clothes torn, head bared, and mouth covered while announcing himself with a shout of warning: "Unclean! Unclean!"

If a similar scaly infection erupts like a mold on wool or linen fabric, the priest shall determine if it can merely be washed or if burning is necessary.

JAMIE GLASSMAN

tinea cru·ris [kroo r-is], (*noun*), (*medical*). A dermatophyte fungal infection, or ringworm, involving especially the groin region in any sex, though more often seen in teenage males. Also known as eczema marginatum or (*colloquial*) crotch itch, crotch rot, gym itch, jock itch, jock rot, or in Budapest in 1989, *scrot rot*.

W henever I read a portion of the *Tanakh* translated into English, I am taken back to my days as a twelve-year-old boy in Liverpool studying for my bar mitzvah.

This was the moment when I was to become part of the Jewish religion, with its thousands of years of tradition and its code of ethics that had survived numerous catastrophes.

After months of learning, practice, and nerves, it hadn't crossed my mind to translate the words I would be singing to my local Hebrew congregation. I had just assumed that the words that I would sing would surely resonate and move me.

I can remember the moment my heart sank when I discovered that my parashah—a section from Exodus known as *Mishpatim*—was a long list of laws about the treatment of slaves and what to do with your neighbor's lost ox should you see it wandering.

But I pity any poor twelve-year-old child who is saddled with this portion, *Tazri·a*, and reads it for the first time. It is a list of dos and don'ts for any leprosy sufferer. Could there be any less meaningful chunk of the Bible?

Things like *When a person has on the skin of his body a swelling, a rash, or a discoloration that develops into a scaly or leprous affliction on the skin of his body, he shall present himself to the priest.*

Or, *If a white swelling streaked with red develops where the inflammation was, he shall present himself to the priest. The person with a leprous affliction, his clothes shall be rent and burnt, and he shall call out, "Unclean! Unclean!"*

Surely there can be no more proof of the irrelevance of the Bible to our modern lives than this parashah.

That is unless you consider Maimonides' thoughts on *Tazriʻa*. A twelfth-century Jewish philosopher—you may know him as Rambam—Maimonides broadened this parashah into one of the most important lessons any teenage boy could ever learn.

When the Bible says "leprosy," he wrote, think of it as any fungal infection.

I learned Rambam's lesson the hard way. Aged eighteen, I was traveling around Europe with a monthlong rail pass and two unfortunate friends.

Unfortunate because they would have to share train carriages, hotel rooms, and a tent with an overweight young man with a very serious case of tinea cruris.

The author attempts to sanitize his underwear in Budapest, 1989.

Long walks on sweltering summer days through Europe's great capitals with inappropriate polyester clothing might not have been what Maimonides had in mind, but the result was the same.

A mixture of stoicism and pride stopped me from seeing a doctor in a country where I knew only a smattering of the local language, so I walked through the streets of Paris and Rome like John Wayne after three weeks riding on the plains.

The affliction was not without its benefits. There was some tender mercy on the long, crowded night train to Budapest, when it was impossible to get the much coveted banquette compartment in which third-class passengers might catch some sleep. That is, until I walked in stinking of rotting flesh, causing the carriage to empty within minutes. No sooner had the last bunch of young Euro lovelies fled the compartment than the choice of banquettes was ours.

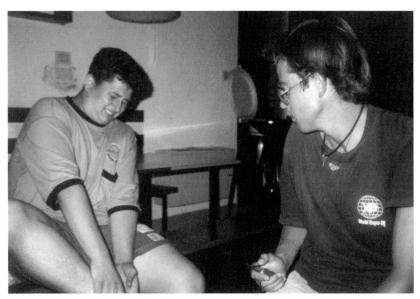

A fellow traveler attempts to scrape off the affliction in Padua, Italy.

Rambam didn't say this, but I have added my own level of interpretation to the great scholar of Cordoba's. Instead of a "priest," perhaps the parashah should say a "pharmacist." For in the back streets of Budapest my pain outweighed my shame when I limped into a local pharmacy and tried to mime my condition to the old man behind the counter.

He spoke no more English than I did Hungarian, so I pointed to my crotch and waved a hand in front of my nose, letting him see the agony on my face as I made each step.

His diagnosis was immediate. "Scrot rot!" he proclaimed with a theatrical clap of his palms, and he handed me a cream that cost me a few forints.

After days of suffering, just one application of his wondrous cream and my "leprosy" had gone.

So *Tarzi·a* is proof of the great wisdom of the Bible across continents and millennia, for this sufferer went to the priest/pharmacist and exclaimed, "I am Unclean! I am Unclean!" and an ointment was procured and the priest/pharmacist did make him clean once more.

And that night, the offending polyester shorts did warm us as they were tossed upon the fire.

If you know of any bar mitzvah boy or any young man in his teens about to embark on a long and possibly sweaty journey, I urge you to point him in the direction of *Tazri·a*. For there can be no greater lesson for a young man of this age.

Tell him that if he should experience a swelling, a rash, or a discoloration that develops into a scaly or leprous affection on the skin of his body, he should wash, dry, and air the affected area as often as possible, together with a generous application of a clotrimazole antifungal cream, available in any pharmacy, in any city in the world.

"This shall be the ritual for a leper at the time that he is to be cleansed." —Leviticus 14:2

M'TZORA (*"Being diseased"*)
LEVITICUS 14:1–15:33

THE SCAPEGOATING OF THE BIRD: **THE LORD** explains to Moses how a leprous or "skin-blanched" patient should be cleansed. The priest is to visit the diseased person outside the camp. If the infection appears to have cleared up, the priest is to take two live, pure birds, cedar wood, crimson stuff, and hyssop. One bird shall be killed, and the other is to be dipped in a mixture of bird blood and the other ingredients. After sprinkling the potion on the patient, the surviving bird is to be let free. The sick person shall wash his clothing, shave off all his hair, bathe, and then be deemed clean.

Once back in camp, the individual must remain outside his tent for seven days, and then shave off all his body hair again, wash his clothing, and bathe before being declared clean. The next day he shall make a series of sacrifices, in the course of which the priest shall dab oil on the head of the cleansed Israelite.

HOME IMPROVEMENT
The Lord then teaches Moses and Aaron how to cope with the case of a mold-infected house in Canaan. The

home is to be evacuated before the priest enters. If the priest identifies green or reddish streaks penetrating the wall, the house shall be closed up for seven days. If the infection continues to spread, the contaminated stone has to be ripped out and cast outside of the city. The rest of the house is to be thoroughly scraped and replastered. If the disease still remains, the house must be torn down and the debris discarded outside the city.

DISCHARGED

The Lord then briefs the brothers on the tender subject of genital discharge, which is considered unclean. Not only is the infected man to wash his clothing and bedding, but anyone he may have spat on has to do likewise, and any earthen vessel he touched has to be broken. After seven days, the infected individual shall bathe and offer two birds as a sin offering.

A gentleman who has experienced an emission of semen is to bathe but still remains unclean until the evening. If he has enjoyed sexual relations with a woman, they both will be considered unclean until the evening. A menstruating woman is considered impure for seven days. Anyone who touches her will be unclean until the evening, unless it is a man enjoying sexual relations with her, in which case he too is considered unclean for seven days. A woman who bleeds when not menstruating must be monitored; she is considered unclean as long as her discharge lasts.

God concludes by warning Moses to make sure that the Israelites guard against disease, so they do not die by defiling the Tabernacle.

TIM SAMUELS

PRESCRIPTION

PATIENT: Mr. Levite

MEDICATION TO BE COLLECTED BY: Moses (Levite family friend)

CONDITION: Patient claims to be suffering from leprosy. Closer examination reveals merely patches of dry skin around the elbows and knees, and some flakiness around the nose. Probably caused by excessive time recently spent wandering around the wilderness without adequate moisturization. However, patient was insistent on full course of treatment, lest the condition develop into full-blown lesions.

TREATMENT: When the symptoms appear to be improving, gather two clean birds (living), cedar wood, something crimson, and a sprig of hyssop. Slaughter one bird, and dip the other bird in the blood, cedar, crimson, and hyssop. Sprinkle the blood on the affected areas seven times and set the living bird free. Wash all clothes, shave off hair, take a long bath, and sleep away from home for seven days. On the seventh day, bathe, and shave off all hair (again), including eyebrows and beard. The following day, sacrifice a lamb and put blood and oil on the right ear, right thumb, and right big toe. If insurance policy does not cover cost of the lamb, Medicare turtledoves or pigeons can be used instead. (All lambs free of charge in Europe, Canada, and other socialist enclaves.)

NOT TO BE TAKEN WITH: The following may exacerbate the condition: idol worship, unchastity, bodily violence, profaning God, blasphemy, robbery, usurping a dignity, overweening pride, evil speech, and casting an evil eye. Haughtiness and general immorality are best avoided, too.

LONG-TERM SIDE EFFECTS: Prolonged obsession with obscure cleansing rituals from 1440 B.C. onward could lead to endemic hypochondria among future generations and an absurd though comforting overrepresentation among medical professionals.

AHAREI MOT (*"After death"*)
LEVITICUS 16:1–18:30

THE LONG-SUFFERING BROTHER. **AFTER THE** death of Aaron's two sons, the Lord warns Moses to forbid his brother from freely entering the Tabernacle's inner sanctuary, known as the Holy of Holies. Exposure to God's presence will kill him, unless he is appropriately clothed and has presented a complicated series of sin offerings and burnt offerings, then laid his hands on the head of a goat and dispatched it into the wilderness to carry away the symbolic sins of the Israelites.

God then commands Moses to make sure Aaron sacrifices only sheep and goats at the Tent of Meeting. Anyone making sacrifices elsewhere is to be cut off from the people. In addition, anyone eating an animal carcass is to be deemed unclean until he has undergone the purification process.

THE NAKED TRUTH

God then makes clear that Moses must understand that the norms of Egyptian society no longer apply to the Israelites. They are to be careful about nudity and avoid seeing many of their relatives naked, including their father, mother, father's wife, sister, half sister, granddaughter, aunt, uncle, daughter-in-law, and sister-in-law. A man is also to avoid marrying both a mother and her daughter or granddaughter, or a woman and her sister in the other's lifetime. A man is also forbidden from enjoying sexual relations with a woman during her period, or with his neighbor's wife. He is also commanded to avoid offering his offspring to a foreign god, or committing bestiality.

An Israelite is to consider defiling himself as grave an act as defiling the land. The tribes who preceded the Israelites may have committed abhorrent acts, but if those practices are maintained, the land will spit them out, too. Those who commit repulsive acts must be cut off from their people.

AMICHAI LAU-LAVIE

BECOMING A MAN: MY BAR MITZVAH
SPEECH THIRTY YEARS LATER

I grew up Orthodox in Israel. By the time of my bar mitzvah—in April 1982—I was living in New York City, a sweet kid in a polyester suit. A little on the chubby side, perhaps. My dark blond mop of hair covered a pimpled forehead.

Being Orthodox had its advantages. Chanting my bar mitzvah portion was no problem. I rattled it off with ease. The problem was the speech. There was so much I wanted to say, but my English wasn't good enough, and anyway, my speech had been written for me by my uncle, a renowned rabbi, who gave me a tired presentation expounding on the laws of charity.

Thirty years on, I would like to think that if the choice had been mine, and I had been able to summon the courage, this is the speech I would have delivered at the Fifth Avenue Synagogue in Manhattan.

As I write it, I imagine my forty-three-year-old self as a man in a black suit with a trim beard, standing directly behind that chubby bar mitzvah boy and visible to him alone.

Esteemed Rabbis, My Dear Parents, Family, and Friends:

Shabbat Shalom.

Thank you for coming to celebrate with me on this day on which I become a man. Many of you have traveled very far to get here. My parents and I appreciate it very much.

My bar mitzvah portion, *Aharei Mot*, is about laws and limitations. Laws, I understand, are necessary, because without them things go wrong, and people can get hurt. The portion begins with the reminder of what had happened to the two sons of Aaron, the high priest, and how they died by a "strange fire" because they did not observe the law, and were not careful enough when they entered the holy Tent of Meeting.

There are many different kinds of laws in this portion. These laws, I was taught, were given to us by God so that each of us can live a holy life, as part of a bigger, healthy society.

I started learning how to chant my Torah portion two years ago, back when we were still in Israel, from a cassette tape. I played it over and over again to memorize the verses by heart. At first, I didn't think about what the words meant.

But over time I started paying more attention, and I began to wonder about the meaning of some of these laws, especially the ones about not seeing people naked.

There is a list, in this portion, of relatives that you are not supposed to see naked.

I figured out that "seeing someone naked" was a euphemism—a biblical way to talk about "having sex." But I couldn't understand why some relatives are on the list and some aren't. And I had other questions, also, about some of the other laws.

My teacher, Rabbi Motti, didn't want to talk about this too much. He said I'd understand when I am more grown up. When I become a man.

And I guess that day is today.

I don't know if I'm as grown up as my teacher intended, and if I'm really already a man, but as I turn thirteen today, I think I'm just old enough to ask you all a question about these laws, and about one of them in particular that I've been thinking a lot about.

The room is stilled. My mother, up in the women's balcony, is looking at me with a grave, strange look. My father, in the front row, turns to my uncle, who is seated next to him, and whispers something in his ear. The uncle shakes his head, confused.

After the list of relatives one is not supposed to see naked there are a few other laws that describe prohibited sexual behaviors. One of the laws forbids sex with animals. Another of the laws prohibits sexual relations between men. It's called an abomination. And whoever does it can be punished by death.

Silence.

I'm sorry if this is weird, and maybe neither appropriate nor the speech you expected me to make today. But a few months ago, when we walked home from this synagogue, I asked my father what it means to be a man, and he told me that to be a man is to be honest and not be afraid of the truth.

And the truth is that I've been thinking a lot about this law, and it makes me afraid and ashamed to think about it and to talk about it, but it also makes me angry and confused.

I know it's wrong to question God and the Torah, and maybe I'm too young to understand. But I don't think that the law about abomination is fair, and I don't think that people who break it deserve to die.

Today, you say, I am a man. But in fact I think that it already happened.

I think that I became a man almost a year ago, when I kissed for the first time, and felt like a grown-up.

I kissed another boy, a friend of mine, a friend I love.

It made us both afraid and nervous, but it didn't feel dirty, or wrong, or like an abomination, whatever that is. It felt holy, whatever that is. It felt right.

DON'T LOOK UP. DON'T LOOK UP. My mouth is dry. My heart beats faster than it ever has. I am aware my life will never be the same again. I read on.

I am not an abomination. I don't deserve to die because of whom I love.

You are all looking at me now, and it's not pleasant, but I've held this secret, this abomination in my stomach, long enough.

If today I am a man, then on this day I tell the truth and face it, like a man. And you, who came from near and far, if you really love me, will love me still, I hope, just the way I am.

I know the Torah says it's wrong.

I know it's disappointing to you, my parents and siblings, relatives, friends.

But maybe the Torah does not mean what I'm feeling, because I don't think—I don't believe—that God thinks I am dirty, or sinning, or an abomination. Because isn't that how God created me, in God's own image, just the way I am?

Today I become a man, and I am who I am, with all of my questions, and doubts, and hard choices, and truths.

I think that's what becoming a man is all about.

I want to thank you, my parents, for helping me so much in preparing for today, and for being the best parents possible. I'm sorry if I surprised you now, but I hope that you understand. Thank you to my brothers, and my sister, for coming all the way from Israel for this occasion and for always being there for me.

My family are all looking at the floor.

Thank you for listening, and for joining me on this most important day of my life.

Shabbat Shalom.

I close the folder and dare to look up. Will somebody say something? Someone please hug me. My mother is crying. My father still stares down. Don't hate me. Please say something.

And there I stand, thirty years later, placing a hand on my thirteen-year-old self's shoulder and whispering, softly, "It's going to be all right."

"You shall not let your cattle mate with a different kind;
you shall not sow your field with two kinds of seed; you shall not
put on cloth from a mixture of two kinds of material." —Leviticus 19:19

K'DOSHIM ("*Holy ones*")
LEVITICUS 19:1–20:27

THE HOLY LIFESTYLE: **THE LORD OUTLINES** the ways the Israelites are to pursue a holy life in the style of God, based around a catalog of loosely connected behaviors, starting with the basics—honoring parents, keeping the Sabbath, shunning idols, and following sacrifice protocol.

Appropriate harvesting techniques are then defined. Israelites are to leave the edges of their fields unharvested, and in the vineyards, fallen fruit is to be left ungathered. The intention of both laws is the same—to create a food supply for the poor.

Stealing, fraud, robbery, deceitful dealings, and withholding wages are prohibited. Ditto for making a false oath in God's name or swearing profanely.

Insulting the deaf or intentionally taking advantage of the blind is forbidden.

Fair judgment is expected. Decisions shall neither intentionally favor the poor nor corruptly support the rich. No one shall benefit from the suffering of their fellow countrymen.

One Israelite can accuse another, but not falsely. Taking vengeance or bearing grudges is not permitted. They are to love others in the same way they love themselves.

Odd combinations are not to be fostered: Different beasts shall not be mated. Two different kinds of seeds shall not be sown in the same field. Two different kinds of material shall not be woven into a piece of cloth.

If a man has sexual relations with another man's slave, he will not be put to death as would be the case if it was someone else's wife, because the woman is not free. A sin offering will suffice to rectify the situation.

Once they enter the land, any new tree that is planted cannot be harvested for three years. In the fourth year, the first fruit must be offered to the Lord before the rest can be eaten.

A rapid round of prohibited acts is then set out:

No animal can be eaten along with its blood.

Soothsaying is outlawed.

Men are not to shave off side-growths from their heads or beards.

No tattoos or gashes can be made in the flesh.

Daughters cannot be turned into whores, thus creating a depraved land.

Sabbaths and the sanctuary must be revered.

Ghosts cannot be engaged with.

The old have to be respected.

Foreigners are to be afforded the same rights as citizens, because the Israelites were once seen as foreigners in Egypt.

Merchants cannot employ false measures and weights.

PUNISHMENT . . . AND REWARD

God proceeds to stipulate a slew of punishments to Moses:

Any Israelite or visitor worshipping false foreign gods like Molech shall be punished with death by stoning.

A person who communes with ghosts shall be cut off from the people.

The death penalty is prescribed for those who insult their parents, commit adultery, or lie with their father's wife or daughter-in-law. If a man lies with another man, it is to be considered an "abhorrent thing"; they both will be put to death. If a man marries both mother and daughter, all three shall be burned to death. If man or woman lies with a beast, both human and animal shall be killed.

Incest—marrying a sister or half sister—is not permitted. Those who indulge in it shall be cut off from their people. A man who lies with a woman when she is unwell will suffer the same fate. Men shall not lie with their aunts or marry their brother's wife. Those who do are doomed to die childless.

The Israelites are specifically instructed to avoid the norms of the Canaanites, whom God is poised to drive out of Canaan as a result of their abhorrent behavior. God reminds Moses that the land will soon flow with the promised milk and honey. The Israelites are to be set apart from other people, and in the same way, they are to set apart the clean beast from the unclean and to carry on as a holy people.

A. J. JACOBS

G-d's Original Edits on Leviticus 19:19

To Hashem
Editor-In-Chief, Leviticus

Dear Hashem,

You had said that you were looking for ideas for Leviticus
19:19, which you want to be a rule about what people
can/cannot wear. Below, some options. Looking forward to your
feedback.

Do not wear a garment that reveals your nakedness. *— Kind of obvious*

Do not wear a garment that was designed by a man who has lain
with another man

↑ — They won't have anything left to wear!

Do not wear a garment consisting of more than two colors

Do not wear jorts *conflicts w/ Joseph story*

Do not wear a garment on which is written the name of your
favorite Tribe of Israel

Do not wear a garment bought at the street bazaar that claims
to be made by one weaver when in truth it was made by a less
skilled weaver.

Do not wear a garment that has but one pocket in the middle
of the garment, as this could lead to sinful behavior

Do not wear a garment made from a fiber that was harvested by a beast that was born at the start of a new month

Do not wear a garment made of two kinds of cloth

Also, I think it would be wonderful to include a short paragraph after the commandment. Just a little exposition — nothing too clunky, to help people understand why you are giving them such specific edicts about clothing. Perhaps something along these lines:

I make this command because rituals can be fulfilling, even if these rituals seem strange from the outside, as with candles on a birthday cake, which is a bizarre custom if ever there was one. I make this command because there is something inherently good and beautiful about following rules, as they give structure to your very lives.

Otherwise, I fear this commandment might just seem kind of, well, crazy.

Eternally yours,

Archangel Michael
Head Writer
Leviticus

שֶׁבֶר תַּחַת שֶׁבֶר עַיִן תַּחַת עַיִן שֵׁן תַּחַת שֵׁן כַּאֲשֶׁר יִתֵּן מוּם בָּאָדָם כֵּן יִנָּתֶן בּוֹ:

"Fracture for fracture, eye for eye, tooth for tooth, the injury he inflicted on another shall be inflicted on him." —Leviticus 24:20

EMOR *("Speak")*

LEVITICUS 21:1–24:23

PRIESTLY RULES: **THE LORD TELLS MOSES** to make sure the priests know not to come into contact with a dead body unless the deceased is a close relative: a mother, father, son, daughter, brother, or a virgin sister who remained unmarried.

Priests are to follow a series of rules. They are not to cut the sides of their beards or make gashes in their own flesh. They cannot bare their heads or tear their clothes. Nor are they to take the name of God in vain.

When it comes to marriage, it is imperative that the priest marry a virgin. Because of this, priests can never marry a prostitute or divorcee. If a priest's daughter becomes a prostitute, she will have defiled her father and so must be burned to death.

If a priest's son is blind or lame, a hunchback or a dwarf, or cursed by a growth on his eye, scurvy, or "crushed testes," the son will no longer be qualified to make offerings by fire. The defect removes his ability to come behind the curtain to the altar and to enter places that have been sanctified by God.

If the priests are unclean, they are to avoid touching the sacrifices until they are clean again. A number of objects that can make a priest unclean are described, including a dead body, semen, or a "swarming thing."

Non-priests are prohibited from eating donated offerings unless they are from the priests' slaves, or a priest's daughter who has been widowed and become dependent on her father again.

SACRIFICE WORTHINESS . . . PLUS THE CALENDAR REVEALED

A sacrifice must not be defective. Defects listed include animals that are blind or maimed or suffering from crushed testes. Offerings have to be at least eight days old, but no animal can be sacrificed alongside its young.

God then articulates the days that will be considered holy.

• No work shall be done on Sabbath, the seventh day.

• Passover will start on the fourteenth day of the first month and last seven days, with the first and last days considered sacred.

• A Harvest Festival will occur fifty days later.

• Rosh Hashana, on the first day of the seventh month, will be marked by complete rest and shofar blasts.

• Yom Kippur will be on the tenth day of the seventh month. Any person who does not participate will be cut off from his kin, and those who ignore the day and work shall be put to death.

• Sukkot, on the fifteenth day of the seventh month, will involve dwelling in huts for seven days and employing palm and citrus trees in celebration.

These are listed as the Lord's sacred occasions in which sacrifices should be offered.

Moses is advised to make sure the Israelites bring clear oil to kindle the Temple lights and keep them burning. They also have to provide bread for the altar every Sabbath.

A story is then told of a man whose mother is Israelite and whose father is Egyptian. The man had a fight with another Israelite, during which he used God's name in vain; the "half-Israelite" is placed in custody to await the Lord's ruling. God commands that he be taken outside the camp and stoned before those who witnessed the blasphemy, and he is.

God commands that blasphemers be put to death, as well as murderers. An Israelite who kills another man's beast has to make restitution. Those who maim others will have to suffer the same injury in return: fracture for fracture, eye for eye, tooth for a tooth.

DANA ADAM SHAPIRO

We

I've been thumping the Bible
And thinking of truth
Of an eye for an eye
And a tooth for a tooth.
Of revenge, retribution
AYIN TACHAT AYIN,
That dish best served cold
Was it cooked on Mount Zion?

To wish for the murdering man to drop dead
Got me thinking of what Dr. Seuss might have said.
So I sat, then I stood.
Then I sat back and wondered
Of times when I've stumbled and bumbled and
   blundered,
Of times I've been too cool or too proud to say
That "I'm sorry,
I'm sorry for being that way."

But it's not just a lack of I'm sorrys that sway
Peaceful people to huff and to puff in that way

That we all know can lead to a POW!
Or a THWACK!
Or a monkey Velcro-ing itself to your back.
It's the triumph of ego.
A hex laid upon us.
That need to get even
Or LEX TALIONIS.

Now think of the eye for the eye
And the tooth—
Why, it sounds so unfriendly,
It sounds so uncouth.
Though intended to moderate vengeance, instead
It makes people grow eyes in the back of their head.

But imagine if "eye" became "I"
As in: You
And if TOOTH became TRUTH.
Tell me, what would you do?
Yes, an I for an I
And some truths for some truces,
We'll unplug the chairs
And unravel the nooses.
An eye for an eye equals blindness,
You'll see,
But an I for an I
Makes for something called
We.

"But in the seventh year the land shall have a Sabbath of complete rest,
a Sabbath of the Lord; you shall not sow your field
or prune your vineyard." —Leviticus 25:4

B'HAR (*"On the Mount"*)
LEVITICUS 25:1–26:2

THE LORD BROACHES THE NOTION OF A Sabbatical for the land with Moses. Every seven years, the fields are to be left unsown and the vineyards untended, so the land can recuperate. In the year after the seventh Sabbatical, the fiftieth year, the Israelites are to celebrate a jubilee with a loud horn blast. The jubilee year is akin to a Sabbatical year where the land will lie fallow, but in addition, all property will revert to the possession of its original owners, unless it is an urban dwelling in a walled city.

INDEBTED
If an Israelite falls on such hard times that he has to borrow money, interest cannot be charged. If the Israelite is unable to repay the debt and has to offer his own services instead, he cannot be treated as a slave. He shall work as a hired laborer and be freed in the jubilee year, because no one Israelite can rule over another.

MIREILLE SILCOFF

I liked my school, because my school was quiet. In retrospect it was also a dour place: The heavy shoes of rabbis and the stern heels of French teachers echoed through dark green hallways that smelled like old wet paper. This is not the sort of place a child would normally relish. More like something out of Pink Floyd's *The Wall*.

But I liked it. You could hunker down there, between the pencil shavings and the monolithic walls of books with burgundy pleather covers. I believed I had a secret. It was one of those innately childish beliefs, like thinking that your voice is deeper than everyone else's, because that's how it sounds in your ears. My mother imagined I did well in school because I had smarts. But I knew my scholarly success as a third grader had nothing to do with intellect. It had to do with stillness. I liked sticking my head into something and then leaving it there for a while. It felt, somehow, homey.

This was not the sort of home my mother approved of. An active woman of Tel Aviv provenance, an Israeli folk dancer in both calling and profession, she held that life, the childhood phase of it in particular, was synonymous with movement. This meant that if any of my time was in her hands, it would most likely be spent in a leotard.

Witness: It's 1981. I am eight years old. I am just minding my own business, reading a cereal box while eating its cereal for breakfast. My mother is playing a cassette of unspeakably bad Israeli folk music while reminding me of my week:

"Okay! Today, Monday! After school you have rhythmic gymnastics, Wednesday you have Broadway, Thursday you have modern dance, and Friday, *danse ouverte.*"

My mother knew that I was a hopeless dancer. But four days a week, she had her rehearsals, and they went late, and she needed somewhere to put me. She didn't want me to be one of those sad kids with a key tied around my neck, sitting in a house, doing nothing. And I suppose in early 1980s

Quebec, extracurriculars were limited. And so dance and dance and dance and dreaded *open dance* it was.

On some mornings, I pleaded with her to just let me come home after school, to the silent house. I would imagine the darkening at 4:00 p.m. in the Petits Anges dance studio with Gerry Laframboise, the rhythmic gymnastics instructor, who wore a black scoop-neck with chest hair sprouting forth, like a bearish Marcel Marceau, and I would feel bone tired: the overheated locker room; the running around in leg warmers with an unfurling ribbon on a stick (and for what purpose? this ribbon on a stick?); the hungry lineup for miniature boxes of hard raisins; the chattering car pool home.

In school, most of the books I had for my classes contained central sections of calligraphic-looking Hebrew writing framed by columns of smaller Hebrew writing. The school was always cold. You kept your head in your weekly Torah portion, the big writing, and then the small. You used the heat of your eight-year-old mind to make the blocks of text come apart.

I chose to write about this parashah—*B'har*, a far-from-exciting bit, largely about leap years in farming practice—because it is, even over anything in the big bang of *B'reishit,* the one I remember best from my primary school years.

This is because I took *B'har* out of the book and put it into my life. Children are capable of surprisingly lateral thinking. I thought, *For every extended period of planting, the farmer gives the land a period to rest. God says the farmer has to, or everything will get too exhausted. The farmer does not plow, or dig, or sow, or prance about in French Canadian dance studios balancing ball on chest like a trained seal. The farmer, might, say, kick back in a cozy bedroom with a nice chapter book in a quiet, empty house at dusk.*

There was no way I could have persuaded my mother to cut my extracurriculars by quoting Bible passages about taking breaks. So, God on my side, I began lying instead. One week I made my modern dance instructor sick, and the next Gerry Laframboise "canceled class." The week after that I had a sudden headache for Broadway, and the week after that my mother may have understood something: I got a key, and it went around my neck. And sometimes, when I was sure I was alone, I danced like crazy in my bedroom.

B'HUKKOTAI ("*By my decrees*")
LEVITICUS 26:3–27:34

REWARD! **GOD REMINDS MOSES OF THE** covenant. As long as it is maintained, God will supply rain at the appropriate time and guarantee a bountiful harvest so the Israelites can eat their fill and dwell securely in their land.

Peace shall reign. The Israelites will not be threatened by either man or beast. All enemies will be put to the sword. Just five Israelites will be imbued with sufficient power to rout 100 of their enemies. One hundred can make ten thousand flee.

The Lord will ensure that the Israelites multiply, while residing in their midst.

AND THE PUNISHMENT
However, if the Israelites do not maintain the covenant and keep the Lord's commandments, misery will befall them. The Israelites will be beset by consumption and fever. They will sow their seed fruitlessly. Their enemies will dominate them. Their land will yield no produce. Wild beasts will kill their children and cattle. The Israelites will withdraw into their cities, yet an epidemic will run among them and their enemies will control them.

Hunger will set in, and they will be forced to cannibalize their sons and daughters. They will be scattered among the nations as their land becomes desolate and their cities ruined. The Israelites will be made so nervous that the sound of a leaf will make them flinch, and they will fall over though no one is pursuing them. They will rot in the lands of their enemies.

Those who survive will confess their guilt and the guilt of their fathers, and they will atone, and God will remember the covenant made with Isaac and with Abraham and will remember the land.

A COSTLY VOW

As an appendix, God affixes values for Israelites who want to consecrate or sanctify their lives to the Lord, or the lives of family members, as a ritual and voluntary act of dedication to God. The cost of consecration is set out as follows:

- 50 shekels of silver for a male aged 20–60 years old

- 30 shekels for a woman aged 20–60 years old

- 20 shekels for a boy aged 5–20 years old

- 10 shekels for a girl aged 5–20 years old

- 5 shekels for a boy aged 1 month to 5 years

- 3 shekels for a girl aged 1 month to 5 years

- 15 shekels for a man 60 years or over

- 10 shekels for a woman 60 years or over

If the person who wants to make a vow cannot afford the above sums, a priest is to fix a fair price.

CHRISTOPHER NOXON

Gomer & Gazzam*

*BIBLICAL FOREBEARERS of GOOFUS & GALLANT!

Gomer faithfully observes the commandments. Gazzam doesn't!

G-d grants peace in Gomer's land.

G-d lets loose wild beasts against Gazzam.

Gomer lies down untroubled by anyone.

Gazzam is struck by consumption and fever!

The earth yields its produce for Gomer, the trees yield their fruit.

The sky above Gazzam is like iron; the earth is like copper.

Gomer's enemies fall before him by the sword.

Gazzam is routed by his enemies

Gomer eats his fill of bread.

Gazzam eats the flesh of his sons and the flesh of his daughters!

PART FOUR

NUM

BERS

WELCOME TO THE BIBLICAL SMOR-gasbord. Numbers is a grab bag of text, akin to a movie made of the discarded scenes that hit the cutting-room floor only to be resurrected and rush-released.

The promised land is close. The twelve tribes are polled, organized, and detailed. Yet insurrection is never far away, and it often seems like the Israelites' greatest threat is their own self-doubt: They continue to grumble their way ungratefully toward self-actualization.

Despite this, the Israelites have become a hard-ened, martial people—one their opponents can only gaze at fearfully when their armies are scattered across the valley floor.

ELI HOROWITZ
B'MIDBAR (*"In the desert"*) Numbers 1:1–4:20

JUSTIN ROCKET SILVERMAN
NASO (*"Lift up"*) Numbers 4:21–7:89

EDDY PORTNOY
B'HA·ALOT'KHA (*"When you step up"*) Numbers 8:1–12:16

CAITLIN ROPER
SH'LAKH L'KHA (*"Send to you"*) Numbers 13:1–15:41

ADAM LEVIN
KORAH (*"Korah"*) Numbers 16:1–18:32

RACHEL AXLER
HUKKAT (*"Decrees"*) Numbers 19:1–22:1

SHOSHANA BERGER
BALAK (*"Balak"*) Numbers 22:2–25:9

LARRY SMITH
PINHAS (*"Pinhas"*) Numbers 25:10–30:1

GABE DELAHAYE
MATTOT (*"Tribes"*) Numbers 30:2–32:42

REBECCA BORTMAN
MASEI (*"Journeys"*) Numbers 33:1–36:13

וַיֹּאמֶר יְהוָה אֶל מֹשֶׁה פְּקֹד כָּל בְּכֹר זָכָר לִבְנֵי
יִשְׂרָאֵל מִבֶּן חֹדֶשׁ וָמַעְלָה וְשָׂא אֵת מִסְפַּר שְׁמֹתָם׃

"The Lord said to Moses: Record every firstborn male
of the Israelite people from the age of one month up,
and make a list of their names." —Numbers 3:40

B'MIDBAR (*"In the desert"*)
NUMBERS 1:1–4:20

CENSUS II. ON THE FIRST DAY OF THE second month of the second year since the Exodus, God instructs Moses to take a census of the Israelite community. He and Aaron are to record the names of every male twenty years and older who can wage war.

The census determines the tribes to be sized as follows:

Reuben: 46,500; Simeon: 59,300; Gad: 45,650; Judah: 74,600; Issachar: 54,400; Zebulun: 57,400; Ephraim: 40,500; Manasseh: 32,200; Benjamin: 35,400; Dan: 62,700; Asher: 41,500; Naphtali: 53,400. A grand total of 603,550.

MEET THE LEVITES
God instructs the Levite class to dedicate themselves to looking after the Tabernacle—carrying and guarding it as well as setting it up and breaking it down. The responsibility is the Levites' alone. Any outsider who encroaches upon it will be put to death.

The Lord then informs Moses how the Israelites should march and camp, tribe by tribe, in fixed positions around the Tent of Meeting.

The Levites' responsibilities are further delineated. They are to serve the priestly class. Moses records the name of every Levite aged over one month, spread amongst the Kohathites, Gershonites, and Merarites—a total of 22,200. Each is given a separate task.

God decrees that the Levites will be treated as substitutes for the firstborn sons who had to be ritually redeemed in God's eyes, causing Moses to record the names of the 22,273 firstborn sons.

Finally, Moses is instructed to take a census of the Kohathites, aged thirty to fifty years old, who are responsible for the most sacred objects in the Tent of Meeting surrounding the Ark of the Covenant. God reminds Moses and Aaron to prohibit the Kohathites from entering the sanctuary while they are performing their duties, to protect them from instant death.

ELI HOROWITZ

T he Bible is, of course, full of excitement: fighting and feasts and sex and weird food rules and weird sex rules. It's a real page-turner, no doubt. But amid those rollicking good times, every now and then there's a ... pause. A moment of reflection, or a meditation on core values—or, in this case, the logistical procedure for a regional census, followed by detailed results of said census and also some discussion of campground zoning.

Of course, that's just a rough summary. The actual text gets much juicier. I mean, this census isn't going to just organize *itself*, is it? Of course not, and don't worry—the Lord has thought of *everything*. For example, you were probably wondering who was going to help Moses and Aaron count the members of the Asher clan; well, that'd be Ochran's son Pagiel. That is hammered out tribe by tribe, and then we learn the exciting results: There are 54,400 adult males in the Issachar clan, 57,400 in Zebulun, a mere 32,200 in Manasseh, and so on.

If this is sounding a little dull: Yes. It is. Fortunately, it's followed by a lengthy description of where each clan should camp: who's next to whom, who's down south, who marches in what order. It's actually somewhat soothing, sort of like reading box scores—and much like box scores, little narratives sometimes start to emerge: Hmm, looks like Asher got kind of screwed, placed all the way up north and squashed next to those noisy Naphtalites. Mostly, though, it's about as exciting as a wedding seating chart read aloud by Werner Herzog. (Which is pretty much what it *is*, depending on one's religious feelings toward Werner Herzog.)

What I haven't mentioned, though, is that one clan got excluded from all this fun, all the camping and counting: the Levites. The Lord forbade Moses from including them in the census, instead reserving them as the special Tabernacle-tending squad. Hmm! Starting to get interesting, maybe? Wait, not so fast, says the Lord. Remember how I said not to include the Levites in that census? Well, that's because I want them counted in a *separate* census, all 22,000 of them. Okay, and now that we're rolling, how about just one more census, this time just to see how many Kohathites are among those Levites.

And so *now* we're ready for some action: the Tabernacle, the Ark of the Pact. There are blue cloths and purple cloths and a crimson cloth. There are lamps and tongs and ladles, and there's a surprising amount of dolphin skin. It's all described in great detail (of course), and guess who gets to carry it all? The lucky Kohathites, well counted thanks to those dogged census-takers.

And then it ends.

And so I am left looking for lessons, the essential truths at the heart of this seemingly mundane recitation. Does this passage teach us the benefits of taking stock, counting up who we are and what we have? Or is it, perhaps, a meditation on neighborhood dynamics, urban planning, the diverse roles that make up a community? Maybe. It's possible. But maybe what we're reading here is more just a reminder that sometimes things are a little ... boring. Some days you might find yourself spending hours rearranging your living room, or alphabetizing your record albums, or choosing which among your children will serve as specialized ark-porters. These days can feel futile and irrelevant, and maybe they are. But these futile days stretch back as far as days have been counted, and most likely will stretch forward as far as there are any left to count. Moses had to organize a team of census-takers. Shelumiel son of Zurishaddai had to find his camping spot on a seating chart. All our days are counted—even the dull ones.

"The priest shall adjure the woman, saying to her, 'If no man has lain with you, if you have not gone astray in defilement while married to your husband, be immune to harm from this water of bitterness that induces the spell.'" —Numbers 5:19

NASO (*"Lift up"*)
NUMBERS 4:21–7:89

L EVITE LABOR: **THE LORD TELLS MOSES TO** take a census of the Levite clans known as the Gershonites, the Merarites, and the Kohathites. Those aged thirty to fifty years old are tasked with hauling specific components of the Tabernacle and Tent. Moses supervises a count: there are 2,750 Kohathites, 2,630 Gershonites, and 3,200 Merarites in this age range.

The Lord instructs Moses to ensure that any Israelite with a contagious disease—a skin rash or genital discharge—or one who has been defiled by a corpse is set outside the camp to minimize the threat of viral infection.

THE RITUAL OF SOTAH

A procedure is created to defuse a situation in which a man suspects his wife of infidelity. If he is overcome by a fit of jealousy, he has to bring her to a priest, along with a sacrifice of barley flour, so they can undergo a trial by ordeal known as *sotah*.

The procedure begins with the priest taking the woman's hair down, then placing the sacrifice into her palms. He then holds up holy water mixed with earth from the sanctuary floor, and declares that if she is innocent, the bitter water will not affect her, but if she is guilty, her thigh will sag and her belly will swell. As soon as the accused woman drinks the water, her guilt or innocence will be revealed.

THE NAZIRITE

The Lord then describes the voluntary vow of the Nazirite—an Israelite who dedicates him- or herself to God by abstaining from wine, grape products, and the use of razors, and avoiding all corpses. The process by which Nazirites can choose to end their terms is also explained.

BLESS YOU

The Lord reveals the words of the blessing Aaron and his sons should make over the Israelites:

> THE LORD BLESS YOU
> AND PROTECT YOU!
> THE LORD DEAL KINDLY AND
> GRACIOUSLY WITH YOU!

> THE LORD BESTOW
> HIS FAVOR UPON YOU AND
> GRANT YOU PEACE.

CONSECRATION DAY

When Moses finishes setting up the Tabernacle and anointing it, he takes carts and oxen donated by the tribes and regifts them to the Gershonites and Merarites, so that they can perform their hauling duties. The Kohathites, who have the job of caring for the most sacred objects, are instructed to carry them on their shoulders. The chiefs of each tribe then bring forth more offerings—a silver bowl and basin filled with flour and oil, a gold ladle filled with incense, a bull, oxen, rams, goats, and lambs.

Moses' method of communication with God is then described: God's voice will sound in the Tent of Meeting from above the ark cover between the two cherubim.

JUSTIN ROCKET SILVERMAN

S he did him.

Everyone knows it. Everyone except me. My own brother calls me a fool for not seeing, and maybe he's right. But how could I? Even now, even now I don't want to.

My love. The only one. I won't believe it. And yet . . . there is something in the curl of her lips when she denies ever sleeping with *him*.

Defilement. Defilement of our sacred marriage. That's the real danger here. A union is sacred only when it is. She knows what that means. And she knows I'm not a jealous man. Ask anyone. If I had walked in on them together, I wouldn't have responded the way other men do. There would have been no blood sprayed upon the walls. I simply would have walked away. Never looking back. Never needing to.

It's the unknowing that's impossible. The nagging doubt. God does not like sexual deviance. And neither do I.

So there is only one solution. Never did I think it would come to this. Yet as the entire village witnessed early this morning as we left for Jerusalem, I decided she was to endure the ritual of the *sotah*—a unique test of purity for the wayward wife.

Some of the teenage boys yelled taunts as we walked past, until their mothers hushed them. Everyone else whispered, and the sound followed us for miles into the desert.

We entered the bustling city and made our way to the temple gates. There we were made to wait, side by side, amid the beggars, thieves, and prostitutes.

I looked at my wife and saw her shivering gently. It was not a cold morning. I tried to look at her eyes beneath her shawl, but her head was downcast. In shame or in fear I could not tell. It seemed fear.

She sensed me watching her and breathed a single word: "Please."

I reached out and almost took her hand. To reassure her that my love was still strong. But we do not touch our women in public.

Only the image of *him* in my mind succeeded in hardening my heart. Otherwise I never would have been able to risk the life of my love in this manner.

"If you are innocent, no harm will come to you," I told her. "If you are innocent, God will reward you with renewed fertility."

"I am innocent," she whispered.

"Then you have nothing to fear!"

It sounded untrue even as I said it.

The temple's gold and silver walls became blinding in the noon sun. We were finally ushered through the outer gates and into a round chamber lit by torchlight. A small sacrificial fire burned on the stone altar.

In no other instance does our Torah command such a trial by ordeal. God does not otherwise intervene so directly in matters of legal justice. The Creator gave us the laws, and we are left to make them work. Only in the ritual of the *sotah* does God judge guilt or innocence.

It's an enigma, yes.

* * *

The priest looked from my wife to me, from me to my wife. Then he held out his hands for the sacrificial offering I had carried from home. It was only a small sack of coarse barley. And so cheap! Hardly fit for animals. Yet this is the only sacrifice acceptable for the ritual of the *sotah*, as ordained by the word of God.

The priest accepted the barley and then commanded me to stand back against a wall. Only then did I notice the other men gathered there. They were strangers and did not meet my gaze.

Then the priest tore off my wife's shawl.

She let out a sharp cry. I wanted to go to her. This was the first time any man but me had seen her naked hair since our marriage. It was shameful to her, and to me. But before I could act, two strong attendants rushed from the shadows. They held my wife on either side as the priest undid her careful braids, letting the soft brown locks fall about her face. The sight stirred an unexpected desire in me. I tried to remember the last time I'd felt it. Not since we'd accepted defeat in our attempts to have a child.

Just then I regretted that we'd stopped trying.

* * *

The priest bade my wife to kneel before him, and then laid the barley into her hands. From the altar he lifted a tiny clay bowl of water. It was just water. But the power of God made it more than water. In this fearsome place, water was poison.

He reached down and gathered a pinch of dust from the temple floor, then sprinkled it into the water.

"If no man other than your husband has been with you, this water will be harmless," the priest intoned, his loud voice echoing along the rounded walls. "But if you have been with someone besides your husband . . . this water of bitterness will destroy your insides and make your flesh fall away."

My wife turned and captured my gaze. She was so pretty. I was suddenly overcome with panic. It was wrong to bring her here.

"Amen," she said. "Amen."

With that, the two attendants left my wife's side and brought the priest a small parchment, upon which he wrote out the very same words he'd just intoned. Then he laid this parchment into the bowl of water, so that the ink bled away.

I wondered if somehow the ink itself was the poison that could make my wife's flesh rot. Or perhaps it was simply absorbing the name of God that made the water so dangerous. We Jews are not in the habit of erasing God's name from anything. In fact, doing so is against the rules.

And my wife was going to drink the transgression.

The priest lifted the pitiful sack of barley from her hands and held it over the sacrificial fire. The odor of singed grain filled the chamber. The smell made me think of a night with my wife back in our village, not long after our wedding. She had burned the Sabbath bread, and there was no time to make more before the sun set. She wanted to go around to the neighbors to see who might have extra, but I insisted that even her burnt bread was superior to the most moist and chewily delicious that any neighbor baked. So we sat there eating the bread, laughing as we washed it down with large pours of wine, yet still hardly able to chew. Blackened crumbs poured over the table and the floor, and I loved her then. Trusted her completely. So much that I let her see my own darkness, my own regrets. She's the only one who has. It was expected that I would take other wives, or at least enjoy the company of unmarried women, but I didn't want to. Because that charred husk was the best bread I'd ever tasted.

The priest commanded my wife to lift the bowl of water to her lips.

"Don't do it!" I cried, charging forth. "I withdraw the accusation of adultery. It was a mistake! In the name of . . ."

My protest was cut short as my face plowed into the ground.

My wife looked at me, her eyes empty and numb. The priest looked, too, his filled with scorn. I understood then that this was no longer about me. This was a private matter between my wife and God—a point driven home by the weight of the attendant's foot on the back of my neck.

"Remember," the priest told her, "if you are innocent of adultery, then this same water will make it so you can conceive children. This is God's gift to the falsely accused."

"Amen," my wife whispered, and then she lifted the bowl. Her hands trembled, and she paused just as the inky water touched her lips. Perhaps praying for mercy. Perhaps cursing the day she had ever met him. Perhaps cursing the day she had ever met me. In one rushing gulp she finished the bowl clean, drinking the name of God.

The attendant removed his foot, and I was able to stand. The chamber was filled with silence. We men stood around and watched my wife. Her eyes closed, her lips moist.

Then it happened. The sacrificial fire on the altar suddenly flared bright and then went utterly cold. This was not supposed to be. The priest and his attendants rushed to the altar to get the flames going again. So it was only me left to watch as my wife opened her eyes.

* * *

I may be mistaken, and to this day cannot be certain, but I believe she was smiling as she tossed the empty bowl into the dust, stood up, and strolled out of the chamber.

I caught up with her in the courtyard outside, where she had paused to retie her braids.

"My love!" I exclaimed, my heart filled with joy. "This is wonderful! God's will has been done. Now we can finally have a child together."

She looked at me for a long moment before she spoke, her smile gone.

"No. No, we cannot." With that she walked away. Alone.

Like me.

ויהי העם כמתאננים רע באזני יהוה וישמע יהוה
ויחר אפו ותבער בם אש יהוה ותאכל בקצה המחנה:

"The people took to complaining bitterly before the Lord.
The Lord heard and was incensed."—Numbers 11:1

B'HA·ALOT'KHA
("*When you step up*")
NUMBERS 8:1–12:16

EVITE LABOR, CONT'D: **THE LORD DESCRIBES** how Aaron should light the lamps around the Tabernacle. The cleansing of the Levites is prescribed, a process that necessitates being sprinkled with water of purification, receiving a full body shave, and sacrificing two bulls. The Levites are to serve between the ages of twenty-five and fifty, after which they can still act as guards but shall perform no labor.

A SHIFTING PASSOVER
At the start of the second year of freedom, God instructs Moses to prepare to offer the Passover sacrifice; however, it is discovered that some of the Israelites are unclean because they have touched a corpse. As a remedy, God suggests that the group celebrate Passover the following month, but lets it be known that if others fail to perform the sacrifice at the right time without good reason, they will be cut off from the community.

SOUND CLOUD
Once the Tabernacle is established, a

253

cloud covers it by day, morphing into fire by night. When the cloud lifts, the Israelites prepare to follow it on their journey. Wherever it settles, they know to pitch camp.

The Lord commands Moses to craft two silver trumpets for the priests to blow and summon the community. Long blasts are the signal to assemble at the Tent of Meeting. A single trumpet sound instructs the chieftains to assemble. Short blasts command the right flank to move forward. Further short blasts instruct the rear to shift. An additional set of signals will act to mobilize the army during a time of war; others will be used to celebrate festivals and joyous occasions.

The order by which the Israelites embark on a journey is described, tribe by tribe—from Judah, who leads with the Tabernacle behind them, all the way through to the tribe of Dan, who act as rear guard.

The Israelites march for three days from Mount Sinai. As the ark sets out, Moses cries these words:

"Advance, Lord!
May Your enemies be
scattered, And may Your foes
flee before You."

And when the ark stops, he exclaims:

"Return, Lord,
You who are Israel's
myriads of thousands."

LET THEM EAT MEAT

The Israelites soon revert to their complaining ways, moaning about the hardships of desert wandering. A furious God unleashes fire on the outskirts of camp until Moses intercedes on the people's behalf. Tired of their manna-centric diet, the people beg for meat, nostalgic for their Egyptian diet of fish and fruit.

The people weep. God is furious. Stuck in the middle, Moses wonders aloud what he has done to deserve a leadership role that he compares to breast-feeding an infant; he tells the Lord he would prefer to die rather than hear more complaints about the lack of meat.

A solution-oriented God tells Moses to bring seventy elders to the Tent of Meeting so they can begin to share the burden of leadership. Moses also instructs the people to purify themselves, telling them meat will be delivered the next day. Stung by the people's whining, God reveals a devious intention: So much meat will be provided that the Israelites will have it coming out of their nostrils until they are sick of it.

Moses doubts God's ability to conjure up that much meat in the middle of the desert, but the Lord snorts, reminding him there is no limit to God's power.

The seventy elders convene before God, who comes down in a cloud to extend Moses' leadership abilities to them. God then summons a wind, which causes quail to blow into the camp from the sea. The people greedily gather them up, but before they have a chance to chew the meat, an angry God inflicts a plague.

SIBLING RIVALRY

Moses' own brother and sister, Aaron and Miriam, spread gossip about their sibling, wondering aloud why he alone has been put in a position of leadership when he is not perfect. After all, they say, he married a Cushite woman.

When God hears the rumormongering, he calls the three to the Tent of Meeting and descends in a pillar of cloud to validate Moses' unique stature. Unlike other prophets, to whom God appears in visions and dreams, Moses communicates with the Lord directly, "mouth to mouth." Moses has even been permitted to see a likeness of the Lord. Furious, God withdraws, but not before turning Miriam's skin a deathly snow white. Moses begs God to heal his sister, but God wants her to be shamed and instructs her to leave camp for seven days.

EDDY PORTNOY

B *'ha·alot'kha* reads like the biblical equivalent of Tourette's syndrome. The narrative weaves around like slop, as if the redactor was handed a pile of scriptural detritus and told to figure out some way—any way—to string them together into a sad corned beef hash suitable for vellum.

What do we have here? Levites shaving their pubic hair, menorah-makers, trumpets, Passover, complaining, a horrific rain of dead birds, more complaining, some moving around, murder, more complaining, racism, and even a skin rash.

What takes place here is the afterbirth of a nation. The Israelites' national symbol, the menorah, is created. The first national music is commanded to be played. The first national holiday, Passover, is celebrated. But above all, our cardinal trait for all eternity begins to manifest itself: bitter dissent. We are portrayed as a nation of grumbling whiners, of ultracritical, nattering nitpickers of negativism, of miserable, whiny, unreconstructed nudniks. Freedom isn't good enough. The manna isn't good enough for our people, evidently ill-equipped to be desert wanderers.

It's a wonder that our national symbol isn't an image of someone with a deep frown and a wagging finger telling a waiter to send the meal back, or that our national anthem isn't called "It's Not Good Enough." An invisible deity has freed you from the bonds of slavery, given you a sacred covenant by which to live, and sustained you in the desert with copious amounts of food? But, meh! What have You done for me lately? The food was better in Egypt. From the outset, the Israelites were Olympians of complaining. Right there from our founding, this national trait was our birthright.

The glut of dead quail that blanketed the Israelites' encampment was also a problem. What are we going to do with all of these dead birds, Motl? Nu, we'll put them on sale. Although God intended it as a punishment, hoping the gluttons would eat until they puked, the quail turned out to be an integral element in the development of another national trait, the "Going Out of Business" sale. Two-for-one quail. The revered commercial abilities of the nation received an early start.

When I read this portion, I can't help but be taken back to the debunked pseudosciences of the nineteenth century. Nasologists often raged about the Hebrews' "vending acumen," linking it to their "commercial noses." According to the tenets of nasology, as outlined by Eden Warwick, the author of its central tome, personal and national traits determine the shape of one's nose. Its nasal taxonomy holds that a nose of the hooked variety is Hebraic in origin and commercial in nature. Ms. Warwick further argued that although the Hebraic-Mercantile nose was "good and practical," it did not "elevate [its owner] to any exalted pitch of intellectuality." Moreover, owners of such noses, although undoubtedly inclined commercially, were considered to be "curious wranglers, ingenious cabalists,

The Nose as a Sign of Character.

By Jessie Allen Fowler.

Lavater once said that a nose physiognomically good is of unspeak-

spicuous feature of the face. Porta. De La Chambre, Albert and others

A VARIETY OF NOSES.

able weight as an indication of character, and we have only to go back to the early days to realize how much the people then thought of the proper development of this most con-

speculate a good deal as to the sign of character that the nose indicates. To-day even more than in olden times the nose is studied as an index to a person's disposition.

A VARIETY OF NOSES

FROM *Nasology, Or Hints Towards a Classification of Noses*, by Eden Warwick, London, 1848.

Class IV. The Jewish, or Hawk Nose, is very convex, and preserves its convexity like a bow, throughout the whole length from the eyes to the tip. It is thin and sharp.

It indicates considerable Shrewdness in worldly matters; a deep Insight into character, and facility of turning that insight to profitable account.

fine splitters of hairs, shrewd perverters of texts, sharp detecters of discrepancies, clever concocters of analogies, and finders of mysteries in a sun-beam"[1]—in other words, irritating, whiny nudniks with nothing better to do after they'd sold out their stock in dead quail.

A subsequent interpreter of nasological sciences, Gustavus Cohen, held that the Hebraic nose was inherently a "combative nose, receiving its peculiar form principally from an extraordinary development of the sign of apprehension." A combative nose. "Combative," indeed. An allusion, perhaps, to the biblically established tradition of "it's not good enough."[2] Combative. Because saying "everything's fine" is an affront to the nation. As much as they were pilloried and discredited, even the pseudosciences understood the Israelites.

The Hebrew Skater is always Strapped
No money will he spend;
He 'knows' it cheaper to use one skate
His "NOSE" goes to that end.

FROM THE PERSONAL COLLECTION OF EDDY PORTNOY

[1] FROM *Nasology, Or Hints Towards a Classification of Noses*, by Eden Warwick (London: Rich. Bentley, 1848).

[2] FROM *On the Manners and Customs of Modern Judaism*, by Gustavus Cohen (Nottingham: J. Derry, 1880).

ויוציאו דבת הארץ אשר תרו אתה אל בני ישראל לאמר הארץ אשר עברנו
בה לתור אתה ארץ אכלת יושביה הוא וכל העם אשר ראינו בתוכה אנשי מדות:

"Thus they spread calumnies among the Israelites about the land they had
scouted, saying, 'The country that we traversed and scouted is one that devours its
settlers. All the people that we saw in it are men of great size.'" —Numbers 13:32

SH'LAKH L'KHA ("Send to you")

NUMBERS 13:1–15:41

THE LORD ORDERS MOSES TO RECRUIT ONE man from each of the twelve tribes to scout Canaan. Moses explains the mission to them. The twelve are to report back on the region's topography, military strength, resources, and fortifications.

The scouts explore as far as Hebron, cutting down a branch of grapes so large that it takes two men to carry it. The mission lasts forty days. When it is over, the returning scouts exhibit the giant grapes and breathlessly tell the Israelites how the land is inhabited by powerful, well-fortified tribes. Only one scout, Caleb, confidently predicts an Israelite victory. His telling is soon supported by that of a second scout, Joshua. The rest fearfully tell tales of giants swarming the area and suggest that the region is a land that devours its settlers.

The effect of these fear-driven reports is immediate. The Israelites begin to wail, questioning Moses and the decision to leave the comparative safety of Egyptian slavery. Moses and Aaron, siding with Caleb, urge the Israelites to remain rational. They reaffirm that Canaan is a land of milk and honey: If God is with them, the

Israelites should have no fear. Their words have no effect. As the community prepares to pelt them with stones, God is forced to make an appearance.

God speaks to Moses, demanding to know how long the people will lack faith, despite all that has been done for them, and threatening to unleash a disease that will destroy them. Moses protects the Israelites by asking God to imagine the pleasure the Egyptians will derive from such an act; will not the Lord appear impotent?

God promises to be patient; however, because of their incessant moaning, of those who left Egypt, only the loyal scouts, Caleb and Joshua, will live to see Canaan. All those aged twenty years and older will die in the course of the forty years the Israelites will wander in the wilderness. (The number forty is selected to represent one year for each of the forty days the scouts spied on Canaan.) The ten failed scouts die immediately of a plague.

In their grief, a group of Israelites vow that they have seen the error of their ways and will set forth for the promised land of Canaan immediately. Moses warns them that they cannot enter the land without the Lord's permission, but they ignore his advice and are instantly cut down by the Amalekites and Canaanites.

SACRIFICES FOR THE PROMISED LAND

The Lord then offers a list of sacrifices required to mark the moment the Israelites enter Canaan, and reminds the Israelites about the role of the sin offering, repeating that those who defiantly break a commandment will be cut off from the community.

An example is soon provided: An Israelite is found collecting wood on the Sabbath. God instructs Moses to have him stoned to death.

The Lord then tells Moses that he must ensure that the Israelites wear fringes on the corner of their garments as a visual reminder of the Lord's commandments and the role God played in freeing them from Egypt.

CAITLIN ROPER

TRUTH V. PEACE, OR HOW MY TINY LIFE REMINDS ME A LITTLE BIT OF SH'LAKH L'KHA

I married the wrong man. Before that, I'd had misgivings. When I would tell him I was upset about something that had happened between us, he'd say, "I'm sorry you feel that way."

I talked about my worries to close friends, and to some family. But though they listened and advised, no one told me not to get married. More than one friend recalled the trepidation they'd felt before committing to marriage.

You can't blame other people for not telling you the truth[1]—truth is often the enemy of peace. Most of us would rather stay safe than say what we feel is true.[2] That is how I married the wrong man, after all.

One friend told me the truth.[3] She told me not to marry him. She asked a few cutting questions. Could I share my feelings with him? Could he talk to me about what I cared most about? Did he want to? Was the sex good enough? Did I feel connected to him? She told me she didn't think I should do it.

---

[1] Unless you're God. It really pisses Him off. When He told Moses to send spies to the promised land, and they came back shaking and mewling about undefeatable giants mucking up the milk and honey, full of crap and unmotivated to press forward at God's command, He was furious.

[2] As desperate as the Israelites were to find a home, they wanted to stay safe more than move forward into the unknown.

[3] Brave spies Caleb and Joshua told the truth about the promised land.

I remember where I stood while she said these things. I was clutching my cell phone, pacing the sidewalk across the street from the house I shared with my boyfriend. Looking up at the light from the windows as darkness shaded me in. My friend was thousands of miles away, but she could hear me.

I didn't feel angry that she'd told me the truth.[4] But I didn't listen either.[5] Months later, she came to my wedding, flying across the country to be there, knowing I was making a mistake.

It wasn't long before I left him.[6] We divorced. I was sad for a long time. It was a mess of guilt and pain, but there is one indelible thing from that time—that single conversation, the voice of truth, the one person who put truth before peace. I aim to be more like her.

---

[4] Clearly, I'm not God. He was SO MAD.

[5] Neither did the Israelites. I mean, they didn't listen to Caleb and Joshua; they were fearful, and they mucked up.

[6] The Israelites had to walk in the desert for forty years for their mistake. I was married for four months.

"They combined against Moses and Aaron and said to them, 'You have gone too far! For all the community are holy, all of them, and the Lord is in their midst. Why then do you raise yourself above the Lord's congregation?'"—Numbers 16:3

KORAH ("*Korah*")
NUMBERS 16:1–18:32

KORAH'S REBELLION! **MOSES' AND AARON'S** leadership is challenged by Korah. Abetted by Dathan, Abiram, and On, he rounds up 250 respected chieftains and demands to know why the brothers are exalted more than any other Israelite.

Moses meets the challenge with a challenge. He suggests that Korah and his confidants return in the morning with fire pans and incense so the Lord can demonstrate exactly who should be considered holy and worthy of communicating with God. He finishes by suggesting that Korah has overstepped his bounds and proclaiming that he and his band—Levites all—should have settled for the honor of being priestly assistants without aspiring to be priests themselves.

Moses sends for Dathan and Abiram, but they refuse to recognize his command. Moses is annoyed, yet he instructs Korah and his band to return the following morning.

The next day, the whole community assembles to watch the spectacle. The Lord's presence appears, commanding Moses and Aaron to stand back so the rebels can be annihilated. Moses questions whether God should punish the collective for one man's sins, and God relents, instructing Moses to evacuate the area around Korah, Dathan, and Abiram's tents: They are wicked and must be wiped out accordingly.

Just as Moses does this, the three men wander out of their abodes accompanied by their wives and children. Moses declares that if these men end up dying a natural death, he should be considered a false prophet. But if they are spectacularly swallowed up by the ground, then it should be taken as a sign that Moses is acting on behalf of the God they spurned.

No sooner have the words tumbled from Moses' mouth than the earth opens to swallow up the families and their possessions. The 250 chieftains are simultaneously burned to death by fire dispatched by the Lord.

The Lord orders the fire pans of the dead rebels to be turned into plating for the altar to serve as a warning to the people. Yet the following day the entire community rails against Moses and Aaron, disgusted by the death and destruction they have wrought.

As they menace Moses and Aaron, God's presence appears in cloud form, ready to annihilate the people. Moses realizes that God is prepared to unleash a plague and quickly orders Aaron to make an offering on behalf of the people. The plague descends nonetheless. Aaron begs for penitence, but is unable to check it before 14,700 lives are lost.

VOTE OF CONFIDENCE FOR AARON

God instructs Moses to take a staff from each of the tribal chiefs, plus one from Aaron, and deposit them in the Tent of Meeting. The staff of the individual whom God deems the elected leader will sprout into flower as a sign that will end the Israelites' incessant grumbling.

The next day, Moses enters the Tent and discovers Aaron's rod has sprouted blossoms and borne almonds. God orders that it be left in the Tent as proof of Aaron's elevated status. But the Israelites continue to moan, voicing a collective fear that they will be struck down if they approach the Tabernacle. God responds by carefully articulating the roles of Aaron and the priests as well as the Levites, in regard to safe maintenance of the Tabernacle.

ADAM LEVIN

Like so many conflicts in the Torah, the basic one described in Numbers 16 is fairly straightforward: good Jew versus dummkopf Jew. And like so many other times that this conflict arises in the Torah, the good Jew in Numbers 16 is Moses, and the dummkopf Jew, a man called Korah, is little more than a redshirt with a speaking part. Korah thinks Moses—who gave up an extremely easy and unimaginably privileged life as an Egyptian prince to murder a slave driver, go into exile, turn prematurely gray, then return to Egypt to bring Korah and all the other enslaved Jews out of Egypt by walking them through the middle of a sea God split open on his (Moses'!) cue, only to spend what he shortly came to realize would be the rest of his life listening to people whine in a desert—is hogging God.

Korah thinks Moses is hogging God, and, having convinced a bunch of Jews that Moses is hogging God, Korah gets these Jews to stand behind him while he complains to Moses about the perceived hogging, and demands that he and his family (i.e., Korah and his family) get more access to God. Moses finds this so hilarious that he falls "on his face." But then Korah makes it clear he's not kidding at all, and Moses tries to explain that who gets access to God and who doesn't isn't up to Korah or Moses, but God, and that God wants to deal pretty much exclusively with Moses and Moses' brother, Aaron.

Korah's not having any of it, though, and Moses, still hopeful, tries to talk sense to two of Korah's friends, Dathan and Abiram, but Dathan and Abiram make it clear that they agree with Korah; they too think Moses is hogging God. They even go so far as to refer to Egypt as a "land of milk and honey."

Moses tells the lot of them to break out some incense and shut their pieholes.

So a bunch of them break out some incense and shut their pieholes, at which point God appears. He tells Moses and Aaron to get away from all the incense-lighting piehole-shutters because He's going to do something extremely violent. At the mention of extreme violence, Moses and Aaron *both* fall "on their faces," not so much because they think extreme violence is as funny as all that, but because they know that God appreciates a well-executed face-plant, and since, after all, He's just a man without a body (unless everything that exists plus everything that will exist and has formerly existed and might or might not one day eventually exist can be said to be a body), they know that if they can get Him to laugh, He'll be more likely to listen to reason. And it turns out, they're right. He listens to reason. They tell Him He shouldn't kill all those thousands of people—people who can pratfall as good as anyone—just because Korah and a couple of his pals are dummkopfs, and God tells Moses to warn anyone who doesn't want to experience extreme violence firsthand to get out of the way. And though Moses warns as commanded, Korah, Dathan, Abiram, and their wives and babies and their extended families stand firm. The rest of the Jews get out of the way.

And then God opens a sinkhole beneath all the members of the families of Dathan and Abiram and Korah who aren't holding burning incense (all the wives and children), and He does so quickly enough to scare them crazy, but gradually enough to prevent them from dying at impact. And then they stand there, in the darkness at the bottom of the sinkhole—which, being a miracle sinkhole, then covers over, but doesn't fill in completely—and they scream until they die of fright or dehydration.

Korah, Dathan, Abiram, and all the other guys from their extended families who *are* holding burning incense, however, are killed in a trice with a wall of Godfire, and that's that.

Double face-plant notwithstanding, what makes this episode stand out among others of the good Jew versus dummkopf Jew genre is that the dummkopfiest of the dummkopf Jews seem to get off quite a bit easier than the less dummkopfy of the dummkopf Jews. That Korah, Dathan, and Abiram, having played the most active roles in the rebellion, are nonetheless granted a quicker and seemingly more merciful death than are the members of their families, who were, when the sinkhole opened up beneath them, only honoring their husbands and fathers as the law commands, is . . . *interesting*. God—quite possibly overcompensating for His own feelings of self-hatred—seems to be insisting that it's more reprehensible to have an angry, stubborn man for a father or husband than it is to *be* an angry, stubborn man. Either that, or it's better to die screaming beneath a desert than it is to die suddenly by fire.

"Instruct the Israelite people to bring you a red cow without blemish, in which there is no defect and on which no yoke has been laid." —Numbers 19:2

HUKKAT (*"Decrees"*)

NUMBERS 19:1–22:1

THE INCREDIBLY STRANGE RITUAL OF THE red heifer: God breaks down the esoteric ritual law of the red heifer for Moses and Aaron. The Israelites are commanded to offer an unblemished red cow that has never once worn a yoke. One of the priests, Aaron's son Eleazar, is to slaughter it outside of the camp, sprinkle its blood toward the front of the Tent of Meeting, and burn it with cedar wood, hyssop, and crimson stuff. The ashes are then to be swept up and kept as "water of lustration," which can cleanse any Israelite who comes into contact with a corpse.

Instructions for its usage are then provided. The ashes are to be mixed with fresh water and hyssop and sprinkled on objects and humans exposed to corpses. Any individual who fails to follow these procedures shall be cut off from the community.

THE DEATHS OF MIRIAM AND
AARON, PLUS MORE GRUMBLING,
AND A TOUGH PATCH FOR MOSES
The Israelites arrive at the Wilderness of Zin. Miriam dies and is buried there.

The Israelites begin to complain loudly about their lack of water, repeating their now familiar line of questioning to Moses and Aaron: "Why did you bring us out of Egypt to suffer like this?"

The Lord commands Moses to solve the drought by taking his rod, assembling the community in front of a rock, and commanding it to spring forth water. Moses does so, but after informing the Israelites of the wonder he is about to perform with God, strikes the rock twice. Water pours forth, but God expresses displeasure that Moses has not struck the rock according to the Lord's instructions. This act of disobedience is perceived as a symbol of Moses' lack of trust for which he receives a severe punishment: He will not be able to lead the Israelites into the land that has been promised to them.

Moses dispatches messengers to the king of Edom requesting safe passage through his kingdom, promising not to plunder food or drink along the way. The king refuses the request and assembles a large military force that compels the Israelites to turn away.

On Edom's borderland at Mount Hor, God advises Aaron to prepare for death by transferring his priestly garb to Eleazar. Aaron does as he is told and dies on the mountaintop. The community mourns for thirty days.

THE RIGORS OF JOURNEYING AND MILITARY CAMPAIGNING

The Israelites then enter battle with the Canaanites around Arad, destroying them with God's help. But the people grow restless once more as they cross the Sea of Reeds; the Lord dispatches snakes to kill a number of them as punishment. Once the people recognize their sin, Moses intercedes on their behalf and God tells Moses to forge a copper snake and mount it on a pole. Any Israelite who is bitten need only look at it to recover.

The Israelites dispatch messengers to Sihon, king of the Amorites, asking for safe passage through his kingdom. Sihon refuses and sends his people to attack the Israelites. The Israelites prove victorious and soon take possession of the Amorite towns.

King Og of Bashan also attacks them—with a similar outcome. The Israelites continue their march, camping on the grasslands of Moab, across the Jordan from Jericho.

RACHEL AXLER

SONG OF THE RED COW

Moo.

Please no murder me.

I am red cow. Know you how many of me there is in world? Not many! More particular: I am red cow, no blemish. See how pretty! No yoke has been laid on me. This mean inside of egg, make me sticky and yellow. I no sticky! My hide soft, clean. Nice for petting, if you into that sort of thing.

I being told this not what mean. Yoke is saddle thing that impede movement. Who care! Point is: I happy, red, and free. I enjoy graze, ruminate, deep talk with cow friends. My milk taste gooooooood.

Lord say bring me to Eleazar Priest for kill me. I know Eleazar Priest. He nice man once fed me dandelion. Eleazar Priest no want kill me any more than you want hole in head. You no look gift horse in mouth. Why, then, it okay you look gift cow in eye, chop off head?

Lord say Eleazar Priest take me outside camp for murder. I no want go outside camp, for no reason! I like camp. Camp where other cows roam, sleep warm, make good talks. Many color cows: white or brown or with spots or Bovis who look like funny zebra. I am ONLY RED COW. Hard not think Lord specifically talking about me. Like maybe have thing against me, maybe no like me, maybe I talk too much, cannot help, I ruminate, things make worry in my cow head. Maybe Lord just not appreciate gingers. Apology for heresy, I just saying.

Lord say Eleazar Priest take my blood on finger, sprinkle seven times toward tent, then make me burn in fire. I have many question, but first is why seven? Seven is odd number to choose. Get it? Odd number. Ha ha. Red cow make math joke. Okay back to topic of kill me in fire. Lord say burn my hide, flesh, blood, and poop. Yes, Lord specifically mention my poop. Although this may be funny idea for put in bag, leave on doorstep of nasty neighbor, this seem particular stupid for making broth of cleansing. You know what smell like when burn cow poop? Smell like burnt cow poop. I think is gross, but hey, what I know, I just red cow you want make dead.

Then come recipe. For most cow, after slaughter, chop up strategic by master butcher, rub with spice or marinade, put on grill, serve medium rare with nice potato. For me, Lord suggest cedar wood, hyssop, crimson stuff. This sound disgusting. Then I not even eaten! I left overnight for burn away to black, and priest go home, take nice bath.

Then Lord command clean man take my ashes, mix in water. Then clean man bathe. You notice trend here? Anyone touch me have to take bath. Here a secret: BECAUSE SLAUGHTER RED COW POOP ASH VERY DIRTY. Even when mix with water!!

But Lord suddenly up and say: Law for all time is unclean man for cleansing must use Red Cow Poop Ash Water? And just because He Lord, you listen?? And they say cow is stupid!

Here. Before kill me forever, just you try test? For me, because maybe once you pat my pretty red body and it is soft? Maybe because I once look at you with big brown cow eyes, as if say: "Hello, friend"? For me before call priest to sprinkle blood on tent you try once this test, please, okay?

Poop in fire. I know, is human poop, but poop anyway. Add side beef, get at any grocer, plus blood. Add more red thing—food dye, berry, what have. Add leather jacket. Lots smoke now, yes? Good. Wait for nightfall.

Take some of mixture, put in water. Like disgusting soup.

Now take thing that is unclean. Maybe jeans? You know it been at least two weeks since you wash them, do not front. Dip jeans in bloody poop soup. Let dry.

I make you bet. I bet you jeans dirtier than before. Now not just normal dirty. Now need throw away dirty. Now friend look at you when wear like you maybe into weird S&M stuff dirty.

I know Lord spake. But this between Lord and me. I will pray to Lord, ask what did wrong, ask how fix it. Maybe He make me do crazy thing—venture into strange pasture near university, stand until drunk frat boy tip me over. Maybe He ask me slaughter own calf. Lord ask some weird things. But let me resolve on own, okay?

You no call Eleazar Priest. You had awful day anyway, probably touched corpse, why else you need cleansing? You go back to Tent, run bubble bath, no ash, no blood. Maybe light nice candle in scent like jasmine or Fresh Laundry. You get clean like normal human.

Afterward, come see me—happy red cow who not dead in own feces—and I promise: make you most delicious, warm milk.

BALAK (*"Balak"*)

NUMBERS 22:2–25:9

T HE STORY OF BALAK. **A KING OF MOAB NAMED** Balak monitors Israel's destruction of the Amorites with alarm. After consulting with his elders, he summons a prophet named Balaam to curse the Israelites on his behalf. Balaam refuses the invitation when a vision of God appears and warns him off.

Balak refuses to take no for an answer and promises to reward Balaam richly. Balaam tells Balak's messengers that it is irrelevant what they offer him, as he is powerless in the face of the Lord. But God appears to Balaam overnight, granting permission for him to go, so when he awakes in the morning, the prophet saddles his ass and departs with the Moabite dignitaries.

Once the journey begins, the Lord becomes incensed and dispatches an angel to interfere with Balaam's mission. First the prophet's ass senses the angel's presence and refuses to stay on the road. When Balaam beats the animal, it squashes him against a wall before lying down.

The Lord then gives the ass the power of speech. She asks Balaam to explain why he is beating her. Balaam explains that he has been embarrassed by her behavior and informs her that if he had carried a sword, she would be dead. At that, the Lord suddenly reveals the angel, who appears with sword in hand.

Balaam immediately bows to the ground as the angel explains the Lord's role in his humiliation, adding that the prophet is the one who deserves to die, not the ass. Balaam offers to turn back, but the angel suggests he continue on the journey, as long as he does the Lord's bidding from now on.

As Balaam approaches, Balak eagerly runs out to greet him, only for the prophet to inform him that he can utter only the words God puts in his mouth.

Balaam goes with Balak to an overlook, where they can see the Israelites on the valley floor below. The prophet orders the king to build seven altars and prepare rams and bulls for sacrifice. He then channels the words of God, advising Balak that he cannot doom Israel as God has not doomed them, for they are a people who dwell apart.

Balak immediately expresses his displeasure to Balaam, reminding him that he has been summoned to curse the Israelites, not praise them. Balaam defends himself by explaining how prophecy works: He can repeat only the words God places in his mouth.

Balak suggests they move to another location where they can see only a fraction of the Israelites, and the process is repeated. This time Balaam reveals that God is not like a mortal who will change His mind. He has been told to bless the Israelites and cannot reverse God's support of the Israelites, which is compared to the horns of a wild ox. Israel is described as a people who will rise like a lion, the king of beasts who feeds on its prey.

Balak tries once more, suggesting Balaam need no longer curse the Israelites but should attempt to refrain from blessing them. The king and the prophet relocate again, but this time Balaam looks down on the camps of Israel and gushes with poetic praise, predicting they will devour enemy nations, crush their bones, and smash their arrows.

Balak is furious at Balaam's impudence, but the prophet refers to the message he has delivered constantly since his arrival: He can repeat only the Lord's commands. To reinforce that, he predicts the fate of Moab in the days to come, describing imminent destruction at the hands of a triumphant Israel.

MEANWHILE, BACK AT THE
CAMP . . .

While the Israelites encamp, they enrage God by whoring with Moabite women and worshipping the Moabite god, Baal-peor. The only way to calm the Lord's wrath is to impale the ringleaders; Moses demands that all those who worshipped the foreign god be killed. At that very moment, an Israelite is spotted bringing a Midianite woman over to his companions, so Eleazar's son Pinhas picks up a spear, pursues them, and then stabs them both in the belly. His actions check a plague, which had claimed the lives of 24,000 Israelites.

SHOSHANA BERGER

L isten to your ass. Your ass knows more than you do. And by ass I mean both the humblest member of the Equidae family and the beastliest part of you. That your animal could be better—closer, even—to God than you are may sound like a lark. But that's the lesson I take from the story of Balak, Balaam, and his talking donkey. Our language-larded, sweaty brains are not the part of us with the clearest vision. Our asses apprehend God before we do.

As Old Testament books go, Numbers is considered the flyover part. Like Leviticus' recitation of laws, the very title "Numbers" suggests that we're in for a slog of accounting. It pales when compared with the pyrotechnics of Genesis and Exodus. But just as you're nodding off, along comes chapter 22, a madcap fable in which Balak, overlord of the Moab tribe, asks Balaam, a freelance seer, to curse the Israelites, lest they "nibble away" all of the local resources as they settle into nearby land. This may be the first biblical characterization of Jews as resource-nibblers. It's a short jump to moneylender.

Balaam accepts this mission, which promises handsome riches and fame, even though God had originally come to him in a dream and warned him against it, saying, to paraphrase, "Back off, them's my people." Balaam saddles his donkey and heads off to put a hex on the Israelites. But when the Lord's messenger blocks the road with his sword drawn, Balaam's ass swerves away to protect his master, eventually buckling and refusing to go farther, even as Balaam, who sees nothing, beats his hind with a stick.

In a Looney Tunes turn, God gives the abused animal the power of speech: "The Lord opened the ass's mouth" to ask Balaam why he's beating the crap out of her when she's always been a dutiful donkey and is stopping for a good reason. At that moment the wool is pulled from

Balaam's eyes and he sees the divine spirit standing before him. Horrified by his misdeeds, he face-plants. Picture the gesture: head down, ass in the air. Balaam ends up as lowly as his animal. Only then is he righteous in the eyes of God.

I feel close to Balaam. When offered bank for his services, he jumps at it, even though his more instinctual side—a message delivered in a dream—forbids the task at hand. I've done so many things that required a dose of ethical Dramamine. These days you needn't be a criminal to cross the line—just buying an iPhone is suspect. You know somewhere down the line people will suffer, may even be "cursed" by what you do, but those people are far away in a Chinese factory. You cannot see their faces.

I was hired as a Balaam-like seer once. After getting my start as a journalist, I took a cue from Matt Drudge and began publishing an early online newsletter about cultural trends, called *D.I. Wire* (DIYer, get it?). I stole the email addresses of hotshot execs from group emails in which people had forgotten to blind copy, and sent my weekly dispatch out unsolicited. It caught the attention of a big advertising agency, and I was christened a "futurist" in my late twenties. They hired me to translate the whims of my generation into marketing plans for Sony and Mattel and Shell Oil and Ford Motors. It paid more zeroes than I'd ever dreamed of. And as I interviewed teenagers all around the world and wrote fun-loving reports based on their answers, I told myself there was no harm in it—if I didn't do it, someone else would.

I wish I could say that a visit from the Lord's messenger set me back on the righteous path, but in the end I just got fed up with my boss and quit. I did listen more closely to my inner donkey after that, though. I took the money I'd earned and started an anticonsumerist magazine. I was broke and happy. My soul felt clean. And it paid off. After six years the magazine got bought. I'd created something of real value.

But the kids I'd interviewed during those years continued to haunt me. Especially a group of Czech teens I'd met one afternoon at a coffeehouse in 1999. As I was asking them pro forma questions about what they thought was cool and what colors they liked and what they feared, I couldn't help but notice their threadbare backpacks and terrifically outdated headphones. American goods were so out of reach, the idea of using this information to try to sell them a Ford Escort in the next five years seemed like a cruel joke.

I read the story of Balaam and Balak through the lens of Robert Alter, the Hebrew language and comparative literature prof at Berkeley who delivers stirring sermons at our local synagogue. In his translation of the five books of Moses, Alter writes that chapter 22 is all about sight and vision. Balaam may be a seer, but at a decisive moment, his sight is obstructed by a sclerotic artery of greed. He sells out, and it nearly kills him.

The lesson? Being a true seer, not just a two-buck huckster, means listening to your inner donkey. It might just save your ass.

ולפני אלעזר הכהן יעמד ושאל לו במשפט האורים לפני יהוה
על פיו יצאו ועל פיו יבאו הוא וכל בני ישראל אתו וכל העדה:

"Let the Lord, Source of the breath of all flesh, appoint someone over the
community who shall go out before them and come in before them,
and who shall take them out and bring them in, so that the Lord's community
may not be like sheep that have no shepherd." —Numbers 27:21

PINHAS (*"Pinhas"*)
NUMBERS 25:10–30:1

CENSUS III: **GOD IS DELIGHTED WITH** Pinhas' act of loyalty and vows to attack the Midianites for the role they played in persuading the Israelites to act immorally and worship their god. To prepare, God commands Moses and Eleazar to perform a new census, counting every Israelite aged twenty and up who is able to bear arms. The total number comes to 601,730 plus 23,000 Levite males aged one month and older. The Lord instructs Moses to apportion shares of Canaan accordingly.

SISTERHOOD IS POWERFUL

The five daughters of Zelophehad stand before Moses and explain their plight. Since their father has died in the wilderness without leaving a male heir, the women request his landholding. Moses consults God, who determines that the claim is just. From then on, if a man dies without leaving a son, his property rights can be assigned to his daughters, brothers, or, failing that, nearest relatives.

A SUCCESSION PLAN

The Lord tells Moses to scale the heights of Mount Abarim, savor the land God has given the Israelites from afar, and then prepare for his death in the same style as Aaron. Moses begins to ponder which man has the leadership ability to replace him and prevent the Israelites from becoming a sheep without a shepherd. God suggests Joshua and tells Moses to single him out to begin the succession plan.

Moses announces the change by laying his hands on Joshua before the entire community.

The Lord then details the appropriate presentation of offerings due at different times—a complex array of rams, goats, bulls, and lambs, presented as burnt offerings, meal offerings, libations, and offerings of well-being.

LARRY SMITH

HYBRID VIGOR

Lou Smith

Larry Smith

The Last of the Jewish Smiths?

Lou Smith looked down from above—the modest eight-to-twelve-inch perch afforded by his La-Z-Boy chair, with the permanent stains from where the back of his head regularly met the soft brown leather—and surveyed all before him. His gaze commanded respect. He appraised his small kingdom:

- his eldest child, Saralee;
- his youngest child, Susan Elizabeth;
- his middle child, Laurence David, the last male Smith in the line and keeper of the Smith family name.

He reviewed the choices each had made with regard to their faith.

- His eldest experienced panic as her bat mitzvah prep commenced. At once sensing her trepidation and seeing an opening for an item on his own agenda, Lou Smith, lifetime litigator, offered her two choices: (a) your big day as planned; (b) reallocate those funds to redo the family basement. She chose the latter. Years later it was with a certain degree of irony, not to mention snickering from her siblings, that after falling in love with a tall Catholic man, she rediscovered her religion. Her husband, Dave, was one of ten siblings, and out of duty/desire attended church each Sunday with his mother. In a last-minute deal brokered by Saralee that even Lou Smith had to admit was pretty genius, Dave agreed to raise the kids Jewish, so long as he could get a dog.

- His youngest similarly came down with massive stage fright as her own bat mitzvah approached. Lou was known for many personality traits: He was an obsessive-compulsive neat freak, a fanatical Philly sports fan, a lover of French pastry—but above all, a man with a sense of fair play. He let his youngest know that he wished her to have her bat mitzvah as planned. But, he noted by way of another option, the deposit on the banquet room was refundable, and those monies might be moved into a trip to Israel, where Susie would be encouraged to have a quick and speedy bat mitzvah. And would it kill us to stop in Paris for a couple of days on the way over? Susie Smith chose door number two. Years later, she met and fell in love with a Mormon. Sure, Michael had left the church. But still. As discussions of matrimony began, she suddenly started roasting chickens on Shabbat. Shortly thereafter she demanded and received Jewish children.
- His middle child—his son, his only son—offered an easier case, at least on paper. He dutifully finished Hebrew school and became a bar mitzvah (theme: baseball) and dated each and every one of the attractive Jewish girls from among the dozen or so Jewish families found in his small, suburban, wasp-y hometown. So it was surprising that he would fall in love with an Episcopalian lesbian, one willing to abandon her taste for the opposite sex but not her faith. As his wife did not feel the need to procreate, the Jewish question was largely avoided.

I am that middle child. The only son. The last of the Jewish Smiths.

The first Smith was Morris Smith, my grandfather, known to one and all as Smitty. Smitty died with most of his hair after an excellent run that began in 1911 in a small suburb of Minsk and ended ninety-one years later in a small suburb of Philadelphia. Upon his arrival at Ellis Island, his family name was changed to "Smith" from "Kuznets," a loose translation of "blacksmith," an irony not lost on the generations of Smith family men more comfortable at a racetrack than in a metal shop. His name would end with me, his only grandson. "It's up to you," the first Smith said wistfully at my older sister's wedding.

The woman I would eventually wed did not want children. She was very stubborn and very beautiful, a combination that means you'll rarely change her mind and that the risks of even trying are formidable. If you were to bet on our procreation, you'd probably bet against me. But that would also be a bet against my faith: the resourceful, stubborn, steely DNA that got my people out of Egypt, my grandfather out of Russia, and me to marry my heretofore elusive bride. "You finally broke her down," my astonished friend Tim said to us upon telling him we were expecting a half-Jewish baby. At this point, even Lou Smith would agree that attempting to negotiate a religious preference was foolhardy.

And so it is that the Smith family name continues. Two years into our son's life, we're raising him both Jewish and Episcopalian. This year we managed to light the world's ugliest menorah (theme: sports candleholders) a couple of nights, and placed a star with six points atop our Christmas tree. Our boy will be exposed to both our faiths, without a lot of fanfare and an unspoken agreement to keep lobbying for saviors or chosen people to a minimum.

Today, when Lou looks down at his grandchildren, he sees six mixed-faith mutts, each and every one of them stronger, smarter, and more gorgeous than his parents or grandparents. There's a term for what my father now sees before him: hybrid vigor. It's a phrase usually applied to plants and animals and describes superior qualities that come from genetic crossbreeding. Purebred dogs, for example, often have more health problems and die younger than mixed breeds. And Russian Jews who marry Russian Jews are more likely to get Gaucher's disease, as my own family can attest. My older sister's first son is handsome, a math genius, and a baseball star. The purebred golden retriever her husband received in the deal was sweet . . . and dumb.

When Lou Smith looks at my boy, his youngest grandson, the last Smith in the line, he sees my cheeks, my wife's fair skin, a big, funny mouth, and the most beautiful tangle of blond curly hair imaginable. Is my hybrid-vigor boy a superior breed? Who knows, but he sure looks good to me. With each interfaith union, my father has mellowed or maybe just become resigned; either way, from that La-Z-Boy our family's Grand Poo-Bah looks quite pleased these days. The Smith family name continues. It does so without the bloodshed of Pinhas' day, or the eye rolling of mine. Will there be Jewish Smiths down the line? Only one person can say.

אִישׁ כִּי יִדֹּר נֶדֶר לַיהוָה אוֹ הִשָּׁבַע שְׁבֻעָה לֶאְסֹר
אִסָּר עַל נַפְשׁוֹ לֹא יַחֵל דְּבָרוֹ כְּכָל הַיֹּצֵא מִפִּיו יַעֲשֶׂה:

"If a man makes a vow to the Lord or takes an oath imposing
an obligation on himself, he shall not break his pledge; he must
carry out all that has crossed his lips."—Numbers 30:3

MATTOT ("*Tribes*")
NUMBERS 30:2–32:42

A VOW IS A VOW, EXCEPT WHEN IT IS NOT. Moses gathers the tribal heads and explains the laws of "vows" or legal commitments to them. If a man makes a vow to the Lord, it has to be fulfilled, but the rules are more complex for women, depending on their marital status and age.

If a young woman assumes a vow while she is still living with her parents, it will stand only if her father authorizes it.

A divorcée or widow's vow is considered binding, but a married woman needs her husband's authorization if the vow is to stand. If he waits longer than a day to make his decision, he will assume her guilt if the vow goes unfulfilled.

CRUSHING MIDIANITES

God orders Moses to take vengeance on the Midianites, reminding him that this military campaign will be the last act before his death. Moses calls up a thousand men from each of the twelve tribes. Pinhas is appointed as the priest for the operation, overseeing the choreography of the all-important trumpet blasts. With the Lord on their side, the Israelites slay every male foe, including the kings of Midian: Evi, Rekem, Zur, Hur, and Reba. Balaam is also put to the sword, yet the Israelites do not suffer a single casualty.

The Midianite women and children are taken captive; beasts, herds, and possessions are seized. Their towns and camps are burned to the ground.

BOOTY-LICIOUS

When the generals present the booty and slaves to Moses, he berates them for sparing the women, as they are the ones who have tempted so many of his men back in camp. He orders all of them, except for the virgins, to be put to death. Meanwhile, Eleazar, the priest, oversees the purification process for the soldiers, as many have understandably been in contact with corpses.

God tells Moses to oversee the division of booty with Eleazar, suggesting they make a careful inventory before dividing it equally among the soldiers and the rest of the community. Each man is instructed to rededicate a portion of his booty (including 675,000 sheep and 32,000 virgins) to the Lord.

COW COUNTRY

The chieftains of Reuben and Gad approach Moses with a proposition.

The fertile region that has just been conquered is perfect cow country. Because both tribes are cattle-rich, they want permission to settle down and exploit it without moving into the land God has promised.

Moses is initially lukewarm to the idea: He is reminded of the scouts who angered God by turning the people away from the Lord's master plan. He worries that the tribes of Reuben and Gad will become a distraction to the rest of the community as they continue their journey; he asks the other chieftains whether they think it would be fair if the two tribes detached themselves from the national mission.

But the leaders of Gad and Reuben counter by offering to act as shock troops to protect the Israelite vanguard, insisting that the military role will be their priority. Moses agrees to the idea—if the two tribes will first cross the Jordan with the Israelites to protect their rear and then take possession of the land only once the fight is over.

The Gadites and the Reubenites agree to settle their wives, children, and flocks east of the Jordan while their men proceed with Moses and the rest of the Israelite army.

GABE DELAHAYE

I wish you an easy fast. Right? Right.

  God takes promises very seriously, no duh, in a way that is totally respectable but also makes Him seem like the kind of guy who, if He was your roommate, would put up a chore wheel on the very first day, color-coded so everyone knew who was responsible for taking out the trash or cleaning up the living room that week. You wouldn't even have your boxes unpacked and already He would be calling a house meeting, complaining that someone ate the low-fat coffee-flavored yogurt in the fridge that was clearly marked "G-d." He has a point. Other people would come over to watch a movie or for a dinner party and compliment you on how nice and neat the apartment was, and you'd have to admit that it was all God's doing, and He would emerge from the kitchen with a frilly, old-fashioned apron tied over His oxford shirt and slap your knuckles with a wooden spoon slicked with red sauce because you were hogging too many curried-chicken endive boats and weren't leaving enough for the guests. It's not always easy, but He's the one who found the apartment in the first place, so you really only have a place to live because of Him. It's hard to complain too much. But you find a way.

  The one exception God makes is virgins. They're allowed to break their promises to Him. Hahaha. That is just classic God. Dude loves virgins! But then again, who doesn't?! He also says that married women are allowed to break their vows to Him if they made them before they were married and their husband says okay. It's all very '90s. Everyone else is stuck, though.

  So God tells Moses (who used to live here but had to move out after he broke his lease. This is a good metaphor, let's just keep doing this metaphor forever) that he's going into a battle where he will for sure die and there are no two buts about it. But? No. No buts! And you know what Moses does? Runs right up in there! High knees even! That is the depth to which God (and Moses, I guess) takes promises seriously. Even in the face of certain death, your vows must be upheld. Well, fair enough! The truth is, it's a pretty apt metaphor for just about everything that we do, whether we believe in Him or not. Not to get all college-sophomore-single-credit-survey-course-in-existentialism on anyone, but whether you believe in an all-powerful creator who sits on a throne made of clouds and worries over who is going to get cancer and who is going to get the latest iPhone, or you believe that the universe is a Godless farce of absolute absurdity with zero rules or consequences, the result is 100 percent the same. SPOILER ALERT: We die in the end. Life itself is a fight from which we will not, not a one of us, return. The singular promise we have all inherently made to the world is that we will disappear one day. And it's the one promise that we will for sure keep. But? No.

So get in there. Thrash around a little bit. Get those knees up. And if you say you're going to do something, you better damn well do it. You promised, and besides, not doing it won't save you. Nothing will.

אלה מסעי בני ישראל אשר יצאו מארץ מצרים לצבאתם ביד משה ואהרן:

"These were the marches of the Israelites who started out from the land of Egypt, troop by troop, in the charge of Moses and Aaron." —Numbers 33:1

MASEI (*"Journeys"*)
NUMBERS 33:1–36:13

THE INVASION IS PLANNED: **THE ISRAELITES'** journeys are faithfully recorded after they follow God out of Rameses, and then in the grasslands of Moab, near Jericho, the Lord provides Moses with the military strategy to dispossess the inhabitants of Canaan. The Israelites are under orders to destroy all idols, demolish temples, and settle the land, sharing it among themselves in the way God apportioned. Joshua and Eleazar will oversee that process. God warns Moses to show no mercy to the Midianites, to prevent them from becoming thorns in the Israelites' sides.

CITIES OF REFUGE
The Levites are assigned forty-eight towns, six of which are to be known as "Cities of Refuge," where a man who has unintentionally killed another can escape those seeking vengeance. The man can then wait to stand trial and benefit from the application of justice. God explains the difference between manslaughter and murder. Someone who kills another with an iron bar, stone, or wooden tool is a murderer who can be put to death by the victim's avenger. The avenger can also kill the

offender if he or she ever steps outside the City of Refuge.

Rules of evidence are detailed. More than one witness must provide testimony in a murder case. Convicted murderers cannot pay ransoms to save their lives. They have to suffer the death penalty. Bloodshed pollutes the land, and only the blood of the murderer can compensate for that.

THE DAUGHTERS OF ZELOPHEHAD, ROUND II

Members of the Daughters of Zelophehad's tribe approach Moses for a clarification of the law. The daughters have successfully inherited their father's land, but the tribe is worried they will lose the land to another tribe if the daughters marry, as all of their possessions would automatically be reassigned to their husbands. The Lord solves the problem neatly by decreeing that the daughters can marry only within their own tribe. The daughters follow the law, marrying their cousins.

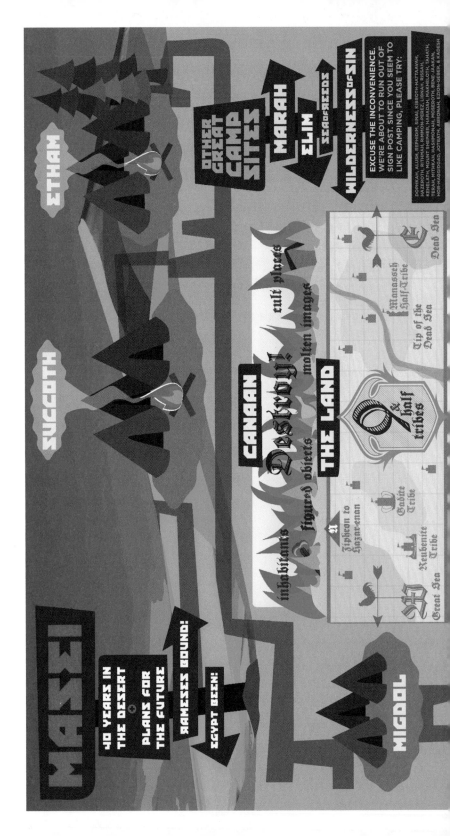

REBECCA BORTMAN

THE DREAM TEAM

ELEAZAR **1**
JOSHUA **2**
CALEB **3**
SAMUEL **4**
ELIDAD **5**
BUKKI **6**
HANIEL **7**
KEMUEL **8**
ELIZAPHAN **9**
PALTIEL **10**
AHIHUD **11**
PEDAHEL **12**

THE LEVITES

LEVITES ♥ TOWNS!

LEVITES ♥ CULTURE!

GIVE LEVITES TOWNS!

THEY'LL MAKE CULTURE!

MANSLAYERS

IS IT A MISHAP OR MURDER?

ROCKS
WOOD TOOLS
IRONS
BLOOD AVENGERS
MISTAKES
MISHAP
MURDER

POLLUTION

Keep Canaan beautiful!

MAN! GREAT! **CAMPING**

ZALMONAH

PUNON

OBOTH

IYE-ABARIM

ALSO: DIBON-GAD, ALMON-DIBLATHAIM, + ABARIM TOO!

▲ **STEPPES**•**MOAB**

AT THE JORDAN NEAR JERICHO

MT. **HOR**

R.I.P. AARON
123 YRS YOUNG

DAUGHTERS OF ZELOPHEHAD ASK:
How do we keep our land? All we've got are daughters?

LAND-KEEPING PRO TIP:
Marry anyone you want as long as he's your uncle!

PART FIVE

DEUTER

ONOMY

WITH HIS DEATH APPROACHING, Moses uses the time he has left to preach, beg, suggest, threaten, urge, and pray that the Israelites keep the covenant. Having been refused entry to the promised land, the aging Israelite relives the adventures of the wilderness experiences, then states and restates the blessings and curses that await his people once he is no more.

The flawed leader, born with a speech impediment, has become an orator, and although many men would seek to burnish their own legend, Moses appears almost maniacally focused on the lethal threat posed by idols. Upon handing the mantle of leadership over to Joshua, he ascends the mountain and views the promised land from a distance, knowing he will never enter it.

JESSE AARON COHEN
D'VARIM (*"Words"*) Deuteronomy 1:1–3:22

ARIEL KAMINER
VA-ETHANNAN (*"And I pleaded"*) Deuteronomy 3:23–7:11

CHARLES LONDON
EIKEV (*"If you follow"*) Deuteronomy 7:12–11:25

SAMANTHA SHAPIRO
RE'EH (*"See"*) Deuteronomy 11:26–16:17

DAVID KATZNELSON
SHOF'TIM (*"Judges"*) Deuteronomy 16:18–21:9

DAVY ROTHBART
KI TETZEI (*"When you go"*) Deuteronomy 21:10–25:19

ANONYMOUS
KI TAVO (*"When you enter"*) Deuteronomy 26:1–29:8

ELI ATTIE
NITZAVIM (*"Ones standing"*) Deuteronomy 29:9–30:20

GILLIAN LAUB
VA-YE'LEKH (*"Then he went out"*) Deuteronomy 31:1–30

RICK MEYEROWITZ
HA'AZINU (*"Listen"*) Deuteronomy 32:1–52

ROGER BENNETT
VEZOT HABERAKHAH (*"And this is the blessing"*)
Deuteronomy 33:1–34:12

"See, I place the land at your disposal. Go, take possession of the land
that the Lord swore to your fathers, Abraham, Isaac, and Jacob,
to assign to them and to their heirs after them." —Deuteronomy 1:8

D'VARIM (*"Words"*)

DEUTERONOMY 1:1–3:22

OSES REVIEWS HIS FORTY YEARS OF leadership: Aware that his death is imminent, Moses reviews the forty years of wandering he has overseen. He reminds the Israelites of the journeys they have taken and the laws they have received on the way to fulfilling God's promise to Abraham, Isaac, and Jacob by entering Canaan.

Moses remembers the time he told the Israelites they would become as numerous as the stars in the sky and reminds them of the day he admitted he could no longer stand their bickering on his own. He reviews the governance structures he has created, engaging wise men, chieftains, and magistrates.

He then reminisces about the journeys they have undertaken together, retelling the story of the twelve spies, which resulted in God decreeing that the generation who escaped Egypt would die in the desert.

The Israelites' military campaigns are revisited, beginning with failure in the Amorite hill country when the Israelites attacked against the Lord's advice and were defeated. The Lord advises Moses to ask the Ammonite kings for safe passage, as their lands have been set aside for Lot's descendants. Moses recounts the Israelites' victorious military campaigns beginning with the attack on the king of Heshbon, a triumph in which every enemy male, female, and child was slaughtered, making future foes fear Israel's name. The defeat of the giant King Og is also revisited, along with the resulting deal struck by the tribes of Reuben and Gad that saw them settle the land.

Finally, Moses recounts the words of advice he has provided his successor, Joshua, telling him to fear no enemies, as the Lord will do battle for him.

JESSE AARON COHEN

AN ARCHIVIST'S SCRAPBOOK:
SELECTIONS FROM THE
YIVO SCRAPBOOK

I started working at the YIVO Institute for Jewish Research straight out of college in 2002. I stayed, working mostly as a photo archivist, for the next ten years (though I had a music career going simultaneously). YIVO was founded in Vilna, Poland, in 1925 as a library, archives, and research institute dedicated to preserving and enriching the history and culture of Yiddish-speaking Eastern European Jews. Despite spending a big portion of my life as a musician—traveling, expanding my personal horizons—I kept returning to YIVO. It was a weird, wonderful, fascinating little corner of the world that I considered my own. Staring at old photographs all day, I felt like I spent half of my time in New York in the twenty-first century and the other half in Poland in the 1920s. One of the principles that YIVO was founded on is *doikayt* or "hereness," which means, simply, that the diaspora is the Jewish homeland. Rather than looking for a new home, advocates of *doikayt* worked to legitimize Jewish culture and improve the lives of Jews in the countries in which they had lived their entire lives.

YOUTH BOXING at the Educational Alliance. Lower East Side, New York City, early 1950s. The Educational Alliance was, and still is, an important community center for the immigrant generation on the Lower East Side and their children. This photo comes from a series of photos of kids boxing. I like the mix of boredom and fascination among the people in attendance, but the thing I relate to most is the terrified-looking skinny kid *desperately* trying his best.

A COPY of this photograph of an anonymous girl sitting on a bench, some-where in Europe before World War II, was on my desk for most of the ten years I worked at YIVO. Any information about who she was or why her photograph ended up in our collection has been lost, but I do know that the photo is part of one of the original collections at YIVO from Vilna. There are innumerable photos with the same story, but this has always been my favorite. When you look at one of the photos—"orphaned works," they're called—you inevitably fill in the blanks for yourself. Who was she? What happened to her? It's actually a creative process. They say that a picture is worth a thousand words, and most of the time, those words are your own.

THIS PHOTOGRAPH comes from a large collection that historian and YIVO founder Elias Tcherikover amassed to document the pogroms—mob attacks—that followed the Russian Civil War. Many of these photographs were presented as evidence in the Paris trial of the Jewish anarchist assassin Sholom Shwartzbard. The official caption that we have at YIVO for this photo reads, "Chernobyl, 1919: Studio portrait of a member of Struk's rebel band, which carried out pogroms, wearing a fur hat, a holster, and a saber across his chest; pointing a pistol and sitting on a hobbyhorse."

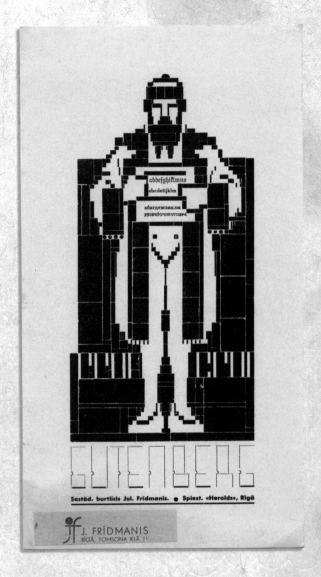

abbefghiklmno
abcdetijklm

абвгдежзиклм
уроальмолефонкар

GUTENBERG

Sastäd. burtlicis Jul. Fridmanis. ● Spiest. «Herolds», Rīgā

ʃf J. FRĪDMANIS
RĪGĀ, TOMSONA IELĀ 11

THIS IS A PIECE of art made entirely out of typographical materials by a man named Julius Fridmanis in Riga, Latvia, in the 1930s. I don't believe he was ever a well-known person anywhere, but I found an amazing folder full of mementos from the printing press that he ran with his father, Abraham, and all the experimental typographical work they did on the side, in which they took an enormous amount of pride. I think it is very similar to early examples of the graphic design art known as ASCII.

אַ שמועס

THIS PHOTOGRAPH, with the caption "A Discussion," is from a 1930s album documenting the activities of the communally run Jewish Home for the Aged in Vilna, at 17 Portowa Street.

THIS PACKAGE of Maseltov Filled Fish Slices speaks for itself.

ROSE PESOTTA was an anarchist, feminist, and prominent organizer for the International Ladies' Garment Workers' Union. This telegram, sent to her in Montreal in 1936, relays a common motif throughout Jewish history.

NAI JUDA

★ **RECRUITING**

The NAI JUDA movement is now signing up ablebodied young men and women willing to join a

JEWISH ARMY

of SOLDIER-SETTLERS for service in a new Independent Jewish State within the American Hemisphere.

 Service will include opening up a large unoccupied territory to settlement and civilization, police and border patrol duty, farming, construction, roadbuilding. Volunteers who pass physical fitness requirements will receive free training in agriculture, engineering, transportation, aviation, seamanship and military defense. In the new Jewish State each soldier-settler will be given a house and four acres of land for life in accordance with the NAI JUDA program.

Further information and application forms may be obtained in person or by mail from Joseph Otmar Hefter, National Leader - 145 East 34th Street, New York, N. Y.

NAI JUDA RECRUITMENT FLYER, 1930S. This artifact is a bit of a mystery. Nai Juda was apparently an ill-fated and barely existent utopian non-Zionist Jewish territorialist movement created by Joseph Otmar Hefter. It seems that this recruitment flyer and an anthem are about as far as he got in pursuing his dream. YIVO actually has very little on the subject, and this flyer is from a collection at YIVO of material that the Nazis collected in their quest to understand the "Jewish Question." This collection somehow made its way from Frankfurt to New York after the war.

THESE TWO BUSINESS CARDS were among some possessions donated to YIVO during the time when I worked there. The "bullshitter" one is obviously really funny, but I have to admit that I don't fully get the "All Schmucks Pick 3" card, although I know it's funny, too. I'm not sure who Cy Constantine is or was or how his card ended up in this collection, but I once Googled him and found an article from 1989 about an adman named Cy Constantine from Northeast Philadelphia who also performed magic on the weekends for sick children. The article is about how his life changed when his son was the victim of a devastating hit-and-run accident that left him partially paralyzed and in a wheelchair. I believe it's the same man who handed these cards out, but I have no way of knowing that for sure.

MY CARD SIR:

I AM SOMEWHAT OF A BULLSHITTER MYSELF BUT OCCASIONALLY I LIKE TO LISTEN TO A

Professional

PLEASE CARRY ON

Pick A Number

1 2 3 4

... All Schmucks Pick 3

Compliments CY CONSTANTINE
(215) 725-5983

"Let me, I pray, cross over and see the good land on the other side of the Jordan, that good hill country, and the Lebanon. But the Lord was wrathful with me on your account and would not listen to me. The Lord said to me, 'Enough! Never speak to Me of this matter again!'" —Deuteronomy 3:25–26

VA-ETHANNAN (*"And I pleaded"*)
DEUTERONOMY 3:23–7:11

MOSES PLEADS WITH THE LORD TO BE allowed to cross into the promised land, but the Lord furiously denies his request and commands Moses to climb Mount Pisgah, survey the region from a distance, and prepare Joshua to be his successor.

Moses then urges the Israelites to follow the entirety of God's commandments, reminding them of the cruel deaths suffered in the past by those tempted to worship the Moabite idol Baal-peor. Fidelity to the legal system will ensure that the Israelites become renowned as a wise and discerning people to their neighbors in the region.

Moses reminds the Israelites of their experience at the foot of Mount Sinai when the Lord spoke to them amid the flames and articulated the commandments on two stone tablets. Although they had heard God's voice only at Sinai, Moses begs them to resist the urge to craft idols of the Lord's image. Such an act will cause God to destroy them and scatter survivors across the earth.

The upside of the covenant is briefly restated: God will never desert the Israelites or let them perish. Moses reminds the people of their exalted status. Only they have heard God speak in a fire and survived. No other people have been led into war by the Lord, or freed from Egypt as they have.

I AM THE LAW

God's laws are recounted so the Israelites know to study and observe them faithfully. Moses reminds the community that the covenant is not a relic of history, but something that binds every one of them in the present. He then restates the Ten Commandments, conjuring the fearsome specter of the scene at Sinai to ensure that the Israelites and their children always maintain them.

THE SHEMA

The Israelites are exhorted to love the Lord with all their heart, soul, and might; to remember the laws and teach them to their children; and to recite the laws continually, bind them on their hands and foreheads, and inscribe them on their doorposts. They should never forget the Lord who freed them from Egypt and should worship no other gods, unless they want to be wiped off the face of the earth. Indeed, they are to tell the stories of the Exodus and Sinai to their children so they develop a keen appreciation of the commandments' origins.

APPETITE FOR DESTRUCTION

The Israelites are informed that once they enter the land, they will encounter seven nations who greatly outnumber them—the Hittites, Girgashites, Amorites, Canaanites, Perizzites, Hivites, and Jebusites. God will deliver victory, but the Israelites must destroy their enemies and smash their temples. Any form of intermarriage is strictly forbidden, as it is a gateway step toward idolatry, which will ultimately force God to obliterate them all.

Finally, Moses reinforces an evident truth: God sees the Israelites as a sacred people. Out of all the nations on earth, they have been chosen as the Lord's treasures. The decision was made not on the basis of size—the Israelites are one of the smallest tribes—but on account of the covenant.

ARIEL KAMINER

That's it?" he asked, when Moses finished speaking. From a rocky outcropping toward the back of the crowd, he hadn't been able to quite hear the whole speech. He had missed some of the interminable dos and don'ts. But the part about Moses' fate had come through loud and clear. "That's what Moses gets for the forty years in the desert with God's chosen pains in the ass? For forty years of hassle?"

"For forty years of manna," his wife said with a slight shudder. Yes, the manna was a miracle. But try eating the same damn miracle for four decades. "Man, I never thought I'd miss those matzohs we made the night we first fled."

"But you never heard Moses complain. He was always, *What's for dinner tonight? Ooh, manna? I love manna!*"

"Actually, I find that routine a bit tiresome," she said.

"Me, too. Him, too, I bet! But what's his reward? 'Thanks for your efforts on behalf of the tribes of Israel. Request to enter promised land denied.'"

"Was he working on our behalf? Or God's? To be honest, I was never entirely sure," she replied. "And I got the feeling he wasn't always that sure who he was working for either. Or why."

Another round of hosannahs rose up from the crowd. *It's always hosannahs with them,* he thought. Except at the first sound of trouble. Then they start crying that they were better off with Pharaoh.

"I dunno," he said. "His sandals got good and wet before the waters parted, and the guy didn't look down once. Just kept marching into the sea like that broad sandy path had been there all along. I don't think you can do that if you're less than a hundred percent."

"No one's really that confident," she said with a wave of her hand, "not even when you've got the Lord whispering in your ear. *Especially* when you've got the Lord whispering in your ear."

"Still," he said. "Seems like a hell of a way to thank him. He never gets to see the promised land."

"He did see it," she reminded him. "That one time, from the top of Mount Pisgah."

"I forgot." He thought for a moment. "So he got to see it but not enter it. That seems almost worse, somehow."

"Maybe it was supposed to be a consolation prize."

"Doesn't seem very consoling to me," he said. "Seems kind of sadistic. But think about it—he knew he'd never make it across the finish line, but he stuck around anyway, for all that thankless go-betweening."

"Hey, God, could you move the awesome fire just a bit farther from the tent?" she said. She could still crack him up with a good Moses impression. *"You're singeing the chosen people's hair. Also, maybe could You go easy with the smiting? Thanks."*

"Seriously. He didn't let on for a minute, just kept right on selling the word of God. Even now, after giving this humiliating speech, he's right back with the commandments. That is some unbelievable devotion." They were both silent for a while. Finally he asked, "So, what now?"

The sleeping bundle strapped to her back squirmed a bit, then nestled back down again. She sighed. Having a baby when she was eighty-nine didn't feel like it had when she was seventeen, that's for sure. "Let's get back to camp. It's almost dark."

"Great. I'm starved," he said. "What's for dinner tonight?"

"Very funny," she said.

"And teach them to your children—reciting them when you stay at home and when you are away, when you lie down and when you get up."—Deuteronomy 11:19

EIKEV (*"If you follow"*)
DEUTERONOMY 7:12–11:25

THE OBEDIENCE IMPERATIVE: MOSES restates the rewards that await those who maintain the covenant. The Lord will favor the Israelites and ensure they are fertile, healthy, and agriculturally prosperous. All of their enemies will be destroyed without pity or fear. Their defeat will be thoughtfully paced so that wild beasts do

not multiply and fill the sudden absence of humans, but the Lord will make sure they are ultimately wiped out so the Israelites can burn their idols.

In return, the Israelites are to keep the Lord's laws and remember their long wilderness journey, when God tested them and taught them there is more to life than eating bread alone. Once they enter the resource-rich land, they are instructed to give thanks to the Lord for the vines, figs, wheat, and precious metals they will mine. Surrounded by riches, they must remember the deprivation of the desert experience so they do not take everything for granted. To do so would be to forget God, a crime for which they would perish.

Moses then warns the Israelites that they should prepare to be outnumbered by physically stronger foes who fight behind sky-high walls, yet they should fear no one, as God will destroy their enemies, punishing them for their wicked ways.

Moses lingers on the times in which the Israelites forgot the Lord—most egregiously during the golden calf incident—reminding the community just how close they came to being destroyed by God and reliving the role he played to calm the Creator's wrath.

Moses mentions God's gift of the Ten Commandments and the ark, and how they will remind the Israelites to revere the Lord and remember the

Creator's role in freeing them from slavery. If they respect God, they will be provided with grain, wine, and oil from the land. But if they disobey the Lord, the land will dry up and they will soon perish.

God's instructions to the Israelites are repeated. Moses tells the community to bind these words on their hands, wear them as symbols on their foreheads, etch them on their doorposts, and teach them to their children. Should they do so, they will retain the land they were promised, and all of their enemies will live in fear.

CHARLES LONDON

The story is an old one, but not this version. This is the story of the children of South Sudan, tens of thousands of kids who crossed the border from Sudan to Ethiopia, then back to Sudan, then into Kenya, boys and girls of all ages lost, sick, dying. They became refugees; they lived on the mercy of international NGOs and charities and the passing whims of passing journalists. They learned a word, which they repeated again and again, over the years. The word sustained them: *repatriation*. They all wanted to go to the promised land, America.

I came along one summer, a twenty-two-year-old journalist, new to the desert. I was always thirsty. I was thirsty for water and for stories, and I drank them both greedily during sweltering interviews. The boys told me stories about being bombed by the government forces of Sudan and of being attacked by lions. The girls told me the same stories, and also told me of drownings and abductions, of parents lost, siblings lost, friends lost. All lost. They alluded to rapes. I balked at the plural. The girls got more specific, each rape a story, each story told in the hope it would be remembered and repeated and eventually, that it would unlock the doors to America. Repatriation. Their stories had national aspirations.

"I tell the other [girls]," Charity, a lanky teenage orphan, explained to me. "I tell them that no matter how hard it is to tell, they must tell their story. They must keep telling it and telling it and telling it. It is only through people knowing our story that [foreigners] will understand what we have been through and will help us."

She told me her story, as filled with murder, rape, and pillage as any biblical tale of kings and chiefs. The pillars of fire in her stories were, however, man-made.

And that was that. Present-day refugees in the desert learned what had been commanded to the Hebrews in ancient times, in the forty-sixth parashah, *Eikev*, among other places: Tell your story. Tell it *"in order that your days may increase and the days of your children . . . "*

Of course, I did my promised duty to Charity and the other girls like her. I wrote her story down. I told it over and over. I published it.

It worked for some of the girls, and they received word from on high: repatriation. They moved to Pennsylvania and to Michigan and to the Greater Atlanta area. Others did not, and they are living in Kakuma Refugee Camp still, their desert sojourn the only life they know. The duration is not quite forty years, but coming around to half of that.

I left the refugee camp that same summer a decade ago and came back to my own promised land, New York City, taking the stories of these girls and the stories of other refugee children from around the globe, and I published a book and published articles and did well for myself by telling their stories. No wandering in the desert for me. I bought property in Brooklyn; I settled in.

But by what right did I get to live so well while those boys and girls still suffered? I was haughty and covetous. I worked on the Sabbath and I ate shellfish and pork and I gossiped and broke all those desert-decreed commandments from ancient times. I didn't even inscribe said commandments on the doorpost of my house, once I had said house. It can't be because of my righteousness that I live the good life. But it could not be because of their wickedness that these refugee children do not.

At least, not yet. That's the difference between the masses of today's dispossessed and the ancient Anakites and Moabites and Ammonites. All those forgotten-ites never got to tell their stories. There is the logic of *Eikev*. We are instructed to repeat the story of the blessings we have received through no virtue of our own so that we may keep receiving those blessings. Storytelling is the key. Those other tribes whose wickedness incurred the wrath of the Hebrew Lord would no doubt have different stories to tell had they not been so thoroughly written out of history. The privilege of survival is the ability to tell your story. So it was with the Hebrews; so it was with the children of South Sudan. So it will be again, when new peoples rise up and others fall down, and the righteous and the wicked keep trying to claim their own little piece of the desert by telling stories. Not all the stories will survive, but as long as someone is listening, someone else will be stiffnecked enough to keep telling them.

לא תאכלו כל נבלה לגר אשר בשעריך תתננה ואכלה או מכר
לנכרי כי עם קדוש אתה ליהוה אלהיך לא תבשל גדי בחלב אמו:

"You shall not eat anything that has died a natural death; give it to the
stranger in your community to eat, or you may sell it to a foreigner.
For you are a people consecrated to the Lord your God. You shall not
boil a kid in its mother's milk." —Deuteronomy 14:21

RE'EH ("See")

DEUTERONOMY 11:26–16:17

OSES EXPLICITLY SETS THE CHOICE
of blessing or curse before the Israelites. If they
obey the commandments, they will be blessed.
If they fail and worship other gods, they will
be cursed. To that end, the Israelites are instructed to destroy
their enemies' altars and burn down their idols, while offering

their own sacrifices in the way God instructed and adhering to the notions of cleanliness.

The dire threat of worshipping idols is restated. Moses warns that once an Israelite begins to express curiosity about foreign gods, he will soon find himself partaking in immoral behavior and human sacrifice. He also warns against believing in false prophets and dream diviners who might rise up. God's orders are the only ones to be followed. Anyone—even close kin—seeking to lead an Israelite astray should be stoned to death. If a town turns against God, every resident should be killed and the town burned to the ground.

KOSHER RESTATED

As a holy people, the Israelites should not mutilate their bodies or shave the front of their heads. Nor are they to eat anything deemed abhorrent. A list of permitted animals is provided: the ox, the sheep, the goat, the deer, the gazelle, the roebuck, the wild goat, the ibex, the antelope, the mountain sheep—any animal that has cleft hooves and that chews the cud. Camels, the hare, and the daman lack proper hooves, and pigs do not regurgitate the cud so are taboo. Fish can be eaten as long as they have fins and scales. Birds of prey are unclean, as are winged, swarming things. It is also prohibited to boil a kid in its mother's milk.

THE OBLIGATIONS OF HOLY PEOPLE

The Israelites are instructed to set aside a tenth of their harvest every year and to make a pilgrimage to a destination God will name. Every seventh year they are to forgive all debts and release all slaves. They are also to ensure there are no needy or poor members of their community. If a slave does not want to be freed, the master will have to execute a ritual in which the slave's ear is pierced with an awl.

The festivals of Passover, Shavuot, and Sukkot are restated—Passover to commemorate the exodus from Egypt, the agrarian festival of Shavuot, and the booth-dwelling festival of Sukkot, a time of "nothing but joy." All three of the festivals will involve male Israelites traveling to worship with offerings to a place God will determine.

SAMANTHA SHAPIRO

The command issued in this parashah to not-eat (*lo tochlu*) certain foods has had amazing staying power. From juice fasters to political vegans to the gluten-free, the carb-free, Lent observers, halal eaters, hippies avoiding "nightshade" plants, and those swearing off sugar, it is not hard to find people of any faith or no faith who still believe that some form of *lo tochlu*, not-eating, will purify them.

In *Re'eh* Moses restates the basic rules for Jewish not-eating, also known as keeping kosher. We are told not to eat the camel, the griffin vulture, animals with undivided hooves like pigs, and "creeping things" like bugs or eel or calamari. Blood is also a no-no, as is "cooking a kid in its mother's milk."

Those laws alone are a handful but still pretty workable—the logistics of collecting and storing the milk of a mother cow seem difficult, and who wants a burger boiled in milk anyway? But thousands of years of rabbinic interpretation have added layers of complication to Jewish not-eating. For starters, the law against cooking a kid in its mother's milk has been expanded to mean not serving the milk of *any* animal and the meat of *any* animal together (see: cheeseburger) and not eating foods that contain any dairy product until six hours after you have finished eating meat. The rabbis also determined that silverware, dishes, and cookware acquire a status of dairy, meat, or unkosher animals through heat, and that this status is retained and can be further transferred, depending on the porousness of materials. This ruling is what really limits kosher eating. Cooking a ham renders one's stove, pan, utensils, and serving dishes unkosher; those items then have the power to turn something kosher, like a spear of asparagus, into something unkosher.

In my twenties I decided to keep strictly kosher. This meant I couldn't eat any cooked food unless it was prepared in a kosher kitchen or at minimum, a kitchen about which I had a detailed historical record. Switching at this late date from eating pretty much everything to not-eating so much taught me something really important about food. Birthdays are celebrated, jobs won, and boy problems dissected over food. It's not enough to go and not eat; people expect that something material will be shared. The alchemy of transforming a kosher apple into an unkosher apple cake—the heat, the care, and time invested—does not just matter to ancient rabbis, it actually still matters to most everyone. I have interviewed a Saudi prince in the rooftop restaurant at Dubai's Burj Al Arab and a North Korean refugee sleeping on the floor of a suburban condo, and both cared very much, almost as a condition of the interview, that I eat something they laid out for me. When the host at a family event discovered I wasn't partaking of the refreshments, he drove off mid-party to pick up salmon, which he roasted in tin foil (the tin foil shields the salmon from the unkosher oven). The other two kosher cousins and I found ourselves surrounded by relatives demanding that we immediately eat the huge, steaming side of salmon.

The first time I wondered if I could truly keep strictly kosher for the rest of my life was not when faced with turning down one of the more expensive and beautiful meals I'd ever been offered during a work lunch at a trendy restaurant. It was when, one afternoon leaving my parents' Manhattan apartment, I was caught downwind of the vent outside Mariella Pizza. Like a hydraulic dredge, the rush of pizza air lifted submerged memories to the top of my mind: the yellow plastic kiddie furniture my brother and I used to eat the pizza off of, the time I got Kareem Abdul-Jabbar's autograph at a street fair next to a five-foot-wide Mariella Pizza, a snowstorm in sixth grade that stranded me at school and the Mariella sub I requested when I got picked up. It was impossible to imagine that I might really never eat another slice of Mariella.

Not-eating expresses a rejection of some aspect of the world or one's body, and a hope for a change in it. Some see kosher eating and not-eating as a rejection of the non-Jewish world. I haven't experienced it that way. In the not-eating of *kashrut*, I hear an echo of the *lo tochlu* imparted to Adam and Eve. The command not to eat from that seemingly harmless apple tree in the garden of Eden is at least as counterintuitive as the one associated with the ham sandwich. Failure to comply with the first *lo tochlu* is what got us kicked out of Eden into sorrow, labor, and violence. I don't know what was so bad about that apple, or Twinkies for that matter, but I do know that better control over appetites—for vengeance, greed, selfishness—could prevent much suffering.

In *Re'eh*, dietary laws come before the laws about the Sabbatical year. In the Sabbatical year, the Torah tells us, no one should work, the land must rest, slaves should be freed, and all loans should be forgiven. What could run more counter to our impulses than voluntarily giving up everything we have worked for? Perhaps this is why the Torah calls the Sabbatical year the year of "release"—it entails letting go of the idea that you own people or possessions.

To let go of the urge to build up the self demands a radical reconfiguring of appetites. The Torah places the dietary rules before the laws of the Sabbatical year and so provides a daily practice for retraining appetites, an almost hourly negotiation between a base appetite and a spiritual concept. Perhaps from these negotiations, our appetites will emerge no less fierce, but more clearly joined with spiritual hungers for justice, love, and connection.

In keeping kosher, I could not eat so much—the enchiladas sold out of a Coleman cooler on my street, a friend's wedding cake—and I came to better understand what I really wanted from those foods. There are many ways to connect to people and place, but few that go as deep as quickly as eating. In the not-eating, I see that what the rabbis said about food was exactly right: Everything is transferred and absorbed in heat. A pizza vent can unleash a string of memories, shining and dense like pearls.

נביא אקים להם מקרב אחיהם כמוך ונתתי
דברי בפיו ודבר אליהם את כל אשר אצונו:

"I will raise up a prophet for them from among their own people,
like yourself: I will put My words in their mouth and he will
speak to them all that I command him." —Deuteronomy 18:18

SHOF'TIM ("*Judges*")
DEUTERONOMY 16:18–21:9

USTICE, JUSTICE SHALL YOU PURSUE: MOSES continues his final instructions to the Israelites, commanding them to appoint magistrates and officials in every settlement God gives them. The justice system shall be fair and bribe-free.

Israelites should avoid erecting stone pillars or posts by altars in case they lead to idolatry. They are reminded to make sure sacrifices are unblemished and to condemn those who worship idols to death by stoning. Two witnesses are required in such a case, and the witnesses have to be the first to cast the deadly stones.

If any case baffles the community, it shall be presented to the priests, who will make a ruling. Anyone disregarding their decision shall be put to death to maintain the people's faith in the legal system.

The Israelites are given permission to appoint a king, but on a few conditions. First, he cannot be a foreigner. A king is also prohibited from living lavishly: He cannot keep an abundance of horses, marry numerous wives, or amass riches of silver and gold. He must follow God's laws without deviating from them.

SACRED SUSTENANCE

As the Levite class is receiving no land of their own, they are to sustain themselves by eating offerings and are free to choose where to live. However, the priests are to receive the shoulder, cheeks, and stomach of any sacrifice, and the first fruits of the field, as well as the first shearing of the flock.

SOOTHSAYERS WILL HAVE SEEN THIS COMING . . .

Once they enter the land, the Israelites are not to replicate the rituals practiced by the locals—human sacrifice, sooth-saying, or sorcery. Such activities are deemed abhorrent and linked to the Lord's decision to evict the people from the land in the first place.

The Lord will provide a prophet who will rise up and become a Godly mouth-piece. Any self-appointed prophet shall be deemed false and must die.

CITY OF REFUGE, AGAIN

Three cities are to be set aside for those involved in manslaughter so that they can flee their avengers. These cities will be augmented by three more once the Lord enlarges the size of the territory. However, the sanctuary is not to be misused by an enemy who kills another. Such an act warrants the death penalty.

The Israelites are not to move the country's landmarks, nor are they to allow a single witness to condemn the accused, as it can encourage malicious testimony. However, they are not to offer pity and must follow the value of a life for a life, an eye for an eye, a tooth for a tooth, a hand for a hand, a foot for a foot.

THE RULES OF ENGAGEMENT

The Israelites should feel no fear when they take to the battlefield and encounter armies larger than theirs. Before engaging in combat, a priest shall address the troops to remind them how the Lord will march beside them and guarantee victory. Soldiers who have not yet dedicated newly built homes, harvested their vineyards, or married a woman for whom they have paid a dowry shall be granted leave to return home and complete those tasks. Those who are afraid shall also be allowed to stand down. Military commanders will then assume control of the forces.

Before attacking any town, the Israelites should offer to broker peace. If those terms are accepted, their enemies will be permitted to serve as forced labor. If the offer is refused, a siege shall be set, and once the Lord delivers victory, all the males shall be put to the sword and the women and children treated as spoils of war. However, if the town lies within the land the Lord has promised, the townspeople must be killed on account of their previous abhorrent behavior.

During a siege, the Israelites are forbidden from cutting down trees that bear food, though their produce can be savored.

COLD CASE

If a body is found and the case remains unsolved, the elders and magistrates shall measure the distance between the corpse and nearby towns. Those towns will sacrifice a heifer to signify that they are not responsible for the death, and ask God for absolution.

DAVID KATZNELSON

I believe in prophets because I have met one.

I am a music enthusiast. I started young; collecting records before I knew how to read, ushering at rock-and-roll shows, and deejaying on the radio before I could drive. I began working at a major record label at voting age and grew to become one of the youngest vice presidents in the A&R Department, catching the end of the industry's renaissance era.

I learned my craft while working with musicians I revered—from the Flaming Lips and Nick Cave to Shane MacGowan. Although each of these artists was different, they all shared a commonality: the ability to articulate a complex vision of the world rife with challenging and inspiring ideas.

In a way, all my musical appreciation stems from the blues: the Afro-American art form that has bled its way into so much of the music that has come after it and in many ways is the root of everything I hold so dear. Like many late-twentieth-century music enthusiasts, I had learned about the blues through the modern artists I grew up with. The Who and the Rolling Stones covered blues tunes, incorporating song structures and melodic lines into original compositions, resurrecting some of the genre's forgotten legends like Son House or Mississippi John Hurt in the process. In so doing, they rescued these artists from obscurity and brought them to a new public.

My understanding deepened the day producer and friend Jim Dickinson sent me the field recordings his son Luther had made of local Mississippian legend Otha Turner, one of the last purveyors of the fading blues fife tradition. Turner's band, the Rising Star Fife and Drum Band, kept alive a type of music that was the oldest practiced in postcolonial America. It was the only form of blues the slave owners allowed their charges to play, because of its similarity to military marching music.

But the slaves, and the sharecroppers who followed them, reveled in the tradition, infusing it with their own rhythms and stories.

Otha had taken Luther under his wing, embracing the young guitarist as both student and collaborator. The recordings he sent me were unlike anything I had heard before: crazy, repetitive rhythms that swayed and grooved, with the angelic blow of the fife on top, the low pulse of the bass drum on the bottom, and Otha's deep, sultry vocals carried in between. Otha was ninety years of age and had been leading his band for more than fifty years. Yet he had never released his own record. The first time I heard Luther's recordings of the Rising Star Fife and Drum Band, the music weighed so heavily on my ears that I knew I had to travel down in person, meet him, and preserve his work.

A few months later, I ventured down to Mississippi for the first time. It was a cool, dry winter day when I drove into Senatobia, Mississippi. Otha's place was on the outer part of town, down a gravel road that took you through a rural land dotted with double-wide trailers and circles of chairs around fire pits. Black country dogs tried to play fetch with every car that drove by. I met Luther at a crossroad, and we drove on to Otha's house, which the bluesman had built himself on a small piece of land he had farmed since he was a young man.

Luther led me into the main room of the house, which was heated and lit by a wood-burning stove. In the corner sat Otha. The brown and yellow lights of the room were reminiscent of a Rembrandt painting, and when the aged bluesman rose to greet me, this statuesque figure with sharp cheekbones and translucent blue eyes offered me a wiry, firm handshake. He knew I had come because I wanted to release his record. But first, he wanted to have a few words, his way.

He started by talking about the centrality of worship. "Sunday, every Sunday, you need to make sure you went to church," he declared, adding that it was critical that every human be a good community citizen so you could "keep yourself right." And after he was sure I got that message, he pulled a bottle of moonshine out from under his couch, passed it to me, and started telling me about women, about his family, and about his approach to life.

Jim Dickinson would often say that Otha was the "most whole" human I would ever meet . . . a man who lived life on his own terms, battling extreme poverty while crafting a livelihood and building a family of four children, countless grandchildren, and a growing number of great-grandchildren who all lived nearby. His band was comprised of his daughter and his grandkids. His band was his voice, family, and community intertwined.

Since the 1950s, Otha had a tradition of convening a two-day picnic for the local community around Labor Day. By the time I first attended, the event had grown. It felt like the entire region was there, along with people who had flown in from far-flung states and even other countries: a crazy mix of Otha's followers who all shared a sense that the two-day festival was to be a time of pause from a hard, trying existence, a time to celebrate the goodness of being alive. Even as a white Jew from California, I was warmly embraced by the Turner family, who made me fit right in.

The picnic started in the morning with Otha ceremonially killing a goat that would be cooked up for the night's festivities. It would end with a wild party driven by the Fife and Drum Band walking through the crowd, blowing and blasting as the participants clapped and shook. Their message was simple, delivered through Otha's rendition of traditional blues songs, like "Work done got hard, and now she's gone, but I don't worry, I'm sitting on top of the world." Those words, along with the drumming, blasted electricity into the congregated mass. We were all suddenly sitting on top of the world, despite whatever it was that had been trying to hold us down. Amen.

Otha used his music to connect his history, his family's story, the history of a people, a history that arguably goes back to his African roots. Jim Dickinson captured this when he wrote the record's liner notes: "Otha is a human treasure merging life and art into a single testimony." And in his signature number, "Shimmy She Wobble," an instrumental, no words were needed to convey the deep, rich tradition he needed to share. It is a dark, driving anthem, a work song—the sound of prophecy—and often at the picnic, he would play it all night long.

I left Senatobia and released Otha's debut record. Reflecting on the picnic, it was titled *Everybody Hollerin' Goat*, a tip of the cap to those great goat sandwiches that were the symbol of the picnic.

The hardest part of being a record man is waiting for the first responses to a newly released disc . . . all the more so with Otha, as I felt a deeply personal responsibility to bring his message and sound to the world. Yet this release was initially received with confused questioning. The Fife and Drum material did not seem like any other blues record. It was hard for critics to classify.

Then a *Rolling Stone* review was able to locate its true place as an essential document of America's folk-music heritage, ultimately hailing the disc as one of the five best blues records of the decade. Slowly, the release became seen as a classic. Martin Scorsese featured it in his PBS-produced miniseries on the blues. Otha's message had been amplified, working its way into the fabric of America's musical culture and out into the world.

Otha passed away in 2003. He had battled pneumonia early that year. Aware that his time was ending, he had spent his days meeting with everyone he knew to say good-bye. I last saw him a few months before his death, when I went down to visit him and Bernice, his daughter and bandmate, who was fighting cancer. As I left her home, I was greeted by the entire Turner family, Otha's granddaughter Sharde among them, the woman who had elected to carry on the tradition of the Fife blower since she was a small child.

Up until Otha's final days he was the patriarch of his family, sitting on top of his world. Indeed, he ultimately died on the same day as Bernice.

Of Otha's favorite sayings, one has always stayed with me—a phrase he would always offer to his family and friends when they were faced with a difficult life decision: "Don't nothing make a fail but a try!" Its meaning was clear to me: Trying to do something is not enough. You simply must do it. Given the obstacles we are faced with in life, the only way to meet them is head-on. Happiness, community, and justice must be pursued with conviction and determination. Expecting them simply to be given to us is like walking through the desert, hoping for an oasis that might never come.

I have tried to heed Otha's words and teach them to my children. To remain connected I bought a small house with an old barn down in the promised land of Mississippi not too far away, ironically, from a town named Egypt. The place is meant to be an anchor for my kids so they can connect to the people, the culture, and its way of thinking. And although Otha is no longer with us, the beauty in his recordings will outlive us all, ensuring that his prophetic voice will always be heard.

"A woman must not put on man's apparel, nor shall a
man wear woman's clothing; for whoever does these things is
abhorrent to the Lord your God." —Deuteronomy 22:5

KI TETZEI (*"When you go"*)
DEUTERONOMY 21:10–25:19

THE BEAUTIFUL CAPTIVE: **IN THE WAKE OF** a military conquest, if an Israelite encounters a beautiful female captive, he is permitted to marry her. The woman must first be brought home, cleaned up, and allowed to spend a month mourning the loss of her own parents. Marriage can then ensue. If the Israelite wishes to dispose of the relationship, the woman must be released outright. She cannot be turned into a slave.

If a man has two wives, loves only one, yet produces sons with both, the birth order still matters when it comes to inheritance. The man is prohibited from treating the younger as if he were the firstborn just because he loves his mother more. The law of birthright takes precedence.

A defiant son who will not listen to his parents shall be taken before the town elders in public, disowned, and stoned to death.

If a guilty man is given the death penalty and impaled on a stake, his corpse should not be left out overnight, as it is an affront to God.

ANIMAL FARM
Stray animals shall be returned to their

owners. If the owner is unknown or lives far away, the animal should be cared for until it is claimed. The same rule applies to any object or possession.

If an Israelite encounters an animal in distress on the road, aid must be given.

A woman shall not wear men's clothing. A man shall not don women's garb. Cross-dressing is abhorrent in God's eyes.

If a traveler chances across a bird's nest in which a mother tends to chicks or eggs, only the young may be taken.

When you build a new home, a small safety barrier must be built around the roof to ensure people do not fall off.

Two different kinds of seed must not be sown in the same vineyard. An ox and an ass shall not be made to plow side by side. Wool and cloth should not be spun into the same clothing. All garments shall have tassels dangling from the corners.

LIKE A VIRGIN

If a married man despises his wife and begins to fabricate allegations that she was not a virgin on their wedding night, the girl's parents shall produce evidence of her virginity for the elders at the town gate. If the elders deem

the evidence to be conclusive, the man shall be punished for defaming a virgin in Israel—a flogging and a fine will suffice, and the man loses the right to divorce his wife. Alternatively, if his charges are discovered to be true, the men of the town shall stone the woman to death for fornicating while under her father's authority.

If a man commits adultery, both the male and female shall be put to death. If a man rapes a virgin engaged to marry, both shall be stoned to death at the city gates. The man deserves to die because he violated another man's wife, and the woman shall be punished because she did not cry for help when the act was committed. If the act occurs in the wide-open countryside, only the man shall be punished: Even if the woman cried out, there was no one to hear her. If the raped virgin is not engaged and the man is caught, he must pay her father fifty shekels, then take his victim as his wife and never divorce her. No man shall marry his father's former wife, as it would be akin to seeing him naked.

MEMBERS ONLY

No man with crushed testes or a damaged member shall be allowed into the congregation of the Lord. No illegitimate child or one descended from ten generations of illegitimate lineage shall be permitted either. Ammonites and Moabites are not to be admitted on account of their failure to offer food and water to the Israelites upon their liberation from slavery, then hiring Balaam to curse them. The children of Edomites and Egyptians can be admitted in the third generation.

A SMORGASBORD OF LEGISLATION

If a soldier experiences a nocturnal emission while on military maneuvers, he shall be deemed unclean and forced to leave camp until he has bathed in the evening. The Israelites are to ensure they defecate outside their camp so they remain holy even in the field.

A slave seeking refuge from his master shall be sheltered without being ill-treated. No Israelite shall be a cult prostitute involved in sacred sexual rituals, nor should a whore be brought into the Temple to fulfill a vow.

Israelites can charge interest on loans only when dealing with foreigners. Interest shall not be added to loans between members of the community.

Any vow made shall be fulfilled with speed.

In a vineyard, any man can pluck grapes off the vine and eat them, but no one can fill up a bag or container. Similarly, in a field, Israelites can pluck another man's wheat with their hands but are not permitted to use a sickle.

LOVE AND (RE)MARRIAGE

When a man divorces a woman, he cannot take her back if she marries another man. If the second husband also divorces her or dies, she shall be judged to have become defiled.

A newlywed is exempt from military service for one year. His obligation is to give happiness to his new wife.

A SMORGASBORD OF LEGISLATION II

A handmill or millstone should not be taken as security on a loan, as it is akin to taking someone's livelihood.

Kidnapping is an offense punishable by death.

Victims of skin infections shall follow the priest's instructions with care.

Debt collectors shall not enter a debtor's home to reclaim what is owed. They should wait outside. If the debtor remains needy, the loan shall be rolled over. The lender will receive the Lord's favor.

A destitute laborer should also be

treated fairly and paid promptly or else he will cry out to the Lord and the offender will be considered guilty.

Parents should not be put to death for their children's crimes nor children held responsible for their parents'. Only the person responsible for the crime shall be put to death.

Foreigners and orphans shall be granted their rights. A widow's possessions shall not be taken in pawn. The Israelites will always remember they were once slaves in Egypt and needed God to redeem them. Any sheaves in the field mistakenly unharvested should be left for the needy to take. The same rule applies in vineyards and in regard to olive crops.

Guilty men may be lashed up to forty times; any more would be degrading.

An ox should not be muzzled while being forced to thresh.

THE UNSANDALED ONES

In a family where there are two brothers, if one dies leaving a wife and no male heir, the brother is obliged to marry her and ensure a son is produced so that the deceased's name will not be forgotten. If the brother elects to shun this duty, the bereaved wife must appear before the town elders and inform them. He must confirm his decision. The woman must then perform the ritual of pulling off his sandal, spitting in his face, and declaring that henceforth, the living brother should be known as "the family of an unsandaled one."

If two men are fighting and one of the combatant's wives intercedes by grabbing his opponent's genitals, her hand shall be cut off.

Honest weights must be used. Dishonesty will not be tolerated by the Lord.

BLOTTING THE AMALEK

The Israelites shall never forget how the tribe of the Amalek attacked them from the rear, cutting down the weak and the weary. The Amalek must be blotted out in their entirety.

DAVY ROTHBART

T. J. MAX

One particularly dead Sunday night, nursing my fourth PBR on a stool at the 8-Ball, I caught sight of my old friend Sam, with whom I'd been close in high school but hadn't seen in years. We hugged and slammed down a couple of whiskey shots. Then he looked at me somberly and said, "Today was my grandfather's funeral."

I remembered meeting the guy a few times when Sam and I were in high school. His name was Max—a cheery, talkative old-timer who always got after me for wearing a baseball cap indoors. "Better show off your hair while you've still got it," he'd say with a smile. His story, as I'd heard from Sam, was that he'd been a barber in a small town in Poland and during the war had been shipped to Treblinka, his young wife to another camp. He'd survived only because the Nazi soldiers needed someone to cut their hair, and he was apparently damn good at it. His wife, meanwhile, had perished. Later, after the war, he lived in Denmark for a couple of years, and then tracked down a distant cousin who'd found his way to Detroit and followed him there, marrying again, eventually, and raising a family. For decades, he'd helped his cousin manage a small-appliances store and had cut hair for family members and friends from synagogue on a barber's chair he kept in his garage. In high school, I'd had my hair cut by him twice myself.

I bought Sam another shot, and he wound from one story about his grandfather to another. Sam had gotten to know the guy pretty well the summer between tenth and eleventh grade, when he'd spent three months working at the appliances store and living with his grandparents in Royal Oak.

One night, Sam said, after he'd been there for a month, he'd bounded into his grandfather's bedroom to ask him a question and come upon an eerie, astonishing sight—his grandfather was half naked in the middle of the room, dressed in only a woman's antique slip and high-heeled shoes, struggling to pull a skinny, frayed dress over his head. "I turned and bolted right outta there," Sam said. "I was pretty sure he had no idea what I'd seen, which made things less awkward, I guess, while still being somewhat awkward. I mean, it was like I'd caught him in the dressing room at some crappy women's clothing store at the mall. But I never told anyone what I saw." Sam paused. "Although, for most of that summer, I used to refer to my grandfather as 'T. J. Max.' You remember that?"

I shook my head. This all felt like a pretty weird story to relate to someone the night of your grandfather's funeral. On the other hand, we'd both been drinking heavily, and Sam seemed relieved to have run into someone with whom to share stories of Max, especially since I'd actually known him.

"Well, whatever," he said. "I didn't use that nickname long." At the end of the summer, his grandfather had called him into his room, saying he wanted to talk to him, that he had something to show him. Laid out on the bed, Sam said, were the same old-school women's underwear, ornate high-heeled shoes, and the worn but pretty dress that he'd seen his grandfather wriggling into a couple of months before.

I stopped him. "Wait, did you guys *bone*?" This was my lame ploy to inject levity into a story that seemed, to me, like it was creeping toward some kind of unknowable heartbreak or dark twist that I was afraid to hear about.

"Yeah, we humped like dogs!" Sam cried, his face gone mad. Then his smile skedaddled and his eyes drooped. "No," he said. "My grandfather just told me he wanted to explain something to me. He knew I'd seen him in women's underwear and wanted to explain who these clothes belonged to." Sam looked me in the eye. "Well, you can guess. They belonged to his first wife. The one who died. The one who was killed. It was her favorite dress, he said. Her favorite pair of shoes. Years and years after she died, I guess, some relative of hers tracked down Max and gave him the clothes and a couple of other trinkets of hers. 'I love your grandmother more than anything,' he told me that day, 'but it doesn't mean I don't miss Hedda sometimes. When I'm missing her, I put on her clothes. Maybe it's just my imagination, but when I'm in her clothes, I feel her close to me, like I can still smell her, can still feel her touch.'"

"Wow. What did you say?" I asked.

"What could I say? I just said, 'Okay, Pops.' He never mentioned it again. I never brought it up, either. But then, we were going through his stuff yesterday, me and my mom. I was helping her clean out his house, sort through all his stuff, empty out the closets. And I saw the dress. I'm sure it was the dress."

At this point, I realized that Wolfie, the bartender, and a few other guys close by whom Sam and I half-knew had been pulled into the story. "So, what'd you do with it?" Wolfie asked.

"What do you think? I tried that damn thing on!" Sam roared. "When my mom was out of the room!" He laughed too hard, then seized up. "Well, it didn't fit me. I don't know, man. Shoot. We just donated it to Goodwill, with all the rest."

Wolfie poured one last round of shots and silently passed them around. "These are on me," he said.

Sam held up his glass, whiskey spilling over the edge, down his fingers, dripping to the floor. "To T. J. Max," he said quietly.

"Cheers," we said. "To Max." And we all drank.

יככה יהוה בשחין רע על הברכים ועל השקים
אשר לא תוכל להרפא מכף רגלך ועד קדקדך:

"The Lord will afflict you at the knees and thighs with a severe inflammation
from which you shall never recover—from the sole of your foot to the
crown of your head."—Deuteronomy 28:35

KI TAVO ("*When you enter*")
DEUTERONOMY 26:1–29:8

BLESSINGS . . . AND CURSES: MOSES continues to prepare the Israelites for his death. He begins by instructing them to dedicate the first fruit of the harvest to God in a place to be revealed once they enter the land. As the priests offer the fruit on the altar, each Israelite is obliged to recite a paragraph retelling the

Exodus story and the journey to the promised land.

Upon setting aside a tenth of their yield as a tithe and giving it to the Levites and the needy, the people are to announce the fulfillment of the commandment to God.

The Lord commands the Israelites to follow all the laws. Following the laws will ensure they remain a treasured people resting high above all

other nations—a holy people.

The elders join Moses to reinforce his point. The Israelites are told to coat large stones in plaster and inscribe the Torah on them once they have crossed the Jordan into the land of milk and honey. Moses commands Simeon, Levi, Judah, Issachar, Joseph, and Benjamin to stand on Mount Gerizim and bless the people. Reuben, Gad, Asher, Zebulun, Dan, and Naphtali are instructed to stand on Mount Ebal and curse any-one who worships idols. Others who deserve to be cursed include

- those who insult their parents;

- those who shift their neighbors' border lines;

- those who trick blind people;

- those who subvert the rights of the powerless and needy;

- those who have relations with their father's wife, a sister, their mother-in-law, or an animal;

- those who kill a countryman without witnesses;

- an official who accepts a bribe during a murder case; and

- those who do not uphold the Torah.

The rewards for observing God's laws are repeated: God will set the Israelites high above all other nations. Their wombs, harvest, and herds will be blessed. Enemies will be routed. All other people will fear them. They will be a creditor to many nations but a debtor to none.

However, if the Israelites fail the Lord . . . well, the consequences are detailed in painstaking fash-ion. Calamity and panic will ensue. Pestilence will torture them until they are wiped out. Sickness and inflam-mation will run amok. Drought shall reign, the crops shall fail, and dust storms will devour them. The descrip-tions of ultimate doom become ever more graphic, gruesome, and imagina-tive. They end with the few surviving Israelites being sent back to Egypt in galleys, begging to be bought as slaves, yet finding no buyers.

Moses reminds the Israelites of the wonders of the Exodus. He asks them to consider how in forty years their clothes and shoes did not wear out once, and sustenance was never lacking, and to remember how military battles were won and the land was conquered.

He begs the Israelites to observe the covenant's terms so their prosperity will be guaranteed.

ANONYMOUS

I like to think of the opening books of the Bible as a slightly wordy, occasionally inaccessible buddy road movie. Two initially ill-suited characters—in *Rain Man*, Tom Cruise and Dustin Hoffman, in *Exodus*, God and the Israelites—are thrown together by a life-threatening experience and become bound at the hip.

Through Leviticus and Numbers, the Lord and His chosen people have their share of high jinks. Wilderness living. Hunger. Thirst. Enemies from King Sihon of Heshbon to King Og of Bashan have been introduced to the meaning of one of God's favorite words, *smite*.

Strange then, after four decades of a relationship forged in sweat, sand, and death, that God suddenly elects to depart from the buddy genre. With our heroes poised to cross the Jordan and enter the promised land, the Lord delivers a speech of such curdling horror that it makes a mockery of the common wisdom, "The devil gets all the best lines."

God's middleman, Moses, is forced to do the dirty work. He starts on familiar territory, trotting out a routine reminder of some of the Lord's pet peeves. The biggies—no idols or lying "with any beast"—are relayed alongside what one hopes would have been rarer transgressions. Those seized by the frankly incomprehensible idea of "lying with their mother-in-law" are reminded that such copulation is frowned upon.

But God is just getting started, and Moses moves up a gear to race through the familiar legalese of the Israelites' covenant with God. If they can resist the allure of their in-laws, they will be blessed. It is still easy to detect a touch of the "blah blah blahs" in Moses' voice as he works toward his finale. "But if you do not obey the Lord your God to observe faithfully all His commandments and laws which I enjoin upon you this day, all these curses shall come upon you and take effect."

Moses pauses dramatically for a beat before launching into this final act with a bombastic venom. Some highlights:

Verse 22: *"The Lord will strike you with consumption, fever, and inflammation, with scorching heat and drought, with blight and mildew."*

Verse 25: *"You shall become a horror to all the kingdoms of the earth. Your carcasses shall become food for all the birds of the sky and all the beasts of the earth, with none to frighten them off."*

By now, Moses has worked up quite the head of steam. These are lines that can only be delivered bug-eyed with spittle foaming from the corner of his mouth:

Verse 27: *"The Lord will strike you with the 'Egyptian inflammation,' with hemorrhoids, boil-scars, and itch, from which you shall never recover."*

Can it get worse? It can. The climax:

Verse 49: *"The Lord will bring a nation against you from afar, from the end of the earth, which will swoop down like the eagle . . . shut you up in all your towns throughout your land until . . . you eat your own issue, the flesh of your sons and daughters."*

Ten lines of carrot have been delivered by rote with all the passion of an air steward trotting out preflight emergency precautions. Fifty-two verses of sadistic stick are then preached with fire and brimstone.

What kind of a God conjures threats like these, with the kind of creative violence typically found only in the Yiddish cursing tradition? ("May all your teeth fall out—except one, and may that one cause you great pain.") And just as important, isn't belief in the God of the heavens tarnished just a little by this reliance on threat and force?

The knee-jerk disgust I experience is quickly tempered by the realization that if anyone knows humans, it should be God. After all, She allegedly created us.

At the risk of having delusions of grandeur, I would assess the situation through God's eyes as such: She knows the Israelites are on the brink of an epic societal transformation. For forty years they have been utterly dependent on Her for food, clothing, and protection. Now they are not only preparing to enter the promised land but are about to create their own social order and morality. This speech is Her one last chance to influence their actions.

Effective storytelling demands that you know your audience—in God's case, humans. She knows we are weak, fallible, and easily tempted. At the very least, I am. And with those truths self-evident, there are few more effective ways to deliver a memorable message than employing the rigid conventions of the horror genre.

"Here's Johnny!"[1]

"They're he-e-e-re."[2]

"Whatever you do, don't fall asleep."[3]

We remember terror-filled tales because of the stimulation and catharsis they provide, and for the strict moral code that is reinforced by their retelling. Well-worn horror dictates are as familiar as they are clichéd: Don't pick up a deranged hitchhiker when it is lightning; try to get to third base with your girlfriend while in a vehicle, late at night, in a deserted parking lot when a serial killer is on the loose; or perhaps worst of all, be the guy who dismissively quips, "I'll prove to you that nothing will happen if I read from this book . . ." Decapitation, flaying, or asphyxiation is guaranteed to ensue.

I like this God of Horror. Think of Her not as some kind of puritanical televangelist wallowing in self-righteousness but more a human manipulator, like Alfred Hitchcock or Wes Craven—a master storyteller like Edgar Allan Poe or Stephen King, a writer who once reduced his methodology to "terror as the finest emotion, and so I will try to terrorize the reader."

Picture the Lord crafting a draft of this speech in a writers' room with Moses, giggling as they brainstorm scenarios of doom, searching for the perfect, fear-inducing combination that would not just be listened to, but heard and repeated for generations.

An NC-17 God. The kind of deity I can believe in.

---

[1] *The Shining*   [2] *Poltergeist*   [3] *A Nightmare on Elm Street*

כי המצוה הזאת אשר אנכי מצוך היום לא נפלאת הוא ממך ולא רחקה הוא:

"Surely, this instruction which I enjoin upon you this day is
not too baffling, nor is it beyond reach." —Deuteronomy 30:11

NITZAVIM (*"Ones standing"*)
DEUTERONOMY 29:9–30:20

MOSES REMINDS ALL THE ISRAELITES that they stand before God, and that all of them have the choice to enter into the covenant. Anyone who is tempted to worship the gods of other nations shall be warned that a furious God will blot them out of existence. Moses proceeds to paint an apocalyptic portrait of the destruction experienced by any tribe who breaks the covenant, detailing the plagues, diseases, and famine they will suffer.

If the Israelites become cursed and experience suffering, they can always return to God and follow the commands while in exile. The Lord will then restore their fortunes and reunite them, reinstating the blessings.

Moses sets out the stark choice for his people and makes sure they understand how simple the decision should be. Their fate does not depend on the heavens, or foreign affairs. It will be determined by their very words and deeds. Moses offers the Israelites the choice of life or death and asks heaven and earth to act as a witness for their decision.

ELI ATTIE

Int. sleek, ultra-modern conference room--day
     MOSES sits at a big glass conference table, across from
two PAUNCHY, MIDDLE-AGED MEN in suits. A fresh-faced
TWENTYSOMETHING sits behind them, also in a suit. Moses
is wearing dusty, threadbare robes. He looks tired, even
older than his 120 years, like a guy who has just crossed
the desert by foot. You might say he's a little out of his
element. The paunchy men look at him expectantly. After a
long, awkward beat--

                         MOSES
Look, I don't know how to--I appreciate your sitting down
with me today.

                    PAUNCHY MAN #1
Oh, it's a real thrill for us--

                    PAUNCHY MAN #2
We're big fans, have all your albums and--

     The twentysomething nudges paunchy man #2 and points
     to the name on a FILE that's in front of him.

                PAUNCHY MAN #2 (CONT'D)
I'm so sorry. I thought this was the--

     [To twentysomething]
When's the Willie Nelson meeting?

                    TWENTYSOMETHING
He's your two fifteen--

                         ———

                    PAUNCHY MAN #1

    [To twentysomething]
Let's get a big fruit plate or something--

                    PAUNCHY MAN #2

    [To Moses]
"Always on My Mind" slays me every time--

                         MOSES
I've been in the desert for forty years.
I'm still on lute music.

    The paunchy men LAUGH at this, until they realize he's
    not joking.

                    MOSES (CONT'D)
Honestly? I'm not sure I need any . . . what do you
call this again?

                    PAUNCHY MAN #1
Crisis management's what we generally--

                    PAUNCHY MAN #2
Or strategic communications. No one's saying there's a
crisis in this . . . movement of yours--

                         MOSES
It's a religion. And I wouldn't say it's mine.

                    PAUNCHY MAN #2

    [To paunchy man #1]
See, that's a branding opportunity right there--

                    PAUNCHY MAN #1
Gotta sell YOURSELF every bit as much as your--

                    ___
                    343

PAUNCHY MAN #2

[To paunchy man #1]
How 'bout we smarten up his clothes first--

[To the twentysomething]
Get him in to see Karen as soon as--

MOSES
No, look, here's the thing. I'm sure Karen's terrific.

PAUNCHY MAN #1
She's the best.

MOSES
And again, I appreciate your time. Abraham insisted I sit
down with you guys. I know you really helped him out when
he had that problem with his kid.

PAUNCHY MAN #1
Not to beat our chests, but one day he's an infanticidal nutbag,
the next he's starring in biblical epics. I'm just sayin'.

MOSES
And that's great. But my situation's different. We had a
rough patch as we were nearing the Holy Land, some folks
started turning away from the Lord our God, I ended up
being the heavy. But we got through it, and I don't know
that I have a P.R. problem at all.

The paunchy men are skimming some NEWS CLIPPINGS from
the file. They share a look: another client in denial.

MOSES (CONT'D)
Fine, I've gotten some bad press lately. I don't always
say things in the most . . . elegant way.

The paunchy men share another look: Who's gonna lower
the boom on this guy? Then--

                    PAUNCHY MAN #2
Mr. Moses--

                         MOSES
Just Moses is fine--

                    PAUNCHY MAN #2
You compared your own membership to--

    [Reading from clipping]
"Poison weed and wormwood"--

                         MOSES
That's way out of context, no one ran the full quote--and
they're not "members," they're--

                    PAUNCHY MAN #1

    [Another clipping]
You said if they didn't follow your "covenant"--

                         MOSES
It's GOD'S covenant--

                    PAUNCHY MAN #1
You said their soil would be "devastated by sulfur and
salt"--you think the EPA gives a rat's ass whose covenant
it is?

                         MOSES
People were hungry, tired, false idols were bandied about.
And yeah, maybe I was a little harsh in the way I phrased
certain--

                    PAUNCHY MAN #1
"A little harsh"? This "religion" of yours sounds more
like a protection racket.

                         MOSES
Again, it's not MY--

                      _____

Moses has had enough of this, starts to rise to
leave--

                    MOSES (CONT'D)
Never mind. I don't know why I let Abe talk me into--

                    PAUNCHY MAN #2
Hang on, don't get your tunic in a bunch here, all we're
saying is, does it have to be so doom-and-gloom? Look at
some of the other religions--glitzy promises of salvation,
seventy-one virgins--

                    PAUNCHY MAN #1
That's been really popular lately--

                    PAUNCHY MAN #2
Mega-church choirs that make U2 sound like a jug band--

                    PAUNCHY MAN #1
We're working with Bono on his debt-relief stuff. That's
confidential--

                    PAUNCHY MAN #2
Point is, you're in a brutally tough marketplace, and
instead of sweetening the pot, you're saying, Follow these
endless laws and rules and whatever--

                    MOSES
Commandments--

                    PAUNCHY MAN #2
Whatever, or you're cursed for generations. "Yahweh or the
highway." THAT'S gonna grow your market share?

                    PAUNCHY MAN #1
    [To paunchy man #2]
How 'bout a prize giveaway?

    Moses is getting visibly agitated.

                    PAUNCHY MAN #2
Punchier slogan might do it. "Want faith? Jew got it." Get
it? "JEW got it."

                        MOSES

    [Annoyed]
I get it.

                    PAUNCHY MAN #2
Goes down easier than your plagues and wormwood and
what-have-you.

    Moses can't take any more of this. He rises, creating
    a small cloud of DUST--

                        MOSES
Let's talk about my "what-have-you." Yes, it can be demanding,
unforgiving, at times contradictory. One minute God's
ushering in abounding prosperity, the next he's wielding a
tire iron like Tony Soprano--I can't always figure it out
myself. And if we gave away prizes and had cutesy slogans,
maybe we'd be the biggest religion on the planet. But you know
what? That's not the TRUTH. That's not his WORD, his COMMAND.

    [Building a head of steam]
And the TRUTH happens to be beautiful and ugly and
confounding and uplifting AT THE SAME TIME, because IT is
THAT WAY, because ALL OF life IS THAT WAY. It's a riddle.
An undertaking. There are CONSEQUENCES. It doesn't fit on a
bumper sticker. The prizes go to those who SWEAT for 'em. AND
I DON'T CARE WHAT THEY SAY ABOUT ME IN THE GODDAMN NEWSPAPERS.

    A stunned silence. And then--

                    PAUNCHY MAN #1

    [To twentysomething]
Are we ready for the Willie Nelson meeting?

    AND WE--
    CUT TO BLACK.

                        ———

ויאמר אלהם בן מאה ועשרים שנה אנכי היום לא אוכל
עוד לצאת ולבוא ויהוה אמר אלי לא תעבר את הירדן הזה:

"He (Moses) said to them: 'I am now one hundred and twenty years old,
I can no longer be active. Moreover, the Lord has said to me,
'You shall not go across yonder Jordan.'"—Deuteronomy 31:2

VA-YE'LEKH (*"Then he went out"*)
DEUTERONOMY 31:1–30

HE CLIMAX: **MOSES INFORMS ISRAEL THAT** at the age of 120 he is no longer able to lead them. The Lord has forbidden him to cross the Jordan into the promised land, so Joshua will inherit his mantle. Despite the transition, it will still be the Lord who will go before them and wipe out the nations who currently live on the land.

Moses calls Joshua before him, and in front of the entire community, transfers the reins of power. He instructs the priests, Levites, and elders to read the entire Torah to the Israelites every seven years as they gather together for Sukkot.

The Lord informs Moses that his time to die is nearing and suggests he bring Joshua to the Tent of Meeting. The Lord meets them in a pillar of cloud and expresses a concern that Moses' death will encourage a spate of infractions among the Israelites, who might worship other gods and force the Lord to abandon them. As a precautionary measure, God presents a poem that will remind the people of the covenant and the curses and blessings it offers.

Moses writes the poem down and teaches it to the Israelites, charging

Joshua with the courage to lead them. Then he orders the Levites to take the book he has written and place it beside the ark as a reminder to obey the Lord.

Despite this, Moses confides his fear that the people were defiant while he was alive and will be worse once he dies. He orders them to gather the entire Israelite community so he can read the Lord's poem to them one last time.

GILLIAN LAUB

GRANDMA FEELING MY BELLY
Mamaroneck, New York   October 2012
Grandma is ninety-three. She can't see anymore, but she knows her eighth great-grandchild is in my belly. We spent the afternoon in her bedroom waiting to feel kicks.

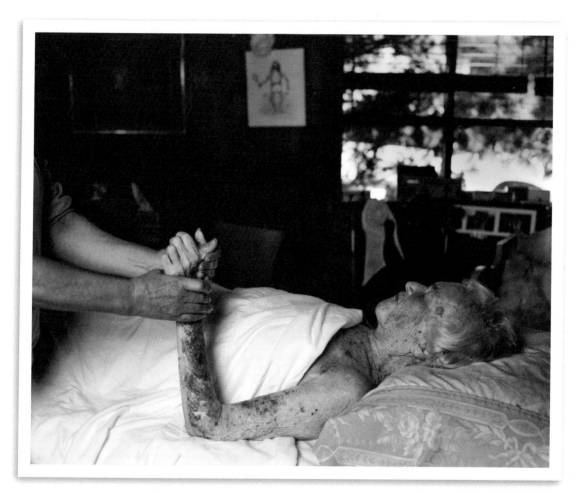

GRANDMA HAVING A MASSAGE
Mamaroneck, New York October 2012
Grandma is in the den, getting her weekly massage. Sometimes when she dozes off, she starts to talk to my grandfather. Even though he passed away five years ago, she thinks he's in the room.

הַצּוּר תָּמִים פָּעֳלוֹ כִּי כָל־דְּרָכָיו מִשְׁפָּט אֵל אֱמוּנָה וְאֵין עָוֶל צַדִּיק וְיָשָׁר הוּא:

"The Rock!—His deeds are perfect, Yea, all His ways are just;
A faithful God, never false, True and upright is He." —Deuteronomy 32:4

HA'AZINU (*"Listen"*)

DEUTERONOMY 32:1–52

OSES ADDRESSES THE ISRAELITES WITH a final, lengthy poem, fittingly known as the Song of Moses.

In the course of 142 lines he proclaims the glory of God, lambastes human weakness, celebrates the role the Lord played in blessing the Israelites, yet predicts a future in which they grow fat with wealth and start to worship idols. An incensed God is then compelled to inflict an arsenal of punishments, including famine, plague, and pestilence.

The only reason God will not destroy the Israelites is revealed: a desire to prevent their enemies from forming the misconception that their gods have ultimately prevailed. If the Israelites are smart, they will have already realized God's power and know it surpasses that of their enemies. Once their foes are defeated, God will goad them, demanding to know where their gods have disappeared to.

There is one God: an eternal power with a flashing blade, who will bring forth justice and vengeance to the world.

When Moses completes his poem, he commands the people to take his words to heart and teach them to their children, observing that the Torah is not a small thing. It is life itself.

That same day, the Lord tells Moses to ascend the heights of Mount Nebo and look out over the land of Canaan, which will become the Israelites' possession. God tells Moses he will die in the same fashion as his brother, Aaron, reminding him of his error in the wilderness for which he is being punished. He is doomed to view the promised land from a distance, without ever being able to enter it.

RICK MEYEROWITZ

"A FAITHFUL GOD, NEVER FALSE. TRUE AND UPRIGHT IS HE."

RICK MEYEROWITZ

אשריך ישראל מי כמוך . . .

"O happy Israel! Who is like you . . ." —Deuteronomy 33:29

VEZOT HABERAKHAH
("*And this is the blessing*")
DEUTERONOMY 33:1–34:12

A FINAL BLESSING: **MOSES, A MAN OF GOD,** says farewell to the Israelites with a somewhat cryptic blessing for every tribe.

He begins by recapping God's election of the Israelites and his own role as leader, then blesses the tribe of Reuben by expressing the hope that they will not become extinct due to a scarcity of members. For Judah, Moses asks for wartime protection from God. For the Levites—who carry God's prophetic yet mysterious devices, the "Thummim and Urim," and forsake their families to serve the Lord, teach the laws of the covenant, and place incense and offerings on the altar—he asks for favor and that they have the ability to smash their enemies.

For Benjamin, the Lord's friend, he requests security; for Joseph, copious quantities of dew, sun crops, and favor. Moses then compares the tribe to a firstborn bull that gores people with its horns.

For the tribes of Zebulun and Issachar, he urges them to savor their journeys. Moses compares God to a lion savoring the prime part of the kill; Dan, to a lion's cub. Moses urges God to favor Asher and maintain their physical security, and then he concludes the blessings by recounting God's role in driving out Israel's enemies and enabling them to live securely within a land of grain and wine. He asks the Israelites to consider how unparalleled a position they find themselves in, with God's protection striking fear into their enemies.

THE END

Moses goes up to Mount Nebo and the Lord lets him survey the land that had been promised to Abraham, Isaac, and Jacob, reminding him that he can glimpse it but never enter.

Moses dies there and is buried in a place that has not been found. He was 120 and his energy was unabated. The Israelites mourn him for thirty days, and Joshua inherits the mantle of leadership. Yet Israel never again has a prophet like Moses, who had been face-to-face with God; confronted Pharaoh, his court, and the Egyptian nation; and displayed his immense power before Israel.

ROGER BENNETT

When New York City's Metropolitan Transit Authority commissioned the illustrator Sophie Blackall to design a poster for their Arts for Transit program, she created a piece that perfectly captured the everyday theater of subway car life. In her eclectic juxtaposition of passengers crushed together by New York City's rush hour, an old lady nods off to sleep, slumped against a plump stranger steadying a bucket overflowing with freshly caught fish; a Midwestern family of tourists glance around anxiously as two skinny-jeans-clad teens make out, their hormones practically popping off the page. But no matter the chaos depicted in the poster, the eye is drawn to its center, where a man clad in a full bear costume lolls casually against a pole as a black-hatted Hasid, engrossed in his Torah, appears oblivious to the world around him.

Worlds collide in Sophie Blackall's subway poster.

There is *always* someone reading a Bible on a New York subway. Before I embarked on this book, I often wondered how they had the stamina to read and reread the same volume, endlessly, without ever becoming bored. In my limited imagination, few things could, quite literally, feel more like the Hebrew School I had been expelled from than plowing through pages stuffed with cloying characters acting out black-and-white depictions of saints and sinners, in comforting tales that shut out the real world and reduce life to a trite message of reward and punishment, good and evil.

And then I worked on this project—a two-year task that necessitated taking the part of life most normal men use to train for a marathon, work on their golf short game, or brew their own craft beer, and devoting it to the Lord's word. I found plunging into the Torah and wallowing in its stories to be a humbling experience, one that has forced me to consider the difference between what I know, and what I think I know.

I was instantly hooked by the book's breathless narrative. As Genesis gave way to Exodus and Moses was elected to build a nation, the time I had to spend away from the text began to feel like time wasted. Though slogging through the precise details of ritual sacrifice or vows at times felt like being back in a law school torts class, the tempo soon picked up again as Moses edged the Israelites—and the reader—toward the promised land.

Counter to my previously held, ill-informed assumptions, the storytelling was nuanced and its portrayals human and complex. The lead characters were presented flaws and all, as each struggled, under survival conditions, to tell the difference between right and wrong, the godly and the godless, without always being able to conjure the correct decisions. And this was true with few more than with Abraham: a man who circumcised himself, aged ninety-nine, amid the desert plains no less. Kierkegaard may have elevated the moral predicament at the heart of the story of the Binding of Isaac, but the fact that the patriarch was willing to pass his wife off as his sister, and profit as she entered Pharaoh's harem, appeared equally fascinating to me.

I was also thrilled by the panoply of minor characters and their experiences: Hagar's suffering, Rebekah's nobility, Esau's anguish, Laban's greed, the doomed ambition of Nadab and Abihu, Miriam's frustration, the Daughters of Zelophehad's courage, and after the exodus, the incessantly demanding Israelite people, an emotional Greek chorus before such a concept had been invented. As I discovered, the Torah is home to a complex universe that rivals anything found in a *Star Wars* cantina.

Above all, I was struck by the complexity of God. The omnipotent creator is heralded as being slow to anger and quick to forgive, yet, as the Torah concludes with Moses' death scene, it is hard not to be struck by the lack of sentimentality on display. Mustache-twirling villains in silent movies at times exhibited more.

At the outset of their partnership, the Lord had appeared so aware of, and even tender toward, Moses' leadership limitations. The Egyptian prince turned Israelite prophet directed an untrusting people through decades of grueling military campaigning in the wilderness, managing to write the Torah along the way. And then, a single moment of human fallibility undermined every one of those achievements. Antagonized by the thirst of his followers, and under conditions of wilderness hysteria, Moses had taken his anger out on a rock God had commanded him merely to speak to—a symbolic lack of faith for which he pays dearly, as he is permitted to glimpse yet not enter the promised land.

The end of the Torah marks a new beginning. Moses dies. Joshua assumes the role of leader for a new era. And though we are assured there will never again be "in Israel a prophet like Moses," Moses' burial place is immediately cloaked in mystery so it cannot be worshipped. Amid change, God is the only constant. And as Moses discovered, not even he could rise above the shock of divine justice.

Yet it is more than just the surprise of this cruel conclusion that keeps people reading as the weekly rhythm of the Torah now starts again from the beginning on an endless loop, like the seasons, against which readers can mark time. The Mishnah quotes a mysterious, yet fantastically named rabbi, Ben Bag Bag, who enthuses about the subtle layers of the Torah, declaring, "Turn it and turn it again, for everything is in it, pore over it and wax gray and old over it."

I think of Rabbi Ben Bag Bag now whenever I see someone on the 3 train reading the Bible, be it a church lady or a black-hatted Orthodox Jew. Before, I had thought they were attempting to shut out real life. Now I imagine they are engrossed as Jacob's vengeance-seeking sons brutally massacre the men who had raped their sister, or marveling when Bezalel is miraculously able to procure the dolphin skins necessary to complete the Tabernacle in the middle of the wilderness, or stunned as the earth opens up to swallow the leaders of Korah's rebellion whole: realities that are even more chaotic, complicated, and engrossing than the most colorful rush hour subway car in New York City could possibly be.

CONTRIBUTORS

ELI ATTIE is an Emmy-winning television writer and recovering political operative. His credits include *The West Wing* and *House, M.D.*, and he served as chief White House speechwriter for former vice president Al Gore. He has always preferred Ess-a-Bagel to H&H.

DAVID AUBURN is a playwright (*The Columnist*, *Proof*), filmmaker (*The Girl in the Park*), and theater director. He lives in New York City.

RACHEL AXLER is a playwright and Emmy-winning TV writer. She's written for a number of wonderful shows, including *The Daily Show with Jon Stewart*, *Parks and Recreation*, and *How I Met Your Mother*. Her play *Smudge* has been published in English and German, one of which she speaks.

AIMEE BENDER is the author of four books, including *The Girl in the Flammable Skirt* and *The Particular Sadness of Lemon Cake*, and her latest short story collection, *The Color Master*. She has been published in *Granta*, *Harper's*, the *Paris Review*, *Tin House*, *McSweeney's*, and more, as well as heard on *This American Life* and *Selected Shorts*. She lives in Los Angeles and teaches creative writing at the University of Southern California.

ROGER BENNETT is a writer, broadcaster, and cofounder of Reboot.

SHOSHANA BERGER worships at the same altar as Professor Robert Alter, the famed biblical scholar, and stole everything she knows about the Bible from him. Berger is editorial director of IDEO and was director of special projects at *Wired* and the founding editor of *ReadyMade* magazine. She lives in Berkeley, California, with all the other deli-starved Jews.

DENNIS BERMAN is an editor and columnist at the *Wall Street Journal*. He grew up in Kentucky and lives in Brooklyn, New York, with his wife and son.

STEVE BODOW is coexecutive producer and former head writer of *The Daily Show with Jon Stewart*, which he has plagued since 2002. He has also directed theater (Elevator Repair Service), written for magazines, and played a lot of Werewolf. He lives with his wife and two daughters in New York.

REBECCA BORTMAN is a visual designer, living in colorful San Francisco and working on Snapguide, an app for making how-to guides. Before venturing into the start-up world, she spent three years at YouTube, leading design on the site's first visual refresh. Rebecca is also the art director for the Disposable Film Festival, sings in the punk band Happy Fangs, and formerly sang in the indie pop band My First Earthquake. She was bat mitzvahed two days before turning fourteen at Temple Emanuel in Pittsburgh.

JESSE AARON COHEN spent ten years working at the YIVO Institute for Jewish Research, mostly as a photo and film archivist. His work now is writing, producing, and performing music as one half of the group Tanlines. He lives in New York City.

RICH COHEN is the author of several books, including *Tough Jews, Sweet and Low*, and *The Fish That Ate the Whale*. His stories have appeared in the *New Yorker*, the *Atlantic*, and *Vanity Fair*, where he is a contributing editor. He is working on a book about the 1985 Chicago Bears.

SLOANE CROSLEY is the author of the *New York Times* bestselling books *How Did You Get This Number* and *I Was Told There'd Be Cake*. She is a frequent contributor to *GQ, Elle*, and the *New York Times*. She lives, writes, and teaches in Manhattan.

REBECCA DANA is an author and journalist in New York. Her book, *Jujitsu Rabbi and the Godless Blonde*, was published by Putnam in January 2013. She was a staff writer for the *Wall Street Journal* and *Newsweek*, and her writing has appeared in the *New Republic, Rolling Stone*, the *New York Times*, and elsewhere. Find her at rebeccadana.com.

GABE DELAHAYE is a writer and comedian just like everybody else. His work has appeared on Videogum, *This American Life, McSweeney's, Gawker*, CNN, PBS, Comedy Central, ESPN,

VH1, Facebook, Instagram, and Twitter.

SUSAN DOMINUS is a staff writer at the Sunday *New York Times Magazine*.

JOSHUA FOER is the author of the international bestseller *Moonwalking with Einstein: The Art and Science of Remembering Everything*.

JAMIE GLASSMAN is a writer and performer living in merry old London. He was a writer for HBO's *Da Ali G Show*, and his company, Double Gusset Productions, makes shorts for the BBC and Comedy Central. His characters and films have been entertaining tens of people all across the World Wide Interweb.

BEN GREENMAN is an editor at the *New Yorker* and the author of several acclaimed books of fiction, including *Superbad*, *Please Step Back*, and *What He's Poised to Do*. His most recent book is *The Slippage*, a novel.

ELI HOROWITZ is the cocreator of the Silent History, a serialized, exploratory app for the iPhone and iPad. He was the managing editor and then publisher of *McSweeney's* for eight years, working closely with authors including Nick Hornby, Michael Chabon, Joyce Carol Oates, William Vollmann, and Stephen King. He is the coauthor of *The Clock Without a Face*, a treasure-hunt mystery, and *Everything You Know Is Pong*, an illustrated cultural history of Ping-Pong, and his design work has been honored by *I.D.*, *Print*, and the American Institute of Graphic Arts.

A. J. JACOBS is the author of *The Year of Living Biblically*. He once had his wardrobe examined by an Orthodox mixed-fiber inspector, and was disturbed to learn that his wedding suit contained both wool and linen. He pledges that any and all of his future marriages will involve a kosher suit.

ARIEL KAMINER is a reporter at the *New York Times*. She and the Bible are fairly distant acquaintances.

DAVID KATZNELSON is a Grammy-nominated producer, independent-record label head, and problematic vinyl collector. He is the cofounder of the San Francisco Appreciation

Society and the Idelsohn Society for Musical Preservation. He is also director of strategy for the San Francisco Jewish Community Federation. But mainly, he is father to Kaya and Asher and husband to Barbara.

SAKI KNAFO reports on a wide range of subjects for the *Huffington Post*. He has written about homeless kids living in a hotel outside of Disney World, the shady politics of Staten Island real-estate development before and after Hurricane Sandy, and Internet pranksters. He grew up in Brooklyn and basically never left.

JOSH KUN is a professor in the Annenberg School for Communication and Journalism at the University of Southern California, where he directs the Popular Music Project of the Norman Lear Center. He is the author or editor of several books, including *Audiotopia: Music, Race, and America*, *And You Shall Know Us by the Trail of Our Vinyl* (with Roger Bennett), and *Songs in the Key of Los Angeles: Sheet Music and the Making of Southern California*. His writing has also appeared in the *New York Times*, the *Los Angeles Times*, and many other publications.

MARC KUSHNER is partner at HWKN Architects (Hollwich Kushner) and CEO of Architizer.com, the largest platform for architecture online. HWKN won the prestigious MoMA PS1 Young Architect Program in 2012 and specializes in architecture projects that communicate to the broadest population. Marc is a good yeshiva boy from northern New Jersey who is obsessed with the murky history of "Jewish Architecture."

MARK LAMSTER is an occasional humorist, sometimes even on purpose, who recently moved to Texas, a land of biblical scale and fundamentalist fervor. He is the architecture critic of the *Dallas Morning News*, an associate professor at the University of Texas at Arlington, and the author of several works of nonfiction. He is at work on a biography of the late architect Philip Johnson.

GILLIAN LAUB is a photographer. Her practice is deeply rooted in the tradition of portraiture. *Testimony*, Laub's first monograph, was published by *Aperture* in 2007 to critical acclaim. Laub contributes regularly to the *New York Times Magazine* and *Time*, among many other publications. She is represented by Bonni Benrubi Gallery in New York and is widely exhibited and collected. Laub is working on a project centered on the American South that will consist of a documentary film, her next book, and a traveling exhibition.

AMICHAI LAU-LAVIE is an Israeli-born Jewish educator and performance artist who in 1999 founded Storahtelling. He Reboots often and is enrolled in the rabbinical studies program at the Jewish Theological Seminary in New York City.

ADAM LEVIN is the author of the novel *The Instructions*, winner of both the 2011 New York Public Library Young Lions Fiction Award and the inaugural Indie Booksellers Choice Award. For his short stories, Levin has won the Summer Literary Seminars Fiction Contest, as well as the Joyce Carol Oates Fiction Prize. His collection of short stories, *Hot Pink*, was published by McSweeney's in 2012. He lives in Chicago.

RACHEL LEVIN is the executive director of Steven Spielberg's Righteous Persons Foundation and the head of

a consulting practice that helps individuals and families of high net worth increase their philanthropic impact. She is a cofounder of Reboot.

DAMON LINDELOF is a writer and producer of silly television shows and films that feature magic islands, space aliens, and lots and lots of time travel. He is also a husband and a father, which is much harder but a thousand times more rewarding. Lindelof is on a continuum of asking questions that can never be definitively resolved, but he has just enough hubris to occasionally try answering them himself. The results have been mixed thus far. He also wrote this bio.

SAM LIPSYTE is the author of five books of fiction. He teaches at Columbia University and lives in New York City.

CHARLES ALEXANDER LONDON writes books for children, teens, and adults. He is the author of the Accidental Adventures and Dog Tags series for children, *Proxy* for young adults, and for less young adults, *One Day the Soldiers Came* and *Far from Zion: In Search of a*

Global Jewish Community, which was a finalist for the National Jewish Book Award. He lives in Brooklyn, New York, and on the Web at calexanderlondon.com.

ADAM MANSBACH is the author of the #1 *New York Times* bestseller *Go the F**k to Sleep*, as well as the novels *Rage Is Back*, *The End of the Jews*, and *Angry Black White Boy*. His work has appeared in the *New Yorker*, the *New York Times Book Review*, *Esquire*, and the *Believer*, and on National Public Radio's *All Things Considered*.

ROSS MARTIN has won Emmy and Peabody awards as executive vice president at Viacom Media Networks and runs Scratch, a creative SWAT team working across the company. He is the author of a book of poems, *The Cop Who Rides Alone*, and has taught creative writing at the Rhode Island School of Design, The New School, and Washington University. Ross is a member of the Academy of Television Arts & Sciences, the Viacom Marketing Council, and the advisory board of St. Jude's Children's Hospital. In 2012, he was named one of *Fast Company*'s 100 Most Creative

People in Business and a "Media Maven" by *Advertising Age*.

RICK MEYEROWITZ began contributing illustrated articles to the *National Lampoon* in the first issue published in April 1970. He painted the poster for *Animal House*, and the magazine's trademark visual, the *Mona Gorilla*, which has been called "one of the enduring icons of American humor." Shortly after 9/11, Rick and Maira Kalman created the most talked-about *New Yorker* cover of this century, *NewYorkistan*, about which the *New York Times* wrote: "When their cover came out, a dark cloud seemed to lift." Rick would like to point out that the lifting of one lousy cloud hardly puts a dent in the pall hovering over us these days, but he doesn't want to be a bummer. His most recent book is *Drunk Stoned Brilliant Dead: The Writers and Artists Who Made the National Lampoon Insanely Great*, published by Abrams in 2010.

CHRISTOPHER NOXON is a writer, doodler, and flaming *shaygutz* who weirdly but strenuously identifies as a cultural Jew, active in Reboot, the Silver Lake Jewish Community, and the East Side Jews. He's the author of the nonfiction *Rejuvenile* and a forthcoming novel. His work has appeared in the *New Yorker*, *Salon*, and the *New York Times Magazine*.

REBECCA ODES has coauthored and illustrated four books. She lives in New York.

EDDY PORTNOY is a short, bespectacled Jew with curly hair and a big nose. He teaches Yiddish at Rutgers University and has a Ph.D. from the Jewish Theological Seminary.

MICHELLE QUINT is an editor at TED Books. Her young adult novel, *The Defiant*, will be published by McSweeney's in 2014.

JOSH RADNOR is best known for playing Ted Mosby on the Emmy-nominated CBS comedy *How I Met Your Mother*. He has written and directed two feature films, *happythankyoumoreplease* and *Liberal Arts*, both of which premiered to great acclaim at the Sundance Film Festival (the former winning the festival's 2010 Audience Award). He has many film and TV credits and has appeared on

and off Broadway, and his writing has been published in the *Los Angeles Times Magazine*, the *Huffington Post*, *MovieMaker*, *Indiewire*, and *Guilt & Pleasure*.

CAITLIN ROPER is a senior editor at *Wired* magazine in San Francisco.

TODD ROSENBERG (also known as "Odd Todd") produces short-form animated segments for television, Internet, and corporate clients. His cartoons focus on taking economic, scientific, or logistical concepts and making them quick, simple, and fun. His clients include *ABC World News*, PBS, *National Geographic*, HP, and American Express. He is currently fighting a ticket for having his dog off-leash in a public park.

DAVY ROTHBART is the creator of *Found Magazine*, a frequent contributor to public radio's *This American Life*, and the author of a book of personal essays, *My Heart Is an Idiot*, and a collection of stories, *The Lone Surfer of Montana, Kansas*. He writes regularly for *GQ* and *Grantland*, and his work has appeared in the *New Yorker*, the *New York Times*, and the *Believer*.

His documentary film, *Medora*, about a resilient high-school basketball team in a dwindling town in rural Indiana, premiered in March 2013 at the SXSW Film Festival. Rothbart is also the founder of Washington II Washington, an annual hiking adventure for inner-city kids. He divides his time between Los Angeles and his hometown of Ann Arbor, Michigan.

TIM SAMUELS is a documentary maker and broadcaster based in London. For his films for the BBC, he has won three Royal Television Society awards as well as an award for best documentary at the World Television Festival. He has also written for the *New York Times Magazine*, *GQ*, and the *Guardian*.

DAVID SAX is a writer and journalist from Toronto. He is the author of *Save the Deli: In Search of Perfect Pastrami, Crusty Rye, and the Heart of Jewish Delicatessen*, a James Beard Award–winning book that was dubbed "an epic journey, akin to *The Odyssey* but with Rolaids" by one observer, and the upcoming book *The Tastemakers*, which looks into the business of food trends and the bacon-cupcake–food truck industrial complex. Sax's writing has also appeared in *Bloomberg Businessweek*, the *New York Times Magazine*, *Saveur*, and other august publications.

DANA ADAM SHAPIRO was nominated for an Academy Award for his first film, *Murderball*. His second film, *Monogamy*, was nominated for a 2010 Independent Spirit Award. He is a former senior editor at *Spin* magazine, and his debut novel, *The Every Boy*, was a *New York Times Book Review* Editors' Choice and a Book Sense notable book. His latest work, a nonfiction book about divorce called *You Can Be Right (or You Can Be Married)*, was published by Scribner in 2012.

SAMANTHA SHAPIRO is a contributing writer for the *New York Times Magazine*. Her writing has also appeared in a number of other publications, including *Wired*, *Slate*, *Mother Jones*, *Glamour*, and the *Stranger*.

MIREILLE SILCOFF is a columnist with the *National Post* and a frequent contributor to magazines, including the *New York Times Magazine*. She is the founding editor of *Guilt & Pleasure* quarterly and the author of several books on drug and youth culture. She is finishing her first work of fiction. Mireille lives in Montreal.

JUSTIN ROCKET SILVERMAN has covered nightlife, tasers, meditation, politics, and other salacious topics for the *New York Post*, *Wired*, *Fast Company*, and many more publications. He lives in Brooklyn, but in a part far more hip than where the really famous writers are.

LARRY SMITH is the founder of *SMITH Magazine* (smithmag.net), home of the Six-Word Memoir project and book series, including *Oy! Only Six? Why Not More? Six-Word Memoirs on Jewish Life*. He's the editor of an anthology, *The Moment: Wild, Poignant, Life-Changing Stories from 125 Writers and Artists Famous & Obscure*, and a frequent speaker on storytelling at companies, nonprofits, and schools around the world.

JILL SOLOWAY is a writer and director. She won the U.S. Dramatic Directing Award for her first feature, *Afternoon Delight*, at the 2013 Sundance Film Festival. Jill is a three-time Emmy

nominee for her work writing and producing *Six Feet Under*. She authored *Tiny Ladies in Shiny Pants*, a humorous post-feminist manifesto/memoir. She is a cofounder of the community organization East Side Jews and lives with her husband and two sons in Silver Lake, Los Angeles.

JOEL STEIN grew up in Edison, New Jersey, went to Stanford, and in 1997, became a staff writer for *Time*. In 1998, he began writing his sophomoric humor column that now appears in the magazine every week. He's also written fourteen cover stories for *Time*, and has contributed to the *New Yorker*, *GQ*, *Esquire*, *Details*, *Food & Wine*, *Travel & Leisure*, *Bloomberg Businessweek*, *Wired*, *Real Simple*, *Sunset*, *Playboy*, *Elle*, the *Los Angeles Times*, and many more magazines, most of which have gone out of business. He has appeared as a talking head on any TV show that has asked him, taught a class in humor writing at Princeton, and wrote a weekly column for the back page of *Entertainment Weekly* and the opinion section of the *Los Angeles Times*. His first book, *Man Made: A Stupid Quest for Masculinity*, was published in 2012. This is the most he's ever written in third person.

MICHAELA WATKINS is an actress who has appeared in movies such as *Wanderlust*, *Thanks for Sharing*, the upcoming *In a World*, and *Afternoon Delight*, and TV shows such as *New Girl*, *Enlightened*, *The New Adventures of Old Christine*, *Modern Family*, *Curb Your Enthusiasm*, *Children's Hospital*, *Parenthood*, *Grey's Anatomy*, and *Californication*. She hails from the Los Angeles main stage company the Groundlings, and appeared on *SNL* in the 2008–2009 season.

ANONYMOUS is a film critic for one of the last big newspapers in the U.S. that still employs film critics.

ABOUT REBOOT

EBOOT WAS FOUNDED ELEVEN YEARS AGO AS a strange experiment. We wanted to see what would happen if you engaged a creative cast of characters in a no-holds-barred conversation about how identity, community, and meaning are changing in America today.

The project was launched in the spirit of innovation and adventure. While it had no premeditated outcomes, we had a hunch that if an eclectic, intelligent, inventive network was let loose and given the freedom to discuss the personal questions they harbored about their own identities, they would quickly forge new concepts that would encourage a wider audience to do the same.

We arrived at that hunch after spending a year interviewing 800 creative types in New York, San Francisco, and Los Angeles about their own identities and experiences. These frank and honest conversations uncovered a large, young Jewish audience who expressed an eagerness to explore questions about history, theology, ritual, culture, and philosophy, yet professed slightly less interest in the universe of traditional Jewish organizations then in existence, most of which had been established before the 1940s when issues of survival and fighting anti-Semitism predominated.

Where others had suggested this widespread lack of interest was just an anxiety-inducing symptom of assimilation, we sensed it could be a springboard for reclamation. The United States had changed radically in the postwar period, and while America's Jews had been transformed along with it—a large segment moving en masse from the city to the suburbs, from tradition to modernity—the organizations had not always kept pace. Reboot was formed to experiment with closing that gap by catalyzing forms of

Jewish life that would encourage participants to define identity, community, and meaning self-confidently, on their own terms.

In the course of the last decade, Reboot has spawned over 100 projects, including digital projects like 10Q (doyou10q.com), enabling thousands to reflect on their year, prior to Yom Kippur; Sabbath Manifesto (nationaldayofunplugging.com), promoting the notion of a technology-free Shabbat; the Idelsohn Society (idelsohnsociety.com), exploring postwar history by taking re-releases of lost Jewish vinyl onto the *Billboard* chart; and Sukkah City (sukkahcity.com), a global architectural design contest building a dozen avant-garde *sukkot* (the temporary huts built for the festival of Sukkot) in the heart of Union Square, New York City.

For more on this Unscrolled project go to unscrolled.org and @unscrolled.

REBOOT WOULD LIKE TO THANK . . .

Every project that Reboot has birthed is a testament to the passion, energy, and collective curiosity of the Reboot network, an always remarkable, occasionally unexpected cast of characters willing to run through walls in order to bring a production line of ideas into life. The network is too sprawling to mention name by name, but we are especially indebted to Reboot's board: Scott Belsky, Roger Bennett, Greg Clayman, Ben Elowitz, Kate Frucher, Jeremy Goldberg, Julie Hermelin, Courtney Holt, David Katznelson, Samantha Kurtzman-Counter, Rachel Levin, Steven Rubenstein, Jill Soloway, and Anne Wojcicki. We are especially grateful to those who have served as Reboot's chair over the years: the mighty Erin Potts, the strategic Scott Belsky, and the dynamic, inimitable David Katznelson. Special thanks also to those who have given their time to work as Reboot's staff over the years, especially Amelia Klein, Shane Hankins, Robin Kramer, Maria Arsenieva, Melissa Buscemi, Lisa Grissom, Dina Mann, and Tanya Schevitz.

Reboot is also proud and honored to have partnered with more than 500 community organizations around the world. Yet none of our projects would have come to life without the encouragement and support of the many foundations, individual donors, friends, colleagues, and partners that have supported Reboot financially over the years. As a 501(c)3 non-profit, we know that investing in an experiment demands real courage, and we are grateful to each and every one of you for believing in us. We are ever indebted to the late Andrea Bronfman, whose vision Reboot made manifest.

We are also grateful to Rabbi Barry Schwartz and the Jewish Publication Society for their support with this project. We used their brilliant Torah, *The Jewish Bible: Tanakh: The Holy Scriptures—The New JPS Translation According to the Traditional Hebrew Text*, as our core text, and encourage all those who intend to follow the portions week to week to do the same. JPS is currently raising money to create a digital version of their translation. Please support them.

ROGER BENNETT WOULD LIKE TO THANK . . .

The concept that became *Unscrolled* came from the mind of Damon Lindelof. It was his idea that led to the creation of this book, and we are grateful to the fifty-four writers who agreed to jump into the project with such abandon. Working with you all over the past two years has been a delight, though it has also made me realize that Moses simply had the commandments handed to him for a reason. We are also indebted to Adam Walden who came up with the name for this tome.

It has taken a collective as large as a biblical tribe to bring this book to life.

Thanks to my agent, Elyse Cheney, and her team. I am grateful to Kate Lee for introducing me to Suzie Bolotin, who has edited this book. Suzie, I cannot tell you how much I adore being in your company. When I am with you I am overcome by a sadly ephemeral belief that every global problem can be solved and overcome. Thanks also to the creative and patient design duo of Raquel Jaramillo and Jean-Marc Troadec, as well as Selina Meere, Jessica Wiener, Courtney Greenhalgh, Beth Levy, Samantha O'Brien, Barbara Peragine, Jarrod Dyer, the entire sales and marketing team, and everyone at Workman.

On the Reboot front, I am grateful to Harrison Owen, whose Open Space methodology is at the core of the Reboot project. I am also indebted to the magical Amichai Lau-Lavie for his textual and educational brilliance. A gent who possesses the most eclectic mix of attributes I have ever encountered in one human being, he patiently worked with many of the writers as they thought through their contributions. (For more on Amichai and his work go to www.amichai.me.)

Rachel Levin has long been the most insightful, patient, and determined professional partner I could have had. She has been blessed with every skill set that I lack, including style, grace, wisdom, and an ability to bring the best out of everyone she encounters.

I am also utterly indebted to Dana Ferine, who has long demonstrated an unparalleled ability to work with boundless passion on some of the most arcane projects in America.

Finally, love to my family—the Bennetts and the Krolls. As someone who was expelled from Hebrew school when my father was president, I know nothing will ever erase the shame I brought to the family name. I hope this project goes some way to repairing the damage. Massive love to the kids I have "begat:" Samson, Ber, Zion, and Oz; and most of all, to my wife, Vanessa. You are all the proof I need to know that behind every biblical patriarch, there is a biblical matriarch acting as the puppet master.

twitter: @rogbennett

IN THE
BEGINNING . . .